HOLLYWOOD STATION

A NOVEL

JOSEPH WAMBAUGH

LITTLE, BROWN AND COMPANY

LARGE PRINT

Little, Brown and Company
Hachette Book Group USA
1271 Avenue of the Americas, New York, NY 10020
Visit our Web site at www.HachetteBookGroupUSA.com

First Large Print Edition: November 2006
The Large Print Edition is published in accord with
the standards of the N.A.V.H.

The characters and events in this book are fictitious. Any
similarity to real persons, living or dead, is coincidental and
not intended by the author.

Library of Congress Cataloging-in-Publication Data
Wambaugh, Joseph.
Hollywood Station : a novel /
Joseph Wambaugh. — 1st ed.
p. cm.
ISBN-10: 0-316-06624-9
ISBN-13: 978-0-316-06624-2
1. Police — California — Los Angeles — Fiction.
2. Hollywood (Los Angeles, Calif.) — Fiction. I. Title.
PS3573.A475H65 2006
813'.54 — dc22   2006015759

10 9 8 7 6 5 4 3 2 1

Q-FF

Interior design by Nancy Singer Olaguera,
ISPN Publishing Services

Printed in the United States of America

ACKNOWLEDGMENTS

Special thanks for the terrific anecdotes and wonderful cop talk goes to officers of the Los Angeles Police Department:

Chate Asvanonda, Matt Bennyworth, Michael Berchem, Wendi Berndt, Vicki Bynum, Elizabeth Estupinian, Laura Evens, Heather Gahry, Brett Goodkin, Chuck Henry, Craig Herron, Jack Herron (ret.), Brian Hospodar, Andy Hudlett, Jeff Injalls, Rick Jackson, Dennis Kilcoyne, Al Lopez, Tim Marcia, Kathy McAnany, Roger Murphy, Bill Pack, Mike Porter, Rosie Redshaw, Tom Redshaw, Dave Sigler, Bill Sollie, Olivia Spindola, Joe Witty

And to officers of the San Diego Police Department:

Mark Amancio, Pete Amancio, Andra Brown, Brett Burkett, Laurie Cairncross, Blaine

Ferguson, Pete Griffin (ret.), Mike Gutierrez, Vanessa Holland, Gerry Kramer, Charles Lara, Vic Morel, Tony Puente (ret.), Andy Rios, Steve Robinson, Steve Sloan, Elliott Stiasny, Alex Sviridov, Don Watkins, Joe Winney

And to officers of the Palm Springs Police Department:

Dave Costello, Don Dougherty, Steve Douglas, Mitch Spike

And to special agents of the Federal Bureau of Investigation:

Matt Desarno, Jack Kelly (ret.)

And to author James Ellroy for urging this return to LAPD roots

HOLLYWOOD STATION

ONE

"WANNA PLAY PIT bull polo, dude?"

"What's that?"

"It's something I learned when I worked Metro Mounted Platoon."

"It's weird thinking of you as a cowboy cop."

"All I know about horses is they're assholes, man. But we got the overtime there. You know my little Beemer? I wouldn't have that if I hadn't worked Metro. My last year in Metro I made a hundred grand plus. I don't miss those crazy horses but I miss that OT money. And I miss wearing a Stetson. When we worked the mini-riot at the Democrats convention, a hot little lobbyist with nipples big enough to pack up and leave home said I looked like a young Clint Eastwood in that Stetson. And I didn't carry a Beretta nine then. I carried a six-inch Colt

1

revolver. It looked more appropriate when I was sitting on a horse."

"A wheel gun? In this day and age?"

"The Oracle still carries a wheel gun."

"The Oracle's been on the job nearly fifty years. He can wear a codpiece if he wants to. And you don't look like Clint Eastwood, bro. You look like the guy in *King Kong,* except you got even more of a beak and your hair is bleached."

"My hair is sun-streaked from surfing, dude. And I'm even two inches taller in the saddle than Clint was."

"Whatever, bro. I'm a whole foot taller on the ground than Tom Cruise. He's about four foot ten."

"Anyways, those pacifist demonstrators at the convention center were throwing golf balls and ball bearings at our horses, when twenty of us charged. And dude, when you get stepped on by a fifteen-hundred-pound animal, it sucks *bad.* Only one horse went down. He was twenty-eight years old, name of Rufus. That fried him. Had to retire him after that. One of those Jamba Juicers threw a lit trash bag at the one I was riding, name of Big Sam. I beat that bitch with my koa."

"Your what?"

"It's like a samurai sword made of koa wood. The baton's about as useless as a stalk of celery when you're up there on a horse seventeen hands high. Supposed to strike them in the clavicle, but guess what, she juked and I got her upside the head. Accidentally, wink wink. She did a loop de loop and ended up under a parked car. I saw a horse get stuck with a knitting needle by one of those tree fuckers. The horse was fried after that. Too much stress. They retired him to Horse Rescue. They all get fried sooner or later. Just like us."

"That sucks. Sticking a horse."

"That one got a TV interview at least. When cops get hurt, nothing. Who gives a fuck? When a horse gets hurt, you get on TV, maybe with that Debbie D-cup news bunny on Channel Five."

"Where'd you learn to ride?"

"Griffith Park. A five-week course at the Ahmanson Training Center. Only horse I ever rode before that was on a merry-go-round, and I don't care if I ever ride another one. Got the job 'cause my sister-in-law went to high school with the platoon lieutenant. Horses're assholes, man. An RTD bus can pass you three inches away at sixty miles an hour and the horse doesn't blink. A little piece of paper blows in his face all of a sudden and he bucks you clear over a pile of tweakers and baseheads sleeping on a skid-row sidewalk at Sixth and San Pedro. And you end up in Momma Lucy's shopping cart with her aluminum cans and refundable bottles. That's how I got a hip replacement at the age of thirty. Only thing I wanna ride now is a surfboard and my Beemer."

"I'm thirty-one. You look a lot older than me."

"Well I ain't. I just had a lot to worry about. They gave me a doctor that was so old he still believed in bleeding and leeches."

"Whatever, bro. You might have progeria. Gives you those eyelid and neck wrinkles, like a Galapagos turtle."

"So you wanna play pit bull polo or not?"

"What the fuck is pit bull polo?"

"Way I learned, they trailered ten of us down to Seventy-seventh Street on a night when they decided to sweep a three-block row of crack houses and gangsta cribs. Whole fucking area is a crime scene. Living next to that is what razor wire was made for. Anyways, all those Bloods and Crips have pit bulls and rotties and they let them run loose half the time, terrorizing the 'hood and eating any normal dogs they see. And the whole fucking pack of gangsta dogs flew into a blood lust the second they saw us coming in and they attacked like we were riding T-bones and ribeyes."

"How many did you shoot?"

"Shoot? I need this job. You gotta be richer than Donald Trump and Manny the plumber to fire your piece in today's LAPD, especially at a dog. You shoot a human person and you get maybe two detectives and a team from Force Investigation Division to second-guess you. You shoot a dog and you get three supervisors and four detectives plus FID, all ready to string yellow tape. Especially in the 'hood. We didn't shoot them, we played pit bull polo with the long sticks."

"Oh, I get it. Pit bull polo."

"Man, I rode through them, whacking those killer bulls, yelling, 'One chukker for my team! Two chukkers for my team!' I only wish I coulda whacked their owners."

"Bro, a chukker is a period of play. I know 'cause I watched a special on the Royal Family. Horny old Charles was playing a chukker or two for Camilla with big wood in his jodhpurs. That old babe? I don't see it."

"Whatever. You down with that or not?"

"Yeah, I'm down. But first I wanna know, did

anyone beef you for playing polo with the gangsta bulls?"

"Oh yeah, there's always an ABM who'll call IA, his councilman, and maybe long distance to Al Sharpton, who never saw a camera he didn't hug."

"ABM?"

"You ain't a 'hood rat, are ya? ABM. Angry black male."

"Spent my nine years in Devonshire, West Valley, and West L.A. before I transferred here last month. ABMs ain't never been filed on my desktop, bro."

"Then don't go to a police commission or council meeting. ABMs are in charge. But we don't have hardly any living in Hollywood. In fact, nowadays most of south L.A. is Latino, even Watts."

"I been reading that the entire inner city is mostly Latino. Where the fuck have the brothers gone to? I wonder. And why is everybody worrying about the black vote if they're all moving to the suburbs? They better worry about the Latino vote, because they got the mayor's office now and they're about one generation away from reclaiming California and making us do the gardening."

"You married? And which number is it?"

"Just escaped from number two. She was Druid-like but not as cuddly. One daughter three years old. Lives with Momma, whose lawyer won't be satisfied till I'm homeless on the beach eating seaweed."

"Is number one still at large?"

"Yeah, but I don't have to pay her nothing. She took my car, though. You?"

"Divorced also. Once. No kids. Met my ex in a cop bar in North Hollywood called the Director's Chair. She wore a felonious amount of pancake. Looked too slutty for the Mustang Ranch and still I married her. Musta been her J Lo booty."

"Starter marriages never work for cops. You don't have to count the first one, bro. So how do we play pit bull polo without horses? And where do we play?"

"I know just the place. Get the expandable baton outta my war bag."

The Salvadoran gang *Mara Salvatrucha,* aka MS-13, began at Los Angeles High School less than twenty years earlier but was now said to have ten thousand members throughout the United States and seven hundred thousand in

Central American countries. Many residents of state prison displayed tattoos saying "MS" or "MS-13." It was an MS-13 crew member who was stopped on a street in North Hollywood in 1991 by Officer Tina Kerbrat, a rookie just months out of the LAPD academy, who was in the process of writing him a citation for drinking in public, nothing more than that, when the MS-13 "cruiser" shot her dead. The first LAPD woman officer to be murdered in the line of duty.

Later that evening a besieged Mexican resident living east of Gower Street called Hollywood Station to say that she saw an LAPD black-and-white with lights out driving loops around a dirty pink apartment building that she had reported to the police on several occasions as being full of *Mara Salvatrucha* gang members.

On the other occasions, the officers at the desk kept trying to explain to the Mexican woman about gang injunctions and probable cause, things she did not understand and that did not exist in her country. Things that apparently denied protection to people like her and her children from the criminals in that ugly pink building. She told the officer about how their vicious dogs had mauled and killed a collie belonging to her neighbor Irene, and how all the children were unable to walk safely in the streets. She also said that two of the dogs had been removed by people from the city pound but there were still enough left. More than enough.

The officers told her they were very sorry and that she should contact the Department of Animal Services.

The Mexican woman had been watching a Spanish-language channel and was almost ready for bed when she first heard the howling that drew her to the window. There she saw the police car with lights out, speeding down the alley next to the apartment building, being pursued by four or five barking dogs. On its second pass down the alley, she saw the driver lean out the window and swing something that looked like a snooker stick at one of the brutes, sending it yelping and running back into the pink building. Then the car made another loop and did it to another big dog, and the driver yelled something that her daughter heard from the porch.

Her daughter stumbled sleepily into the tiny living room and said in English, "Mamá, does chukker mean something very bad, like the *F* word?"

The Mexican woman called Hollywood Station and spoke to a very senior sergeant whom all the cops called the Oracle. She wanted to say thank you for sending the officers with the snooker stick. She was hopeful that things might improve around the neighborhood. The Oracle was puzzled but thought it best not to question her further. He simply said that he was glad to be of service.

When 6-X-32's lights were back on and they were cruising Hollywood Boulevard, the driver said, "Dude, right there's where my career with the Mounted Platoon ended. That's where I decided that overtime pay or not, I was going back to normal patrol."

His partner looked to his right and said, "At Grauman's Chinese Theater?"

"Right there in the courtyard. That's where I learned that you never ride a horse on the Hollywood Walk of Fame."

"Bad juju?"

"Bad footing."

Sid Grauman's famous theater seemed somehow forlorn these days, dwarfed and sandwiched by the Hollywood & Highland Center, better known as the Kodak Center, containing two blocks of shopping and entertainment. It was home to the Kodak Theatre and the Academy Awards and was overrun by tourists day and night. But the Chinese Theater still held its own when it came to Hollywood weirdness. Even this late, there were a number of costumed creatures posing for photos with tourists who were mainly photographing the shoe and handprints in the famous forecourt. Among the creatures were Mr. Incredible, Elmo, two Darth Vaders, Batman, and two Goofys, one short, one tall.

"They pose with tourists. Pix for bucks," the driver said to his partner. "The tourists think the creatures work for Grauman's, but they don't. Most of them're crackheads and tweakers. Watch little Goofy."

He braked, making the nighttime traffic go around their black-and-white. They watched the shorter of the two Goofys hassling four Asian tourists who no doubt had refused to pay him for taking his photo or hadn't paid enough. When Goofy grabbed one of the two Asian men by the arm, the cop tooted his horn. When Goofy looked up and saw the black-and-white, he gave up panhandling for the moment and tried to disappear into the throng, even though his huge Goofy head loomed over all but the tallest tourist.

The driver said, "The subway back there is a good escape route to the 'hood. Dealers hang out by the trains, and the hooks hang around the boulevard."

"What's a hook?"

"A guy that approaches you and says, 'I can hook you up with what you need.' These days it's almost always crystal. Everybody's tweaking. Meth is the drug of choice on the Hollywood streets, absolutely."

And that made him think of his last night at Metro, which was followed by the replacement surgery and a right hip more accurate than a barometer when it came to predicting sudden temperature drops and wind-chill factor.

On that last night in the Mounted Platoon, he and another mounted cop were there for crowd suppression, walking their horses along Hollywood Boulevard all calm and okey-dokey, along the curb past the Friday-night mobs by the subway station, moseying west, when he spotted a hook looking very nervously in their direction.

He'd said to his partner, who was riding a mare named Millie, "Let's jam this guy."

He dismounted and dropped his get-down

rope. His partner held both horses and he approached the hook on foot. The hook was a sweaty, scrawny white guy, very tall, maybe even taller than he was, though his LAPD Stetson and cowboy boots made him tower. That's when it all went bad.

"I was talking to a hook right about there," he said to his partner now, pointing to the sidewalk in front of the Kodak Center. "And the dude just turned and rabbitted. Zip. Like that. And I started after him, but Major freaked."

"Your partner?"

"My horse. He was fearless, Major was. Dude, I'd seen him chill in training when we were throwing firecrackers and flares at him. I'd seen other horses rear up on their hind legs and do a one-eighty while Major stood his ground. But not that night. That's the thing about horses, they're assholes, man."

"What'd he do?"

"First, Major reared clear up tall and crazy. Then he bit my partner on the arm. It was like somebody cranked up his voltage. Maybe a tweaker shot him with a BB gun, I don't know. Anyways, I stopped chasing the hook, fuck him, and ran back to help my partner. But Major wouldn't calm down until I made like I was going to climb in the saddle. Then I did something very stupid."

"What's that?"

"I climbed in the saddle, intending to ride him back to the trailer and call it a night. I did that instead of leading him back, which anybody without brain bubbles woulda done under the circumstances."

"So?"

"He freaked again. He took off. Up onto the sidewalk."

The moment would be with him forever. Galloping along the Walk of Fame, kicking up sparks and scattering tourists and panhandlers and purse snatchers and tweakers and pregnant women and costumed nuns and SpongeBob and three Elvises. Clomping over top of Marilyn Monroe's star or James Cagney's or Elizabeth Taylor's or fucking Liberace's or whoever was there on this block of the Walk of Fame because he didn't know who was there and never checked later to find out.

Cursing the big horse and hanging on with one hand and waving the creepy multitudes out of his way with the other. Even though he knew that Major could, and had, run up a flight of concrete steps in his long career, he also knew that neither Major nor any horse belonging to the Mounted Platoon could run on marble, let alone on brass inserts on that marble sidewalk where people spilled their Starbucks and Slurpees with impunity. No horse could trample Hollywood legends like that, so maybe it *was* the bad juju. And very suddenly Major hydroplaned in the Slurpees and just . . . went . . . *down.*

His partner interrupted the sweat-popping flashback. "So what happened, bro? After he took off with you?"

"First of all, nobody got hurt. Except Major and me."

"Bad?"

"They say I ended up in John Wayne's boot prints right there in Grauman's forecourt. They say the Duke's fist print is there too. I don't remember boots or fists or nothing. I woke up on a gurney in an RA with a paramedic telling me yes I was alive, while we were screaming code three to Hollywood Pres. I had a concussion and three cracked ribs and my bad hip, which was later replaced, and everybody said I was real lucky."

"How about the nag?"

"They told me Major seemed okay at first. He was limping, of course. But after they trailered him back to Griffith Park and called the vet, he could hardly stand. He was in bad shape and got worse. They had to put him down that night." And then he added, "Horses are *such* assholes, man."

When his partner looked at the driver, he thought he saw his eyes glisten in the mix of light from the boulevard — fluorescence and neon, headlights and taillights, even reflected glow from a floodlight shooting skyward — announcing to all: This is Hollywood! But all that light spilling onto them changed the crispness of their black-and-white to a wash of bruised purple and sickly yellow. His partner wasn't sure, but he thought the driver's chin quivered, so he pretended to be seriously studying the costumed freaks in front of Grauman's Chinese Theater.

After a moment the driver said, "So anyways, I said fuck it. When I healed up I put in for Hollywood Division because from what I'd seen of it from the saddle it seemed like a pretty good place to work, long as you got a few hundred horses under you instead of one. And here I am."

His partner didn't say anything for a while. Then he said, "I used to surf a lot when I worked West L.A. Lived with my leash attached to a squealy. I had surf bumps all over my knees, bro. Getting too old for that. Thinking about getting me a log and just going out and catching the evening glass."

"Awesome, dude. Evening glass is way cool. Me, after I transferred to Hollywood I sorta became a rev-head, cruising in my Beemer up to Santa Barbara, down to San Diego, revving that ultimate driving machine. But I got to missing being in the green room, you know? In that tube with the foam breaking over you? Now I go out most every morning I'm off duty. Malibu attracts bunnies. Come along sometime and I'll lend you a log. Maybe you'll have a vision."

"Maybe I'll get a brain wave out there on evening glass. I need one to figure out how to keep my second ex-wife from making me live under a tree eating eucalyptus like a fucking koala."

"Of course you're gonna get a surf jacket soon as these hodads around Hollywood Station find out. Everybody calls me Flotsam. So if you surf with me, you *know* they're gonna call you . . ."

"Jetsam," his partner said with a sigh of resignation.

"Dude, this could be the beginning of a choiceamundo friendship."

"Jetsam? Bro, that is wack, way wack."

"What's in a name?"

"Whatever. So what happened to the Stetson after you played lawn dart in Grauman's courtyard?"

"No lawn in that courtyard. All concrete. I figure a tweaker picked it up. Probably sold it for a few teeners of crystal. I keep hoping to someday find that crankster. Just to see how fast I can make his body heat drop from ninety-eight point six to room temperature."

As they were talking, 6-X-32 got a beep on the MDT computer. Jetsam opened and acknowledged the message, then hit the en route key and they were on their way to an address on Cherokee Avenue that appeared on the dashboard screen along with "See the woman, 415 music."

"Four-fifteen music," Flotsam muttered. "Why the hell can't the woman just go to her neighbor and tell them to turn down the goddamn CD? Probably some juice-head fell asleep to Destiny's Child."

"Maybe Black Eyed Peas," Jetsam said. "Or maybe Fifty Cent. Crank up the decibels on that dude and you provoke homicidal urges. Heard his album called *The Massacre*?"

It wasn't easy to find a parking place near the half block of apartment buildings, causing 6-X-32 to make several moves before the patrol car was able to squeeze in parallel between a late-model Lexus and a twelve-year-old Nova that was parked far enough from the curb to be ticketed.

Jetsam hit the at-scene button on the keyboard, and they grabbed their flashlights and got out, with Flotsam grumbling, "In all of Hollywood tonight there's probably about thirteen and a half fucking parking places."

"Thirteen now," Jetsam said. "We got the half." He paused on the sidewalk in front and said, "Jesus, I can hear it from here and it ain't hip-hop."

It was the *Schreckensfanfare,* the "Fanfare of Terror," from Beethoven's Ninth.

A dissonant shriek of strings and a discordant blast from brass and woodwinds directed them up the outside staircase of a modest but respectable two-story apartment building. Many of the tenants seemed to be out this Friday evening. Porch lights and security lights were on inside some of the units, but it was altogether very quiet except for that music attacking their ears, assaulting their hearing. Those harrowing

passages that Beethoven intended as an intro-
duction to induce foreboding did the job on
6-X-32.

They didn't bother to seek out the com-
plainant. They knocked at the apartment from
which that music emanated like a scream, like a
warning.

"Somebody might be drunk in there," Jetsam
said.

"Or dead," Flotsam said, half joking.

No answer. They tried again, banging louder.
No answer.

Flotsam turned the knob, and the door
popped open as the hammering timpani served
the master composer by intensifying those fear-
ful sounds. It was dark except for light coming
from a room off the hallway.

"Anybody home?" Flotsam called.

No answer. Just the timpani and that sound of
brass shrieking at them.

Jetsam stepped inside first. "Anybody home?"

No answer. Flotsam reflexively drew his nine,
held it down beside his right leg and flashed his
light around the room.

"The music's coming from back there." Jetsam
pointed down the dark hallway.

"Maybe somebody had a heart attack. Or a stroke," Flotsam said.

They started walking slowly down the long, narrow hallway toward the light, toward the sound, the timpani beating a tattoo. "Hey!" Flotsam yelled. "Anybody here?"

"This is bad juju," Jetsam said.

"Anybody home?" Flotsam listened for a response, but there was only that crazy fucking music!

The first room off the hall was the bedroom. Jetsam switched on the light. The bed was made. A woman's pink bathrobe and pajamas were lying across the bed. Pink slippers sat on the floor below. The sound system was not elaborate, but it wasn't cheap either. Several classical CDs were scattered on a bookcase shelf beside the speakers. This person lived in her bedroom, it seemed.

Jetsam touched the power button and shut off that raging sound. Both he and his partner drew a breath of relief as though bobbing to the surface from deep water. There was another room at the far end of the hallway, but it was dark. The only other light came from a bathroom that served this two-bedroom unit.

Flotsam stepped to the bathroom doorway first and found her. She was naked, half in, half out of the bathtub, long pale legs hanging over the side of the tub. She had no doubt been a pretty girl in life, but now she was staring, eyes open in slits, lips drawn back in that familiar snarl of violent death he'd seen on others: Don't take me away! I'll fight to stay here! Alive! I want to stay alive!

Jetsam drew his rover, keyed it, and prepared to make the call. His partner stayed and stared at the corpse of the young woman. For a few seconds Flotsam had the panicky idea that she might still be alive, that maybe a rescue ambulance would have a chance. Then he moved one step closer to the tub and peeked behind the shower curtain.

There were arterial spurts all over the blue tile of the wall even to the ceiling. The floor of the tub was a blackening vat of viscosity and from here he could see at least three chest wounds and a gaping gash across her throat. At that second but not before, the acrid smell of blood and urine almost overwhelmed him, and he stepped out into the hallway to await the detectives from Hollywood Station and from Scientific Investigation Division.

The second bedroom, apparently belonging to a male roommate, was tidy and unoccupied at the moment, or so they thought. Jetsam had shined his light in there in a cursory check while talking on the rover, and Flotsam had glanced in, but neither had bothered to enter the bedroom and look inside the small closet, its door ajar.

While the two cops were back in the living room making a few notes, careful not to disturb anything, even turning on the wall switch with a pencil, a young man entered from the darkened hallway behind them.

His voice was a piercing rasp. He said, "I love her."

Flotsam dropped his notebook, Jetsam the rover. Both cops wheeled and drew their nines.

"Freeze, motherfucker!" Flotsam screamed.

"Freeze!" Jetsam added redundantly.

He was frozen already. As pale and naked as the young woman he'd murdered, the young man stood motionless, palms up, freshly slashed wrists extended like an offering. Of what? Contrition? The gaping wrists were spurting, splashing fountains onto the carpet and onto his bare feet.

"Jesus Christ!" Flotsam screamed.

"Jesus!" Jetsam screamed redundantly.

Then both cops holstered their pistols, but when they lunged toward him the young man turned and ran to the bathroom, leaping into the tub with the woman he loved. And the cops gaped in horror as he curled himself fetally and moaned into her unhearing ear.

Flotsam got one latex glove onto his hand but dropped the other glove. Jetsam yelled into the rover for paramedics and dropped both latex gloves. Then they jumped onto him and tried to drag him up, but all the blood made his thin arms slip through their hands, and both cops cursed and swore while the young man moaned. Twice, three times he pulled free and plopped onto the bloody corpse with a splat.

Jetsam got his handcuff around one wrist, but when he cinched it tight the bracelet sunk into the gaping flesh and he saw a tendon flail around the ratchet and he yelled, "Son of a bitch! Son of a bitch!" And he felt ice from his tailbone to his brain stem and for a second he felt like bolting.

Flotsam was bigger and stronger than Jetsam, and he muscled the rigid left arm out from under the chest of the moaning young man and forced it up behind his back and got the dangling bracelet around the wrist. And then he got to see it sink into the red maw of tendon and tissue and he almost puked.

They each got him by a handcuffed arm and they lifted him but now all three were dripping and slimy from his spurting blood and her thickening blood and they dropped him, his head hitting the side of the tub. But he was past pain and only moaned more softly. They lifted again and got him out of the tub and dragged him out into the hallway, where Flotsam slipped and fell down, the bleeding man on top of him still moaning.

A neighbor on her balcony screamed when the two panting cops dragged the young man down the outside stairway, his naked blood-slimed body bumping against the plastered steps in a muted plop that made the woman scream louder. The three young men fell in a pile onto the sidewalk under a street lamp, and Flotsam got up and began ransacking the car trunk for the first-aid kit, not knowing for sure what the hell was in it but pretty sure there was no tourniquet. Jetsam knelt by the bleeding man, jerked his Sam Browne free, and was trying to tie off one arm with an improvised tourniquet made from his trouser belt when the rescue ambulance came squealing around the corner onto Cherokee, lights flashing and siren yelping.

The first patrol unit to arrive belonged to the sergeant known as the Oracle, who double-parked half a block away, leaving the immediate area to RA paramedics, Hollywood detectives, evidence collectors from Scientific Investigation Division, and the coroner's team. There was no mistaking the very old patrol sergeant, even in the darkness. As his burly figure approached, they could see those pale service stripes on his left sleeve, rising almost to his elbow. Forty-six years on the Job rated nine hash marks and made him one of the longest-serving cops on the entire police department.

"The Oracle has more hash marks than a football field," everybody said.

But the Oracle always said, "I'm only staying because the divorce settlement gives my ex half my pension. I'll be on the Job till that bitch dies or I do, whichever comes first."

The bleeding man was unmoving and going gray when he was blanketed and belted to the gurney and lifted into the rescue ambulance, both paramedics working to stem the now oozing blood but shaking their heads at the Oracle, indicating that the young man had probably bled out and was beyond saving.

Even though a Santa Ana wind had blown into Los Angeles from the desert on this May evening, both Flotsam and Jetsam were shivering and wearily gathering their equipment which was scattered on the sidewalk next to a concrete planter containing some hopeful pansies and forget-me-nots.

The Oracle looked at the blood-drenched cops and said, "Are you hurt? Any injuries at all?"

Flotsam shook his head and said, "Boss, I think we just had a tactical situation they never covered in any class I've taken at the academy. Or if they did, I fucking missed it."

"Get yourselves to Cedars for medical treatment whether you need it or not," the Oracle said. "Then clean up real good. Might as well burn those uniforms from the looks of them."

"If that guy has hepatitis, we're in trouble, Sarge," Jetsam said.

"If that guy has AIDS, we're dead," Flotsam said.

"This doesn't look like that kind of situation," the Oracle said, his retro gray crew cut seeming to sparkle under the streetlight. Then he noticed

Jetsam's handcuffs lying on the sidewalk. He flashed his beam on the cuffs and said to the exhausted cop, "Drop those cuffs in some bleach, son. I can see chunks of meat jammed in the ratchets."

"I need to go surfing," Jetsam said.

"Me too," Flotsam said.

The Oracle had acquired his sobriquet by virtue of seniority and his penchant for dispensing words of wisdom, but not on this night. He just looked at his bloody, hollow-eyed, shivering young cops and said, "Now, you boys get right to Cedars ER and let a doc have a look at you."

It was then that D2 Charlie Gilford arrived on the scene, a gum-chewing, lazy night-watch detective with a penchant for bad neckties who was not a case-carrying investigator, his job being only to assist. But with more than twenty years at Hollywood Station, he didn't like to miss anything sensational that was going down and loved to offer pithy commentary on whatever had transpired. For his assessments they called him Compassionate Charlie.

During that evening's events on Cherokee Avenue, after he'd received a quick summary from the Oracle and called a homicide team from home, he took a look at the gruesome scene of murder and suicide, and at the bloody trail marking the grisly struggle that failed to save the killer's life.

Then Compassionate Charlie sucked his teeth for a second or two and said to the Oracle, "I can't understand young coppers anymore. Why would they put themselves through something like that for a self-solver? Shoulda just let the guy jump in the tub with her and bleed out the way he wanted to. They coulda sat there listening to music till it was over. All we got here is just another Hollywood love story that went a little bit sideways."

TWO

IT HAD ALWAYS seemed to Farley Ramsdale that the blue mailboxes, even the ones on some of the seedier corners of Hollywood, were much more treasure-laden and easier to work than the resident boxes by most of the upmarket condos and apartments. And he especially liked the ones outside the post office because they got really full between closing time and 10 P.M., the hour he found most propitious. People felt so confident about a post office location that they dropped a bonanza in them, sometimes even cash.

The hour of 10 P.M. was midday for Farley, who'd been named by a mother who just loved actor Farley Granger, the old Hitchcock thriller *Strangers on a Train* being one of her favorites. In that movie Farley Granger is a professional tennis player, and even though Farley Ramsdale's mother had signed him up for private lessons when he was in middle school, tennis had bored him silly. It was a drag. School was a drag. Work was a drag. Crystal meth was definitely not a drag.

At the age of seventeen years and two months, Farley Ramsdale had gone from being a beads 'n' seeds pothead to a tweaker. The first time he smoked crystal he fell in love, everlasting love. But even though it was far cheaper than cocaine, it still cost enough to keep Farley hopping well into the night, visiting blue mailboxes on the streets of Hollywood.

The first thing Farley had to do that afternoon was pay a visit to a hardware store and buy some more mousetraps. Not that Farley worried about mice — they were scampering around his rooming house most of the time. Well, it wasn't a rooming house exactly, he'd be the first to admit. It was an old white-stucco bungalow just off Gower Street, the family home deeded to him by his mother before her death fifteen years ago, when Farley was an eighteen-year-old at Hollywood High School discovering the joys of meth.

He'd managed to forge and cash her pension checks for ten months after her death before a county social worker caught up with him, the meddling bitch. Because he was still a teenager and an orphan, he easily plea-bargained down to a probationary sentence with a promise to pay restitution, which he never paid, and he began calling the two-bedroom, one-bath bungalow a rooming house when he started renting space to other tweakers who came and went, usually within a few weeks.

No, he didn't give a shit about mice. Farley needed ice. Nice clear, icy-looking crystal from Hawaii, not the dirty white crap they sold around town. Ice, not mice, that's what he worried about during every waking hour.

While browsing through the hardware store, Farley saw a red-vested employee watching him when he passed the counter where the drill bits, knives, and smaller items were on display. As if he was going to shoplift the shitty merchandise in this place. When he passed a bathroom display and saw his reflection in the mirror, now in the merciless light of afternoon, it startled him. The speed bumps on his face were swollen and angry, a telltale sign of a speed freak, as his kind used to be known. Like all tweakers he craved candy and sweets. His teeth were getting dark and two molars were hurting.

And his hair! He had forgotten to comb his fucking hair and it was a whirling tangle with that burnt-straw look, hinting at incipient malnutrition, marking him even more as a longtime crystal-smoking tweaker.

He turned toward the employee, an East Asian guy younger than Farley and fit-looking. Probably a fucking martial arts expert, he thought. The way Korea Town was growing, and with a Thai restaurant on every goddamn street and Filipinos emptying bedpans in the free clinics, pretty soon all those canine-eating, dog-breath motherfuckers would be running City Hall too.

But come to think of it, that might be an improvement over the chili-dipping Mexican asshole who was now the mayor, convincing Farley that L.A. would soon be ninety percent Mexican instead of nearly half. So why not give the slopes and greasers knives and guns and let them waste each other? That's what Farley thought should happen. And if the south end niggers ever started moving to Hollywood, he was selling the house and relocating to the high desert, where there were so many meth labs he didn't think the cops could possibly hassle him very much.

Since he couldn't shake that slit-eyed asshole watching him, Farley decided to stop browsing

and headed for the shelf containing the mouse-
traps and rat poison, whereupon the Asian employee walked up to him and said, "Can I help
you, sir?"

Farley said, "Do I look like I need help?"

The Asian looked him over, at his Eminem
T-shirt and oily jeans, and said in slightly accented English, "If you have rats, the spring-
loaded rattraps are what you want. Those glue
traps are excellent for mice, but some larger ro-
dents can pull free of the glue pads."

"Yeah, well, I don't have rats in my house," Farley said. "Do you? Or does somebody eat them
along with any stray terriers that wander in the
yard?"

The unsmiling Asian employee took a deliber-
ate step toward Farley, who yelped, "Touch me
and I'll sue you and this whole fucking hardware chain!" before turning and scuttling away
to the shelf display of cleaning solutions, where
he grabbed five cans of Easy-Off.

When he got to the checkout counter, he
grumbled to a frightened teenage cashier that
there weren't enough English-speaking Americans left in all of L.A. to gang-fuck Courtney
Love so that she'd even notice it.

Farley left the store and had to walk back to

the house, since his piece-of-shit white Corolla had a flat tire and he needed some quick cash to replace it. When he got to the house, he unlocked the dead bolt on the front door and entered, hoping that his one nonpaying tenant was not at home. She was a shockingly thin woman several years older than Farley, although it was hard to tell, with oily black hair plastered to her scalp and tied in a knot at the nape of her neck. She was a penniless, homeless tweaker whom Farley had christened Olive Oyl after the character in *Popeye.*

He dumped his purchases on the rusty chrome kitchen table, wanting to catch an hour of shut-eye, knowing that an hour was about all he could hope for before his eyes snapped open. Like all tweakers, he was sometimes awake for days, and he'd tinker with that banged-up Jap car or maybe play video games until he crashed right there in the living room, his hand still on the controls that allowed him to shoot down a dozen video cops who were trying to stop his video surrogate from stealing a video Mercedes.

No such luck. Just as he fell across the unmade bed, he heard Olive Oyl clumping into the house from the back door. Jesus, she walked heavy for a stick of a woman. *Riverdance* was quieter. He wondered if she had hep C by now. Or Christ! Maybe AIDS? He'd never shared a needle on the rare occasions when he'd skin-popped ice, but she'd probably done it. He vowed to quit boning her and only let her blow him when he was totally desperate.

Then he heard that tremulous little voice. "Farley, you home?"

"I'm home," he said. "And I need to catch some z's, Olive. Take a walk for a while, okay?"

"We working tonight, Farley?" She entered the bedroom.

"Yeah," he said.

"Want a knobber?" she asked. "Help you to sleep."

Jesus, her speed bumps were worse than his. They looked like she scratched them with a garden tool. And her grille showed three gaps in front. When the hell had she lost the third tooth? How come he hadn't noticed before? Now she was skinnier than Mick Jagger and sort of looked like him except older.

"No, I don't want a knobber," he said. "Just go play video games or something."

"I think I got a shot at some extra work, Farley," she said. "I met this guy at Pablo's Tacos. He does casting for extras. He said he was looking for someone my type. He gave me his card and said to call next Monday. Isn't that cool?"

"That's so chill, Olive," he said. "What is it, *Night of the Living Dead, Part Two*?"

Unfazed, Olive said, "Awesome, ain't it? Me, in a movie? Of course it might just be a TV show or something."

"Totally awesome," he said, closing his eyes, trying to unwire his circuits.

"Of course he might just be some Hollywood Casanova wanting in my pants," Olive said with a gap-toothed grin.

"You're perfectly safe with Hollywood Casanovas," Farley mumbled. "You got nothing to spank. Now get the fuck outta here."

When she was gone he actually succeeded in falling asleep, and he dreamed of basketball games in the gym at Hollywood High School and boning that cheerleader who had always dissed and avoided him.

Trombone Teddy had a decent day panhandling on Hollywood Boulevard that afternoon. Nothing like the old days, when he still had a horn, when he'd stand out there on the boulevard and play cool licks like Kai Winding and J.J. Johnson, jamming as good as any of the black jazzmen he'd played with in the nightclub down on Washington and La Brea forty years ago, when cool jazz was king.

In those days the black audiences were always the best and treated him like he was one of them. And in fact he had gotten his share of chocolate cooz in those days, before pot and bennies and alcohol beat him down, before he hocked his trombone a hundred times and finally had to sell it. The horn had gotten him enough money to keep in scotch for oh, maybe a week or so if he remembered right. And no trash booze for Teddy. He drank Jack then, all that liquid gold sliding down his throat and warming his belly.

He remembered those old days like it was this afternoon. It was yesterday he couldn't recall sometimes. Nowadays he drank anything he could get, but oh, how he remembered the Jack and the jazz, and those sweet mommas whispering in his ear and taking him home to feed him gumbo. That's when life was sweet. Forty years and a million drinks ago.

While Trombone Teddy yawned and scratched and knew it was time to leave the sleeping bag that was home in the portico of a derelict office building east of the old Hollywood Cemetery, time to hit the streets for some nighttime panhandling, Farley Ramsdale woke from his fitful hour of sleep after a nightmare he couldn't remember.

Farley yelled, "Olive!" No response. Was that dumb bitch sleeping again? It burned his ass how she could be such a strung-out crystal fiend and still sleep as much as she did. Maybe she was shooting smack in her twat or someplace else he'd never look and the heroin was smoothing out all the ice she smoked? Could that be it? He'd have to watch her better.

"Olive!" he yelled again. "Where the fuck are you?"

Then he heard her sleepy voice coming from the living room. "Farley, I'm right here." She'd been asleep, all right.

"Well, move your skinny ass and rig some mail traps. We got work to do tonight."

"Okay, Farley," she yelled, sounding more alert then.

By the time Farley had taken a leak and splashed water on his face and brushed most of the tangles out of his hair and cursed Olive for not washing the towels in the bathroom, she had finished with the traps.

When he entered the kitchen, she was frying some cheese sandwiches in the skillet and had poured two glasses of orange juice. The mouse-traps were now rigged to lengths of string four feet long. He picked up each trap and tested it.

"They okay, Farley?"

"Yeah, they're okay."

He sat at the table knowing he had to drink the juice and eat the sandwich, though he didn't want either. That was one good thing about let-ting Olive Oyl stay in his house. When he looked at her, he knew he had to take better care of himself. She looked sixty years old but swore she was forty-one, and he believed her. She had the IQ of a schnauzer or a U.S. congressman and was too scared to lie, even though he hadn't laid a hand on her in anger. Not yet, anyway.

"Did you borrow Sam's Pinto like I told you?" he asked when she put the cheese sandwich in front of him.

"Yes, Farley. It's out front."

"Gas in it?"

"I don't have no money, Farley."

He shook his head and forced himself to bite into the sandwich, chew and swallow. Chew and swallow. Dying for a candy bar.

"Did you make a couple auxiliary traps just in case?"

"A couple what?"

"Additional different fucking traps. With duct tape?"

"Oh yes."

Olive went to the little back porch leading to the yard and got the traps from the top of the washer, where she'd put them. She brought them in and placed them on the drain board. Twelve-inch strips of duct tape, sticky side out with strings threaded through holes cut in the tape.

"Olive, don't put the sticky side down on the fucking wet drain board," he said, thinking that choking down the rest of the sandwich would take great willpower. "You'll lose some of the stickiness. Ain't that fucking obvious?"

"Okay, Farley," she said, looping the strings around knobs on the cupboard doors and hanging them there.

Jesus, he had to dump this broad. She was dumber than any white woman he'd ever met with the exception of his aunt Agnes, who was a certifiable re-tard. Too much crystal had turned Olive's brain to coleslaw.

"Eat your sandwich and let's go to work," he said.

Trombone Teddy had to go to work too. After sundown he was heading west from his sleeping bag, thinking if he could panhandle enough on the boulevard tonight he was definitely going to buy some new socks. He was getting a blister on his left foot.

He was still eight blocks from tall cotton, that part of the boulevard where all those tourists as well as locals flock on balmy nights when the Santa Anas blow in, making people's allergies act up but making some people antsy and hungry for action, when he spotted a man and woman standing by a blue mailbox half a block ahead of him at the corner of Gower Street. The corner was south of the boulevard on a street that was a mix of businesses, apartments, and houses.

It was dark tonight and extra smoggy, so there wasn't any starlight, and the smog-shrouded moon was low, but Teddy could make them out, leaning over the mailbox, the man doing something and the woman acting like a lookout or something. Teddy walked closer, huddling in the shadows of a two-story office building where he could see them better. He may have lost part of his hearing and maybe his chops on the trombone, and he'd lost his sex drive for sure, but he'd always had good vision. He could see what they were doing. Tweakers, he thought. Stealing mail.

Teddy was right, of course. Farley had dropped the mousetrap into the mailbox and was fishing it around by the string, trying to catch some letters on the glue pad. He had something that felt like a thick envelope. He fished it up slowly, very slowly, but it was heavy and he didn't have enough of it stuck to the pad, so it fell free.

"Goddamnit, Olive!"

"What'd I do, Farley?" she asked, running a few steps toward him from her lookout position on the corner.

He couldn't think of what to say she'd done wrong, but he always yelled at her for something when life fucked him over, which was most of the time, so he said, "You ain't watching the streets. You're standing here talking is what."

"That's because you said 'Goddamnit, Olive,'" she explained. "So that's why I —"

"Get back to the fucking corner!" he said, dropping the mousetrap into the blue mailbox.

Try as he might, he couldn't hook the glue trap onto the thick envelope, but after giving up on it, he did manage to sweep up several letters and even a fairly heavy ten-by-twelve-inch envelope that was nearly as thick as the one he couldn't catch. He tried the duct tape, but it didn't work any better than the mousetrap.

He squeezed the large envelope and said, "Looks like a movie script. Like we need a goddamn movie script."

"What, Farley?" Olive said, running over to him again.

"You can have this one, Olive," Farley said, handing her the envelope. "You're the future movie star around here."

Farley tucked the mail under Olive's baggy shirt and inside her jeans in case the cops stopped them. He knew the cops would bust him right along with her but he figured he'd have a better shot at a plea bargain if they didn't actually find any evidence on his person. He was pretty sure that Olive wouldn't snitch him off and would go ahead and take the rap. Especially if he promised that her bed in the house would be there when she got out. Where else did she have to go?

They walked right past one of the old homeless Hollywood street people when they rounded the corner by the car. He scared the shit out of Farley when he stepped out of the shadows and said, "Got any spare change, Mister?"

Farley reached into his pocket, took out an empty hand and said to Teddy, "April Fool, shit-bag. Now get the fuck outta my face."

Teddy watched them walk to an old blue Pinto, open the doors, and get in. He watched the guy turn on the lights and start the engine. He stared at the license plate for a minute and said the number aloud. Then he repeated it. He knew he could remember it long enough to borrow a pencil from somebody and write it down. The next time a cop rousted him for being drunk in public or panhandling or pissing in somebody's storefront, maybe he could use it as a get-out-of-jail-free card.

THREE

THERE WERE HAPPIER partners than the pair in 6-X-76 on Sunday of that May weekend. Fausto Gamboa, one of the most senior patrol officers at Hollywood Station, had long since surrendered his P3 status, needing a break from being a training officer to rookies still on probation. He had been happily working as a P2 with another Hollywood old-timer named Ron Le-Croix, who was at home healing up from painful hemorrhoid surgery that he'd avoided too long and was probably just going to retire.

Fausto was always being mistaken for a Hawaiian or Samoan. Though the Vietnam veteran wasn't tall, only five foot nine, he was very big. The bridge of his nose had been flattened in teenage street fights, and his wrists, hands, and shoulders belonged on a guy tall enough to easily dunk a basketball. His legs were so massive he probably could have dunked one if he'd un-coiled those calf and thigh muscles in a vertical leap. His wavy hair was steel-gray and his face was lined and saddle leather–brown, as though he'd spent years picking cotton and grapes in the Central Valley as his father had done after ar-riving in California with a truckload of other ille-gal Mexican immigrants. Fausto had never set eyes on a cotton crop but somehow had inher-ited his father's weathered face.

Fausto was in a particularly foul mood lately, sick and tired of telling every cop at Hollywood Station how he'd lost in court to Darth Vader. The story of that loss had traveled fast on the concrete jungle wireless.

It wasn't every day that you get to write Darth Vader a ticket, even in Hollywood, and everyone agreed it could only happen there. Fausto Gam-boa and his partner Ron LeCroix had been on patrol on an uneventful early evening when they got a call on their MDT computer that Darth Vader was exposing himself near the cor-ner of Hollywood and Highland. They drove to that location and spotted the man in black cy-cling down Hollywood Boulevard on an old Schwinn three-speed bike. But there was often more than one Darth Vader hanging around Grauman's, Darths of different ethnicity. This one was a diminutive black Darth Vader.

They weren't sure they had the right Darth until they saw what had obviously prompted the call. Darth wasn't wearing his black tights under his black shorts that evening, and his manhood was dangling off the front of the bike saddle. A motorist had spotted the exposed trekker's meat and had called the cops.

Fausto was driving and he pulled the car behind Darth Vader and tooted the horn, which had no effect in slowing down the cyclist. He tooted again. Same result. Then he turned on the siren and blasted him. Twice. No response.

"Fuck this," Ron LeCroix said. "Pull beside him."

When Fausto drew up next to the cyclist, his partner leaned out the window and got Darth's attention by waving him to the curb. Once there, Darth put down the kickstand, got off the bike, and took off his mask and helmet. Then they saw why their attempts to stop him had been ineffective. He was wearing a headset and listening to music.

It was Fausto's turn to write a ticket, so he got out the book and took Darth's ID.

Darth Vader, aka Henry Louis Mossman, said, "Wait a minute here. Why you writing me?"

"It's a vehicle code violation to operate a bike on the streets wearing a headset," Fausto said. "And in the future, I'd advise you to wear underwear or tights under those short shorts."

"Ain't this some shit?" Darth Vader said.

"You couldn't even hear our siren," Fausto said to the littlest Darth.

"Bullshit!" Darth said. "I'll see you in court, gud-damnit! This is a humbug!"

"Up to you." Fausto finished writing the ticket.

When the two cops got back in their car that evening and resumed patrol, Fausto said to Ron LeCroix, "That little panhandler will never take me to court. He'll tear up the ticket, and when it goes to warrant, we'll be throwing his ass in the slam."

Fausto Gamboa didn't know Darth Vader.

After several weeks had passed, Fausto found himself in traffic court on Hill Street in downtown L.A. with about a hundred other cops and as many miscreants awaiting their turn before the judge.

Before his case was called, Fausto turned to a cop in uniform next to him and said, "My guy's a loony-tune panhandler. He'll never show up."

Fausto Gamboa didn't know Darth Vader.

Not only did he show up, but he showed up in costume, this time wearing black tights under the short shorts. All courtroom business came to a standstill when he entered after his name was called. And the sleepy-eyed judge perked up a bit. In fact, everyone in the courtroom — cops, scofflaws, court clerk, even the bailiff — was watching with interest.

Officer Fausto Gamboa, standing before the bench as is the custom in traffic court, told his story of how he'd gotten the call, spotted Darth Vader, and realized that Darth didn't know his unit was waving in the breeze. And that he couldn't be made to pull over because he was wearing a headset and listening to music, which the cops discovered after they finally stopped the spaceman.

When it was Darth's turn, he removed the helmet and mask, displaying the headset that he said he wore on the day in question. He did a recitation of the vehicle code section that prohibits the wearing of a headset while operating a bike on city streets.

Then he said, "Your Honor, I would like the court to observe that this headset contains only one earpiece. The vehicle code section clearly refers to both ears being blocked. This officer did not know the vehicle code section then and he don't know it now. The fact is, I did hear the officer's horn and siren but I did not think that it was for me. I wasn't doing nothing illegal, so why should I get all goosey and pull over jist because I hear a siren?"

When he was finished, the judge said to Fausto, "Officer, did you examine the headset that Mr. Mossman was wearing that day?"

"I saw it, Your Honor," Fausto said.

"Does this look like the headset?" the judge asked.

"Well . . . it looks . . . similar."

"Officer, can you say for sure that the headset you saw that day had two earpieces, or did it have only one, like the headset you are looking at now?"

"Your Honor, I hit the siren twice and he failed to yield to a police vehicle. It was obvious he couldn't hear me."

"I see," the judge said. "In this case I think we should give the benefit of the doubt to Mr. Mossman. We find him not guilty of the offense cited."

There was applause and chortling in the courtroom until the bailiff silenced it, and when business was concluded, Darth Vader put on his helmet and with every eye still on him said to all, "May the force be with you."

Now Ron LeCroix and his hemorrhoids were gone, and Fausto Gamboa, still smarting from having his ass kicked by Darth Vader, gave the Oracle a big argument the moment he learned that he was being teamed with Officer Budgie Polk. When Fausto was a young cop, women didn't work regular patrol assignments at the LAPD, and he sneered when he said to the Oracle, "Is she one of them who maybe trades badges with a boyfriend copper like they used to do class rings in my day?"

"She's a good officer," the Oracle said. "Give her a chance."

"Or is she the kind who gets to partner with her boyfriend and hooks her pinkie through his belt loop when they walk the boulevard beat?"

"Come on, Fausto," the Oracle said. "It's only for the May deployment period."

Like the Oracle, Fausto still carried an old six-inch Smith & Wesson revolver, and the first night he was paired with this new partner, he'd pissed her off after she asked him why he carried a wheel gun when the magazine of her Beretta

9-millimeter held fifteen rounds, with one in the pipe.

"If you need more than six rounds to win a gunfight, you deserve to lose," he'd said to her that night, without a hint of a smile.

Fausto never wore body armor, and when she asked him about that too, he had said, "Fifty-four cops were shot and killed in the United States last year. Thirty-one were wearing a vest. What good did it do them?"

He'd caught her looking at his bulging chest that first night and said, "It's all me. No vest. I measure more around the chest than you do." Then he'd looked at her chest and said, "Way more."

That really pissed her off because the fact was, Budgie Polk's ordinarily small breasts were swollen at the moment. Very swollen. She had a four-month-old daughter at home being watched by Budgie's mother, and having just returned to duty from maternity leave, Budgie was actually a few pounds lighter than she had been before the pregnancy. She didn't need thinly veiled cracks about her breast size from this old geezer, not when her tits were killing her.

Her former husband, a detective working out

of West L.A. Division, had left home three months before his daughter was born, explaining that their two-year marriage had been a "regrettable mistake." And that they were "two mature people." She felt like whacking him across the teeth with her baton, as well as half of his cop friends whom she'd run into since she came back to work. How could they still be pals with that dirtbag? She had handed him the keys to her heart, and he had entered and kicked over the furniture and ransacked the drawers like a goddamn crack-smoking burglar.

And why do women officers marry other cops in the first place? She'd asked herself the question a hundred times since that asshole dumped her and his only child, with his shit-eating promise to be prompt with child-support payments and to visit his daughter often "when she was old enough." Of course, with five years on the Job, Budgie knew in her heart the answer to the why-do-women-officers-marry-other-cops question.

When she got home at night and needed to talk to somebody about all the crap she'd had to cope with on the streets, who else would understand but another cop? What if she'd married an insurance adjuster? What would he say when

she came home as she had one night last September after answering a call in the Hollywood
Hills, where the owner of a three-million-dollar
hillside home had freaked on ecstasy and crack
and strangled his ten-year-old step-daughter,
maybe because she'd refused his sexual ad-
vances, or so the detectives had deduced. Nobody would ever know for sure, because the son
of a bitch blew half his head away with a four-
inch Colt magnum while Budgie and her partner were standing on the porch of the home
next door with a neighbor who said she was
sure she'd heard a child screaming.

After hearing the gunshot, Budgie and her
partner had run next door, pistols drawn, she
calling for help into the keyed mike at her shoulder. And while help was arriving and cops were
leaping out of their black-and-whites with shotguns, Budgie was in the house gaping at the
body of the pajama-clad child on the master bedroom floor, ligature marks already darkening,
eyes hemorrhaging, pajamas urine-soaked and
feces-stained. The step-father was sprawled
across the living room sofa, the back cushion
soaked with blood and brains and slivers of
bone.

And a woman there, the child's crack-smoking

mother, was screaming at Budgie, "Help her! Resuscitate her! Do something!"

Over and over she yelled, until Budgie grabbed her by the shoulder and yelled back, "Shut the fuck up! She's dead!"

And that's why women officers seemed to always marry other cops. As poor as the marital success rate was, they figured it would be worse married to a civilian. Who would they talk to after seeing a murdered child in the Hollywood Hills? Maybe male cops didn't have to talk about such things when they got home, but women cops did.

Budgie had hoped that when she returned to duty, she might get teamed with a woman, at least until she stopped lactating. But the Oracle had said everything was screwed during this deployment period, with people off IOD from an unexpected rash of on-duty injuries, vacations, and so forth. He had said, she could work with Fausto until the next deployment period, couldn't she? All of LAPD life revolved around deployment periods, and Fausto was a reliable old pro who would never let a partner down, the Oracle said. But shit, twenty-eight days of this?

Fausto longed for the old days at Hollywood

Station when, after working the night watch, they used to gather in the upper parking lot of the John Anson Ford Theater, across from the Hollywood Bowl, at a spot they called the Tree and have a few brews and commiserate. Sometimes badge bunnies would show up, and if one of them was sitting in a car, sucking face with some cop, you always could be sure that another copper would sneak up, look in the window, and yell, "Crime in progress!"

On one of those balmy summer nights under what the Oracle always called a Hollywood moon, Fausto and the Oracle had sat alone at the Tree on the hood of Fausto's VW bug, Fausto, a young cop back from Vietnam, and the Oracle, a seasoned sergeant but less than forty years old.

He'd surprised Fausto by saying, "Kid, look up there," referring to the lighted cross on top of the hill behind them. "That'd be a great place to have your ashes spread when it's your turn. Up there, looking out over the Bowl. But there's even a better place than that." And then the Oracle told young Fausto Gamboa about the better place, and Fausto never forgot.

Those were the grand old days at Hollywood Station. But after the last chief's "Reign of Terror," nobody dared to drive within a mile of the Tree.

Nobody gathered to drink good Mexican brew. And in fact, this young generation of granola-crunching coppers probably worried about *E. coli* in their Evian. Fausto had actually seen them drinking organic milk. Through a freaking straw!

So here she was, Budgie thought, riding shotgun on Sunset Boulevard with this cranky geezer, easily older than her father, who would have been fifty-two years old had he lived. By the number of hash marks on Fausto's sleeve, he'd been a cop for more than thirty years, almost all of it in Hollywood.

To break the ice on that first night, she'd said, "How long you been on the Job, Fausto?"

"Thirty-four years," he said. "Came on when cops wore hats and you had to by god wear it when you were outta the car. And sap pockets were for saps, not cell phones." Then he paused and said, "Before you were on this planet."

"I've been on this planet twenty-seven years," she said. "I've been on the Job just over five."

The way he cocked his right eyebrow at her for a second and then looked away, he appeared to be saying, So who gives a shit about your history?

Well, fuck him, she thought, but just as night fell and she was hoping that somehow the pain in her breasts would subside, he decided to make a little small talk. He said, "Budgie, huh? That's a weird name."

Trying not to sound defensive, she said, "My mother was Australian. A budgie is an Australian parakeet. It's a nickname that stuck. She thought it was cute, I guess."

Fausto, who was driving, stopped at a red light, looked Budgie up and down, from her blond French-braided ponytail, pinned up per LAPD regulations, to her brightly shined shoes, and said, "You're what? Five eleven, maybe six feet tall in your socks? And weigh what? About as much as my left leg? She shoulda called you 'Storkie.' "

Budgie felt it right then. Worse breast pain. These days a dog barks, a cat meows, a baby cries, she lactates. This bastard's gruff voice was doing it!

"Take me to the substation on Cherokee," she said.

"What for?" Fausto said.

"I'm hurting like hell. I got a breast pump in my war bag. I can do it in there and store the milk."

"Oh, shit!" Fausto said. "I don't believe it! Twenty-eight days of this?"

When they were halfway to the storefront,

Fausto said, "Why don't we just go back to the station? You can do it in the women's locker room, for chrissake."

"I don't want anyone to know I'm doing this, Fausto," she said. "Not even any of the women. Somebody'll say something, and then I'll have to hear all the wise-ass remarks from the men. I'm trusting you on this."

"I gotta pull the pin," Fausto said rhetorically. "Over a thousand females on the Job? Pretty soon the freaking chief'll have double-X chromosomes. Thirty-four years is long enough. I gotta pull the pin."

After Fausto parked the black-and-white at the darkened storefront substation by Musso & Frank's restaurant, Budgie grabbed the carryall and breast pump from her war bag in the trunk, unlocked the door with her 999 key, and ran inside. It was a rather empty space with a few tables and chairs where parents could get information about the Police Activity League or sign up the kids for the Police Explorer Program. Sometimes there was LAPD literature lying around, in English, Spanish, Thai, Korean, Farsi, and other languages for the polyglot citizenry of the Los Angeles melting pot.

Budgie opened the fridge, intending to put

her blue ice packs in the freezer, and left her little thermal bag beside the fridge, where she could pick it up after going off duty. She turned on the light in the john, deciding to pump in there sitting on the toilet lid instead of in the main room, in case Fausto got tired of waiting in the car and decided to stroll inside. But the smell of mildew was nauseating.

She removed the rover from her Sam Browne, then took off the gun belt itself and her uniform shirt, vest, and T-shirt. She draped everything on a little table in the bathroom and put the key on the sink. The table teetered under the weight, so she removed her pistol from the gun belt and laid it on the floor beside her rover and flashlight. After she'd been pumping for a minute, the pain started subsiding. The pump was noisy, and she hoped that Fausto wouldn't enter the storefront. Without a doubt he'd make some wisecrack when he heard the sucking noise coming from the bathroom.

Fausto had clicked onto the car's keyboard that they were code 6 at the storefront, out for investigation, so that they wouldn't get any calls until this freaking ordeal was over. And he was almost dozing when the hotshot call went out to 6-A-77 of Watch 3.

The PSR's urgent voice said, "All units in the vicinity and Six-Adam-Seventy-seven, shots fired in the parking lot, Western and Romaine. Possibly an officer involved. Six-A-Seventy-seven, handle code three."

Budgie was buttoning her shirt, just having stored the milk in the freezer beside her blue ice packs. She had slid the rover inside its sheath when Fausto threw open the front door and yelled, "OIS, Western and Romaine! Are you through?"

"Coming!" she yelled, grabbing the Sam Browne and flashlight while still buttoning her shirt, placing the milk and the freezer bags in the insulated carryall, and running for the door, almost tripping on a chair in the darkened office as she was fastening the Sam Browne around her waspish waist.

There were few things more urgent than an officer-involved shooting, and Fausto was revving the engine when she got to the car and she just had time to close the door before he was ripping out from the curb. She was rattled and sweating and when he slid the patrol car around a corner, she almost toppled and grabbed her seat belt and . . . oh, god!

Since the current chief had arrived, he'd decided to curtail traffic collisions involving officers busting through red lights and stop signs minus lights and siren while racing to urgent calls that didn't rate a code 3 status. So henceforth, the calls that in the old days would have rated only a code 2 status were upgraded to code 3. That meant that in Los Angeles today the citizens were always hearing sirens. The street cops figured it reminded the chief of his days as New York's police commissioner, all those sirens howling. The cops didn't mind a bit. It was a blast getting to drive code 3 all the time.

Because the call wasn't assigned to them, Fausto couldn't drive code 3, but neither the transplanted easterner who headed the Department nor the risen Christ could keep LAPD street cops from racing to an OIS call. Fausto would slow at an intersection and then roar through, green light or not, making cars brake and yield for the black-and-white. But by the time they got to Western and Romaine, five units were there ahead of them and all officers were out of their cars, aiming shotguns or nines at the lone car in the parking lot, where they could see someone ducking down on the front seat.

Fausto grabbed the shotgun and advanced to the car closest to the action, seeing it belonged to the surfers, Flotsam and Jetsam. When he looked over at Budgie trailing beside him, he wondered why she wasn't aiming hers.

"Where's your gun?" he said, then added, "Please don't tell me it's with the milk!"

"No, I have the milk," Budgie said.

"Just point your finger," he said and was stunned to see that, with a sick look on her face, she did it!

After a pause, he said, "I have a two-inch Smith in my war bag. Wanna borrow it?"

Still pointing her long, slender index finger, Budgie said, "Two-inch wheel guns can't hit shit. I'm better off this way."

Fausto came as close to a guffaw as he had in a long time. She had balls. And she was quick, he had to give her that. Then he saw the car door open, and two teenage Latino boys got out with their hands up and were quickly proned-out and cuffed.

The code 4 was broadcast by the PSR, meaning there was sufficient help at the scene. And to keep other eager cops from coming anyway, she added, "No officer involved."

Fausto saw one of those surfers, Flotsam, heading their way. Fausto thought about how back when he was a young copper, there was no way in hell bleached hair would be allowed. And what about his partner, Jetsam, swaggering along beside him with his dark blond hair all gelled in little spikes two inches long? What kind of shit was that? It was time to retire, Fausto thought again. Time to pull the pin.

Flotsam approached Fausto and said, "Security guard at the big building there got hassled by some homies when he caught them jacking up a car to steal the rims. Dumb ass capped one off in the air to scare them away. They jumped in the car and hid, afraid to come out."

"Sky shooting," Fausto snorted. "Guy's seen too many cowboy movies. Shouldn't allow those door shakers to carry anything more than a bag of stones and a slingshot."

"You should see the ride they were working on," Jetsam said, joining his partner. "Nineteen thirty-nine Chevy. Completely restored. Cherry. Bro, it is sweet!"

"Yeah?" Fausto was interested now. "I used to own an old 'thirty-nine when I was in high school." Turning to Budgie, he said, "Let's take a look for a minute." Then he remembered her empty holster and thought they'd better get away before somebody spotted it.

He said to Flotsam and Jetsam, "Just remembered something. Gotta go."

Budgie was thrown back in her seat as they sped away. When she shot him a guilty look, he said, "Please tell me that you didn't forget your key too."

"Oh shit," she said. "Don't you have your nine-nine-nine key?"

"Where's your freaking keys?"

"On the table in the john."

"And where is your freaking gun, may I ask?"

"On the floor in the john. By the keys."

"And what if my nine-nine-nine key's in my locker with the rest of my keys?" he said. "Figuring I didn't have to bother, since I have an eager young partner."

"You wouldn't leave your keys in your locker," Budgie said without looking at him. "Not you. You wouldn't trust a young partner, an old partner, or your family dog."

He looked at her then and seeing a tiny upturn at the corner of her lips thought, She really has some balls, this one. And some smart mouth.

And of course she was right about him — he would never forget his keys.

Fausto just kept shaking his head as he drove back to the storefront substation. Then he grumbled more to himself than to her, "Freaking surfers. You see that gelled hair? Not in my day."

"That isn't gel," Budgie said. "Their hair is stiff and sticky from all the mai tai mix getting dumped on their heads in the beach bars they frequent. They're always sniffing around like a pair of poodles and getting rejected. And please don't tell me it wouldn't be like that if there weren't so many women officers around. Like in your day."

Fausto just grunted and they rode without speaking for a while, pretending to be scanning the streets as the moon was rising over Hollywood.

Budgie broke the silence when she said, "You won't snitch me off to the Oracle, will you? Or for a big laugh to the other guys?"

With his eyes focused on the streets, he said, "Yeah, I go around ratting out partners all the time. For laughs."

"Is there a bathroom window in that place?" she asked. "I didn't notice."

"I don't think there's any windows," he said. "I hardly ever been in there. Why?"

"Well, if I'm wrong about you and you don't have a key, and if there's a window, you could boost me up and I could pry it open and climb in."

His words laden with sarcasm, Fausto said, "Oh, well, why not just ask me if I'd climb in the window because you're a new mommy and can't risk hurting yourself?"

"No," she said, "you could never get your big ass through any window, but I could if you'd boost me up. Sometimes it pays to look like a stork."

"I got my keys," he said.

"I figured," she said.

For the first time, Budgie saw Fausto nearly smile, and he said, "It hasn't been a total loss. At least we got the milk."

At about the same time that Fausto Gamboa and Budgie Polk were gathering her equipment at the substation on Cherokee, Farley Ramsdale and Olive Oyl were home at Farley's bungalow, sitting on the floor, having smoked some of the small amount of crystal they had left. Scattered all around them on the floor were letters they had fished out of seven blue mailboxes on that very busy evening of work.

Olive was wearing the glasses Farley had stolen for her at the drugstore and was laboriously reading through business mail, job applications, notices of unpaid bills, detached portions of paid bills, and various other correspondence. Whenever she came across something they could use, she would pass it to Farley, who was in a better mood now, sorting some checks they could possibly trade and nibbling on a saltine because it was time to put something in his stomach.

The crystal was getting to him, Olive thought. He was blinking more often than usual and getting flushed. Sometimes it worried her when his pulse rate would shoot up to 150 and higher, but if she mentioned it, he just yelled at her, so she didn't say anything.

"This is a lot of work, Farley," she said when her eyes were getting tired. "Sometimes I wonder why we don't just make our own meth. Ten years ago I used to go with a guy who had his own meth lab and we always had enough without working so hard. Till the chemicals blew up one day and burned him real bad."

"Ten years ago you could walk in a drugstore

and buy all the goddamn ephedrine you wanted," Farley said. "Nowadays a checkout clerk'll send you to a counter where they ask for ID if you try to buy a couple boxes of Sudafed. Life ain't easy anymore. But you're lucky, Olive. You get to live in my house. If you were living in a ratty hotel room, it'd be real dangerous to do the work we do. Like, if you used a hot credit card or a phony name to get your room like you always did before, you'd lose your protection against search and seizure. The law says you have no expectation of privacy when you do that. So the cops could kick your door down without a search warrant. But you're lucky. You live in my house. They need a search warrant to come in here."

"I'm real lucky," Olive agreed. "You know so much about the law and everything." She grinned at him and he thought, *Kee-rist,* those fucking teeth!

Olive thought it was nice when she and Farley were at home like this, working in front of the TV. Really nice when Farley wasn't all paranoid from the tweak, thinking the FBI and the CIA were coming down the chimney. A couple times when he'd hallucinated, Olive really got scared. They'd had a long talk then about how much to smoke and when they should do it. But lately she thought that Farley was breaking his own rules when she wasn't looking. She thought he was into that ice a whole lot more than she was.

"We got quite a few credit-card numbers," he said. "Lots of SS numbers and driver's license info and plenty of checks. We can trade for some serious glass when we take this stuff to Sam."

"Any cash, Farley?"

"Ten bucks in a card addressed to 'my darling grandchild.' What kinda cheap asshole only gives ten bucks to a grandchild? Where's the fucking family values?"

"That's all?"

"One other birthday card, 'to Linda from Uncle Pete.' Twenty bucks." He looked up at Olive and added, "Uncle Pete's probably a pedophile, and Linda's probably his neighbor's ten-year-old. Hollywood's full of freaks. Someday I'm getting outta here."

"I better check on the money," Olive said.

"Yeah, don't cook it to death," Farley said, thinking that the saltine was making him sick. Maybe he should try some vegetable soup if there was a can left.

The money was in the tub that Farley had placed on the screened back porch. Eighteen five-dollar bills were soaking in Easy-Off, almost bleached clean. Olive used a wooden spoon to poke a few of them or flip them over to look at the other side. She hoped this would work better than the last time they tried passing bogus money.

That time Olive almost got arrested, and it scared her to even think about that day two months ago when Farley told her to buy a certain light green bonded paper at Office Depot. And then they took it to Sam, the guy who rented them his car from time to time, and Sam worked for two days cutting the paper and printing twenty-dollar bills on his very expensive laser printer. After Sam was satisfied, he told Olive to spray the stack of bogus twenties with laundry starch and let them dry thoroughly. Olive did it, and when she and Farley checked the bills, he thought they were perfect.

They stayed away from the stores like the mini-market chains that have the pen they run over large bills. Farley wasn't sure if they'd bother with twenties, but he was afraid to take a chance. A mini-market clerk had told Farley that if the clerk sees brown under the pen, it's good; black or no color is bad. Or something like that.

So they'd gone to a Target store on that day two months ago to try out the bogus money.

In front of the store was a buff young guy with a mullet passing out gay pride leaflets for a parade that was being organized the following weekend. The guy wore a tight yellow T-shirt with purple letters across the front that said "Queer Pervert."

He'd offered a handbill to Farley, who pointed at the words on the T-shirt and said to Olive, "That's redundant."

The guy flexed his deltoids and pecs, saying to Farley, "And it could say 'Kick Boxer' too. Want a demonstration?"

"Don't come near me!" Farley cried. "Olive, you're a witness!"

"What's redundant, Farley?" Olive asked, but he said, "Just get the fuck inside the store."

Olive could see that Farley was in a bad mood then, and when they were entering, they were partially blocked by six women and girls completely covered in chadors and burkas, two of them talking on cells and two others raising their veils to drink from large Starbucks cups.

Farley brushed past them, saying, "Why don't you take those Halloween rags back to Western Costume." Then to Olive, "Wannabe sand niggers.

Or maybe Gypsies boosting merchandise under those fucking muumuus."

One of the women said something angrily in Arabic, and Farley muttered, "*Hasta lasagna* to you too. Bitch."

There were lots of things that Olive had wanted to buy, but Farley said they were going to maintain control until they tested the money once or twice with small purchases. Farley kept looking at a CD player for $69.50 that he said he could sell in five minutes at Ruby's Donuts on Santa Monica Boulevard, where a lot of tranny streetwalkers hung out.

Olive had always been tenderhearted and she felt sorry for all those transsexuals trapped between two genders. Some of those she'd talked to had had partial gender-changing operations, and a couple of them had endured the complete change, Adam's apple surgery and all. But Olive could still tell they hadn't been born as women. They seemed sad to Olive and they were always nice to her long before she'd met Farley, when she was panhandling and selling ecstasy for a guy named Willard, who was way mean. Many times a tranny who'd just turned a good trick would give Olive five or ten dollars and tell her to go get something to eat.

"You look nervous," Farley said to Olive as they wandered around the Target store.

"I'm only a little nervous," Olive said.

"Well, stop it. You gotta look like a normal person, if that's possible." Farley eyed a very nice twenty-one-inch TV set but shook his head, saying, "We gotta start small."

"Can we just do it now, Farley?" Olive said. "I just wanna get it over with."

Farley left the store and Olive took the CD player to the checkout counter, the most crowded one so that she'd encounter a clerk who was too busy to be looking for bogus money. Except that just as the shopper ahead of her was paying for a purchase of blankets and sheets, a manager stepped over and offered to relieve the harried young checkout clerk. He glanced at Olive when he was taking care of the other customer, and Olive had a bad feeling.

She had a real bad feeling when it was her turn and he said suspiciously, "Will you be paying by check?"

"No, cash," Olive said innocently, just as a roving store employee walked up to the manager and nodded toward Olive.

The roving guy said, "Where's your friend?"

"Friend?" Olive said.

"Yes, the man who insulted the Muslim ladies," he said. "They complained and wanted me to throw him out of the store."

Olive was so shaken, she didn't notice that she'd dropped the three twenties on the counter until the manager picked them up and held them up to the light and ran them through his fingers. And Olive panicked. She bolted and ran past shoppers with loaded carts, through the doors to the parking lot, and didn't stop until she was on the sidewalk in front.

When Farley found her walking on the sidewalk and picked her up, she didn't tell him about the guy and the complaint from the Muslim women. She knew it would just make him madder and get him in a terrible mood, so she said that the checkout clerk felt the money and said, "This paper is wrong." And that's why Farley went back to Sam, who told him to try to get good paper by bleaching real money with Easy-Off.

So today they were trying it again but with real money. She wore her cleanest cotton sweater and some low-rise jeans that were too big, even though Farley had shoplifted them from the juniors section at Nordstrom. And she wore tennis shoes for running, in case things went bad again.

"This time it won't go bad," Farley promised Olive while he parked in front of RadioShack, seemingly determined to buy a CD player.

When they were out and standing beside the car, he said, "This time you got real paper from real money, so don't sweat it. And it wasn't easy to get hold of all those five-dollar bills, so don't blow this."

"I don't know if they look quite right," Olive said doubtfully.

"Stop worrying," Farley said. "You remember what Sam told you about the strip and the watermark?"

"Sort of," Olive said.

"The strip on the left side of a five says five, right? But it's small, very hard to see. The president's image on the right-side watermark is bigger but also hard to see. So if they hold the bill up to the light and their eyes start looking left to right or right to left, whadda you do?"

"I run to you."

"No, you don't run to me, goddamnit!" He yelled it, then looked around, but none of the passing shoppers were paying any attention to them. He continued with as much patience as he could muster. "These dumb shits won't even notice that the strip ain't for a twenty-dollar bill and that the watermark has a picture of Lincoln instead of Jackson. They just go through the motions and look, but they don't see. So don't panic."

"Until I'm sure he's onto me. Then I run out to you."

Farley looked at the low, smog-laden sky and thought, Maintain. Just fucking maintain. This woman is dumb as a clump of dog hair. Slowly he said, "You do not run to me. You never run to me. You do not know me. I am a fucking stranger. You just walk fast out of the store and head for the street. I'll pick you up there after I make sure nobody's coming after you."

"Can we do it now, Farley?" Olive said. "Pretty soon I'll have to go to the bathroom."

The store was bustling when they entered. As usual, there were a few street people lurking around the parking lot begging for change.

One of the street people recognized Farley and Olive. In fact, he had their license number written down on a card, saving it for a rainy day, so to speak. Farley and Olive never noticed the old homeless guy who was eyeballing them as they entered. Nor did they see him enter the store and approach a man with a "Manager" tag on his shirt.

The homeless guy whispered something to the manager, who kept his eye on Farley and Olive for the whole ten minutes that they browsed. When Farley walked out of the store, the manager still watched him, until he was sure that Farley wasn't coming back in. Then the manager reentered the store and watched Olive at the checkout counter.

Slick, Olive thought. It's working real slick. The kid at the checkout took the four bogus twenties from Olive's hand and began ringing up the purchase. But then it happened.

"Let me see those bills."

The manager was talking to the kid, not to Olive. She hadn't seen him standing behind her, and she was too startled by his arrival to do anything but freeze.

He held the bills up to the late-afternoon light pouring through the plate glass, and she saw his eyes moving left to right and right to left, and she didn't care if Farley said they're too dumb to match up strips and watermarks and all that Farley Ramsdale goddamn bullshit! Olive knew exactly what to do and did it right at that instant.

Three minutes later Farley picked her up sprinting across the street against a red light, and he was amazed that Olive Oyl could move that fast, given her emaciated condition. A few minutes after that, Trombone Teddy walked into RadioShack and the manager told him that yes, they were crooks and had tried to pass bogus twenties. He handed Teddy several dollars from his pocket and thanked him for the tip. All in all, Teddy thought that his day was beginning quite fortuitously. He wished he could run into those two tweakers more often.

FOUR

WONDERING WHY IN the hell she'd volunteered to read her paper when none of them knew what she did for a living, Andi McCrea decided to sit on the corner of the professor's desk just as though she wasn't nervous about criticism and wasn't scared of Professor Anglund, who'd squawked all during the college term about the putative abuse of civil liberties by law enforcement.

With her forty-fifth birthday right around the corner and her oral exam for lieutenant coming up, it had seemed important to be able to tell a promotion board that she had completed her bachelor's degree at last, even making the Dean's List unless Anglund torpedoed her. She hoped to convince the board that this academic achievement at her time of life — combined with twenty-four years of patrol and detective experience — proved that she was an outstanding candidate for lieutenant's bars. Or something like that.

So why hadn't she just gracefully declined when Anglund asked her to read her paper? And why now, nearly at the end of the term, at the end of her college life, had she decided to write a paper that she knew would provoke this professor and reveal to the others that she, a middle-aged classmate old enough to be their momma, was a cop with the LAPD? Unavoidable and honest answer: Andi was sick and tired of kissing ass in this institution of higher learning.

She hadn't agreed with much of what this professor and others like him had said during all the years she'd struggled here, working for the degree she should have gotten two decades ago, balancing police work with the life of a single mom. Now that it was almost over, she was ashamed that she'd sat silently, relishing those A's and A-pluses, pretending to agree with all the crap in this citadel of political correctness that often made her want to gag. She was looking for self-respect at the end of the academic trail.

For this effort, Andi wore the two-hundred-dollar blue blazer she'd bought at Banana instead of the sixty-dollar one she'd bought at the

Gap. Under that blazer was a button-down Oxford in eye-matching blue, also from Banana, and no bling except for tiny diamond studs. Black flats completed the ensemble, and since she had had her collar-length bob highlighted on Thursday, she'd figured to look pretty good for this final performance. Until she got the call-out last night: the bloodbath on Cherokee that kept her from her bed and allowed her just enough time to run home, shower and change, and be here in time for what she now feared would be a debacle. She was bushed and a bit nauseated from a caffeine overload, and she'd had to ladle on the pancake under her eyes to even approach a look of perkiness that her classmates naturally exuded.

"The title of my paper is 'What's Wrong with the Los Angeles Police Department,'" Andi began, looking out at twenty-three faces too young to know Gumby, fourteen of whom shared her gender, only four of whom shared her race. It was to be expected in a university that prided itself on diversity, with only ten percent of the student population being non-Latino white. She had often wanted to say, "Where's the goddamn diversity for me? I'm the one in the minority." But never had.

She was surprised that Professor Anglund had remained in his chair directly behind her instead of moving to a position where he could see her face. She'd figured he was getting too old to be interested in her ass. Or are they ever?

She began reading aloud: "In December of nineteen ninety-seven, Officer David Mack of the LAPD committed a $722,000 bank robbery just two months before eight pounds of cocaine went missing from an LAPD evidence room, stolen by Officer Rafael Perez of Rampart Division, a friend of David Mack's.

"The arrest of Rafael Perez triggered the Rampart Division police scandal, wherein Perez, after one trial, cut a deal with the district attorney's office to avoid another, and implicated several cops through accusations of false arrests, bad shootings, suspect beatings, and perjury, some of which he had apparently invented to improve his plea bargain status.

"The most egregious incident, which he certainly did not invent, involved Perez himself and his partner, Officer Nino Durden, both of whom in nineteen ninety-six mistakenly shot a young Latino man named Javier Ovando, putting him into a wheelchair for life, then falsely testified that he'd threatened them with a rifle that they themselves had planted beside his critically wounded body in order to cover their actions. Ovando served two years in prison before he was released after Perez confessed."

Andi looked up boldly, then said, "Mack, Perez, and Durden are black. But to understand what came of all this we must first examine the Rodney King incident five years earlier. That was a bizarre event wherein a white sergeant, having shot Mr. King with a Taser gun after a long auto pursuit, then directed the beating of this drunken, drug-addled African American ex-convict. That peculiar sergeant seemed determined to make King cry uncle, when the ring of a dozen cops should have swarmed and handcuffed the drunken thug and been done with it."

She gave another pointed look at her audience and then went on: "That led to the subsequent riot where, according to arrest interviews, most of the rioters had never even heard of Rodney King but thought this was a good chance to act out and do some looting. The riot brought to Los Angeles a commission headed by Warren Christopher, later to become U.S. secretary of state under President Bill Clinton, a commission that determined very quickly and with very little evidence that the LAPD had a significant number of overly aggressive, if not downright brutal, officers who needed reining in. The LAPD's white chief, who, like several others before him, had civil service protection, was soon to retire.

"So the LAPD was placed under the leadership of one, then later a second African American chief. The first, an outsider from the Philadelphia Police Department, became the first LAPD chief in decades to serve without civil service protection at the pleasure of the mayor and city council, a throwback to the days when crooked politicians ran the police force. His contract was soon bought back by city fathers dissatisfied with his performance and his widely publicized junkets to Las Vegas.

"The next black chief, an insider whose entire adult life had been spent with the LAPD, was in charge when the Rampart Division scandal exploded, making the race card difficult for anyone to play. This chief, a micromanager, seemingly obsessive about control and cavalier about officer morale, quickly became the enemy of the police union. He came to be known as Lord Voldemort by street cops who'd read *Harry Potter.*

"David Mack, Rafael Perez, and Nino Durden

went to prison, where Mack claimed to belong to the Piru Bloods street gang. So, we might ask: Were these cops who became gangsters, or gangsters who became cops?"

Scanning their faces, she saw nothing. She dropped her eyes again and read, "By two thousand two, that second black chief, serving at the pleasure of City Hall, hadn't pleased the politicians, the cops, or the local media. He retired but later was elected to the city council. His replacement was another cross-country outsider, a white chief this time, who had been New York City's police commissioner. Along with all the changes in leadership, the police department ended up operating under a 'civil rights consent decree,' an agreement between the City of Los Angeles and the United States Department of Justice wherein the LAPD was forced to accept major oversight by DOJ-approved monitors for a period of five years but which has just been extended for three years by a federal judge based on technicalities.

"And thus, the beleaguered rank and file of the formerly proud LAPD, lamenting the unjustified loss of reputation as the most competent and corruption-free, and certainly most famous, big-city police department in the country, finds itself faced with the humiliation of performing under outside overseers. Mandated auditors can simply walk into a police station and, figuratively speaking, ransack desks, turn pockets inside out, threaten careers, and generally make cops afraid to do proactive police work that had always been the coin of the realm with the LAPD during the glory days before Rodney King and the Rampart Division scandal.

"And of course, there is the new police commission, led by the former head of the L.A. Urban League, who uttered the following for the *L.A. Times* before he took office. Quote: 'The LAPD has a long-standing institutionalized culture in which some police officers feel that they have the tacit approval of their leadership . . . to brutalize and even kill African American boys and men.' End quote. This baseless and crudely racist slander is apparently okay with our new Latino mayor, who appointed him claiming to want harmony in the racial cauldron where the police must do their job."

Andi looked again at the blank stares as she prepared for her parting shot and said, "Finally, all of the layers of oversight, based on the crimes of a few cops — costing millions annually, encouraged by cynical politicians and biased reporting and fueled by political correctness gone mad — have at last answered the ancient question posed by the Roman poet Juvenal in the first century A.D. He too was worried about law enforcement abuse, for he asked, 'But who would guard the guards themselves?' At the Los Angeles Police Department, more than nine thousand officers have learned the answer: Everybody."

With that, Andi turned to glance at Anglund, who was looking at papers in his lap as though he hadn't heard a word. She said to the class, "Any questions?"

Nobody answered for a long moment, and then one of the East Asians, a petite young woman about the age of Andi's son, said, "Are you a cop or something?"

"I am a cop, yes," Andi said. "With the LAPD, and have been since I was your age. Any other questions?"

Students were looking from the wall clock to the professor and back to Andi. Finally, Anglund said, "Thank you, Ms. McCrea. Thank you, ladies and gentlemen, for your diligence and attention. And now that the spring quarter is so close to officially concluding, why don't you all just get the hell out of here."

That brought smiles and chuckles and some applause for the professor. Andi was about to leave, when Anglund said, "A moment, Ms. Mc-Crea?"

He waited until the other students were gone, then stood, hands in the pockets of his cords, cotton shirt so wrinkled that Andi thought he should either send it out or get his wife an ironing board. His gray hair was wispy, and his pink scalp showed through, flaked with dandruff. He was a man of seventy if he was a day.

Anglund said, "Why did you keep your other life from us until the end?"

"I don't know," she said. "Maybe I only like to don the bat suit when night falls on Gotham City."

"How long have you been attending classes here?"

"Off and on, eight years," she said.

"Have you kept your occupation a secret from everybody in all that time?"

"Yep," she said. "I'm just a little secret keeper."

"First of all, Ms. McCrea . . . is it Officer Mc-Crea?"

"Detective," she said.

"First of all, your paper contained opinions

and assertions that you may or may not be able to back up and not a few biases of your own, but I don't think you're a racist cop."

"Well, thank you for that. That's mighty white of you, if that's an acceptable phrase." Thinking, There goes the Dean's List. She'd be lucky to get a C-plus out of him now.

Anglund smiled and said, "Sorry. That was very condescending of me."

"I bored them to death," Andi said.

"The fact is, they don't really give a damn about civil liberties or police malfeasance or law enforcement in general," Anglund said. "More than half of today's university students cannot even understand the positions put forth in newspaper editorials. They care about iPods and cell phones and celluloid fantasy. The majority of this generation of students don't read anything outside of class but magazines and an occasional graphic novel, and barely contemplate anything more serious than video downloading. So, yes, I think you failed to provoke them as you'd obviously intended to do."

"I guess my son isn't so different after all, then," she said, seeing her first C-plus morphing into a C-minus.

"Is he a college student?"

"A soldier," she said. "Insisted on joining because two of his friends did."

Anglund studied her for a few seconds and said, "Iraq?"

"Afghanistan."

Anglund said, "Despite the flaws in your thesis, I was impressed by the passion in it. You're part of something larger than yourself, and you feel real pain that uninformed outsiders are harming the thing you love. I don't see much of that passion in classrooms anymore. I wish you'd revealed your other life to us earlier."

Now she was confused, fatigued and confused, and her nausea was increasing. "I wouldn't have done it today, Professor," Andi said, "except my forty-fifth birthday is coming up in two weeks and I'm into a midlife crisis so real it's like living with a big sister who just wants to dress up in thigh-highs and a miniskirt and dance the funky chicken. No telling what kind of zany thing I'll do these days. And last night I got called out on a murder-suicide that looked like O.J. Simpson was back in town, and I'm exhausted. But I'm not half as tired or stressed as two young cops who had to wallow in a bloodbath doing a job that nobody should ever have to do. And when it was all over, one of them asked me back at Hollywood Station if I had some moisturizing cream. Because he surfed so much he thought his neck and eyelids looked like they belonged on a Galapagos turtle. I felt like just hugging him."

Then the catch in her voice made her pause again, and she said, "I'm sorry. I'm babbling. I've gotta get some sleep. Good-bye, Professor."

As she gathered her purse and books, he held up his class folder, opened it, and pointed to her name, along with the grade he'd given her presentation when he'd sat there behind her, when she'd thought he wasn't listening. It was an A-plus.

"Good-bye, Detective McCrea," he said. "Take care in Gotham City."

Andi McCrea was driving back to Hollywood Division (she'd never get used to calling it Hollywood Area, as it was supposed to be called these days but which most of the street cops ignored) to assure herself that all the reports from last night's murder-suicide were complete. She was a D2 in one of the three homicide teams, but they were so shorthanded at Hollywood Station that she had nobody else around today who could help with the reports from her current cases, not even the one that had solved itself like the murder-suicide of the night before.

She decided to send an FTD bouquet to Professor Anglund for the A-plus that guaranteed her the Dean's List. That old socialist was okay after all, she thought, scribbling a note saying "flowers" after she wheeled into the Hollywood Station south parking lot in her Volvo sedan.

The station parking lots were more or less adequate for the time being, considering how many patrol units, plain-wrap detectives units, and private cars had to park there. If they were ever brought up to strength, they'd have to build a parking structure, but she knew that it wasn't likely that the LAPD would ever be brought up to strength. And when would the city pop for money to build a parking structure when street cops citywide were complaining about the shortage of equipment like digital cameras and batteries for rifle lights, shotgun lights, and even flashlights. They never seemed to have pry bars or hooks or rams when it was time to take down a door. They never seemed to have anything when it was needed.

Andi McCrea was bone-weary and not just because she had not slept since yesterday morning. Hollywood Division's workload called for fifty detectives, but half that many were doing the job, or trying to do it, and these days she was always mentally tired. As she trudged toward the back door of Hollywood Station, she couldn't find her ring of keys buried in the clutter of her purse, gave up, and walked to the front door, on Wilcox Avenue.

The building itself was a typical municipal shoe box with a brick facade the sole enhancement, obsolete by the time it was finished. Four hundred souls were crammed inside a rabbit warren of tiny spaces. Even one of the detectives' interview rooms had to be used for storage.

By habit, she walked around the stars on the pavement in front of the station without stepping on them. There was nothing like them at other LAPD stations, and they were exactly like the stars on the Hollywood Walk of Fame except that the names embedded in the marble were not the names of movie stars. There were seven names, all belonging to officers from Hollywood Station who had been killed on duty. Among them were Robert J. Coté, shot and killed by a robber, Russell L. Kuster, gunned down in a Hungarian restaurant by a deranged customer,

Charles D. Heim, shot to death during a drug arrest, and Ian J. Campbell, kidnapped by robbers and murdered in an onion field.

The wall plaque said "To Those Who Stood Their Ground When in Harm's Way."

Hollywood Station was also different from any other in the LAPD by virtue of the interior wall hangings. There were one-sheet movie posters hanging in various places in the station, some but not all from cop movies based in Los Angeles. A police station decorated with movie posters let people know exactly where they were.

Andi was passed in the corridor leading to the detective squad room by two young patrol officers on their way out. Although there were several older cops working patrol, Hollywood Division officers tended to be young, as though the brass downtown considered Hollywood a training area, and perhaps they did.

The short Japanese American female officer she knew as Mag something said hi to Andi.

The tall black male officer whose name she didn't know said more formally, "Afternoon, Detective."

Six-X-Sixty-six had been asked by the vice sergeant to pop into a few of the adult bookstores

to make sure there weren't lewd-conduct violations taking place in the makeshift video rooms.
A pair of Hollywood Station blue suits making
unscheduled visits went a long way toward convincing the termites to clean up their act, the
vice sergeant had told them. Mag Takara, an ath-
letic twenty-six-year-old, and the shortest officer
at Hollywood Station, was partnered in 6-X-66
with Benny Brewster, age twenty-five, from
southeast L.A., who was one of Hollywood's
tallest officers.

One morning last month, the Oracle had spotted a clutch of male cops in the parking lot after
roll call convulsing in giggles at Mag Takara,
who, after putting her overloaded war bag into
the trunk, couldn't close the lid because it was
sprung and yawned open out of reach.

Mag's war bag was on wheels, jammed with
helmet and gear. She had also been carrying a
Taser, an extra canister of pepper spray, a beanbag shotgun, a pod (handheld MDT computer),
her jacket, a bag of reports, a flashlight, a side-
handle baton as well as a retractable steel baton,
and the real we-mean-business shotgun loaded
with double-aught buck that would be locked in
the rack inside the car. She was so short she had
to go around to the rear window of the patrol

car and close the trunk by walking her hands along the length of the deck lid until it clicked shut.

The Oracle watched her for a moment and heard the loudest of the cops tossing out lines to the others like, "It's a little nippy, wouldn't you say? A teeny little nippy."

The Oracle said to the jokester, "Bonelli, her great-grandparents ran a hotel on First Street in little Tokyo when yours were still eating garlic in Palermo. So spare us the ethnic wisecracks, okay?"

Bonelli said, "Sorry, Sarge."

While the cops were all walking to their patrol cars, the Oracle said, "I gotta balance that kid out." And he'd assigned Benny Brewster to partner with Mag for the deployment period to see how they got along. And so far, so good, except that Benny Brewster had a cultural hangup about adult bookstores when it came to gay porn.

"Those sissies creep me out," he said to Mag. "Some of the gangstas in Compton would cap their ass, they saw the stuff we see all over Hollywood" is how he explained it.

But Mag told him she didn't give a shit if the fuck flicks were gay or straight, it was all revolting. One of her former cop boyfriends had tried to light her fire a couple of times by showing her porn videos in his apartment after dinner, but it seemed to her that act two of all those stories consisted of jizz shots in a girl's face, and how that could excite anybody was way beyond her.

Despite his hangup about gay men, Benny seemed to her like a dedicated officer, never badge-heavy, never manhandling anybody who didn't need it, whether gay or straight, so she had no complaints. And it was very comforting for Mag when Benny was standing behind her, eye-fucking some of those maggots who liked to challenge little cops, especially little female cops.

They met Mr. Potato Head in the first porn shop they checked out. It was on Western Avenue, a dingier place than most, with a few peep rooms where guys could look at video and jerk off with the door locked, but this one had a makeshift theater, a larger room with three rows of plastic chairs posing as theater seats, and a large screen along with a quality projector hanging from the ceiling.

The theater was curtained off by heavy black drapes and there was no lighting inside, except for what came from the screen. The occasional visit from uniformed cops was supposed to discourage the viewers from masturbating in public, whether alone or in tandem, while they watched two or three or five guys porking whatever got in front of them. To background hip-hop lyrics about rape and sodomy.

Benny walked down one aisle, looking like he wanted to get it over with, and Mag started down the other, when she heard him say, "Do your pants up and come with me!"

The viewer had been so involved in what he was doing that he hadn't seen that very tall black cop in a dark blue uniform until he was standing three feet away. He lost the erection he'd been stroking, as did just about all of the other guys in the room, but Mag figured some of these dudes were so bent that the presence of the law, the danger of it all, probably enhanced the thrill.

She shined her light across the chair to see what was going on but he had already pulled up and belted his pants. He was being led by the elbow toward the black curtain and Benny kept saying, "Damn!"

When they got him out of the video room, Mag said, "What? Six-forty-seven-A?" referring to the penal code section for lewd conduct in public.

Benny looked at the guy, at the black elastic straps wound around his wrists, and said, "What were you doing in there, man? Besides displayin' your willie. What're them straps on your wrists all about?"

He was a fiftyish plump, bespectacled white guy with a pouty mouth and a fringe of brown hair. He said, "I'd prefer not to explain at this time."

But when they took him to a glass-windowed holding tank at Hollywood Station, they found out. He gave a short demonstration that caused Benny to exit the scene shortly after the prisoner dropped his pants and unhooked the intricately connected elastic straps that encircled his waist, wound under his crotch from each wrist, and finally threaded through holes in the end of a potato. Which he reached behind and removed from his anal cavity with a magician's flourish and not a little pride of invention.

Performing before five gaping cops who happened by the glass window, the prisoner then demonstrated that if he sat on one buttock and manipulated the straps attached to his wrists, he could adeptly pull the potato halfway out simply by raising his arms, then force it back into its "magic cave" by sitting on it. He looked like he was conducting an orchestra. Arms raised, potato out, then sit. Arms raised, potato out, then sit. And so forth.

"Probably keeping time with the background music on the video," Mag suggested. The guy was ingenious, she had to give him that.

"I ain't handling the evidence," Benny said to Mag. "No way. In fact, I wanna transfer outta this lunatic asylum. I'll work anywhere but Holly-weird!"

It disappointed her. *Holly-weird.* Why did they all have to say it?

By end-of-watch, Benny would find a gift box tied with a ribbon in front of his locker and a card bearing the name "Officer Brewster." Inside the box was a nice fresh Idaho potato to which someone had attached plastic eyes and lips, along with a handwritten note that said, "Fry me, bake me, mash me. Or bite me, Benny. Love ya. — Mr. Potato Head."

FIVE

THERE WAS ALWAYS a male cop at LAPD with "Hollywood" attached to his name, whether or not he worked Hollywood Division. It was usually earned by the cop's outside interest in things cinematic. If he did an occasional job with a TV or movie company as a technical advisor, you could be sure everyone would start calling him "Hollywood Lou" or "Hollywood Bill." Or in the case of aspiring thespian Nate Weiss — who so far had only done some work as an extra on a few TV shows — "Hollywood Nate." After he got bitten by the show business bug, he enrolled at a gym and worked out obsessively. With those brown bedroom eyes and dark, wavy hair just starting to gray at the temples, along with his newly buffed physique, Nate figured he had leading-man potential.

Nathan Weiss was thirty-five years old, a late bloomer as far as show business was concerned. He, along with lots of other patrol officers in the division, had done traffic control and provided security when film companies were shooting around town. The pay was excellent for off-duty cops and the work was easy enough but not as exciting as any of them had hoped. Not when all those hot actresses only popped their heads out of their trailers for a few minutes to block out a scene if the director wasn't satisfied with a stand-in doing it. Then they'd disappear again until it was time to shoot it.

Most of the time, the cops weren't up close for the shooting itself, and even when they were, it quickly became boring. After the master shot, they'd do two-shots of the principals, with close-ups and reverse angles, and the actors had to do it over and over. So most of the cops would quickly get bored and hang around the craft services people, who supplied all the great food for the cast and crew.

Hollywood Nate never got bored with any of it. Besides, there were a lot of hot chicks doing below-the-line work and ordinary grunt work on every shoot. Some of them were interns who dreamed of someday being above-the-line talent: directors, actors, writers, and producers. When Nate had a lot of overtime opportunities, he actually made more money than just about all of those cinematic grunts. And unlike them, Nate did not have to suffer the biggest fear in show business: My Next Job.

Nate loved to display his knowledge of the Business when talking to some little hottie, maybe a gofer running errands for the first assistant director. Nate would say things like "My usual beat is around Beachwood Canyon. That's old Hollywood. A lot of below-the-line people live there."

And it was one of those gofers who had cost Nate Weiss his less than happy home two years back, when his then-wife, Rosie, got suspicious because every time the phone rang one time and stopped, Nate would disappear for a while. Rosie started making date and time notations whenever one ring occurred, and she compared it with his cell phone bills. Sure enough, Nate would call the same two numbers moments after the one-ring calls she noted. Probably the slut had two cell phones or two home numbers, and it would be just like Nate to think two separate numbers would fool Rosie if she got suspicious.

Rosie Weiss bided her time, and one cold winter morning Nate came home from work at dawn telling her he was just all tuckered out from an overtime hunt for a cat burglar in Laurel Canyon. Rosie thought, Sure, an alley cat, no doubt. And she did a little experiment in Nate's car while he slept, and then managed to just go about her business for the rest of the day and that evening.

The next day, when Nate went to work, he sat in the roll-call room listening to the lieutenant droning on about the U.S. Department of Justice consent decree that the LAPD was under and hinting that the cars that were working the Hispanic neighborhoods on the east side should be turning in Field Data Reports on non-Hispanics, even though there were none around.

Cops did what cops were doing from Highland Park to Watts, those who worked African American 'hoods and Latino barrios. LAPD officers were inventing white male suspects and entering them on FDRs that contained no names or birth dates and were untraceable. Therefore, an abundance of white male field interviews could convince outside monitors that the cops were not racial profiling. In one inner-city division, there was a 290 percent increase in non-Hispanic white male nighttime pedestrian stops, even though nobody had ever seen a white guy walking around the 'hood at night. Even with a flat tire, a white guy would keep riding on the rims rather than risk a stop. Cops said that even a black-and-white had to have a sign in the window saying "Driver carries no cash."

This was the federal consent decree's version of "don't ask, don't tell": We won't ask where you got all those white male names on the FDRs if you don't tell us.

Before the watch commander had arrived at roll call, a cop said aloud, "This FDR crap is so labor-intensive it makes embryonic cloning look like paint matching."

Another said, "We should all just become lawyers. They get paid a lot to lie, even if they have to dress up to do it."

So it seemed that the Department of Justice, instead of promoting police integrity, had done just the opposite, by making liars out of LAPD street cops who had to live under the consent decree for five years and then had to swallow the demoralizing three-year extension.

During that ponderous roll call, Hollywood Nate was dozing through the consent decree sermon and got surprised when the Oracle popped his head in the door, saying, "Sorry, Lieutenant, can I borrow Weiss for a minute?"

The Oracle didn't say anything until they were alone on the stairway landing, when he turned to Nate and said, "Your wife is downstairs demanding to speak to the lieutenant. She wants a one-twenty-eight made on you."

Nate was mystified. "A personnel complaint? Rosie?"

"Do you have any kids?"

"Not yet. We've decided to wait."

"Do you want to save your marriage?"

"Sure. It's my first, so I still give a shit. And her old man's got bucks. What's happened?"

"Then cop out and beg for mercy. Don't try weasel words, it won't work."

"What's going on, Sarge?"

Hollywood Nate got to see for himself what was going on when he, Rosie, and the Oracle stood in the south parking lot beside Nate's SUV on that damp and gloomy winter night. Still baffled, Nate handed his keys to the Oracle, who handed them to Rosie, who jumped into the SUV, started it up, and turned on the defroster. As the windows were fogging prior to clearing, she stepped out and pointed triumphantly at what her sleuthing had uncovered. There they were, in the mist on the windshield in front of the passenger seat: oily imprints made by bare toes.

"Wears about a size five," Rosie said. Then she turned to the Oracle and said, "Nate always did like little spinners. I'm way too zoftig for him."

When Nate started to speak, the Oracle said, "Shut up, Nate." Then he turned to Rosie and said, "Mrs. Weiss . . ."

"Rosie. You can call me Rosie, Sergeant."

"Rosie. There's no need to drag the lieutenant into this. I'm sure that you and Nate —"

Interrupting, she said, "I called my dad's lawyer today while this son of a bitch was sleeping it off. It's over. Way over. I'm moving everything out of the apartment on Saturday."

"Rosie," the Oracle said. "I'm positive that Nate will be very fair when he talks with your lawyer. Your idea of making an official complaint for conduct unbecoming an officer would not be helpful to you. I imagine you want him working and earning money rather than suspended from duty, where he and you would lose money, don't you?"

She looked at the Oracle and at her husband, who was pale and silent, and she smiled when she saw beads of sweat on Nate's upper lip. The asshole was sweating on a damp winter night. Rosie Weiss liked that.

"Okay, Sergeant," she said. "But I don't want this asshole to set foot in the apartment until I'm all moved out."

"He'll sleep in the cot room here at the station," the Oracle said. "And I'll detail an officer to make an appointment with you to pick up whatever Nate needs to tide him over until you're out of the apartment."

When Rosie Weiss left them in the parking lot that evening, she had one more piece of information to impart to the Oracle. She said, "Anyway, since he got all those muscles in the gym, the only time he can ever get an erection is when he's looking in the mirror."

After she got in her car and drove away, Nate finally spoke. He said, "A cop should never marry a Jewish woman, Sarge. Take it from me, she's a terrorist. It's code red from the minute the alarm goes off in the morning."

"She's got good detective instincts," the Oracle said. "We could use her on the Job."

Now, his wife was married to a pediatrician, no longer entitled to alimony, and Nate Weiss was a contented member of the midwatch, taking TV extra work as much as he could, hoping to catch a break that could get him into the Screen Actors Guild. He was sick of saying, "Well, no, I don't have a SAG card but . . ."

Hollywood Nate had hoped that 2006 would be his breakthrough year, but with summer almost here, he wasn't so sure. His reverie ended when he got a painfully vigorous handshake from his new partner, twenty-two-year-old Wesley Drubb, youngest son of a partner in Lawford and Drubb real-estate developers, who had enormous holdings in West Hollywood and Century City. Nate got assigned with the former frat boy who'd dropped out of USC in his senior year "to find himself" and impulsively joined the LAPD, much to the despair of his parents. Wesley had just finished his eighteen months of probation and transferred to Hollywood from West Valley Division.

Nate thought he'd better make the best of this opportunity. It wasn't often he got to partner with someone rich. Maybe he could cement a friendship and become the kid's big brother on the Job, maybe persuade him to chat up his old man, Franklin Drubb, about investing in a little indie film that Nate had been trying to put together with another failed actor named Harley Wilkes.

The cops often called their patrol car their "shop" because of the shop number painted on the front doors and roof. This so that each car could be easily identified by an LAPD helicopter, always called an "airship." When they were settled in their shop and out cruising the streets that Nate liked to cruise no matter which beat he was assigned, the eager kid riding shotgun swiveled his head to the right and said, "That looks like a fifty-one-fifty," referring to the Welfare and Institutions Code section that defines a mental case.

The guy was a mental case, all right, one of the boulevard's homeless, the kind that shuffle along Hollywood Boulevard and wander into the many souvenir shops and adult bookstores and tattoo parlors, bothering the vendors at the sidewalk newsstands, refusing to leave until somebody gives them some change or throws them out or calls the cops.

He was known to the police as "Untouchable Al" because he roamed freely and often got warned by cops but was never arrested. Al had a get-out-of-jail-free card that was better than Trombone Teddy's any old day. This evening he was in a cranky mood, yelling and scaring tourists, causing them to step into the street rather than pass close to him there on the Walk of Fame.

Nate said, "That's Al. He's untouchable. Just tell him to get off the street. He will unless he's feeling extra grumpy."

Hollywood Nate pulled the black-and-white around the corner onto Las Palmas Avenue, and Wesley Drubb, wanting to show his older partner that he had moxie, jumped out, confronted Al, and said, "Get off the street. Go on, now, you're disturbing the peace."

Untouchable Al, who was drunk and feeling very grumpy indeed, said, "Fuck you, you young twerp."

Wesley Drubb was stunned and turned to look at Nate, who was out of the car, leaning on the roof with his elbows, shaking his head, knowing what was coming.

"He's having a bad hair day," Nate said. "A dozen or so are hanging out his nose."

"We don't have to take that," Wesley said to Nate. Then he turned to Al and said, "We don't have to take that from you."

Yes, they did. And Al was about to demonstrate why. As soon as Wesley Drubb pulled on his latex gloves and stepped forward, putting his hand on Al's bony shoulder, the geezer shut his eyes tight and grimaced and groaned and squatted a bit and let it go.

The explosion was so loud and wet that the young cop leaped back three feet. The sulfurous stench struck him at once.

"He's shitting!" Wesley cried in disbelief. "He's shitting his pants!"

"I don't know how he craps on cue like that," Nate said. "It's a rare talent, actually. Kind of the ultimate defense against the forces of truth and justice."

"Gross!" the young cop cried. "He's shitting! Gross!"

"Come on, Wesley," Hollywood Nate said. "Let's go about our business and let Al finish his."

"Fucking young twerp," Untouchable Al said as the black-and-white drove swiftly away.

While Untouchable Al was finishing his business, an extraordinary robbery was taking place at a jewelry store on Normandie Avenue owned by a Thai entrepreneur who also owned two restaurants. The little jewelry store that sold mostly watches was this week going to offer a very special display of diamonds that the proprietor's twenty-nine-year-old nephew, Somchai "Sammy" Tanampai, planned to take home when he closed that evening.

The robbers, an Armenian named Cosmo Betrossian and his girlfriend, a Russian masseuse and occasional prostitute named Ilya Roskova, had entered the store just before closing, wearing stocking masks. Now Sammy Tanampai sat on the floor in the back room, his wrists duct-taped behind his back, weeping because he believed they would kill him whether or not they got what they wanted.

Sammy forced his eyes from roaming to his son's cartoon-plastered lunch box on a table by the back door. He'd placed the diamonds in little display trays and velvet bags and stacked them inside the lunch box next to a partially consumed container of rice, eggs, and crab meat.

Sammy Tanampai thought they might be after the watches, but they didn't touch any of them. The male robber, who had very thick black eyebrows grown together, raised up the stocking mask to light a cigarette. Sammy could see small broken teeth, a gold incisor, and pale gums.

He walked to where Sammy was sitting on

the floor, pulled Sammy's face up by jerking back a handful of hair, and said in heavily accented English, "Where do you hide diamonds?"

Sammy was so stunned he didn't respond until the large blond woman with the sulky mouth, garishly red under the stocking mask, walked over, bent down, and said in less accented English, "Tell us and we will not kill you."

He started to weep then and felt urine soak his crotch, and the man pointed the muzzle of a .25 caliber Raven pistol at his face. Sammy thought, What a cheap-looking gun they are about to shoot me with.

Then his gaze involuntarily moved toward his child's lunch box and the man followed Sammy's gaze and said, "The box!"

Sammy wept openly when the big blond woman opened the lunch box containing more than a hundred and eighty thousand wholesale dollars' worth of loose diamonds, rings, and ear studs and said, "Got it!"

The man then ripped off a strip of duct tape and wrapped it around Sammy's mouth.

How did they know? Sammy thought, preparing to die. Who knew about the diamonds?

The woman waited by the front door and the

man removed a heavy object from the pocket of his coat. When Sammy saw it he cried more, but the duct tape kept him quiet. It was a hand grenade.

The woman came back in, and for the first time Sammy noticed their latex gloves. Sammy wondered why he hadn't noticed before, and then he was confused and terrified because the man, holding the spoon handle of the grenade, placed it between Sammy's knees while the woman wrapped tape around his ankles. The grenade spoon dug into the flesh of his thighs above the knees and he stared at it.

When the robbers were finished, the woman said, "You better got strong legs. If you relax too much your legs, you shall lose the handle. And then you die."

And with that, the man, holding Sammy's knees in place, pulled the pin and dropped it on the floor beside him.

Now Sammy did wail, the muffled sound very audible even with his mouth taped shut.

"Shut up!" the man commanded. "Keep the knees tight or you be dead man. If the handle flies away, you be dead man."

The woman said, "We shall call police in ten

minutes and they come to help you. Keep the knees together, honey. My mother always tell me that but I do not listen."

They left then but didn't call the police. A Mexican dishwasher named Pepe Ramirez did. He was on his way to his job in Thai Town, driving past the boss's jewelry store, and was surprised to see light coming from the main part of the store. It should have been closed. The boss always closed before now so he could get to both his restaurants while they were preparing for the dinner crowd. Why was the boss's store still open? he wondered.

The dishwasher parked his car and entered the jewelry store through the unlocked front door. He spoke very little English and no Thai at all, so all he could think to call out was "Meester? Meester?"

When he got no answer, he walked cautiously toward the back room and stopped when he heard what sounded like a dog's whimper. He listened and thought, No, it's a cat. He didn't like this, not at all. Then he heard banging, a loud muffled series of thumps. He ran from the store and called 911 on his brand-new cell phone, the first he'd ever owned.

Because of his almost unintelligible English

and because he hung up while the operator was trying to transfer the call to a Spanish speaker, his message had been misunderstood. Other undocumented migrants had told him that the city police were not *la migra* and would not call Immigration unless he committed a major crime, but he was uncomfortable around anyone with a uniform and badge and thought he should not be there when they came.

It came out over the air as an "unknown trouble" call, the kind that makes cops nervous. There was enough known trouble in police work. Usually such a call would draw more than one patrol unit as backup. Mag Takara and Benny Brewster got the call, and Fausto Gamboa and Budgie Polk were the first backup to arrive, followed by Nate Weiss and Wesley Drubb.

When Mag entered the store, she drew her pistol and following her flashlight beam walked cautiously into the back room with Benny Brewster right behind her. What she saw made her let out a gasp.

Sammy Tanampai had hopelessly banged his head against the plasterboard wall, trying to get the attention of the dishwasher. His legs were going numb and the tears were streaming down his face as he tried to think about his children, tried to stay strong. Tried to keep his knees together!

When Mag took two steps toward the jeweler, Benny Brewster shined his light on the grenade and yelled, "WAIT!"

Mag froze and Fausto and Budgie, who had just entered by the front door, also froze.

Then Mag saw it clearly and yelled, "GRENADE! CLEAR!" And nobody knew what was going on or what the hell to do except instinctively to draw their guns and crouch.

Fausto did not clear out. Nor did the others. He shouldered past Benny, plunged into the back room, and saw Mag standing ten feet from the taped and hysterical Sammy Tanampai. And Fausto saw the grenade.

Sammy's face was bloody where he'd snagged the tape free on a nail head, and he tried to say something with a crumpled wad of tape stuck to the corner of his mouth. He gagged and said, "I can't . . . I can't . . ."

Fausto said to Mag, "GET OUT!"

But the littlest cop ignored him and tiptoed across the room as though motion would set it off. And she reached carefully for it.

Fausto leaped forward after Sammy unleashed the most despairing terrifying wail that Mag had ever heard in her life when his thigh muscles just surrendered. Mag's fingers were inches from the grenade when it dropped to the floor beneath her and the spoon flew across the room.

"CLEAR CLEAR CLEAR!" Fausto yelled to all the cops in the store, but Mag picked up the grenade first and lobbed it into the far corner behind a file cabinet.

Instantly, Fausto grabbed Mag Takara by the back of her Sam Browne and Sammy Tanampai by his shirt collar and lifted them both off the floor, lunging backward until they were out of the little room and into the main store, where all six cops and one shopkeeper pressed to the floor and waited in terror for the explosion.

Which didn't come. The hand grenade was a dummy.

No fewer than thirty-five LAPD employees were to converge on that store and the streets around it that night: detectives, criminalists, explosives experts, patrol supervisors, even the patrol captain. Witnesses were interviewed, lights were set up, and the area for two blocks in all directions was searched by cops with flashlights.

They found nothing of evidentiary value, and a detective from the robbery team who had been called in from home interviewed Sammy Tanampai in the ER at Hollywood Presbyterian Hospital. The victim told the detective that the male robber had briefly smoked a cigarette but none had been found by detectives at the scene.

Sammy grew lethargic because the injection they had given him was making him sleepy, but he said to the detective, "I don't know how they knew about the diamonds. The diamonds arrived at ten o'clock this morning and we were going to show them tomorrow to a client from San Francisco who requested certain kinds of pieces."

"What kind of client is he?" the detective asked.

"My uncle has dealt with him for years. He is very wealthy. He is not a thief."

"About the blond woman who you think was Russian, tell me more."

"I think they were both Russians," Sammy said. "There are lots of Russians around Hollywood."

"Yes, but the woman. Was she attractive?"

"Perhaps so. I don't know."

"Anything out of the ordinary?"

"Big breasts," Sammy said, opening and closing his aching jaw and touching the wounded flesh around his mouth, his eyelids drooping.

"Have you ever gone to any of the nightclubs around here?" the detective asked. "Several of them are Russian owned and operated."

"No. I am married. I have two children."

"Anything else that you remember about either of them?"

"She made a joke about keeping my knees together. She said that she never did. I was thinking of my children then and how I would never see them again. And she made that joke. I hope you get to shoot them both," Sammy said, tears welling.

After all the cops who'd been in the jewelry store were interviewed back at the station, Hollywood Nate said to his young partner, "Some gag, huh, Wesley? Next time I work on a show, I'm gonna tell the prop man about this. A dummy grenade. Only in Hollywood."

Wesley Drubb had been very quiet for hours since their trauma in the jewelry store. He had answered questions from detectives as well as he could, but there really wasn't anything important to say. He answered Nate with, "Yeah, the joke was on us."

What young Wesley Drubb wanted to say was, I could have died tonight. I could have . . .

been . . . *killed* tonight! If the grenade had been real.

It was very strange, very eerie, to contemplate his own violent death. Wesley Drubb had never done that before. He wanted to talk to somebody about it but there was no one. He couldn't talk about it to his older partner, Nate Weiss. Couldn't explain to a veteran officer like Nate that he'd left USC for this, where he'd been on the sailing team and was dating one of the hottest of the famed USC song girls. He'd left it because of those inexplicable emotions he felt after he'd reached his twenty-first birthday.

Wesley had grown sick of college life, sick of being the son of Franklin Drubb, sick of living on Fraternity Row, sick of living in his parents' big house in Pacific Palisades during school holidays. He'd felt like a man in prison and he'd wanted to break out. LAPD was a breakout without question. And he'd completed his eighteen months of probation and was here, a brand-new Hollywood Division officer.

Wesley's parents had been shocked, his fraternity brothers, sailing teammates, and especially his girlfriend, who was now dating a varsity wide receiver — everyone who knew him was shocked. But he hadn't been sorry so far. He'd thought he'd probably do it for a couple of years, not for a career, for the kind of experience that would set him apart from his father and his older brother and every other goddamn broker in the real-estate firm owned by Lawford and Drubb.

He thought it would be like going into the military for a couple of years, but he wouldn't have to leave L.A. Like a form of combat that he could talk about to his family and friends years later, when he inevitably became a broker at Lawford and Drubb. He'd be a sort of combat veteran in their eyes, that was it.

Yes, and it had all been going so well. Until tonight. Until that grenade hit the floor and he stared at it and that little officer Mag Takara picked it up with Fausto Gamboa roaring in his ears. That wasn't police work, was it? They never talked about things like that in the academy. A man with a hand grenade between his knees?

He remembered a Bomb Squad expert lecturing them at the police academy about the horrific event of 1986 in North Hollywood when two LAPD officers were called in to defuse an explosive device in a residential garage, rigged by a murder suspect involved in a movie studio/labor union dispute. They defused it but were unaware of a secondary device lying there by a copy of *The Anarchist's Cookbook*. The device went off.

What Wesley remembered most vividly was not the description of the gruesome and terrible carnage and the overwhelming smell of blood, but that one of the surviving officers who had just gotten inside the house before the explosion was having recurring nightmares two decades later. He would waken with his pillow soaked with tears and his wife shaking him and saying, "This has *got* to stop!"

For a while this evening, after he'd completed his brief statement, after he was sitting in the station quietly drinking coffee, Wesley Drubb could only think about how he'd felt trying to dig with his fingernails into the old wooden floor of that jewelry store. It had been an instinctive reaction. He had been reduced to his elemental animal core.

And Wesley Drubb asked himself the most maddeningly complex, dizzying, profound, and unanswerable question he'd ever asked himself in his young life: How the fuck did I get here?

When Fausto Gamboa got changed into civvies, he met Budgie on the way to the parking lot.

They walked quietly to their cars, where they saw Mag Takara already getting into her personal car and driving away.

Fausto said, "It used to make me crazy seeing that kid doing her nails during roll call. Like she was getting ready to go on a date."

"I'll bet it won't annoy you anymore, will it?" Budgie said.

"Not as much," Fausto Gamboa conceded.

★ SIX

THIS WAS SUPPOSED to be a routine interview of a missing juvenile, nothing more. Andi McCrea had been sitting in her little cubicle in the detective squad room staring at a computer screen, putting together reports to take to the DA's office in a case where a wife smacked her husband on the head with the side of a roofing hammer when, after drinking a six-pack of Scotch ale, he curled his lip and told her that the meat loaf she'd labored over "smelled like Gretchen's snatch."

There were two things wrong with that: First, Gretchen was her twice-divorced, flirtatious younger sister, and second, he had a panic-stricken look on his face that denuded the feeble explanation when he quickly said, "Of course, I wouldn't know what Gretchen's . . ." Then he began again and said, "I was just trying for a Chris Rock kind of line but didn't make it, huh? The meat loaf is fine. It's fine, honey."

She didn't say a word but walked to the back porch, where the roofer kept his tool belt, and returned with the hammer just as he was taking the first bite of meat loaf that smelled like Gretchen's snatch.

Even though the wife had been booked for attempted murder, the guy only ended up with twenty-three stitches and a concussion. Andi figured that whichever deputy DA the case was taken to would reject it as a felony and refer it to the city attorney's office for a misdemeanor filing, which was fine with her. The hammer victim reminded her of her ex-husband, Jason, now retired from LAPD and living in Idaho near lots of other coppers who had fled to the wilderness locales. Places where local cops only write on their arrest reports under race of suspects either "white" or "landscaper."

Jason had been one of those whom several other women officers had sampled, the kind they called "Twinkies," guys who aren't good for you but you have to have one. Andi had been young then, and she paid the price during a five-year marriage that brought her nothing good except Max.

Her only child, Sergeant Max Edward McCrea, was serving with the U.S. Army in Afghanistan, his second deployment, the first having been in Iraq at a time when Andi was hardly ever able to sleep more than a few hours before waking with night sweats. It was better now that he was in Afghanistan. A little better. Eighteen years old, just out of high school, he had gotten the itch, and there was nothing she could do to keep him from signing that enlistment contract. Nothing that her ex-husband could do either, when for once Jason had stepped up and acted like a father. Max had said he was going into the army with two other teammates from his varsity football team, and that was it. Iraq for him, tension headaches for her, lying awake in her two-story house in Van Nuys.

After getting her case file in order, Andi was about to get a cup of coffee, when one of the Watch 2 patrol officers approached her cubicle and said, "Detective, could you talk to a fourteen-year-old runaway for us? We got a call to the Lucky Strike Lanes, where he was bowling with a forty-year-old guy who started slapping him around. He tells us he was molested by the guy, but the guy won't talk at all. We got him in a holding tank."

"You need the sex crimes detail," Andi said.

"I know, but they're not here and I think the kid wants to talk but only to a woman. Says the things he's got to say are too embarrassing to tell a man. I think he needs a mommy."

"Who doesn't?" Andi sighed. "Okay, put him in the interview room and I'll be right there."

Five minutes later, after drinking her coffee, and after getting the boy a soft drink and advising him for the second time of his rights, she nodded to the uniformed officer that he could leave.

Aaron Billings was delicate, almost pretty, with dark ringlets, wide-set expressive eyes, and a mature, lingering gaze that she wouldn't have expected. He looked of mixed race, maybe a quarter African American, but she couldn't be sure. He had a brilliant smile.

"Do you understand why the officers arrested you and your companion?" she asked.

"Oh, sure," he said. "Mel was hitting me. Everyone saw him. We were right there in the bowling alley. I'm sick of it, so when they asked for our ID I told them I was a runaway. I'm sure my mom's made a report. Well, I think she would."

"Where're you from?"

"Reno, Nevada."

"How long have you been gone?"

"Three weeks."

"Did you run away with Mel?" Andi asked.

"No, but I met him the next day when I was hitchhiking. I was sick of my mother. She was always bringing men home, and my sister and me would see them having sex. My sister is ten."

"You told the officer that Mel molested you, is that right?"

"Yes, lots of times."

"Tell me what happened from when you first met."

"Okay," the kid said, and he took a long drink from the soda can. "First, he took me to a motel and we had sex. I didn't want to but he made me. Then he gave me ten dollars. Then we went to the movies. Then we had Chinese food at a restaurant. Then we decided to drive to Hollywood and maybe see movie stars. Then Mel bought vodka and orange juice and we got drunk. Then we drove to Fresno and parked at a rest stop and slept. Then we woke up early. Then we killed two people and took their money. Then we went to the movies again. Then we drove to Bakersfield. Then —"

"Wait a minute!" Andi said. "Let's go back to the rest stop!"

Twenty minutes later Andi was on the phone

to the police in Fresno, and after a conversation with a detective, she learned that yes, a middle-aged couple had been shot and killed where they'd obviously been catching a few hours' sleep en route from Kansas to a California vacation. And yes, the case was open with no suspects and no evidence other than the .32 caliber slugs taken from the skulls of both victims at the postmortem.

The detective said, "We just don't have any leads."

Andi said, "You do now."

When Andi's supervisor, D3 Rhonda Jenkins, came in late that afternoon after a long day in court testifying in a three-year-old murder case, she said, "My day sucked. How was yours?"

"Tried to keep busy on a typical May afternoon in Hollywood, USA."

"Yeah? What'd you do?" Rhonda asked, just making conversation as she slipped off her low-heeled pumps and massaged her aching feet.

Deadpan, Andi said, "First I made calls on two reports from last night. Then I reread the case file on the pizza man shooting. Then I interviewed a banger down at Parker Center. Then I had some coffee. Then I cleared a double homicide in Fresno. Then I wrote a letter to Max. Then —"

"Whoa!" Rhonda said. "Go back to the double homicide in Fresno!"

"That bitch! You couldn't find her heart with a darkfield microscope," Jetsam complained to his partner.

Flotsam, who was attending community college during the day, said, "Dude, you are simply another victim of the incestuous and intertwined and atavistic relationships of the law-enforcement community."

Jetsam gaped at Flotsam, who was driving up into the Hollywood Hills, and said, "Just shove those college-boy words, why don't you."

"Okay, to be honest," said Flotsam, "from that photo you showed me, she was spherical, dude. The woman looked to me like a fucking Teletubby. You were blinded by the humongous mammary glands is all. There was no real melding of the hearts and minds."

"Melding of the . . ." Jetsam looked at his partner in disbelief and said, "Bro, the bitch's lawyer wants everything, including my fucking fish tank! With the only two turtles I got left! And guess what else? The federal consent decree ain't gonna end on schedule because that asshole of a federal judge says we're not ready. It's all political bullshit."

"Don't tell me that," Flotsam said. "I was all ready to yell out at roll call, 'Free at last, free at last, Lord God Awmighty, free at last!'"

"I'm outrageously pissed off at our new mayor," Jetsam said, "turning the police commission into an ACLU substation. And I'm pissed off at my ex-wife's lawyer, who only wants me to have what I can make recycling aluminum cans. And I'm pissed off living in an apartment with lunging fungus so aggressive it wants to tackle you like a linebacker. And I'm pissed off at my former back-stabbing girlfriend. And I'm pissed off at the Northeast detective who's boning her now. So all in all, I feel like shooting somebody."

And, as it happened, he would.

The PSR radio voice alerted all units on the frequency to a code 37, meaning a stolen vehicle, as well as a police pursuit in progress of said vehicle.

Ever the pessimist, Jetsam said, "Devonshire Division. He'll never come this far south."

The more optimistic Flotsam said, "You never know. We can dream."

Jetsam said, "Since our politician chief won't

let us pursue unless the driver's considered reckless, do you suppose this fucking maniac has crossed the reckless-driving threshold yet? Or does he have to run a cop off the road first?"

They listened to the pursuit on simulcast as it crossed freeways and surface streets in the San Fernando Valley, heading in the general direction of North Hollywood. And within a few minutes it was in North Hollywood and heading for the Hollywood Freeway.

"Watch them turn north again," Jetsam said.

But the pursuit did not. The stolen car, a new Toyota 4Runner, turned south on the Hollywood Freeway, and Jetsam said, "That one has a pretty hot six under the hood from what I hear. Bet he'll double-back now. Probably some homie. He'll double-back, get near his 'hood, dump the car, and run for it."

But the pursuit left the Hollywood Freeway and turned east on the Ventura Freeway and then south on Lankershim Boulevard. And now the surfer team looked at each other and Jetsam said, "Holy shit. Let's go!"

And they did. Flotsam stepped on it and headed north on the Hollywood Freeway past Universal City and turned off in the vicinity of the Lakeside Country Club, where by now a dozen LAPD and CHP units were involved, as well as a television news helicopter, but no LAPD airship.

And it was here that the driver dumped the car on a residential street near the country club, and he was into a yard, over a fence into another yard, onto the golf course, running across fairways, and then back into a North Hollywood residential street where nearly twenty cops were out on foot, half of them armed with shotguns.

Even though a North Hollywood Division sergeant was at the abandoned stolen car, trying to inform the communications operator that there was sufficient help at the scene, cars kept coming, as happens during a long pursuit like this. Soon there were L.A. Sheriff's Department units as well as more CHP and LAPD cars, with the TV helicopter hovering and lighting up the running cops below.

Flotsam drove two blocks west of the pandemonium and said, "Wanna get out and go hunting for a while? You never know."

"Fucking A," Jetsam said, and they got out of their car with flashlights extinguished and walked through a residential alley behind family homes and apartment buildings.

They could hear voices on the street to their

right, where other cops were searching, and Flotsam said, "Maybe we better turn our flashlights on before somebody caps one off at us."

Then a voice yelled, "There he is! Hey, there he is!"

They ran toward the voice and saw a young cop with ginger hair and pink complexion sitting astride an eight-foot block wall dividing an apartment complex from the alley.

He saw them, or rather, he saw two shadow figures in blue uniforms, and said, "Up there! He's in that tree!"

Flotsam shined his light high into an old olive tree, and sure enough, there was a young Latino up there in an oversize white T-shirt, baggy khakis, and a head bandana.

The young cop yelled, "Climb down now!" And he pointed his nine at the guy with one hand while with his other hand he shined his light on the treetop.

Flotsam and Jetsam got closer, and the guy in the tree looked down at the young cop straddling the wall and said, "Fuck you. Come up and get me."

Flotsam turned to Jetsam and said, "Tweaked. He's fried on crystal."

"Ain't everybody?" Jetsam said.

The young cop, who had "probationer" written all over him, pulled out his rover but before keying it said, "What's our location? Do you guys know the address here?"

"Naw," Jetsam said. "We work Van Nuys Division."

Now, that was weird, Flotsam thought. Why would his partner tell the boot that they worked Van Nuys instead of telling the truth?

Then the young cop said, "Watch him, will you? I gotta run out to the street and get the address."

"Just go out front and start yelling," Jetsam said. "There's coppers all over the block."

Flotsam also found it strange that Jetsam had turned his flashlight off and was standing in deep shadow under a second tree. Almost as though he didn't want the kid to be able to see him clearly. But why? That they had driven a short distance out of their division wasn't a big deal.

After the rookie ran out onto the street in front, Jetsam said, "Fucking boot doesn't know what to do about a thief in a tree."

They stood looking up at the guy who squinted down at their light beams, and Flotsam said, "What would you do besides wait for backup?"

Jetsam looked up and yelled, "Hey asshole, climb down here."

The car thief said, "I'm staying here."

"How would you like me to blow you outta that tree?" Jetsam shouted, aiming his .40 caliber Glock at him. "I feel like shooting somebody tonight."

"You won't shoot," the kid said. "I'm a minor. And all I did was joyride."

Now Jetsam was really torqued. And not for the first time he noticed that the young cop had left his Remington beanbag shotgun with the bright green fore and aft stocks propped against the wall.

"Check this out, partner," he said to Flotsam. "That probey grabbed a beanbag gun instead of the real thing. Now he's probably looking for a chain saw to cut the fucking tree down."

Touching his pepper spray canister, Flotsam said, "Wish he was closer, dude. A little act-right spray would do wonders for him." Then Flotsam looked at Jetsam and Jetsam looked at Flotsam and Flotsam said, "No. I know what you're thinking, but no. Stay real, man!"

But Jetsam said in a quiet voice, "That boot never saw our faces, bro. There's coppers all over the neighborhood."

"No," Flotsam said. "A beanbag gun is not to be

used for compliance purposes. This ain't pit bull polo, dude."

"I wonder if it would induce some compliance here."

Flotsam said, "I don't wanna know."

But Jetsam, who had never shot anyone with a beanbag or anything else, reached into his pocket, put on a pair of latex gloves so as to not leave latent prints, picked up the shotgun, pointed it up into the tree, and said, "Hey *vato,* get your ass down here right now or I'll let one go and blow you outta that tree."

The muzzle of the gun looked big enough to hold a popsicle, but it didn't scare the car thief, who said, "You and your *puto* partner can just kiss my —"

And the muzzle flash and explosion shocked Flotsam more than the kid, who let out a shriek when the beanbag struck him in the belly.

"Ow ow ow, you pussy!" the kid yelled. "You shot me, you pussy! Owwwwwww!"

So Jetsam let go with another round, and this time Flotsam ran to the street in front of the apartment complex and saw no less than five shadow figures yelling and running their way while the kid howled even louder and started climbing down.

"Let's get the fuck outta here!" Flotsam said, after running back to Jetsam and grabbing him by the arm.

"He's coming down, bro," Jetsam said with a dazed expression.

"Toss that tube!" Flotsam said, and Jetsam dropped the shotgun on the grass and scurried after his partner.

Both cops ran back down the alley through the darkness toward their car, and neither spoke until Flotsam said, "Man, there'll be IA investigators all over this one, you crazy fucker! You ain't even allowed to shoot white guys like that!"

Still running, and gradually realizing that he'd just violated a whole lot of Department regulations, if not the penal code itself, Jetsam said, "The homie never saw us, bro. The lights were always in his eyes. The little boot copper didn't see our faces neither. Shit, he was so excited he couldn't ID his own dick. Anyways, this is North Hollywood Division. We don't work here."

"The best-laid plans of mice and rats," Flotsam said. Then he had a panicky thought. "Did you go code six?" he said, referring to the safety rule of informing communications of their location when leaving the car. "I can't remember."

Jetsam also panicked for a moment, then said,

"No, I'm sure I didn't. Nobody knows we're here in North Hollywood."

"Let's get the fuck back to our beat!" Flotsam said when they reached their car, unlocked it, and got inside.

He drove with lights out until they were blocks from the scene and heard the PSR voice say "All units, code four. Suspect in custody. Code four."

They didn't talk at all until they were safely back cruising Hollywood Boulevard. Then Jetsam said, "Let's get code seven. Our adventure's made me real hungry all of a sudden. And bro, your shit's kinda weak lately. We gotta jack you up somehow. Why don'tcha get one of those healthy reduced-fat burritos swimming in sour cream and guacamole." Then he added, "It musta been those two shots I gave that homie, but I feel mega-happy now."

And Flotsam could only gape when Jetsam suddenly began to sing the U2 hit: "Two shots of happy, one shot of saaaaad."

"You're scary, dude," Flotsam said. "You're as scary as a doctor putting on one rubber glove."

Jetsam kept on singing: "Two shots of happy, one shot of saaaaaad."

Flotsam kept driving toward Sunset Boulevard

and finally said, "I wanna take you up to the Director's Chair first night we're off together. Have a few beers. Shoot some pool or darts."

"Okay, I got nothing better to do, but I never been fond of the joint. Don't you wanna go someplace where there ain't so many cops?"

Flotsam said, "I love a bar with a sign that says 'No shirt, no shoes, no badge, no service.' Besides, there's always a few badge bunnies around that'll pork any copper, even you."

Jetsam said, "Thank you, Dr. Ruth. Why're you so concerned with my sex life all of a sudden?"

Flotsam said, "It's me I'm thinking about, dude. You gotta take your mind off your ex and her lawyer and that hose monster that dumped you. Either that or in order to protect my career and pension I gotta go find that Northeast detective she's snogging."

"What for?"

"To cap him. We can't go on like this. You hearing me, dude?"

Cosmo Betrossian had always denied that he was even loosely associated with the so-called Russian Mafia. The federal and local authorities called everybody from the former USSR and eastern Europe "Russian Mafia." That is, everyone

Cosmo knew, because everyone Cosmo knew was involved in illegal activity of one sort or another. The designations didn't make any sense to Cosmo, who, even though he had grown up in Soviet Armenia and spoke some bastardized Russian, was no more a Russian than George Bush was. He figured that American cops were just full of shit as far as eastern European immigrants were concerned.

But because of their obsession with Russian Mafia, he had to be careful when he had any business dealing with Dmitri, the owner of the Gulag, a nightclub on Western Avenue that wasn't in the best part of town but had a well-lit, well-guarded parking lot. Young people from all over the west side, even Beverly Hills and Brentwood, were not afraid to drive east to Little Siberia, as some called it.

The Gulag's food was good and they poured generous drinks and Dmitri gave them the recorded familiar rock sounds they wanted, which kept the dance floor jammed until closing time. And on the occasional "Russian Night" Dmitri advertised live entertainment: Russian dancers, balalaikas, violins, and a beautiful singer from Moscow. It brought Dmitri a very wealthy clientele who had emigrated to Los Angeles from all over the former USSR, whether or not they were into legitimate business or smuggling or money laundering. But this night was not going to be one of the Russian nights.

A week had passed since the robbery, and Cosmo felt confident going to Dmitri. The police were even less of a worry. Nobody he knew had even been questioned. Early in the evening, he drove to the Gulag, entered, and went to the bar. He knew the bartender whom the Americans called "Georgie" because he was from the Republic of Georgia, and asked to see Dmitri. The bartender poured him a shot of ouzo and Cosmo waited for the bartender to deal with two cocktail waitresses at the service bar who were giving the bartender more happy hour drink orders than he could handle.

The nightclub was typical for Hollywood in that there was an area set aside for private parties. In the Gulag the private area was upstairs, with plush green sofas lining walls papered in garish streaks of color — somebody's idea of "edgy," that favorite cliché of Hollywood scenesters, the other being "vibe." The Gulag was edgy. The Gulag vibed mysterious.

On this evening, the jock was just setting up

and he spun some soft-rock standards for the end of the extended happy hour. There were two guys repairing some strobes and spots before the crowd arrived and bodies got writhing in the dance-floor pit. Busboys and waiters were wiping off tables and chairs and dusting the seats in the cuddle-puddle booths on the raised level for those customers who tipped the manager Andrei.

After ten minutes, Cosmo was directed upstairs into Dmitri's surprisingly spartan office where he found the club owner at his desk, slippered feet up, smoking a cigarette in a silver holder, and watching S&M porn on his computer screen. Everybody said that Dmitri indulged in all kinds of exotic sex. He was forty-one years old, not tall, had a slight build, soft hands, and bloodshot blue eyes, and was wearing a chestnut hair weave. He looked unexceptional and harmless in a white linen shirt and chinos, but Cosmo was very scared of him. He had heard things about Dmitri and his friends.

The club owner knew that Cosmo's Russian was extremely poor and Dmitri adored current American slang, so he had always spoken

English to Cosmo. Without getting up he said, "Here comes a happen-ink guy! A guy who always has it go-ink on! Hello, Cosmo!"

He reached out with one of those soft hands and slapped palms with Cosmo, who said, "Dmitri, thank you for this talk. Thank you, brother."

"You got some-think I need?"

"Yes, my brother," Cosmo said, sitting in the client chair in front of the desk.

"Not credit-card information, I hope. In genyural I am not into credit cards no more, Cosmo. I am moving into other directions."

"No, brother," Cosmo said. "I have brought for you something to show." And with that he produced a single diamond, one of the larger stones from the jewelry store robbery, and put it gingerly on the desk.

Dmitri lowered his feet onto the floor and looked at the stone. He smiled at Cosmo and said, "I do not know diamonds. But I have a friend who knows. Do you have more?"

"Yes," Cosmo said. "Much more. Many rings and earrings too. All very beautiful stones."

Dmitri looked impressed. "You are grow-ink in America!" he said. "No more business with addicts?"

"Addicts do not have diamonds," Cosmo said. "I think you shall buy all my diamonds and sell for big profit, my brother."

"It is possible that I should be een-wolved with you again, Cosmo," Dmitri said, smiling. "You are perhaps now a big man in America."

"I wish to bring every diamond soon. I wish to sell for only thirty-five thousands. The news lady on TV say the diamonds worth maybe two, three hundred thousands."

"The hand grenade!" Dmitri said with a grin. "So it was you! But thirty-five thousand? You must bring me high-quality stones for thirty-five thousand."

"Okay, brother," Cosmo said. "I shall bring."

"I need perhaps one month to make my deal and to get so much cash for you," Dmitri said. "And to make sure that police do not arrest you in meantime."

"I am very sad to hear that," Cosmo said, sweat popping on his forehead. "I must get money now."

Dmitri shrugged and said, "You may take your treasure to somebody else, Cosmo. No problem."

Cosmo had nobody else for something like this, and he knew that Dmitri was aware of it.

"Okay," Cosmo said. "I wait. Please call me when you have money."

"Now that you are grow-ink into a business-man," Dmitri said as Cosmo bowed slightly and prepared to leave, "you should shave between the eyebrows. Americans like two eyebrows, not one."

On the night that Jetsam fired two shots of happy with no shot of sad, another shooting would take place, this one in Hollywood Division, that would provoke several shots of sad for two of the officers involved.

The code 3 call was given to 6-A-65 of Watch 3, directing them to a residential street on the west side of Hollywood, an area that seldom was the source of such calls. Half the cars on the midwatch rolled on it when the PSR said the words "Man with a gun."

The assigned car, thanks to lights and siren, got there seconds before the others, but two of the midwatch units roared in before the officers of 6-A-65 were out of the car. One of the midwatch units was driven by Mag Takara. Her partner, Benny Brewster, jumped out with a shotgun, and then another car from Watch 3 arrived. Eight cops, four with shotguns, approached the house from which the call had emanated. The porch lights were out, and the street was quite dark.

The decision whether to approach the porch did not have to be made. The front door to the house swung open, and the cops at the scene could scarcely believe what they were seeing.

A thirty-eight-year-old man, later identified as Roland Tarkington, owner of the house, stepped out onto the porch. It would be learned that his father had once owned large chunks of commercial property in Hollywood but had lost it all in bad investments, leaving his only child, Roland, the house and sufficient money to exist. Roland was waving a document in one hand and had the other hand behind his back.

In the glare of half a dozen flashlight beams plus a spotlight trained on him by the closest black-and-white, Roland spoke not a word but held up the paper as though it were a white flag of surrender. He struggled down the concrete steps from his porch and advanced toward the cops.

The thing that had the cops amazed was Roland Tarkington's size. He would be measured the next day during a postmortem at five feet six inches. His weight would be listed on the death report as just over 540 pounds. The shadow of Roland Tarkington thrown onto the walk behind him was vast.

After Benny Brewster shouted, "Let's see the other hand!" there was a cacophony of voices:

"Show us your other hand!"

"Both hands in the air, goddamnit!"

"Get down on the sidewalk!"

"Watch that fucking hand! Watch his hand!"

A probationary cop from Watch 3 left his training officer and crept along the driveway forty feet from the standoff as the obese man stopped, still silently waving the white paper. The probationer was in a position to see behind Roland Tarkington's back and yelled, "He's got a gun!"

As though on cue, another Hollywood performance ended when Roland Tarkington showed them what he was hiding, suddenly aiming what looked like a .9-millimeter semiautomatic pistol at the closest cop.

And he was hit by two shotgun blasts fired by separate officers from Watch 3 and five rounds from pistols fired by two other Watch 3 officers. Roland Tarkington, despite his great bulk, was lit up by bright orange muzzle blasts, lifted off his feet, and thrown down on his back, where he bled out, dying within seconds, his heart literally shredded. Another five police pistol rounds that missed had riddled the front of the house as Roland Tarkington fell.

Neighbors then poured out of their homes, and voices were yelling, and at least two women across the street were wailing and crying. The Oracle, who arrived just as the rounds exploded in the night, picked up the blood-spattered paper lying on the grass beside the dead man. Roland Tarkington's gun turned out to be a realistically designed water pistol.

The second cop to have fired his shotgun said, "What's it say, Sarge?"

The Oracle read aloud: "'I offer my humble apologies to the fine officers of the LAPD. This was the only way I could summon the courage to end my life of misery. I ask that my remains be cremated. I would not want anyone to have to carry my body to our family plot at Forest Lawn Cemetery. Thank you. Roland G. Tarkington.'"

None of the midwatch units had been in a position to fire, and Mag said to Benny, "Let's get outta here, partner. This is bad shit."

When they were back at their car putting the shotgun into the locked rack, Mag heard two cops talking to the Oracle.

One said, "Goddamnit! Goddamn this bastard! Why didn't he take poison? Goddamn him!"

The Oracle said to the cop, "Get in your car and get back to the station, son. FID will be arriving soon."

Another voice said to the Oracle, "I'm not a fucking executioner! Why did he do this to me? Why?"

The final comment was made by the night-watch detective Compassionate Charlie Gilford, who showed up as the black-and-whites were driving away. The RA was double-parked, a paramedic standing over the huge mound of bloody flesh that had been Roland Tarkington, glad that the crew from the coroner's would be handling this one.

Compassionate Charlie picked up the water pistol, squeezed the trigger, and when no water squirted out said, "Shit, it ain't even loaded." Then he shined his light on the blasted gaping chest of Roland Tarkington and said, "You would have to call this a heartrending conclusion to another Hollywood melodrama."

SEVEN

THE FOLLOWING FRIDAY evening saw throngs on Hollywood Boulevard at another of the endless red carpet ceremonies, this one at the Kodak Theatre, where show business back-slaps and hugs itself before returning to every-day backbiting and seething in never-ending bouts of jealousy over a colleague's getting a job that should have been given to Me! Show business's unmentioned prayer: Please, God, let me succeed and let them . . . fail.

The midwatch was in terrible shape as far as deployment was concerned. Fausto was on days off and so was Benny Brewster. Budgie Polk saw the Oracle working at his desk and found it reas-suring to see all those hash marks on his left sleeve, all the way up to his elbow. He wore not his heart on his sleeve, but his life. Forty-six years. Nine service stripes. Who could push him around? The Oracle had said he was going to break the record of the detective from Robbery-Homicide Division who'd retired in February with fifty years of service. But sometimes, like now, he looked tired. And old.

The Oracle would be sixty-nine years old in August, and it was all there around his eyes and furrowed brow, all the years with the LAPD. He'd served seven chiefs. He'd seen chiefs and mayors come and go and die. But in those old glory days of LAPD, he couldn't have imagined he'd be serving under a federal consent decree that was choking the life out of the police department he loved. Proactive police work had given way to police paranoia, and he seemed to internalize it more than anyone else. Budgie watched him unscrew a bottle of antacid liquid and swallow a large dose.

Budgie had been hoping to team up with Mag Takara, but after Budgie walked into the watch commander's office and had a look at the lineup, she took the Oracle aside in the corridor, where she said privately, "Did the lieutenant decide on the assignments tonight, Sarge?"

"No, I did," he told her, but he stopped talking when Hollywood Nate interrupted by bounding in the back door with three rolls of paper, carrying them like they were treasure maps.

"Wait'll you see these, Sarge," he said to the Oracle.

He handed two to Budgie while he carefully unrolled the third, revealing a movie one-sheet for Billy Wilder's *Sunset Boulevard,* starring William Holden and Gloria Swanson.

"Don't we have enough movie posters around the station?" the Oracle said.

"But this one's in great shape! It's a copy, but it's a pretty old copy. And in beautiful condition. I'm getting the frames donated tomorrow."

"All right, put them up in the roll-call room with the others," the Oracle said, running his hand over his gray crew cut. "I guess anything's better than looking at all these inmate green walls. Whoever designed our stations must've got his training in Albania during the cold war."

"Way cool, Sarge," Nate said. "We'll decide where to put the others later. One's for *Double Indemnity,* and the other's for *Rebel Without a Cause,* with James Dean's face right under the title. Lots of great shots of Hollywood in those movies."

"Okay, but pick places where citizens can't

see them from the lobby," the Oracle said. "Don't turn this station into a casting office."

After Hollywood Nate had sprinted up the stairs, the Oracle said to Budgie, "I'm a sucker for young cops who respect old things. And speaking of old things, with Fausto off I thought you wouldn't mind working with Hank Driscoll for a few days."

Budgie rolled her eyes then. Hank aka "B.M." Driscoll was someone nobody liked working with, especially young officers. It wasn't that he was old like Fausto — he had nineteen years on the Job and was only a little over forty — but it was like working with your whiny aunt Martha. The B.M. sobriquet that the other cops hung on him was for Baron Münchhausen, whose invented illnesses resulted in medical treatment and hospitalization, a disorder that came to be known in the psychiatric community as Munchausen syndrome.

B.M. Driscoll probably had more sick days than the rest of the midwatch combined. If they had to arrest a junkie with hepatitis, B.M. Driscoll would go to his doctor with symptoms within forty-eight hours and would listen doubtfully when assured that his claims were medically impossible.

The ten-hour shift of Watch 5 crawled by when you had to work with him. Older cops said that if you felt that life was flying by too quickly, you could bring time almost to a standstill just by working a whole twenty-eight-day deployment period with B.M. Driscoll.

He was tall and wiry, the grandson of Wisconsin farmers who came to California during the Great Depression, which he claimed kept his parents from eating properly, so they passed unhealthy genes down to him. He kept his sparse brown hair clipped almost as close as the Oracle's because he believed it was more hygienic. And he was twice divorced, the mystery being how he found anyone but a psychiatrist to marry him in the first place.

However, there was one event in his career that made him a bit of a police legend. Several years earlier, when he was working patrol in the barrio of Hollenbeck Division, he became involved in a standoff with a drug-crazed, facially tattooed homeboy who was threatening to cut his girlfriend's throat with a Buck knife.

Several cops were there in the middle of the street, pointing shotguns and handguns and cajoling and threatening to no avail. Officer Driscoll was holding a Taser gun, and at one

point during the standoff when the homie lowered the blade long enough to wave it during his
incoherent rant, B.M. Driscoll fired. The dart
struck the homeboy in the left chest area, pene-
trating the pack of cigarettes in his shirt pocket
as well as his butane lighter. Which was ignited
by a lit cigarette. Which caused the guy to burst
into flames. Which ended the standoff.

They got the shirt off the homeboy before he
was seriously burned and threw him into a rescue ambulance, and B.M. Driscoll became something of a celebrity, especially among the Latino
cruisers where he was known as "the dude with
the flame thrower."

But whether he was a legend or not, Budgie
Polk was very unhappy about her assignment.
She said to the Oracle, "Just tell me one thing,
Sarge. Tell me that you're not keeping me and
Mag apart because I'm just back from maternity
leave and she's a little munchkin. I can't explain
to you how degrading it is when that happens to
us women. When male supervisors say stuff like
'We're splitting you up for your own safety.' After
all the shit we women have gone through to get
where we are on this Job."

The Oracle said, "Budgie, I promise you that's
not why I put you with Driscoll instead of Mag. I

don't think of you in those terms. You're a cop. Period."

"And that's not why you put me with Fausto? So the old war horse could look after me?"

"Haven't you caught on by now, Budgie?" the Oracle said. "Fausto Gamboa has been a bitter and depressed man since he lost his wife to colon cancer two years ago. And both their sons are losers, so they don't help him any. When Ron LeCroix had to get his hemorrhoids zapped, it looked like a perfect time to team up Fausto with somebody young and alive. Preferably a woman, to soften him up a little bit. So I didn't assign him to you for your benefit. I did it for him."

They didn't call him the Oracle for nothing, Budgie thought. She was painted into a corner now with nowhere to go. "Hoisted by my own ponytail" was all she could mutter.

The Oracle said, "Put some cotton in your ears for a few days. Driscoll's actually a decent copper and he's generous. He'll buy your cappuccino and biscotti every chance he gets. And not because you're a woman. That's the way he is."

"I hope I don't catch bird flu or mad cow just listening to him," Budgie said.

When they got to their patrol unit, Budgie

driving, B.M. Driscoll threw his war bag into the trunk and said, "Try not to get in my breathing zone if you can help it, Budgie. I know you've got a baby, and I wouldn't want to infect you. I think I could be coming down with something. I'm not sure, but I've got muscle pain and sort of feel chills down my back. I had the flu in October and again in January. This has been a bad year for my health."

The rest was lost in radio chatter. Budgie tried to concentrate on the PSR's voice and tune his out. She was reminded of an event she'd first heard about when she transferred to Hollywood Division and met Detective Andi McCrea. Other women officers particularly enjoyed the story.

It seemed that several years ago an LAPD officer from a neighboring division was shot by a motorist he'd pulled over for a ticket. Andi McCrea was a uniformed cop in Hollywood Division at that time, and several night-watch units were assigned to patrol their eastern border, where the suspect was last seen abandoning his car after a short pursuit.

It was past end of watch, and cars were working overtime, in communication with one another and checking alleys, storage yards, and vacant buildings, with no sign of the shooter.

Then Andi got the word who the officer was: an academy classmate of hers, and he was badly wounded. She'd been relentless that night, shining her spotlight beam onto rooftops, even into trees, and her older male partner, like B.M. Driscoll, was a complainer. Not about imaginary illnesses, but about his need for rest and sleep. He was an unreliable shiftless cop.

Andi McCrea, according to all accounts, endured it for two hours, but after listening to him say, "We ain't gonna find nobody, let's get the hell outta here and go end of watch — this is bullshit," she grimly turned north to the Hollywood Freeway, pulled onto the ramp, and stopped.

When her partner said, "What're we stopping here for?" Andi said, "Something's wrong. Get out and look at the right front tire."

He griped about that too, but complied, and when he was out of the car shining his beam onto the tire, he said, "There's nothing wrong here."

"There sure as hell is something wrong here, you worthless asshole," Andi said and drove off, leaving him on the freeway ramp, his rover still on the seat and his cell phone in his locker at the station.

Andi continued searching for another hour

and only stopped when the search was called off, after which she drove to the station, still hacked off and ready to take her medicine.

The Oracle was waiting for her, and as she was unloading her war bag from the trunk, he said, "Your partner arrived about a half hour ago. Flagged down a car. He's torqued. Stay away from him."

"Sarge, we were hunting a maggot who shot a police officer!" Andi said.

"I understand that," the Oracle said. "And knowing him, I can imagine what you had to put up with. But you don't dump a body on the freeway unless it's dead and you're a serial killer."

"Is he making his complaint official?"

"He wanted to but I talked him out of it. Told him it would be more embarrassing for him than for you. Anyway, he's getting his long-awaited transfer to West L.A., so he'll be gone at the end of the deployment period."

That's how it had ended, except that it was a favorite story of cops at Hollywood Station who knew Andi McCrea. And B.M. Driscoll's whining about his flu symptoms reminded Budgie Polk of the story. It put a little smile on her face, and she thought, How far does he have to push me?

Could I get away with it like Andi did? After all, there is precedent here.

And though Budgie was starting to enjoy certain things about working with Fausto now that he'd mellowed a little, wouldn't it be great to be teamed with Mag Takara? Just for girl talk if nothing else. During code 7, when they were eating salads at Soup Plantation, they could kid around about eye candy on the midwatch, saying things like, "Would you consider doing Hollywood Nate if you thought he could ever keep his big mouth shut about it?" Or, "How much would it take for you to do either of those two logheads, Flotsam or Jetsam, if you could shoot him afterward?" Girl talk cop-style.

Mag was a cool and gutsy little chick with a quiet sense of humor that Budgie liked. And being of Japanese ethnicity, Mag would no doubt be down for code 7 at the sushi bar on Melrose that Budgie couldn't persuade any of the male officers to set foot in. Of course, two women as short and tall as Mag and Budgie would be butts of stupid male remarks, along with the usual sexist ones that all women officers have to live with unless they want to get a rat jacket by complaining about it. The lamest:

What do you call a black-and-white with two fe-males in it? Answer: a tuna boat.

And while Budgie was thinking of ways to trade B.M. Driscoll for Mag Takara without pissing off the Oracle, Mag was thinking of ways to trade Flotsam for anybody at all. With Jetsam on days off, they were teamed for the first time, short and tall, quiet and mouthy. And oh god! He kept sliding his sight line over onto her every time she was looking out at the streets, and if this kept up, he'd be rear-ending a bus or something.

"Where shall we go for code seven?" he asked when they hadn't been on patrol for twenty minutes. "And don't say the sushi bar on Mel-rose, where I've seen your shop parked on nu-merous occasions."

"I won't, then," she said, punching in a license plate on a low rider in the number two lane, fig-uring this surfer probably takes his dates to places with paper napkins and tap water.

Hoping for a smile, he said, "For me an order of sushi is a dish containing unretouched, re-cently dead mollusks. Stuff like that lays all over the beach in low tide. You like to surf?"

"No," Mag said, unamused.

"I bet you'd look great shooting a barrel. All that gorgeous dark hair flowing in the wind."

"A barrel?"

"Yeah, a tube? A pipe? Riding through as the wave breaks over you?"

"Yeah, a barrel." This loghead's had too many wipeouts, she thought. He's gone surfboard-simple, that's what.

"In one of those bikinis that's just a piece of Lycra the size of a Toll House cookie."

Just get me through the night and away from this hormone monster, Mag thought. Then she did some serious eye rolling when Flotsam said, "A surfer might predict that this could be the beginning of a choiceamundo friendship."

Wesley Drubb got to drive, and he liked that. Hollywood Nate was sitting back doing what he did best, talking show business to his young partner, who didn't give a shit about the movie theater that Nate pointed out there at Fairfax and Melrose, one that showed silent films.

"There was a famous murder there in the nineties," Nate informed him, "involving former owners. One got set up by a business partner who hired a hit on him. The hit man is now doing life without. 'The Silent Movie Murder,' the press called it."

"Really," Wesley said, without enthusiasm.

"I can give you a show-business education," Nate said. "Never know when it could come in handy working this division. I know you're rich and all, but would you ever consider doing extra work in the movies? I could introduce you to an agent."

Wesley Drubb hated it when other officers talked about his family wealth and said, "I'm not rich. My father's rich."

"I'd like to meet your dad sometime," Nate said. "Does he have any interest in movies?"

Wesley shrugged and said, "He and my mom go to movies sometimes."

"I mean in filmmaking."

"His hobby is skeet shooting," Wesley said. "And he's done a little pistol shooting with me since I came on the Department."

"Guns don't have it going on, far as I'm concerned," Nate said. "When I talk millimeters, it's not about guns and ammo, it's about celluloid. Thirty-five millimeters. Twenty-four frames per second. I have a thousand-dollar digital video camera. Panavision model. Sweet."

"Uh-huh," Wesley said.

"I know a guy, him and me, we're into film-making. One of these days when we find the right kind of investor, we're gonna make a little indie film and show it at the festivals. We have a script and we're very close. All we need is the right investor. We can't accept just anybody."

They were stopped at a residential intersection in east Hollywood, a street that Wesley remembered hearing about. He looked at a two-story house, home of some Eighteenth Street crew members.

Hollywood Nate was just about to pop the question to Wesley about whether he thought that Franklin Drubb would ever consider including a start-up production company in his investment portfolio, when a head-shaven white guy in faux-leather pants, studded boots, and a leather vest over a swelling bare chest completely covered by body art walked up to the passenger side of the patrol car and tapped loudly on Nate's window.

It startled both of them, and Nate rolled down the window and said, "What can I do for you?" keeping it polite but wary.

The man said in a voice soft and low, "Take me to Santa Monica and La Brea."

Hollywood Nate glanced quickly at Wesley,

then back to the guy, shining his flashlight up under the chin, seeing those dilated cavernous eyes, and said to him, "Step back away from the car." Nate got out and Wesley quickly informed communications that 6-X-72 was code 6 at that location. Then he put the car in park, turned off the engine, tucked the keys in the buckle of his Sam Browne and got out on the driver's side, walking quickly around the front of the car, flashlight in one hand, the other on the butt of his Beretta.

The man was a lot older than he looked at first when Nate walked him to the sidewalk and had a good look, but he was wide shouldered, with thick veins on his well-muscled arms, and full-sleeve tatts. It was very dark and the street lamp on the corner was out. An occasional car passed and nobody was walking on the residential street.

Then the guy said, "I'm a Vietnam vet. You're a public servant. Take me to Santa Monica and La Brea."

Hollywood Nate looked from the guy to his partner in disbelief and said, "Yeah, you're a Vietnam vet and you got napalm eyes to prove it, but we're not a taxi. What're you fried on, man? X, maybe?"

The man smiled then, a sly and secretive smile locked in place just this side of madness. He opened his vest, showing his bare torso, and ran his hands over his own waist and buttocks and groin under the tight imitation-leather pants and said, "See, no weapons. No nothing. Just beautiful tattoos. Let's go to Santa Monica and La Brea."

Hollywood Nate glanced again at his partner, who looked spring-loaded, and Nate said, "Yeah, I see. You got more tatts than Angelina Jolie, but you ain't her. So we're not driving you any-where." Then he uttered the Hollywood Station mantra, "Stay real, dude."

Those eyes. Nate looked again with his flash-light beam under the guy's chin. Where did he find those eyes? They didn't fit his face some-how. They looked like they belonged to some-body else. Or something else.

Nate looked at Wesley, who didn't know what the hell to do. The man hadn't broken any laws. Wesley didn't know if he should ask the guy for ID or what. He waited for a cue from Nate. This was getting very spooky. An unhinged 5150 mental case for sure. Still, all he'd done was ask for a ride. Wesley remembered his academy in-structor saying as long as they weren't a danger to themselves or others, they couldn't be taken to the USC Medical Center, formerly the old county hospital, for a seventy-two-hour hold.

Nate said to the man, "The only place this car goes is jail. Why don't you walk home and sleep it off, whatever it is gave you those eyes."

The man said, "War gave me these eyes. War."

Cautiously, Nate said, "I think we're gonna say good night to you, soldier. Go home. Right now."

Nate nodded to his partner and backed toward the police car, but when he got in and closed the door and Wesley got in on the driver's side and started the engine, the transmission still in park, the man ran to the car and kicked the right rear door with those studded boots, howling like a wolf.

"Goddamn!" Nate yelled, keying the mike and yelling, "Six-X-Seventy-two, officers need help!" He gave the location, then threw open his door and jumped out with his baton, which he lost during the first thirty seconds of the fight.

Wesley jumped from the driver's side, not removing the keys, not even turning off the engine, ran around the car, and leaped onto the back of the madman who had Nate's baton with one hand and Nate in a headlock.

All those muscles that Hollywood Nate had

found in his gym, that had impressed badge bunnies in the Director's Chair saloon, weren't im-
pressing this lunatic one bit. And even when
Wesley hurled his 210-pound body onto the guy,
he still kept fighting and kicking and trying to
bite like a rabid dog.

Wesley tried the Liquid Jesus on him but the
OC can was clogged and it created a pepper-
spray mist in front of his own face that almost
blinded him. Then he tried again but got more
on Hollywood Nate than on the suspect, so he
gave up and dropped the canister.

And pretty soon they had tussled, tumbled,
and rolled across the lawn of a sagging two-
story residence belonging to Honduran immigrants, into the side yard, and then clear into the
backyard, where Hollywood Nate was starting
to panic as he felt his strength waning. And he
thought he might have to shoot this fucking lunatic after he felt the guy trying to grab his
sidearm.

And while the battle was raging, some of the
Eighteenth Street cruisers from another two-
story house looked out the window, and a few
of them came out to get a better look and root
for the guy to kick some LAPD ass. When their

pit bulls tried to follow, they leashed them, knowing that lots of other cops would be coming soon.

The dogs seemed to enjoy the fight even more than the crew did and began snarling and barking, and whenever the leather-clad madman growled and kicked at Wesley Drubb, who was administering LAPD-approved baton strikes, the dogs would bark louder. And then Loco Lennie happened on the scene.

Loco Lennie was not a member of Eighteenth Street but he was oh, such a wannabe. He was too young, too stupid, and too impulsive even for the cruisers to use him as a low-level drug delivery boy. Loco Lennie wasn't watching the fight with the five members of the crew and their crazed dogs. Loco Lennie couldn't take his eyes off the black-and-white that Wesley Drubb had left in gear, engine running, key in the ignition, in his haste to help Hollywood Nate. And Loco Lennie saw a chance to make a name for himself that would live forever in the minds and hearts of these cruisers who had so far rejected him.

Loco Lennie ran to the police car, jumped in, and took off, yelling, "Viva Eighteenth Street!"

Hollywood Nate and Wesley Drubb didn't

even know that their shop had been stolen. By now they had the guy pinned against the single-car garage of the ramshackle house, and young Wesley was learning that all of the leg and arm strikes he'd been taught at the academy weren't worth a shit when battling a powerful guy who was maybe cooked on PCP or just plain psychotic.

And before the first help came screeching around the corner, siren yelping louder than the homie dogs and even louder than this howling mental case who was trying desperately to bite Hollywood Nate, the cop locked his forearm and biceps in a V around the man's throat. Nate applied all the pressure he could manage to the carotid arteries while Wesley exhausted himself, whacking the guy everywhere from the guy's wingspan on down to his lower legs with little effect.

Flotsam and Mag, Budgie and B.M. Driscoll, and four officers from Watch 3 all came running to the rescue just as the guy was almost choked out, his brain oxygen starved from the infamous choke hold, the carotid restraint that had killed several people over the decades but had saved the lives of more cops than all the Tasers and beanbag guns and side-handle batons and Liquid

Jesus and the rest of the nonlethal weapons in their arsenal put together. A form of nonlethal force that, in this era of DOJ oversight and racial politics and political correctness, was treated exactly the same as an officer-involved shooting. And that would require almost as much investigation and as many reports as if Hollywood Nate had shot the guy in defense of his life with a load of double-aught buckshot.

When it looked as though the situation was in hand, one of the dogs belonging to the cruisers did what guard dogs do, after he saw the cops piling out of their black-and-whites and running in the direction of his homeboys. He sprang forward, breaking free of the leash, and raced directly at B.M. Driscoll, who had barely set foot on the sidewalk. When B.M. Driscoll saw those slobbering jaws and those bared fangs and malevolent eyes coming at him, he bellowed, drew his nine, and fired twice, missing once but then killing the dog instantly with a head shot.

The gunfire seemed to stop all action. Hollywood Nate realized that the maniac was choked out, and he let the guy fall to the ground, unconscious. Wesley Drubb looked toward the street for the first time and said, "Where's our shop?"

Now that the entertainment had ended, the

homies and their still-living dogs turned and re-treated to their house without complaint about the unlicensed animal they'd lost. And there was lots of talk among them about how Loco Lennie had *pelotas* made of stainless steel. Maybe they should reconsider Loco Lennie as a cruiser, they agreed, if he didn't get himself dusted by some cop who spotted him in the stolen police car.

When Flotsam saw the leather-clad lunatic lying on the ground, he said to Mag, "Let's do rock-paper-scissors to see who gets the mouth on CPR."

But as Mag was running to the car to look for her personal CPR mask, the unconscious man started breathing again on his own. He moaned and tried to get up but was quickly handcuffed by Hollywood Nate, who then collapsed beside him, his face bruised and swollen.

It was then that Flotsam noticed something clinging to the guy's bald head. He shined his light on it and saw "Weiss." Hollywood Nate's name tag had been pulled off and was sticking to the guy's bare scalp.

"Get me a Polaroid!" Flotsam yelled.

By the time the Oracle had arrived and in-structed Flotsam and Mag to ride with him and to give their car to Hollywood Nate and Wesley

Drubb, the handcuffed man was alert, and he said to Hollywood Nate, "You can only hurt me in a physical state."

And Nate, who was still trying to get his own breathing back to normal, rolled his aching shoulders and answered, "That's the only state we live in, you psycho motherfucker."

The Oracle warned that now they might have two FID teams out there: one on the dog shooting and another because Hollywood Nate had applied the dreaded choke hold. Force Investigation Division would have to be convinced that B.M. Driscoll had acted in fear of great bodily injury and that Hollywood Nate had choked out the madman as a last resort in the immediate defense of a life, namely his own.

"Not one but two FID roll-outs on the same freaking incident," the Oracle moaned.

Flotsam said sympathetically, "LAPD can't get enough layers of oversight, Boss. Somebody flipped the pyramid and we're under the pointy tip. We got more layers than a mafia wedding cake."

When a plain-wrapper detective unit pulled up in front and parked, the Oracle wondered how FID could have gotten there so fast but then saw that it was only the night-watch detective

Compassionate Charlie, as usual experiencing morbid curiosity. He was wearing one of his Taiwanese checked sport coats that made people ask if it was flame retardant. Charlie got out, picked some food from his teeth, and surveyed the scene for one of his sage pronouncements.

Flotsam talked for a few minutes to one of the Eighteenth Street crew who had lingered to be sure the dog was dead, and after the short conversation, the surfer jogged up to the Oracle and said, "Boss, I think we have some extenuating circumstances in this shooting that might help you with those rat bastards from FID."

"Yeah, what's that?"

Pointing to the deceased pit bull, Flotsam said, "A homie told me the dog was just ghetto elk when they found him."

"What?"

"You know, one of those stray dogs that roam around the 'hood? One of the cruisers found the dog down in Watts, brought him here and let him in their pack. But last month the dog came down with terminal cancer and they were just going to put him down any day now."

"So?"

Compassionate Charlie butted into the conversation, saying to the Oracle, "Don't you get it?

Haven't you read about dogs that can smell malignant tumors?"

"Now, what in hell is your point, Charlie?" the Oracle wanted to know. He didn't have time for this goofy surfer or for one of Charlie's on-scene analyses.

Compassionate Charlie shook his head sadly, sucked his teeth, and said, "You can call this just another touching drama among the many that occur nightly on the streets of Hollywood. The fucking mutt knew he had cancer, so he decided to do honor to his crew and commit suicide-by-cop."

Young Wesley Drubb felt sort of dazed for the remainder of the watch. His mind kept wandering away from the issues at hand. For instance, when they drove their prisoner to Central Jail at Parker Center, where medical treatment was available for him, all Wesley could think about when they drove past the parking lot was, Why is the entrance gate blocked with a steel barrier, and the exit gate is wide open with no metal spikes? A terrorist could just drive in the exit. Are we stupid, or what? His mind was wandering like that.

After the prisoner was treated prior to being

booked for battery on a police officer, Hollywood Nate and Wesley Drubb decided to go to
Cedars for treatment of contusions and abra-
sions, and in Nate's case muscle spasms. As to
the prisoner, Nate told Wesley it would be up to
the DA's office to decide if the arrestee was per-
manently nuts or only temporarily nuts from
PCP or whatever a blood test might reveal. Drug-
induced craziness would not be a defense in a
criminal case, but life-induced craziness like his
war experiences might keep him from a jail sentence and put him in a mental ward for a short
vacation.

Wesley Drubb's mind remained unfocused for
more than an hour. He got alarmed by remarks
made by a jail employee who had taken his
sweet time returning from the long lunch break
that their union had recently won for them.

When their prisoner was strip-searched, the
black detention officer studied the darkening
welts all over the guy's body and said, "He looks
like a zebra."

Wesley Drubb had never dreamed a man fifty-
seven years old could fight like that and was still
trying to sort his feelings about the first act of violence he'd ever committed on another human
being in his entire life. And sick from the worry

and stress of having lost his police car, he tried to explain the prisoner's bruises by saying, "We had no choice."

The jailor chuckled at the shaken young cop and said, "Boy, lucky for you he's a peckerwood. If this cat was black, you would be facing the wrath of the city council, the United States Department of Justice, and the motherfuckin' ghost of Johnnie Cochran."

Loco Lennie may or may not have heard the PSR's voice informing all units that 6-X-72's car had been stolen, and he may or may not have opened the text messages sent by other units to 6-X-72 after they'd learned of the incident.

One message said, "When we see you, you are dead meat."

Another said, "We will shoot you and burn your body."

Another, apparently from a K-9 unit, said, "Trooper will eat on your sorry ass for as long as he wants. Before you die."

In any case, Loco Lennie figured he had made his point to the crew, so he abandoned the police car only ten blocks from his house. He found a rock lying beside a chain-link fence, picked it up, and threw it at the windshield, just as a parting shot. Then Loco Lennie sprinted home in glory.

When, at the end of their long and awful duty tour, they were painfully walking to their personal cars, Wesley Drubb, who had been silent most of the night, said to Hollywood Nate, "I don't care what they taught me in my years at USC. I don't care how unscientific it is. All I know is that since coming on this Job, I no longer believe in evolution. I believe in Creationism."

"And why is that?" Nate asked.

"For instance, that guy tonight? An evolved form of life could not resemble something like that."

EIGHT

AFTER STOPPING AT the Gulag for a happy hour drink, Cosmo Betrossian was driving his eighteen-year-old Cadillac east on Sunset to Korea Town, where he was living temporarily, and thinking of how impressed Dmitri had been with him during their meeting last week. This was where he belonged, with people like Dmitri. Cosmo was forty-three years old, too old to be dealing with people addicted to crystal meth. Too old to be buying the paper they'd stolen from mailboxes or from purses left in cars and then shopping the credit-card information to the other freaks at the public libraries and cybercafés, where they sold stolen information and dealt drugs on the Internet.

Cosmo and Ilya had never committed an armed robbery prior to the jewelry store job. The hand grenade idea came from something he had heard from one of the addicts who had read about it in a San Diego newspaper. The reason the addict had mentioned it to Cosmo at all was that the robbers who did it were Armenians who were supposed to be connected with Russian Mafia. Cosmo had to laugh. He had stolen their idea and their modus operandi, and it had been easy. And it had all come to him because he was an Armenian émigré.

The knowledge about the diamonds' arriving on the premises had come to him by way of another of the addicts he had been dealing with for several months. It was information from an invoice receipt acknowledging delivery, sent by the jewelry store to a Hong Kong supplier. Along with that stolen letter had been another one, also bearing the jewelry store's return address, sent to a customer in San Francisco, telling the customer that an "exciting delivery" of stones had arrived and were just what the customer had in mind when last he'd visited the Los Angeles store. The letters had been stolen from a mailbox by an addict who traded a bag full of credit-card and check information along with the letters in question for four teeners of crystal meth that Cosmo had bought for two hundred fifty dollars and used as trade bait.

He'd been doing business with tweakers for over a year and only on one occasion did he and Ilya smoke some crystal with them, but neither had liked the high, although it did sexually arouse them. They preferred cocaine and vodka. Cosmo had told the addicts that he and Ilya were more normal, old-fashioned people.

The thing that really had him excited now was that the robbery had been easy. It gave him a great thrill to make that jeweler weep and piss all over himself. Cosmo had fucked Ilya all night after they had done the robbery. And she too admitted that it had been sexually stimulating. Though she said that she would not participate in any more armed robberies, he thought that he could persuade her.

Ilya was waiting for him when he got back to their apartment. As soon as they sold the diamonds, they would be moving, maybe to a nicer apartment in Little Armenia. Their two-room hovel over a residential garage had been rented to them by a Korean who never asked questions about the men, both white and Asian, who visited Ilya in that apartment for a "massage" and left within an hour or so. Ilya had formerly done a lot of out-call work, until she got arrested in a hotel room on a sting by a handsome vice cop who had flash money and nice clothes and rings on his fingers. Ilya wept when he showed his badge that night. She had been naive enough then to think that the handsome stranger had possibilities beyond a quick blow job.

Ilya was thirty-six years old and without a lot of years left for this kind of life, which is how she got teamed up with Cosmo. He'd promised to take care of her, promising that she'd never get arrested again and that he'd make enough money that she'd seldom have to sell her ass. But so far, she was making more money with her ass than he was making with the addicts who brought him things to trade for drugs.

Cosmo saw the outside light on after he'd parked half a block away and walked through the alley to the garage apartment with its termite-eaten stairway leading up. He was puzzled because she did not have a massage scheduled. He had specifically asked her about that. He felt a rush of fear through his bowels because it could mean a warning from her. But no, he could see her moving past the window. If cops were there, she'd be sitting, probably handcuffed. He took the stairs two at a time stealthily and opened the door without announcing his presence.

"Hi, Cosmo!" Olive Oyl said, with a gap-toothed smile, sitting on the small settee.

"Evening, Cosmo," Farley said with his usual smirk, sitting next to Olive.

"Hello to you, Olive. Hello to you, Farley," Cosmo said. "You did not call me. I am not expecting you to come here tonight."

"They called me," Ilya said, "after you went to Dmitri's."

Cosmo shot her a look. Stupid woman. She mentioned Dmitri in front of these addicts. He turned to Farley and said, "What is it you bring for me?"

"A business proposition," Farley said, still smirking.

Puzzled, Cosmo looked at Ilya. Her blond hair was pulled straight back in a tight bun, which she would never do if she was expecting guests, even addict customers like these. And her makeup was haphazardly applied, and there were dark lines under her eyes. He guessed that she had been taking one of her long afternoon naps when the freaks called, and hadn't really pulled herself together before their arrival. Ilya showed Cosmo a very worried face.

"What business?" Cosmo asked.

"Sort of a partnership," Farley said.

"I do not understand."

"We figure that the last stuff we brought you was worth more than the few teeners you gave us. A whole lot more."

"It is very hard thing to sell credit-card information and the banking paper today. Everyone who do crystal can make many deals today. Everybody know about — how they call it?"

"Identity theft," Farley said.

"Yes," Cosmo said. "So I do not make enough money to pay me back for crystal I give to you, Farley."

"Four lousy teeners," Farley reminded him. "That's one-quarter of an ounce. In your country maybe seven grams, right? What'd you pay, sixty bucks a teener?"

Cosmo was getting angry and said, "We do a deal. It is done. Too late for to complain, Farley. It is done. You go someplace else next time, you don't like us."

Cosmo's tone disturbed Olive, who said, "Oh, we like you, Cosmo, and we like Ilya too! Don't we, Farley?"

"Shut up, Olive," Farley said. "I'm a smart man, Cosmo. A very smart man."

Olive was about to verbally agree, but Farley elbowed her into silence. "Cosmo, I read every fucking thing that I bring to people I deal with. I read those letters from a certain jewelry store. I thought maybe you could do something with it. Like maybe sell the information to some experienced burglar who might tunnel in through the roof when the store was closed and steal the stones. It never occurred to me that somebody might go in with guns and take over the place like Bonnie and Clyde. See, I'm not a violent man and I didn't think you were."

Now Ilya looked like she was about ready to cry, and Cosmo glowered at her. "You talk shit, Farley," he said.

"I watch lots of TV, Cosmo. Smoking glass does that to you. Maybe I don't read the papers much anymore but I watch lots of TV. That hand grenade trick made all the local news shows the night you did it. Shortly after I'd brought the jewelry store's letters to you."

All Cosmo could say was "You talk shit, Farley."

"The description they gave on the news was you." Then he looked at Ilya, saying, "And you, Ilya. I been thinking this over. I can hardly think of anything else."

Cosmo was now glancing wildly from Farley

to Ilya and back again. "I do not like this talk," he said.

"There's one more letter you should have," Farley said. "But I didn't bring it with me. I left it with a friend." Farley felt a pang of fear shoot through him when he added, "If I don't get home safe and sound tonight, he's going to deliver the letter to the Hollywood police station."

Olive looked quizzically at Farley and said, "Me too, Farley. Safe and sound, right?"

"Shut up, Olive," Farley said, smelling his own perspiration now, thinking how the TV news bunny said the guy was waving around a pistol on the night of the robbery.

After a long silence, Cosmo said, "You want from me what?"

"Oh, about fifteen thousand," Farley said.

Cosmo jumped to his feet and yelled, "You crazy! You crazy man!"

"Don't touch me!" Farley cried. "Don't touch me! I gotta arrive home safe and sound or you're toast!"

Olive put her arms around Farley to calm him down and stop his shaking. Cosmo sat back down, sighed, ran his fingers through his heavy black hair, and said, "I give you ten. I give you ten thousands sometime next month. Money will come in the month of June. I have nothing today. Nothing."

Farley figured he'd better settle for the ten, and he was trembling when he and Olive stood. He took her hand. Violence was not his gig. A man like this looking at him with murder in his face? All this was new to Farley Ramsdale.

Farley said, "Okay, but don't try to sneak outta town. I got somebody watching the house twenty-four-seven."

Then, before Cosmo could reply and frighten him again, Farley and Olive scuttled down the staircase, Farley yelping out loud when he almost stepped on a half-eaten rat by the bottom step. A black feral cat hissed at him.

By the time they reached the doughnut shop on Santa Monica where the tweakers hung out, Farley had recovered somewhat. In fact, he was feeling downright macho thinking about the ten large that would be theirs next month.

"I hope you don't think that goat eater had me scared," he said to Olive, even though he'd been so shaky he'd had to pull over and let her take the wheel.

"Of course not, Farley," Olive said. "You were very brave."

"There's nothing to be scared of," he said. "Shit, they used a phony hand grenade, didn't they? I'll bet their gun was phony, too. What'd that news reader with the tits call it? A 'semiautomatic pistol'? I'll bet it was a fucking toy gun dressed up to look bad."

"It's hard to believe Cosmo and Ilya would shoot anybody," Olive agreed.

"Trouble is," Farley reminded her, "we ain't got enough glass to last till next month. We gotta get to the cybercafé and do some business. Like, right away."

"Right away, Farley." She wished they had some money for a good meal. Farley was looking more like a ghost than he ever had.

The cybercafé they chose was in a strip mall. It was a large two-story commercial building with at least a hundred computers going day and night. There was lots of business that could be done on the Internet. A tweaker could buy drugs from an on-line bulletin board or maybe do a little whoring on the Internet — male or female, take your choice. Money could be wired from one account to another. Or a tweaker could just sit there phishing for PIN numbers and credit-card information. The computers were cheap and could be rented by the hour. Just like the dragons working the corner by the cybercafé.

One of the dragons, a six-foot-tall black queen in full drag with a blond wig, short red sheath, three-inch yellow spikes, red plastic bracelets, and yellow ear loops, spotted Farley and Olive and approached them, saying, "You holding any crystal tonight?" The dragon had scored from Farley on a few occasions when he was dealing crack.

"No, I need some," Farley said.

The dragon was about to return to the corner to hustle tricks in passing cars, when a very tall teenage crackhead, also African American, with his baseball cap on sideways, wearing a numbered jersey and baggy knee-length jams and high-top black sneakers, looking goofy enough to be shooting hoops for a living in the NBA, approached the dragon and said, "Hey, Momma, where can I get me some? I needs it bad, know what I'm sayin'?"

"Uh-huh," the dragon said. "I know what you're sayin', doodle-bug."

"Well, whatchoo gonna do about it, Momma? I got somethin' to trade, know what I'm sayin'?"

"And what is that?"

He took several rocks wrapped in plastic from his pocket and said, "This'll take you on a trip to paradise, know what I'm sayin'?"

Pointing to the computer center, the dragon said, "Go in there and sell it, then. Get some United States legal tender and come back and we'll talk."

"I come back and show you tender, I make you do more than talk. I make you scream, know what I'm sayin'?"

"Uh-huh," said the dragon, and when the kid went strutting into the cybercafé, the dragon said to Farley and Olive, "Don't see too many black folk around Hollywood these days 'cept for jive-ass cracked-out niggers like that, come up here from south L.A. to hustle and steal. Jist havin' them around is bad for my bidness. Fuck things up for everyone." Then the dragon grinned and added, "Know what I'm sayin'?"

"If we get any crystal tonight, we'll share with you," Olive said to the drag queen. "I remember when you shared with us."

Farley shot Olive his shut-the-fuck-up look,

and the dragon caught it. "That's okay, honey, your old man needs tweak a lot more than I do, from the looks of him."

Before Olive, which Farley referred to as B.O., he used to do lots of business here. He'd steal a car stereo and sell it at the cybercafé on a rented computer. The money was wired on eBay to the Western Union office, where Farley would pick it up and cash it. Then he was back to the cyber-café to buy his glass. It was hard for him to imagine life away from this place.

They entered and Farley began looking for someone he could work. He saw a dude he'd been arrested with in a drug sweep a few years back, sitting at one of the computers by the door. Farley stood behind the guy for a minute to see if the guy had it going.

The e-mail message said, "Need tickets to Tina Turner concert. And want to sit in 8th row. Have teenager with me."

"That's a fucking cop," Farley said to the tweaker, who jumped and spun around on his chair. "Dude, you are doing e-mail with a fucking cop." He couldn't remember the tweaker's name.

"Yo, Farley," the tweaker said. "What makes you think?"

"Every fucking cop on the planet knows Tina Turner is code for tweak. And eighth row? Dude, think about it. What else could it be but an eight ball, right? And teenager means teener, very fucking obviously. So you're either dealing with the stupidest tweaker in cyberspace or a fucking narc. He's using dopey code that nobody uses anymore 'cause anybody can figure it out."

"Maybe you're right," the tweaker said. "Thanks, man."

"So if I just did you a favor, how about doing me one?"

"I got no ice to share and no cash to loan, Farley. Catch you later."

"Ungrateful, simpleminded motherfucker," Farley said to Olive when he rejoined her. "When we got busted down at Pablo's Tacos two years ago and taken to Hollywood Station in handcuffs, we had to drop our pants and bend over and spread. And crystal went flying out his ass. He told the cop it didn't belong to him. Said he was just holding it for some parolee who pulled a knife and made him put the ice in his ass when the cops surrounded the taco joint."

"Did you see it happen?" Olive asked.

"What?"

"The parolee with the knife, making him put the crystal up there! God, I'll bet your friend was scared!"

Farley Ramsdale was speechless at times like this and thought that she'd be better off dead. Except that she was so stupendously stupid she actually seemed to enjoy living. Maybe that's the way to cope with life, Farley thought. Get as brain-cooked as Olive and just enjoy the ride as long as it lasts.

When he looked at her, she smiled at him, showing her gums, and a tiny bubble popped out from the left gap in her grille when she said, "I think there's a little bit of pot left at home. And we could boost you some candy and a bottle of vodka from the liquor store on Melrose. The old Persian man that works nights is almost blind, they say."

"Persian is a fucking cat, Olive," Farley said. "He's an Iranian. They're everywhere, like cockroaches. This is Iran-geles, California, for chrissake!"

"We'll get by, Farley. You should eat something. And you should not get discouraged, and try to always remember that tomorrow's another day."

"Jesus Christ," Farley said, staring at her. "*Gone with the Fucking Wind*!"

"What, Farley?"

Farley, who, like most tweakers, stayed up for days watching movie after movie on the tube, said, "You're what woulda happened to Scarlett O'Hara in later life if she'd smoked a chuck wagon load of Maui ice. She'd have turned into you! 'Tomorrow is another fucking day'!"

Olive didn't know what in the world he was raving about. He needed to go to bed whether he could sleep or not. It had been a terrible day for him. "Come on, Farley," she said. "Let's go home and I'll make you a delicious toasted cheese sandwich. With mayonnaise on it!"

Nobody on the beach or in the whole state of California was madder than Jetsam that early morning of June 1. That's what he said to Flotsam when he met him at Malibu and unloaded his log from the Bronco and stopped to stare at the ocean. Both were wearing black wet suits.

The sky was a glare of gold rising up, and smudges of gray scudded low over the horizon. Looking away, Jetsam stared at the smog lying low in wispy veils, and at the bruised, glowering clouds that were curdling down onto all the fucking places where people lived in despair. Jetsam turned and looked out to sea, to the hopeful horizon glistening like an endless ribbon of silver, and for a long moment he didn't speak.

"What's wrong, dude?" Flotsam asked.

"I got stung Thursday night, bro!" Jetsam said.

"Stung?"

"A fucking IA sting! If you'da been on duty, you'da got stung with me. I was working with B.M. Driscoll. Poor fucker might as well set fire to homies and shoot dogs. He's always in trouble."

"What happened?"

"You know that IA sting they did down in Southeast — when was it, last year? Year before? The one where they put the gun in the fucking phone booth?"

"I sorta remember the gist of it," Flotsam said while Jetsam waxed the old ten-foot board as he talked.

"On that one, the fucking incompetents working the sting detail at IA leave a gun by a phone booth with one of their undercover guys standing nearby. They put out some kinda phony call to get a patrol unit there. Deal is, a patrol unit they're interested in is gonna come by, see the dude, do an FI, and see the gun there in plain view. The patrol unit's gonna ask what he knows about the gun and the dude's gonna say, 'Who, me?' like the brothers always say down there. Then IA, who's watching from ambush, hope the coppers are gonna arrest the brother and claim he was carrying the gun. And if they're real lucky, maybe slap the brother around after he mouths off to them. And if they hit the jackpot, call him a nigger, which of course will get them a death row sentence and a lethal injection. And then maybe they can have a party for a job well done. But not that time. It goes sideways."

"What happened? A shooting, right?"

"Some homies happen to be cruising by before the black-and-white shows up. These cruisers see a strange brother there who ain't one of their crew and they pop a cap at him. And then the IA cover team comes to the rescue and they fire back but don't really engage. I thought cops're supposed to engage hostile fire, but this is the rat squad. They see life different from regular coppers. So the homies get away, and what does IA do? They grab their sting gun and they get the hell out, and they don't hang around for an FID investigation. So they break every fucking rule the rest of us have to play by during these times. Their excuse was they had to protect the identity of their undercover officer."

"That is bullshit, dude," Flotsam said. "When you apply seven-pound pull on a six-pound trigger, you stay and talk to the Man and make the reports. Undercover is over when the muzzle flashes."

"Except for those rat bastards."

"So how did they sting you Thursday night?"

"That's what makes me so mad. They used the same fucking gag, the unimaginative assholes! I thought at first they must be after B.M. Driscoll. He told me he was involved in a shaky shooting before he transferred to Hollywood and was worried about it. One of those deals where he capped a Mexican illegal who drove his car straight at him when the guy was trying to escape after a long car pursuit. The next day, he gets a phone call at the station from an irate citizen who says, 'You gotta come mow my lawn now. You shot my gardener.'"

Flotsam said, "Yeah, our chief says we're supposed to just jump out of the way of cars coming at us, maybe wave a cape like a matador.

Then start chasing again, long as we don't en-
danger anybody but ourselves. Anything but
shooting a thief who might be a minor. Or
an ethnic. I wish somebody'd make a chart
about which ethnics are unshootable nowadays
and have Governor Arnold give them a sticker
for their license plates. So we'd know."

Jetsam said, "Retreat goes against a copper's
personality traits. Maybe they want us to just go
back to the drive-and-wave policy, like we did
under Lord Voldemort."

"Maybe they should just put trigger locks on
all our guns."

"Anyways, B.M. Driscoll's convinced himself
he's targeted by IA," Jetsam said. "Checks his
house for listening devices every couple weeks.
But you know him, he gets a hay fever cough
and thinks it's cancer."

"So how about Thursday night's sting? Are
you saying they dropped a gun by a phone
booth?"

"Purse," Jetsam said.

Jetsam said it was a phone booth on Hollywood Boulevard of course, where lots of tourists
might do something dumb like that. A phone
booth by the subway station. He remembered

how it had annoyed him when it popped on their computer screen. No big deal. An unnamed person had called in to say that there was a purse left in the phone booth. And the call was assigned to 6-X-32, on a night when B.M. Driscoll was Flotsam's stand-in.

B.M. Driscoll, who was riding shotgun, said, "Shit. Found property to book. What a drag. Oh well, it'll give me a chance to get my inhaler outta my locker. I'm getting wheezy."

"You ain't wheezy," Jetsam said. The guy's imagined health issues were wearing Jetsam down to the ground. "My ex was wheezy. Got an asthma attack every time I put a move on her in bed. That was about once every deployment period. Little did I know that her and the plumber down the street were laying pipe twice a week."

Jetsam parked in a red zone by the intersection of Hollywood and Highland while B.M. Driscoll said, "I don't like steroid inhalers but there's nothing more fundamental than breathing."

When Jetsam was getting out of the car, B.M. Driscoll said, "Be sure to lock it."

He wasn't worried about their shotgun rack getting pried open or their car getting hot-wired. He was worried about his two uniforms they'd just picked up from the cleaners, which were hanging over the backseat.

After locking the car, Jetsam took his baton and ambled toward the phone booth, letting B.M. Driscoll lag behind and finish his medical monologue on the treatment of asthma with steroid inhalers at a distance where Jetsam could hardly hear him.

It was the kind of early summer evening when the layer of smog burnished the glow from the setting sun and threw a golden light over the Los Angeles basin, and somehow over Hollywood in particular. That light said to people: There are wondrous possibilities here.

Feeling the dry heat on his face, looking at the colorful creatures surrounding him, Jetsam saw tweakers and hooks, panhandlers and ordinary Hollywood crazies, all mingling with tourists. He saw Mickey Mouse and Barney the dinosaur and Darth Vader (only one tonight) and a couple of King Kongs.

But the guys inside the gorilla costumes weren't tall enough to successfully play the great ape, and he saw a guy he recognized as Untouchable Al walk up to one of them and say, "King Kong, my ass. You look more like Cheetah."

Jetsam turned away quickly because if there was a disturbance, he wanted no part of Untouchable Al, especially not here on Hollywood Boulevard where the multitudes would witness the dreadful inevitable outcome.

A team of bike cops, one man and one woman whom Jetsam knew from Watch 3, pedaled by slowly on the sidewalk, over those very famous three-hundred-pound slabs of marble and brass dedicated to Hollywood magic and the glamour of the past.

The bike cops nodded to him but continued on their way when he shook his head, indicating that nothing important had brought him here. He thought they looked very uncool in their bike helmets and those funny blue outfits that the other cops called pajamas.

When B.M. Driscoll caught up with him, he said, "Don't this look a little bit strange? I mean, a purse is left here by an unknown person-reporting?"

Jetsam said, "Whaddaya mean?"

B.M. Driscoll said, "They're out to get me."

"Who?"

"Internal Affairs Group. In fact, the whole goddamn Professional Standards Bureau. I got grilled like an Al-Qaeda terrorist by a Force Investigation Team when I popped the cap at the goddamn crackhead that tried to run over me. I tell you, IA's out to get me."

"Man, you gotta go visit the Department shrink," Jetsam said. "You're soaring way out there, bro. You're sounding unhinged."

But B.M. Driscoll said, "I'll tell you something, if that purse is still there in the midst of this god-damn boulevard carnival, it means one thing. An undercover team has chased away every tweaker that's tried to pick it up during the last ten minutes."

And now Jetsam started getting paranoid. He began looking hard at every tourist nearby. Could that one be a cop? That one over there looks like he could be. And that babe pretending to be reading the name on one of the marble stars down on the sidewalk. Shit, her purse is bulging like maybe there's a Glock nine and handcuffs in there.

When they were standing at the phone booth and saw a woman's brown leather handbag on the phone booth tray, B.M. Driscoll said, "The purse is still there. Nobody's picked it up. No tweaker. No do-gooder. It's still there. If there's money in it, you can bet your ass this is a sting."

"If there's money in it, I gotta admit you might

have a point here," Jetsam said, looking behind him for the babe with the bulge in her handbag. And goddamnit, she was looking right at him! Then she gave him a little flirtatious wave and walked away. Shit, just a badge bunny.

B.M. Driscoll picked up the purse and opened it as though he was expecting a trick snake to jump out, removed the thick leather wallet, and handed it to Jetsam, saying, "Tell me I'm wrong."

Jetsam opened it and found a driver's license, credit cards, and other ID belonging to a Mary R. Rollins of Seattle, Washington. Along with $367 dollars in currency.

"Bro, I think you ain't paranoid," Jetsam said. "Forget what I said about the shrink."

"Let's take this straight to the station and make a ten-ten," B.M. Driscoll said, referring to a property report.

"Let's take this to the Oracle," Jetsam said. "Let's call information for a phone number on Mary Rollins. Let's check and see if this ID is legit. I don't like to be set up like I'm a fucking thief."

"It's not you," B.M. Driscoll said, and now he was twitching and blinking. "It's me. I'm a marked man!"

When they got to the station, they found the

Oracle in the john, reading a paper. Jetsam stood outside the toilet stall and said, "You in there, Boss?"

Recognizing the voice, the Oracle replied, "This better be more important than your over-whelming excitement that surf's up tomorrow. At my age, taking a dump is serious business."

"Can you meet Driscoll and me in the roll-call room?"

"In due time," the Oracle said. "There's a time for everything."

They chose the roll-call room for privacy. The Oracle examined the purse and contents, and as he looked at this angry suntanned surfer cop with his short hair gelled up like a bed of spikes, and at his older partner twitching his nose like a rabbit, he said to them, "You're right. This has to be a sting. This is unadulterated bullshit!"

Flotsam and Jetsam were lying in the sand next to their boards, by their towels and water, when Jetsam, reaching this part of the story, stopped to take a long pull from his water bottle.

Flotsam said, "Don't stop, dude. Get to the final reel. What the fuck happened?"

Jetsam said, "What happened was the Oracle came on like El Niño, and everybody stayed outta his way. The Oracle was hacked off, bro. And I got to see what all those hash marks give you."

"What besides death before your time?"

"Humongous prunes and no fear, bro. The Oracle jumped their shit till the story came out. It was a sting, but as usual, Ethics Enforcement Section fucked up. It wasn't meant for B.M. Driscoll. He's so straight he won't even remove mattress tags, but they wouldn't say who it was meant for. Maybe somebody on Watch three. We think communications just gave the call to the wrong unit."

Flotsam said, "EES should stick to catching cops who work off-duty jobs when they're supposed to be home with bad backs. That's all they're good for."

"Being an LAPD cop today is like playing a game of dodgeball, but the balls are coming at us from every-fucking-where," Jetsam said.

Flotsam looked at his partner's thousand-yard stare, saying, "Your display is on screen saver, dude. Get the hard drive buzzing and stay real."

"Okay, but I don't like being treated like a thief," Jetsam said.

Flotsam said, "They gotta play their little games so they can say, 'Look, Mr. Attorney General, we're enforcing the consent decree against the formerly cocky LAPD.' Just forget about it."

"But we got sideswiped, bro."

"Whaddaya mean?"

"They burned us."

"For what?"

"The undercover team saw B.M. Driscoll's uniforms hanging in the car. They had to nail us for something after we didn't fall for their stupid sting, so we're getting an official reprimand for doing personal business on duty."

"Stopping at the cleaners?"

"You got it, bro."

"What'd the Oracle say about that?"

"He wasn't there at the time. He'd already headed out for Alfonso's Tex Mex when a rat from PSB showed up. One of those that can't stop scratching all the insect bites on his candy ass. And the watch commander informed us we were getting burned."

"That is way fucked, dude. You know how many man hours were wasted on that chicken-shit sting? And here we are, with half the bodies we need to patrol the streets."

"That is life in today's LAPD, bro."

"How's your morale?"

"It sucks."

"How would it be if I got you laid Thursday night?"

"Improved."

"There's this badge bunny I heard about at the Director's Chair. Likes midnight swims at the beach, I hear."

"I thought you said you'd fallen in love with Mag Takara?"

"I am in love, but it ain't working too good."

"You said it was hopeful."

"Let's hit it, dude," Flotsam said to change the subject, grabbing his board and sprinting for the surf. He plunged into a cold morning breaker and came up grinning in the boiling ocean foam.

After Jetsam paddled out to his partner, he looked at Flotsam and said, "So what happened between you and Mag? Too painful to talk about?"

"She's got it all, dude. The most perfect chick I ever met," Flotsam said. "Do you know what the Oracle told me? When he walked a beat in Little Tokyo a hundred years ago, he got to know the Takara family. They own a couple of small hotels, three restaurants, and I don't know how much rental property. That little honey might have some serious assets of her own someday."

"No wonder you're in love."

"And she is such a robo-babe. You ever see more beautiful lips? And the way she walks like a little panther? And her skin like ivory and the way her silky hair falls against her gracefully curving neck?"

Sitting astride his surfboard, Jetsam said, "'Gracefully curving' . . . bro, you are way goony! Stay real! This could just be false enchantment because she grabbed that dummy hand grenade and tossed it that time."

Flotsam said, "Then I got way pumped the last night we worked together. I knew after my days off, you and me would be teamed for the rest of the deployment period, so I took the bit in my teeth and I went for it. I said something like, 'Mag, I hope I can persuade you to grab a bikini and surf with me on the twilight ocean with the molten sun setting into the darkling sea.'"

"No, bro!" Jetsam said. "No darkling sea! That is sooo nonbitchin'!" He paused. "What'd she say to that?"

"Nothing at first. She's a very reserved girl, you know. Finally, she said, 'I think I would rather stuff pork chops in my bikini and swim in a tank full of piranhas than go surfing with you at sunset, sunrise, or anytime in between.'"

"That is like, way discouraging, bro," Jetsam said somberly. "Can't you see that?"

Flotsam and Jetsam weren't the only ones complaining about the LAPD watchers that day. One of the watchers, D2 Brant Hinkle, had been biding his time at Internal Affairs Group. He was on the lieutenant's list but was afraid that the list was going to run out of time before an opening came for him. He was optimistic now that all of the black males and females of any race who'd finished lower on the written and oral exam than he had but got preference had already been selected. Even though he wasn't a D3 supervisor, he'd had enough prior supervisory experience in his package to qualify for the lieutenant's exam, and he'd done pretty well on it. He didn't think anyone else could leapfrog over him before the list expired.

It had been an interesting two-year assignment at IAG, good for his personnel package but not so good for the stomach. He was experiencing acid reflux lately and was staring down the barrel at his fifty-third birthday. With twenty-nine years on the Job this was his last realistic chance to make lieutenant before pulling the pin and retiring to . . . well, he wasn't sure where. Somewhere out of L.A. before the city imploded.

Brantley Hinkle was long divorced, with two married daughters but no grandchildren yet, and he tried for a date maybe twice a month after he heard a colleague his age say, "Shit, Charles Manson gets a dozen marriage proposals a year, and I can't get a date."

It made him realize how seldom he had a real date, let alone a sleepover, so he'd been making more of an effort lately. There was a forty-year-old divorced PSR whose honeyed tones over the police radio could trigger an incipient erection. There was an assistant district attorney he'd met at a retirement party for one of the detectives at Robbery-Homicide Division. There was even a court reporter, a Pilates instructor in her spare time, who was forty-six years old but looked ten years younger and had never been married. She'd whipped him into better shape with a diet and as much Pilates as he could stand. His waistband got so loose he couldn't feel his cell phone vibrating.

So he was in decent condition and still had most of his hair, though it was as gray as pewter now, and he didn't need glasses, except for reading. He could usually connect with one of the three women when he was lonely and the need arose, but he hadn't been trying lately. He was more focused on leaving Professional Standards Bureau and getting back to a detective job somewhere to await the promotion to lieutenant. If it came.

At IAG Brant Hinkle had seen complaints obsessively investigated for allegations that would have been subjects of fun and needling at retirement parties back in the days before the Rodney King beating and the Rampart scandal. Back before the federal consent decree.

And they weren't just coming from citizens; they were coming from other cops. He'd had to oversee one where a patrol sergeant his age looked at a woman officer in a halter bra and low-ride shorts who had just come from working out. Staring at her sweaty belly, the sergeant had sighed. That was it, he'd sighed. The woman officer beefed the sergeant, and that very expensive sigh got him a five-day suspension for workplace harassment.

Then there was the wrestling match at arrest-and-control school, where a male officer was assigned to wrestle with a woman officer in order to learn certain holds. The male cop said aloud to his classmates, "I can't believe I get paid for this."

She'd beefed him, and he'd gotten five days also.

Yet another involved a brand-new sergeant who, on his way to his first duty assignment as a sergeant, happened to spot one of the patrol units blow a stop sign on their way to a hot call that the unit had not been assigned. The sergeant arrived at his new post, and immediately he wrote a 1.28 personnel complaint.

Within his first month, that sergeant, a man who wore his new stripes with gusto, called one of the officers on his watch a "dumbbell." The officer made an official complaint against him. The sergeant got a five-day suspension. The troops cheered.

Under the federal consent decree with the legions of LAPD overseers, the cops were turning on each other and eating their own. It was a different life from the one he'd lived when he'd joined the world-famous LAPD, uncontested leader in big-city law enforcement. In Brant Hinkle's present world, even IAG investigators were subjected to random urine tests conducted by Scientific Investigation Division.

The IAG investigators who had preceded him said that during Lord Voldemort's Reign of Terror, they sometimes had six Boards of Rights — the LAPD equivalent of a military court martial — going on at one time, even though there were only five boardrooms. People had to wait in the corridors for a room to clear. It was an assembly line of fear, and it brought about the phenomenon of cops lawyering up with attorneys hired for them by their union, the Los Angeles Police Protective League.

The more senior investigators told him that at that time, everyone had joked grimly that they expected a cop to walk out of his Board of Rights after losing his career and pension and leap over the wrought-iron railing of the Bradbury Building into the courtyard five stories down.

The Bradbury Building, at 304 South Broadway, was an incongruous place in which to house the dreaded Professional Standards Bureau, with its three hundred sergeants and detectives, including the Internal Affairs Group, all of whom had to handle seven thousand complaints a year, both internally and externally generated against a police force of nine thousand officers. The restored 1893 masterpiece, with its open-cage elevators, marble staircases, and five-story glass roof, was probably the most photographed interior in all of Los Angeles.

Many a film noir classic had been shot inside that Mexican-tile courtyard flooded with natural light. He could easily imagine the ghosts of Robert Mitchum and Bogart exiting any one of the balcony offices in trench coats and fedoras as ferns in planter pots cast ominous shadows across their faces when they lit their inevitable smokes. Brant knew that nobody dared light a cigarette in the Bradbury Building today, this being twenty-first-century Los Angeles, where smoking cigarettes is a PC misdemeanor, if not an actual one.

Brant Hinkle was currently investigating a complaint against a female training officer in a patrol division whose job it had been to bring a checklist every day for a sergeant to sign off. After a year of this bureaucratic widget counting, where half the time she couldn't find a sergeant, she'd just decided to create one with a fictitious name and fictitious serial number.

But then the "fraud" was discovered, and no check forger had ever been so actively pursued. IAG sent handwriting exemplars downtown to cement the case against the hapless woman whom the brass was determined to fire. But as it turned out, there was a one-year statute on such offenses, and they couldn't fire her. In fact, they couldn't do anything except transfer her to a division that might cause her a long drive and make her miserable, this veteran cop who had had an unblemished record but had finally succumbed to the deluge of audits and paperwork.

Brant Hinkle and his team were secretly happy that she'd kept her job. Like Brant, just about all of them were using IA experience as a stepping-stone to promotion and weren't the rats that street cops imagined them to be.

As Brant Hinkle put it, "We're just scared little mice stuck in a glue trap."

Once when they were all bemoaning the avalanche of worthless and demoralizing complaints that the oppressive oversight armies had invited, Brant said to his colleagues, "When I was a kid and *Dragnet* was one of the biggest hits on TV, Jack Webb's opening voice-over used to say, 'This is the city. Los Angeles, California. I work here. . . . I'm a cop.' Today all we can say is, 'This is the city. Los Angeles, California. I work here. . . . I'm an auditor.' "

Probably the most talked-about investigation handled by Brant Hinkle during these we-investigate-every-complaint years was the one involving a woman who had become obsessed with a certain cop and made an official complaint against him, signed and dated, maintaining, "He stole my ovaries."

It had to be investigated in full, including with lengthy interviews. There had to be an on-the-record denial by the police officer in question, who said to Brant, "Well, I'm glad IA is taking her complaint seriously. There could be something to this ovary theft. After all, you guys are trying real hard to steal my balls, and you've just about done it."

It was probably at that moment that Brant Hinkle spoke to his boss about a transfer back to a divisional detective squad.

NINE

WATCH 5, THE ten-hour midwatch, from
5:15 P.M. to 4:00 A.M. with an unpaid lunch break
(code 7), had about fifty officers assigned to it.
Five of them were women, but three of those
women were on light duty for various reasons,
and there were only two in the field, Budgie and
Mag. And what with days off, sick days, and light
duty, on a typical weekend night it was difficult
for the Oracle to find enough bodies to field
more than six or eight cars. So when one of the
vice unit's sergeants asked to borrow both of
the midwatch women for a Saturday-night mini-
version of the Trick Task Force, he got an
argument.

"You've got the biggest vice unit in the city,"
the Oracle said. "You've got half a dozen women.
Why don't you use them?"

"Only two work as undercover operators and

they're both off sick," the vice sergeant said. "This isn't going to be a real task force. No motor cops as chase units. No big deal. We only wanna run a couple operators and cover units for a few hours."

"Why can't you put your uniformed women on it?"

"We have three. One's on vacation, one's on light duty, one's pregnant."

"Why not use her?" the Oracle said. "It's a known fact that there's a whole lotta tricks out there who prefer pregnant hookers. Something about a mommy fixation. I guess they want to be spanked."

"She's not pregnant enough to notice, but she's throwing up like our office is a trawler in a perfect storm. I ask her to walk the boulevard, she'll start blowing chunks on my shoes."

"Aw shit," the Oracle said. "How're we supposed to police a city when we spend half the time policing ourselves and proving in writing that we did it?"

"I don't answer trick questions," the vice sergeant said. "How about it? Just for one night."

When the Oracle asked Budgie Polk and Mag Takara if they'd like to be boulevard street whores on Saturday night, they said okay. He only got an argument from Budgie's partner, Fausto Gamboa.

Fausto walked into the office, where three supervisors were doing paperwork, and being one of the few patrol officers at Hollywood Station old enough to call the sixty-eight-year-old sergeant by his given name, he said to the Oracle, "I don't like it, Merv."

"What don't you like, Fausto?" the Oracle asked, knowing the answer.

"Budgie's got a baby at home."

"So what's that got to do with it?"

"Sometimes she lactates. And it's painful."

"She'll deal with it, Fausto. She's a cop," the Oracle said, while the other sergeants pretended to not be listening.

"What if she gets herself hurt? Who's gonna feed her baby?"

"The cover teams won't let her get hurt. And babies don't have to have mother's milk."

"Aw shit," Fausto said, echoing the Oracle's sentiments about the whole deal.

After he'd gone the Oracle said to the other two sergeants, "Sometimes my ideas work too well. Fausto's not only gotten out of his funk, I think he's about to adopt Budgie Polk. Her kid'll probably be calling him Grandpa Fausto in a couple years."

Cosmo Betrossian was a whole lot unhappier than Fausto Gamboa. He had diamonds to deliver to Dmitri at the Gulag soon and he had to kill that miserable addict Farley Ramsdale and his stupid girlfriend, Olive, sometime before then. Farley's claim that he had someone watching Cosmo and Ilya's apartment was so ridiculous Cosmo hadn't given it a thought. And as to Farley's other claim, that he had a letter that would be delivered to the police if something happened to him, well, the addict had seen too many movies. Even if there was a letter, let the police try to prove the truth of it without the writer and his girlfriend alive to attest to its veracity.

Cosmo was going to make them disappear, and he would have liked to talk to Dmitri about that. Dmitri would have some good ideas about how to make someone vanish, but if Dmitri learned about the tweakers, he might see them as potential trouble and back out of the arrangement. No, Cosmo would have to deal with them with only Ilya to help. And it would not be easy.

Other than a gang rival back in Armenia whom he had shot to death when he was a kid of eighteen, Cosmo had never killed anyone. Here in America he had never even committed violent crime until the jewelry store robbery. His criminal life had been relegated to the smuggling of drugs, which he did not use himself, fencing stolen property, and in recent years, identity theft, which he'd learned from a Gypsy.

He'd met the Gypsy in a nightclub on the Sunset Strip. Cosmo had been frequenting the Strip then, doing low-level cocaine sales. But the Gypsy introduced him to a new world. He showed Cosmo how easy it was to walk into the Department of Motor Vehicles, armed with a bit of personal data stolen by common mail thieves like Farley Ramsdale, and tell a DMV employee that he needed a new driver's license because he'd changed his address and misplaced his license. At first the DMV employees would ask for a Social Security number but seldom if ever bothered to pull up the photo of the legitimate license holder to compare it with the face before them. They'd just take a new photo and change the address to the location where the license would be sent, and business would be concluded.

Cosmo and the Gypsy normally used an address of a house or apartment in their neighborhood where the occupant worked during the day. And either Cosmo or the Gypsy would check their neighbor's mailbox every day until the driver's license arrived. Later, when the DMV started asking for a birth certificate, Cosmo learned that with the information from the stolen mail, it was a simple matter for the Gypsy to make a credible birth certificate that would satisfy most DMV employees.

Cosmo and the Gypsy got so lazy that instead of going to the DMV, they started using a CD template that was making the rounds among all the identity thieves. It showed how to make driver's licenses, Social Security cards, auto insurance certificates, and other documents.

Stealing credit-card numbers became a bonanza. They could buy just about anything. They could even buy automobiles, and since car dealers were all covered by insurance, they were the easiest. By the time the legitimate card owners got their statements, Cosmo and the Gypsy would be off that card and on to another. Sometimes the credit-card statements went to bogus addresses supplied by Cosmo and the Gypsy, so legitimate card owners wouldn't discover the account was delinquent until they tried to buy something of value.

The Gypsy had an interior decorator working with them at that time. She said it was amazing how many people on the affluent west side of town kept their old cards, even ATM cards, thrown into a drawer somewhere. Nobody seemed to care much. The credit-card company only took a hit if the card was presented in person by the thief. If the business was done on the Internet or by phone, the credit-card company was not liable. Banks and credit-card companies had long delays in catching up, and identity thefts were so paper intensive the police were overwhelmed.

For a while Cosmo and the Gypsy had gotten so successful they were hoping to deal with the Russians whose eastern European contacts hacked into U.S. banks and lending institutions for card numbers, then ordered high-quality embossing and encoding strips from China. As it was, they just did their business online in the cybercafés or by phone and ordered merchandise to be sent to addresses they'd cased. FedEx would drop the parcels on the porch while the resident was at work, and they would be picked up by Cosmo while the Gypsy waited in their car. The resident would be shocked when, after a few months of this, the police showed up at the home with a search warrant for all that stolen property.

Then one day without warning the Gypsy and the interior decorator moved to New York without notifying Cosmo until they were there. And that was that. Cosmo continued limping through the world that the Gypsy had sailed through, and now Cosmo was dealing with tweaker mail thieves and doing cybercafé networking as best he could. He had almost been arrested twice and was losing confidence now that everybody was doing identity theft.

The big break had come in the batch of mail stolen by Farley Ramsdale, when he had found the letter about the diamonds, and Cosmo had committed his first violent crime in America. He was stunned to learn that he liked it. It had thrilled him, that feeling of power over the jewelry store proprietor. Seeing the fear in his eyes. Hearing him weep. Cosmo had had complete control over everything, including that man's life. The feeling was something he could never put into words, but he believed that Ilya felt some of it too. If another chance at a safe and profitable armed robbery came up, he knew he would take it.

But of immediate concern to him was Farley
Ramsdale and Olive. And Cosmo was very worried about Ilya as a partner in homicide. Could
she do what it took, he wondered. He hadn't
spoken with her about the two addicts, not
since they had come to the apartment with
their blackmail threat. Cosmo sensed that Ilya
knew what had to be done but wanted him to
deal with it alone. Well, it was not going to work
that way. He couldn't do it alone. They wouldn't
trust him. Ilya was a very smart Russian, and he
needed a plan with her involved.

Hollywood Nate Weiss and Wesley Drubb were
having another one of those Hollywood nights,
that is, a night of very strange calls. It always happened when there was a full moon over the
boulevard and environs.

Actually, the Oracle, who'd read a book or two
in his long life, forewarned them all at roll call,
saying, "Full moon. A Hollywood moon. This is a
night when our citizens act out their lives of
quiet desperation. Share your stories tomorrow
night at roll call and we'll give the Quiet Desperation Award to the team with the most memo-
rable story." Then he added, "Beware, beware!
Their flashing eyes, their floating hair!"

Nate's facial bruises from the fight with the veteran who wanted a ride were healing up well, and though he would never admit it to anyone, he was secretly wishing they'd given the psycho the goddamn ride he'd wanted. His black eye had actually cost him a job as an extra on a low-budget movie being shot in Westwood.

Wesley was driving again, and with the Oracle going to bat for him, he hoped that there wouldn't be disciplinary action for letting their shop get stolen and trashed by the little homie who hadn't been arrested yet but whom detectives had identified. The Oracle had written in his report that Wesley's failure to shut off the engine and take the keys when he'd jumped out of the car was understandable given the extreme urgency of helping his partner subdue the very violent suspect.

Hollywood Nate said that since Wesley had just finished his probation it wouldn't cost him his job, but Nate figured he'd be getting a few unpaid days off. "Forgiveness is given in church, in temple, and by the Oracle, but it ain't written into the federal consent decree or the philosophy of Internal Affairs," Nate warned young Wesley Drubb.

Their first very strange call occurred early in

the evening on Sycamore several blocks from the traffic on Melrose. It came from a ninety-five-year-old woman in a faded cotton dress, sitting in a rocker on her front porch, stroking a calico cat. She pointed out that the man who lived across the street in a white stucco cottage "hadn't been around for a few weeks."

She was so old and shriveled that her parchment skin was nearly transparent and her colorless hair was thinned to wisps. Her frail legs were wrapped in elastic bandages, and though she was obviously a bit addled she could still stand erect, and she walked out onto the sidewalk unaided.

She said, "He used to have a cup of tea and cookies with me. And now he doesn't come, but his cat does and I feed her every day."

Hollywood Nate winked at Wesley and patted the old woman on the shoulder and said, "Well, don't you worry. We'll check it out and make sure he's okay and tell him to drop by and have some tea with you and give you his thanks for feeding his cat the past few weeks."

"Thank you, Officer," she said and returned to her rocker.

Hollywood Nate and Wesley strolled across the street and up onto the porch. The few feet of dirt between the house and sidewalk hadn't been tended in a long time but was too patchy and water-starved to have done more than spread a web of crabgrass across its length. There seemed to be several seedy and untended small houses along this block, so there was nothing unusual about this one.

Hollywood Nate tapped on the door and when they received no answer said, "The guy might have gone out of town for the weekend. The old lady doesn't know a few weeks from a few days."

Or a few years, as it turned out.

When Wesley Drubb opened the letter slot to take a look, he said, "Better have a look at this, partner."

Nate looked inside and saw mail piled up nearly to the mail slot itself. It looked to be mostly junk mail, and it completely covered the small hallway inside.

"Let's try the back door," Nate said.

It was unlocked. Nate figured to find the guy dead, but there was no telltale stench, none at all. They walked through a tiny kitchen and into the living room, and there he was, sitting in his recliner in an Aloha shirt and khaki pants.

He was twice as shriveled as his former friend

across the street. His eyes, or what was left of them, were open. He'd obviously been a bearded man, but the beard had fallen out onto his chest along with most of the hair on his head, and the rest clung in dried patches. Beside his chair was a folding TV tray, and on it was his remote control, a *TV Guide,* and two vials of heart medication.

Wesley checked the jets on the kitchen range and tried light switches and the kitchen faucet, but all utilities had been turned off. On the kitchen table was an unused ticket to Hawaii, explaining the Aloha shirt. He'd been practicing.

Nate bent over the *TV Guide* and checked the date. It was two years and three months old.

Wesley asked Hollywood Nate if this could possibly be a crime scene because the dead man's left leg wasn't there.

Nate looked in the corner behind the small sofa and there it was, lying right near the pet door where his cat could come and go at will. There was almost no dried flesh left on the foot, just tatters from his red sock hanging on bone. The leg had apparently fallen off.

"Good thing he didn't have a dog," Nate said. "If grandma across the street had found this on her front porch, she might've had a heart attack of her own."

"Should we call paramedics?" Wesley said.

"No, just the coroner's crew. I'm pretty sure this man's dead," said Hollywood Nate.

When they got back to the station at end-of-watch and everyone was comparing full-moon stories, they had to agree that the Quiet Desperation Award went to Mag Takara and Benny Brewster, hands down.

It began when a homeowner living just west of Los Feliz Boulevard picked up the phone, dialed 911, gave her address, and said, "The woman next door is yelling for help! Her door is locked! Hurry!"

Mag and Benny acknowledged the code 3 call, turned on the light bar and siren, and were on their way. When they got to the spooky old two-story house, they could hear her from the street yelling, "Help me! Help me! Please help me!"

They ran to the front door and found it locked. Mag stepped out of the way and Benny Brewster kicked the door in, splintering the frame and sending the door crashing against the wall.

Once inside the house they heard the cries for help increase in intensity: "For god's sake, help me! Help me! Help me!"

Mag and Benny ascended the stairs quickly,

hearing car doors slam outside as Fausto and Budgie and two other teams arrived. The bedroom door was slightly ajar and Mag stood on one side of it, Benny on the other, and being cops, they instinctively put their hands on their pistol grips.

Mag nudged the door open with her toe. There was silence for a long moment and they could hear the loud tick of a grandfather clock as the pendulum swept back and forth, back and forth.

Then, in the far corner of the large bedroom suite, the voice:"Help me! Help me! Help me!"

Mag and Benny automatically entered in a combat crouch and found her. She was a fifty-five-year-old invalid, terribly crippled by arthritis, left alone that night by her bachelor son. She was sitting in a wheelchair by a small round table near the window, where she no doubt spent long hours gazing at the street below.

She was holding a .32 semiautomatic in one twisted claw and an empty magazine in the other. The .32 caliber rounds were scattered on the floor where she'd dropped them.

Her surprisingly youthful cheeks were tear-stained, and she cried out to them,"Help me! Oh, please help me load this thing! And then get out!"

★ ★ ★

There were two detectives working overtime at Hollywood Station that night. One was Andi Mc-Crea, who had been given the job of finishing what she'd started innocently a few weeks ago as a stand-in for the absent sex crimes detail. But she didn't mind a bit because that was the first time in her career that she had solved a double homicide without knowing a damn thing about it.

The kid from Reno was in Juvenile Hall awaiting his hearing. But more important, his forty-year-old fellow killer, Melvin Simpson, a third-strike ex-con from the San Francisco Bay Area who had been in Reno on a gambling junket, was going to be charged with capital murder.

Now detectives in Las Vegas were also interested in Simpson, since it was discovered through his credit-card receipts that he'd also been in their city for a week. With no means of employment he'd had enough money to gamble in both places, and it turned out that a high-tech engineer from Chicago who was attending a convention had been robbed and murdered at a rest stop outside Las Vegas on the day that Simpson had checked out of his hotel.

The ballistics report hadn't been completed

yet, but Andi had high hopes. Wouldn't this be something to talk about to the oral board at the next lieutenant's exam. It might even rate a story in the *L.A. Times,* except that nobody read the *Times* anymore or any newspaper, so there was no point getting excited about that part of it.

The other detective working late that night was Viktor Chernenko, a forty-three-year-old immigrant from Ukraine, one of two naturalized citizens currently working at Hollywood Station, the other being from Guadalajara, Mexico. Viktor had a mass of wiry, dark hair that he called "disobedient," a broad Slavic face, a barrel of a body, and a neck so thick he was always popping buttons.

Once when his robbery team was called to a clinic in east Hollywood to interview the victim of a violent purse snatching, the receptionist saw Viktor enter and said to a woman waiting in the lobby, "Your cab is here."

And he was just about the most dedicated, hardworking, and eager-to-please cop that Andi McCrea had ever encountered.

Viktor had immigrated to America in September 1991, a month after the coup that led to the collapse of the Soviet Union, at a time when he

was a twenty-eight-year-old captain in the Red
Army. His exit from the USSR was unclear and
mysterious, leading to gossip that he'd defected
with valuable intelligence and was brought to
Los Angeles by the CIA. Or maybe not. No one
knew for sure, and Viktor seemed to like it
that way.

He was the one that LAPD came to when they
needed a Russian translator or a Russian-
speaking interrogator, and consequently he had
become well known to most of the local gangsters from former Iron Curtain countries. And
that was why he was working late. He had been
assigned to assist the robbery team handling the
"hand grenade heist," as the jewelry store robbery came to be called. Viktor had been contact-
ing every émigré that he knew personally who
was even remotely involved with the so-called
Russian Mafia. And that meant any Los Angeles
criminal from the Eastern bloc, including the
YACS: Yugoslavians, Albanians, Croatians, and
Serbs.

Viktor was educated well in Ukraine and later
in Russia. His study of English had helped get
him promoted to captain in the army before
most of his same age colleagues, but the English

he'd studied in the USSR had not included idioms, which would probably confound him forever. That evening, when Andi twice offered to get him some coffee, he had politely declined until she asked if she could bring him a cup of tea instead.

Using her proper name as always, he said, "Thank you, Andrea. That would strike the spot."

During his years in Los Angeles, Viktor Chernenko had learned that one similarity between life in the old USSR and life in Los Angeles — life under a command economy and a market economy — was that a tremendous amount of business was transacted by people in subcultures, people whom no one ever sees except the police. Viktor was fascinated by the tidal wave of identity theft sweeping over Los Angeles and the nation, and even though Hollywood detectives did not deal directly with these cases — referring them downtown to specialized divisions like Bunco Forgery — almost everybody Viktor contacted in the Hollywood criminal community had something or other to do with forged or stolen identity.

After several conversations with the jewelry store victim, Sammy Tanampai, as well as with Sammy's father, Viktor was convinced that neither of them had had any dealings, legitimate or not, with Russian gangsters or Russian prostitutes. Sammy Tanampai was positive that he had heard a Russian accent from the woman, or something similar to the accents he'd heard from Russian émigrés who'd temporarily settled in cheap lodgings that his father often rented to them in Thai Town.

It was during a follow-up interview that Sammy said to Viktor Chernenko, "The man didn't say many words, so I can't be exactly sure, but the woman's accent sounded like yours."

The more that Viktor thought about how these Russians, if they were Russians, had gotten the information about the diamonds, the more he concluded that it could have come from an ordinary mail theft. Sipping the tea that Andi had brought him, he decided to make another phone call to Sammy Tanampai.

"Did you mail letters to anyone about the diamonds?" he asked Sammy after the jeweler's wife called him to the phone.

"I did not. No."

"Do you know if your father did so?"

"Why would he do that?"

"Maybe to a client who wanted the kind of diamonds in your shipment? Something like that?"

And that stopped the conversation for a long moment. When Sammy spoke again he said, "Yes. My father wrote to a client in San Francisco about the diamonds. He mentioned that to me."

"Do you know where he mailed the letter?" Viktor asked.

"I mailed it," Sammy said. "In a mailbox on Gower, several blocks south of Hollywood Boulevard. I was on my way to pick up my kids at the day-care center. Is that important?"

"People steal letters from mailboxes," Viktor explained.

After he hung up, Andi said, curious, "Are you getting somewhere on the jewelry store case?"

With a smile, Viktor said, "Tomorrow I shall be looking through the transient book to see if many homeless people are hanging around Hollywood and Gower."

"Why?" Andi asked. "Surely you don't think a homeless person pulled a robbery that sophisticated?"

With a bigger smile, he said, "No, Andrea, but homeless people can steal from mailboxes. And homeless people see all that happens but nobody sees homeless people, who live even below subculture. My Russian robbers think they are very clever, but I think they may soon find that they have not pulled the fuzz over our eyes."

One of the reasons given for putting Budgie Polk and Mag Takara out on the boulevard on Saturday night was that Compstat had indicated there were too many tricks getting mugged by opportunist robbers and by the whores themselves. And everyone knew that many of the robberies went unreported because tricks were married men who didn't want mom to know where they went after work.

Compstat was the program of the current chief of police that he'd used when he was police commissioner of the NYPD and that he claimed brought down crime in that city, even though it was during a time when crime was dropping all over America for reasons demographic that had nothing to do with his program. Still, nobody ever expressed doubts aloud and everybody jumped onboard, at least feigning exuberance for the big chief's imported baby, pinching its cheeks and patting its behind when anyone was watching.

Brant Hinkle of Internal Affairs Group thought that Compstat might possibly have helped in New York, with its thirty thousand officers, maybe even in Boston, where the chief had served as a street cop. Perhaps it might be a worthwhile tool in many vertical cities where thousands live and work directly on top of others in structures that rise several stories. But that wasn't the way people lived in the transient, nomadic sprawl of the L.A. basin. Where nobody knew their neighbors' names. Where people worked and lived close to the ground with access to their cars. Where everyone owned a car, and freeways crisscrossed residential areas as well as business districts. Where only nine thousand cops had to police 467 square miles.

When crime occurred in L.A., the perpetrator could be blocks or miles away before the PSR could even assign a car to take a report. If she could find one. And as far as flooding an area with cops to deal with a crime trend, the LAPD didn't have half enough cops to flood anything. They could only leak.

There were a few occasions when Brant Hinkle got to see Compstat in action, during the first couple of years after the new chief arrived. That was when the chief, perhaps a bit insecure on the Left Coast, brought in a journalist crony from New York who had never been a police of-

ficer and made a special badge for him saying
"Bureau Chief." And gave him a gun permit so
he'd have a badge and gun like a real cop. That
guy seemed to do no harm, and he was gone
now and the chief of police was more accli-
mated and more secure, but Compstat
remained.

Back then the chief had also brought several
retired cops from New York, as though trying to
re-create New York in L.A. They would put on a
little slide show with two or three patrol captains sitting in the hot seat. On a slide would be
a picture of an apartment building, and one of
the retired NYPD cops with a loud voice and a
Bronx accent would confront the LAPD captains and say, "Tell us about the crime problems
there."

And of course, none of the captains had the
faintest idea about the crime problems there or
even where "there" was. A two-story apartment
building? There were hundreds in each division,
thousands in some.

And the second-loudest guy, maybe with a
Brooklyn accent, would yell in their faces, "Is the
burglary that occurred there on Friday afternoon a single burglary or part of a trend?"

And a captain would stammer and sweat and

wonder if he should take a guess or pray for an earthquake.

However, Brant Hinkle learned that there were some LAPD officers who loved the Compstat sessions. They were the street cops who happened to hate their captains. They got a glow just hearing about their bosses melting in puddles while these abrasive New Yorkers sprayed saliva. At least that's how it was described to the cops who wished they could have been there to watch the brass get a taste of the shit they shoveled onto the troops. The street cops would've paid for tickets.

As far as the troops at Hollywood Station were concerned, the East Coast chief was not Lord Voldemort, and that alone was an answered prayer. And he did care about reducing crime and response time to calls. And he did more than talk about troop morale; he allowed detectives to take their city cars home when they were on call instead of using their private cars. And of great importance, he instituted the compressed work schedule that Lord Voldemort hated, which allowed LAPD cops to join other local police departments in working four ten-hour shifts a week or three twelve-hour shifts instead of the old eight-to-five. This allowed LAPD cops, most of whom could not afford to live in L.A. and had to drive long distances, the luxury of three or four days at home.

As far as Compstat was concerned, the street cops were philosophical and fatalistic, as they always were about the uncontrollable nature of a cop's life. One afternoon at roll call, the Oracle, who was old enough and had enough time on the Job to speak the truth when no one else dared, asked the lieutenant rhetorically, "Why doesn't the brass quit sweating Compstat? It's just a series of computer-generated pin maps is all it is. Give the chief a little more time to settle down in his new Hollywood digs and go to a few of those Beverly Hills cocktail parties catered by Wolfgang Puck. Wait'll he gets a good look at all those pumped-up weapons of mass seduction. He'll get over his East Coast bullshit and go Hollywood like all the clowns at city hall."

When his transfer came through, Brant Hinkle was overjoyed. He had hoped he would get Hollywood Detectives and had had an informal interview months earlier with their lieutenant in charge. He had also had an informal interview with the boss of Van Nuys Detectives, the division in which he lived, and did the same at West L.A. Detectives, pretty sure that he could get one of them.

When he reported, he was told he'd be working with the robbery teams, at least for now, and was introduced around the squad room. He found that he was acquainted with half a dozen of the detectives and wondered where the rest were. He counted twenty-two people working in their little cubicles on computers or phones, sitting at small metal desks divided only by three-foot barriers of wallboard.

Andi McCrea said to him, "A few of our people are on days off, but this is about it. We're supposed to have fifty bodies, we have half that many. At one time ten detectives worked auto theft, now there're two."

"It's the same everywhere," Brant said. "Nobody wants to be a cop these days."

"Especially LAPD," Andi said. "You should know why. You just left IA."

"Not so loud," he said, finger to lips. "I'd like to keep it from the troops that I did two years on the Burn Squad."

"Our secret," Andi said, thinking he had a pretty nice smile and very nice green eyes.

"So where's my team?" he asked Andi, wondering how old she was, noticing there was no wedding ring.

"Right behind you," she said. He turned and suffered an enthusiastic Ukrainian handshake from Viktor Chernenko.

"I am not usually a detective of the robbery teams," Viktor said, "but I am Ukrainian, so now I am a detective of robbery teams because of the hand grenade heist. Please sit and we shall talk about Russian robbers."

"You'll enjoy this case," Andi said, liking Brant's smile more and more. "Viktor has been very thorough in his investigation."

"Thank you, Andrea," Viktor said shyly. "I have tried with all my effort to leave no stone upright."

The Oracle decided maybe he himself should win honorable mention for the Quiet Desperation Award on that full-moon evening. He had just returned from code 7 and had severe heartburn from two greasy burgers and fries, when the desk officer entered the office and said,

"Sarge, I think you need to take this one. A guy's on the phone and wants to speak to a sergeant."

"Can't you find out what it's about?" the Oracle said, looking in the desk drawer for his antacid tablets.

"He won't tell me. Says he's a priest."

"Oh, crap!" the Oracle said. "Did he say his name is Father William, by any chance?"

"How'd you know?"

"There's a Hollywood moon. He'll keep me on the phone for an hour. Okay, I'll talk to him."

When the Oracle picked up the phone, he said, "What's troubling you this time, Father William?"

The caller said, "Sergeant, please send me two strong young officers right away! I need to be arrested, handcuffed, and utterly humiliated! It's urgent!"

TEN

ON SATURDAY, JUNE 3, Officer Kristina Ripatti of Southwest Division was shot by an ex-con who had just robbed a gas station. Her partner killed the robber but got harassed by homies while he was trying to help the wounded officer, whose spinal injury paralyzed her from the waist down. When Fausto learned that Officer Ripatti, age thirty-three, also had a baby girl, he began to agonize over his partner's upcoming assignment.

When Saturday night arrived, Budgie and Mag got whistles from one end of the station to the other. Budgie grinned and flipped them off and tried not to look too self-conscious. She was wearing a push-up bra that wasn't comfortable given her condition, a lime-green jersey with a plunging neck under a short vest to hide the wire and mike, and the tightest skirt she'd ever

251

worn, which the teenager next door had let her borrow.

The neighbor kid had gotten into the spirit of the masquerade by insisting that Budgie try on a pair of her mother's three-inch stilettos, and they fit, for despite being so tall, Budgie had small feet. A green purse with a shoulder strap completed the ensemble. And she wore plenty of pancake and the brightest creamiest gloss she owned, and she didn't spare the eyeliner. Her braided blond ponytail was combed out and sprinkled with glitter.

Flotsam checked her out and said to Jetsam, "Man, talk about bling!"

Fausto looked at her with disapproval, then took a five-shot, two-inch Smith & Wesson revolver from his pocket and said, "Put this in your purse."

"I don't need it, Fausto," Budgie said. "My security team'll be watching me at all times."

"Do like I say, please," Fausto said.

Because it was the first time he'd ever said please to her, she took the gun and noticed him looking at her throat and chest. She reached up and unfastened the delicate gold chain and handed the chain and medal to him, saying,

"What kind of whore wears one of these? Hold it for me."

Fausto took the medal in his hand and said, "Who is this, anyways?"

"Saint Michael, patron saint of police officers."

Handing it back to her, he said, "Keep him in your purse right alongside the hideout gun."

Mag, who wasn't thin like Budgie and was nearly a foot shorter, had all the curves she needed without enhancement, and came off as more of a bondage bitch. She wore a black jersey turtleneck, black shorts, black plastic knee boots that she had bought for this occasion, and dangling plastic earrings. She'd tied back her glossy blunt cut in a severe bun.

Her look said, "I will hurt you but not too much."

When the rest of the midwatch gave Mag the same catcalls and whistles, she just struck a pose and slapped her right hip and shot them a steaming look, saying, "How would you like me to whip you with a licorice rope?"

During the regular roll call, the vice cops escorted their borrowed undercover operators to their office to get them wired and briefed about the elements of 647b of the penal code, which criminalized an offer of sex for money. The decoys had to remain passive without engaging in an entrapment offer, while the cagier of the tricks would try to make them do it, knowing that entrapment would vitiate an arrest if it turned out that the hookers were cops.

After roll call, the Oracle took Fausto Gamboa aside and said privately, "Stay away from Budgie tonight, Fausto. I mean it. You start hovering around the boulevard in a black-and-white, you'll screw it up for everybody."

"Nobody should be giving that job to a new mother is all I got to say," Fausto grumbled and then turned and went to partner with Benny Brewster for the night.

When Budgie and Mag were sitting in the backseat of a vice car being driven out onto east Sunset Boulevard, Mag, who had been loaned to the Trick Task Force on one other occasion, and Budgie, who had never worked as an undercover operator, kept their energy up with a lot of nervous chatter. After all, they were about to step out onto the stage, find their marks, and wait for the vice cop director to say "Action!" All the time knowing that the part they were playing brought with it an element of danger that higher-paid Hollywood performers never had to face. But both women were eager and wanted to do well. They were smart, ambitious young cops.

Budgie noticed that her hands were trembling, and she hid them under the green plastic purse. She wondered if Mag was as nervous and said to her, "I wanted to wear a little halter top but I figured if I did, they wouldn't be able to hide the wire."

"I wanted my belly ring showing," Mag said. "But I thought the same thing about concealing the mike. I still like my ring but I'm glad I resisted the impulse to get the little butterfly above the tailbone when it was so popular."

"Me too," Budgie said, finding that just doing girl talk calmed her. "Tramp stamps are out. And I'm even thinking of losing my belly ring. My gun belt rubs on it. Took almost a year to heal."

"Mine used to rub," Mag said, "but now I put a layer of cotton over it and some tape before I go on duty."

"I got mine right after work one day," Budgie said. "I wore my uniform to work in those days to save time for a biology class I was taking at City College. You should've seen the guy when I walked in and took off my Sam Browne. He gawked at me like, I'm putting a belly ring on a cop? His hands were shaking the whole time."

Both women chuckled, and Simmons, the older vice cop, who was driving, turned to his partner Lane in the passenger seat and said, "Popular culture has definitely caught up with the LAPD."

Before they were dropped off at separate busy blocks on Sunset Boulevard, the older vice cop said to Mag, "The order of desirability is Asian hookers first, followed by white."

"Sorry, Budgie," Mag said with a tense grin.

"Bet I'll catch more," Budgie said also with a tense grin. "I'll get all the midgets with a tall blonde fantasy."

"For now I want you just one block apart," Simmons said. "There's two chase teams of blue suits to pull over the tricks after you get the offer, and two security teams including us who'll be covering you. One is already there watching both corners. You might have some competition who'll walk up to you and ask questions, suspecting you're cops. You're both too healthy looking."

"I can look very bad very easily," Budgie said.

"Won't that mess up our play?" Mag asked. "If we get made by some hooker?"

"No," he said. "They'll just catch a ride ten blocks farther east and stay away from you. They know if you're cop decoys, we're close by watching out for you."

Lane said, "Most tricks're sick scum, but this early in the evening you might catch some ordinary businessmen driving west from the office buildings downtown. They know that better-class whores work the Sunset track and once in a while they look for a quickie."

Budgie said, "I haven't been in Hollywood all that long, but I've been in on some drug busts as transporting officer for trannies and dragons. One of them might recognize me."

"The trannies mostly work Santa Monica Boulevard," Simmons explained. "They do good business with all those parolees-at-large who like that track because they got a taste for dick and ass when they were in the joint. They're disease-ridden. They avoid needles for fear of AIDS, then smoke ice and take it up the toboggan run. Does that make sense? Meth is an erotic drug. Don't even shake hands with trannies or dragons without wearing gloves."

Knowing it was Budgie's first show, Lane said to her, "If you should see an Asian hooker on the Sunset track you can figure she might be a transsexual. Sometimes Asian trannies make good money up here because they can fool the straight tricks. Goose bumps from shaving don't show as much on them. They might arrive just before the bars close, when the tricks're too drunk to see straight. But all trannies and dragons should be considered violent felons in dresses. They like to steal a trick's car when they can, and most tricks don't like to admit how the car got stolen, so the tranny or dragon never ends up on the stolen report as a suspect."

Simmons said, "Just avoid all the other hookers if possible — straights, dragons, and trannies."

"*Other* hookers?" said Budgie.

He said, "Sorry, you're starting to look so convincing I got confused."

When the women were dropped off half a block from the boulevard, Simmons said, "If a black trick hits on you, go ahead and talk but look for a too-cool manner and a cool ride. He may be one of the pimps from a Wilshire track checking out the competition, or trying to muscle in. He may talk shit and try to pimp you out and we would love that to happen, but keep both feet on the sidewalk. You never load up. Never get in a car. And remember, sometimes there's interference on the wire and we can't always make out exactly what the tricks're saying to you, so we take our cues from what you say. The wires have been known to fail completely. If you ever get in trouble, the code word is 'slick.' Use it in a sentence and we'll all come running. If necessary yell it out. Remember: 'slick.' "

After all that, they were both back to being nervous when they got out. Each spoke in a normal voice into their bras and then heard the cover unit say to Simmons and Lane on their radio band, "Got them loud and clear."

The older vice cop seemed clearly more safety conscious, and he said, "Don't take this wrong. I hope I'm not being sexist, but I always tell new operators, don't take foolish chances for a misdemeanor violation like this. You're competent cops but you're still women."

"Hear me roar," Budgie said without conviction.

The younger vice cop said, "Showtime!"

Both women had some twilight action within the first ten minutes. Budgie traded looks with a blue-collar white guy in a GMC pickup. He circled the block only once, then pulled off Sunset and parked. She walked over to his car, mentally rehearsing the lines she might use to avoid an accusation of entrapment. She needn't have worried.

When she bent down and looked at him through the passenger window, he said, "I don't have time for anything but a very sweet head job. I don't want to go to a motel. If you're willing to get in and do it in the alley behind the next corner, I'll pay forty bucks. If you're not, see you later."

It was so fast and so easy that Budgie was stunned. There was no parrying back and forth, no wordplay to see if she might be a cop. Nothing. She didn't quite know how to respond other than to say, "Okay, stop a block down Sunset by the parking lot and I'll come to you."

And that was all she had to do, other than signal to her security team by scratching her knee that the deal was done. Within a minute a black-and-white chase unit from Watch 3 squealed in behind the guy, lit him up with their light bar and a horn toot, and in ten minutes it was over. The trick was taken back to the mobile command post, a big RV parked two blocks from the action taking place on Sunset Boulevard.

At the CP were benches for the tricks, some folding party tables for the arrest reports, and a computerized gadget to digitally fingerprint and photograph the shell-shocked trick, after which he might be released. If he failed the attitude test or if there were other factors such as serious priors or drug possession, he would be taken to Hollywood Station for booking.

If it turned out to be a field release, the trick would find his car outside the command post, having been driven there by one of the uniformed cops, but the trick wouldn't be driving it home. The cars were usually impounded, the city attorney's office believing that impound is a big deterrent to prostitution.

Budgie was taken in a vice car to the command post, where she completed a short arrest report after telling the guy who wired her that she didn't need to hear the tape of her conversation with the trick. He was sitting there glaring at her.

He said, "Thanks a lot." And mouthed the word "cunt."

Budgie said to a vice cop, "Maybe it's just a hormonal funk I'm in, but I'm starting to hate his guts."

The vice cop said to Budgie, "He's the kind of shit kicker that spent his happiest days line dancing and blowing up mailboxes."Then to the glowering trick he said, "This is Hollywood, dude. Let's do this cinema vérité."

The trick scowled and said, "What the fuck's that?"

The vice cop said, "You just keep mouthing off, and pretend we're not in your face with a hidden video camera for a scene maybe you can later interpret for momma and the kiddies."

Mag's first came a few minutes after Budgie's. He was a white guy driving a Lexus, and from the looks of him, one of those downtown business-men on his way home to the west side. He was more cautious than Budgie's trick and circled the block twice. But Mag was a trick magnet. He pulled around the corner after his second pass and parked.

The vice cops had said that they expected long tall Budgie to get some suspicious questions about being a police decoy, but Mag was so small, so exotic, and so sexy that she should reassure anybody. And indeed, the businessman was not interested in her bona fides.

He said, "You look like a very clean girl. Are you?"

"Yes, I am," she said, tempted to try a Japanese accent but changing her mind. "Very clean."

"I think you're quite beautiful," he said. Then he looked around warily and said, "But I have to know you're clean and safe."

"I'm a very clean girl," Mag said.

"I have a family," he said. "Three children. I don't want to bring any diseases into my home."

To calm him down, Mag said, "No, of course not. Where do you live?"

"Bel-Air," he said. Then he added, "I've never done anything like this before."

"No, of course not," she said. Then came the games.

"How much do you charge?"

"What're you looking for?"

"That depends on how much you charge."

"That depends on what you're looking for."

"You're truly lovely," he said. "Your legs are so shapely yet strong."

"Thank you, sir," she said, figuring that matching his good manners was the way to go.

"You should always wear shorts."

"I often do."

"You seem intelligent. So obliging. I'll bet you know how to cater to a man."

"Yes, sir," she said, thinking, Jesus, does he want a geisha or what?

"I'm old enough to be your father," he said. "Does that trouble you?"

"Not at all."

"Excite you?"

"Well . . . maybe."

And with that, he unzipped his fly and withdrew his erect penis and began masturbating as he cried out, "You're so young and lovely!"

For the benefit of the cover team and because of her genuine surprise, Mag yelled into her bra, "Holy shit! You're spanking the monkey! Get outta here!"

For a minute she forgot to scratch her knee.

Within two minutes the uniformed chase team lit up and stopped the Lexus, and when her vice cop security team pulled up, Mag said, "Damn, he just jizzed all over his seventy-five-thousand-dollar car!"

After arriving back at the mobile CP, where the guy was booked for 647a of the penal code, lewd conduct in a public place, Mag was feeling a little bit sorry for the sick bastard.

Until after his digital photographing and fingerprinting, when he turned to Mag and said, "The truth is, you have fat thighs. And I'll just bet you have father issues."

"Oh, so you're a psychologist," Mag said. "From looking at my thighs you have me all figured out. So long, Daddy dearest."

Then she turned to leave and noticed a handsome young vice cop named Turner looking at her. She blushed and involuntarily glanced at her thighs.

"They're gorgeous like the rest of you," Turner said. "Father issues or not."

Mag Takara hooked three tricks in two hours, and Budgie Polk got two. When Budgie's third trick, a lowlife in a battered Pontiac, offered her crystal for pussy, Budgie popped him for drug possession.

"How's that? Felony prostitution," she said, grinning at Simmons when she arrived back at the CP.

"You're doing great, Budgie," Simmons said. "Have fun, but stay alert. There's lotsa real weird people out here."

Mag met one of them ten minutes later. He was a jug-eared guy in his early forties. He drove a late-model Audi and wore clothes that Mag recognized as coming from Banana. He was the kind of guy she'd probably have danced with if he'd asked her at one of the nightclubs on the Strip that she and her girlfriends sometimes visited.

He'd been hanging back when other tricks flitted around her, making nervous small talk for a moment but then driving away in fear. Fear of cops, or fear of robbery, or fear of disease — there was plenty of fear out there mingling with the lust and sometimes enhancing it. There were plenty of neuroses.

When the guy in the Audi took his turn and talked to Mag, broaching the subject of sex for money very tentatively, he became the second guy of the evening to get so excited so fast that he unzipped his pants and exposed himself.

Mag said into her bra, "Oh my! You're masturbating! How exciting!"

"It's you!" he said. "It's you! I'd pay you for a blow job, but I'm tapped out. And I can't get old Jonesy stiff, goddamnit!"

And while the chase team was speeding toward the corner, the headlights from a large van lit up the interior of the Audi. Mag looked more closely, and it was true: Jonesy was not stiff. But it was bright crimson!

"Good god!" Mag said. "Are you bleeding down there?"

He stopped and looked at her. Then he released his flaccid member and said, "Oh, that. It's just lipstick from the other three whores that sucked it tonight. That's where all my money went."

A bit later, Budgie violated an order from Simmons by not keeping her feet on the pavement. She couldn't believe it when a big three-axle box truck hauling calves pulled around the corner and parked in the only place he could, in the first alley north.

She couldn't resist this one, approaching the cab of the truck, even though it was very dark in the alley. She climbed up on the step and listened nervously when the scar-faced trucker in a wife beater and cowboy hat said, "Fifty bucks. Here. Now. Climb on up and suck me off, honey."

This one was so bizarre that when the second cover team showed up, one of the vice cops said to the guy, "Wonder what your boss would say if we booked you into jail and impounded your vehicle."

Budgie said to the cowboy, "Are they going to be slaughtered?"

The cowboy was so pissed off he didn't answer at first but then said, "I suppose you don't eat veal? I suppose you shoot your goddamn lobsters before you put them in boiling water? Gimme a break, lady."

This one presented so many logistical problems that after a field release the cowboy was allowed to continue on his way with his cargo.

When Budgie was finished at the CP and taken back to her corner on Sunset Boulevard, she tried not to remember the doomed calves bawling. It was the first time that evening that she was truly sad.

Budgie wasn't standing on Sunset Boulevard for three minutes when a Hyundai with Arkansas plates pulled up with two teenagers inside. She was still feeling depressed about the calves and about the pathetically reckless husbands and fathers she and Mag had hooked tonight, and she wondered what diseases all these losers would bring home to their wives. Maybe the fatal one. Maybe the Big A.

She could see right away what she was dealing with here: a pair of Marines. Both had tan lines from the middle of their foreheads down, and skinned whitewalls with an inch or two of hair on top. Both were wearing cheap T-shirts with glittery names of rock groups across the front, shirts that they'd probably just bought from a souvenir shop on Hollywood Boulevard. Both had dopey nervous smiles on their dopey young faces, and after being inexplicably sad, Budgie was now inexplicably mad.

The passenger said to her, "Hey, good-lookin'!"

Budgie walked to the car and said, "If you say, 'Whatchya got cookin'?' I might have to shoot you."

The word "shoot" changed the dynamic at once. The kid said, "I hope you're not carrying a gun or something?"

"Why?" Budgie said. "Can't a girl protect herself out here?"

The kid tried to recover some of his bravado and said, "Know where we could get some action?"

"Action," Budgie said. "And what do you mean by that?"

The passenger glanced at the driver, who was even more nervous, and said, "Well, we'd like to party. Know what I mean?"

"Yeah," Budgie said. "I know what you mean."

"If it's not too expensive," he said.

"And what do you mean by that?" Budgie said.

"We can pay seventy bucks," the kid said. "But you have to do both of us, okay?"

"Where're you stationed?" Budgie asked, figuring a chase or cover team was getting ready.

"Whadda you mean?" the passenger said.

"I was born at night, but not last night." They're no more than eighteen, she thought.

"Camp Pendleton," the kid said, losing his grin.

"When're you leaving for Iraq?"

The kid was really confused now, and he looked at the driver and back to Budgie and trying to retrieve some of the machismo said, "In three weeks. Why, are you going to give us a free one out of patriotism?"

"No, you dumb little jarhead asshole," Budgie said. "I'm gonna give you a pass so you can go to Iraq and get your dumb little ass blown up. I'm a police officer and there's a team of vice cops one minute away, and if you're still here when they arrive you'll have some explaining to do to your CO. Now, get the fuck outta Hollywood and don't ever come back!"

"Yes, ma'am!" the kid said. "Thank you, ma'am!"

And they were gone before her cover team

drove slowly past the corner, and Budgie saw that cute vice cop named Turner shake his head at her, then shrug his shoulders as if to say, It's okay to throw one back, but don't make a habit of it.

The vice cops knew that their operators would need a break about now, so they suggested code 7 at a nearby Burger King, but Mag and Budgie asked to be dropped at a Japanese restaurant farther west on Sunset. They figured that the male officers wouldn't eat raw fish, and they'd had enough of that gender for a while. Thirty minutes to rest their feet and talk about their night's work would be a blessing. The vice cops dropped them and said they'd pick them up for one more hour and then call it a night.

Turner said, all the time looking at Mag, "Another hour and it's a wrap."

When Budgie and Mag got inside the restaurant, Budgie said, "Jesus, in this division *all* the coppers use movie expressions."

Mag ordered a plate of mixed sashimi, and Budgie a less courageous sushi plate, trying to observe protocol and not blatantly scrape the wooden chopsticks together, as so many round-eyes did at sushi joints. She lowered them to her lap and did it, dislodging a few splinters from the cheap disposable utensils.

Budgie said, "Do I ever regret borrowing these stilettos."

"My canines are barking too," Mag said, looking down.

"How many you hooked so far?"

"Three," she said.

"Hey, I pulled ahead by one," Budgie said. "And I threw a pair back. Jarheads from Camp Pendleton. I was the righteous bitch from hell they'll always remember."

"I haven't found any worth throwing back," Mag said. "Lowest kind of scum is what I've met. Maybe I shouldn't have worn the S&M wardrobe."

"You still into competitive shooting?" Budgie asked. "I read about you in the *Blue Line* when I worked Central."

"Kinda losing interest," Mag said. "Guys don't like to shoot with me. Afraid I'll beat them. I even stopped wearing the distinguished expert badge on my uniform."

"Know what you mean," Budgie said. "If we girls even talk about guns, we're gay, right?"

"U.S. Customs had a recent shoot that I was

asked to compete in. Until I saw it was called 'Ladies' Pistol Shoot.' Can you believe that? When I got asked, I said, 'Oh, goody. With high tea and cotillion?' The guy from Customs didn't get it."

Budgie said, "I had three guys tonight ask me if I was a cop. I was tempted to say, 'Would you like to ask that again with your dick in my mouth?'"

Both laughed, and Mag said, "I got a feeling Simmons would call that entrapment. Did you get a good look at Turner? Mr. Eye Candy?"

"I got a good look at him getting a good look at you," Budgie said.

"Maybe he's into bondage bitches," Mag said.

"I got a feeling he'd be interested if you wore overalls and combat boots."

"Wonder if he's married."

"God, why do we inbreed with other cops?" Budgie said. "Why not cross-pollinate with firemen or something?"

"Yeah, there must be other ways to fuck up our lives," Mag said. "But he sure is cute."

"Probably lousy in bed," Budgie said. "The cute ones often are."

Mag said, "Couldn't be as bad as a twisted detective from Seventy-seventh Street I used to date. The kind that buys you two drinks and expects to mate in his rape room within the hour. He actually stole one of my thongs, the creep."

Budgie said, "I hooked a drunk tonight who could hardly drive the car. When the cover team called a shop to take him to jail, he asked me if I was seeing someone. Then he asked me if I could get him out of jail. He asked me a dozen questions. When they took him away I had to tell him, 'Yes, I'm seeing someone. No, I can't get you out of jail. No, I can't help it that you have strong feelings for me. And no, this encounter was not caused by fate, it was caused by Compstat.' Christ, I just turn on my dumb-blonde switch and they can't let go. The guy tried to hug me when they were writing the citation! He said he forgave me."

Mag said, "One trick wanted to really hurt me when they badged him, I could tell. He was eye-fucking me the whole time they were writing him up, and he said, 'Maybe I'll see you out on the street sometime, Officer.'"

"What'd you say?"

"I said, 'Yeah, I know you're bigger than me. I know you can kick my ass. But if I ever run into you and you ever try it, I will shoot you until you are dead. I will shoot you in the face, and you'll have a closed-casket funeral.'"

Budgie said, "When I was a boot I used to say to creepy vermin like that, 'You don't get any status points for hitting a girl. But if you try it, my partners will pepper-spray you and kick *your* ass big time.'"

"Whadda you tell them these days?"

"I don't. If nobody's looking, I just take out the OC spray and give them a shot of Liquid Jesus. For a while my partners were calling me 'OC Polk.'"

Mag said, "The only really scary moment I had tonight was when one trick pulled a little too far off Sunset, and I had to walk past the parking lot. And a big rat ran right across my foot!"

"Oh, my god!" Budgie said. "What'd you do, girl?"

"I screamed. And then I had to quick tell the cover team that everything was okay. I didn't want to admit it was only a rat."

Budgie said, "I'm terrified of rats. Spiders too. I would've cried."

"I almost did," Mag said. "I just had to hang on."

"How's your sashimi?"

"Not as fresh as I like it. How's your sushi?"

"Healthy," Budgie said. "With Fausto I eat burritos and get more fat grams than the whole female population of Laurel Canyon consumes in a week."

"But they burn calories shopping for plastic surgeons and prepping their meals," Mag said. "Imagine laying out a weekly diet of celery stalks and carrot strips according to feng shui."

Budgie thought about how pleasant and restful it was just to sit there and drink tea and talk to another girl.

During the last hour, Budgie hooked one more trick, and Mag wanted to soar past her with two, but business was slowing. They had only thirty minutes to go when Mag saw a cherry-red Mercedes SUV with chrome wheels drive slowly past. The driver was a young black man in a three-hundred-dollar warm-up suit and pricey Adidas. He made one pass, then another.

Mag didn't return his smile the way she had been doing to other tricks that night, including two who were black. This guy made her think one word: "pimp." Then she realized that if she was right, this could be the topper of the evening. A felony bust for pimping. So on his next pass, she returned the smile and he pointed just around the corner and parked the SUV. A hip-hop album was blasting out, and he turned it down to talk.

When she approached cautiously, he said, "What's a matter, Momma, ain't you into chocolate delight?"

Yeah, he's a pimp, she thought, saying, "I like all kind of delights."

"I bet you do," he said. "Jump on in here and le's talk bidness."

"I'm okay out here."

"What's wrong?" he said. "You a cop or somethin'?"

He smiled big when he said it, and she knew he didn't believe it. She said, "I can talk out here."

"Come on in, baby," he said, and his pupils looked dilated. "I might got somethin' for you."

"What?" she said.

"Somethin'."

"What something?"

"Get in," he said, and she didn't like the way he said it this time. He was amped, all right. Maybe crack, maybe crystal.

"I don't think so," she said and started to walk away. This wasn't going right.

He opened the door of the SUV and jumped out, striding around the back and standing between her and Sunset Boulevard.

She was about to use the code word "slick" but thought about what it would mean if she brought down a pimp. She said, "You better talk fast because I don't have time for bullshit."

And he said, "You think you gonna come and work this corner? You ain't, not without somebody lookin' out for you. And that ain't no bullshit. That is righteous."

"Whadda you mean?" Mag said.

"I'm gonna be your protector," he said.

"Like my old man?" she said. "I don't need one."

"Yes, you do, bitch," he said. "And the protection has started. So how much you made tonight so far? Workin' on my corner. On my boulevard."

"I think you better get outta the way, Slick," Mag said. And now she was definitely scared and could see one of the vice cops running across Sunset Boulevard in her direction.

She was still looking for her mobile cover team when he said, "I'm gonna show you what is slick."

And she was shocked when his fist struck. She hadn't seen it coming at all. Her face had been turned toward the boulevard while she waited for her security, thinking, Hurry up. Her head hit the pavement when she fell. Mag felt dizzy and sick to her stomach and tried to get up, but he was sitting on top of her, big hands all over her, looking for her money stash.

"In yo pussy?" he said, and she felt his hands down there. Felt his fingers exploring inside her.

Then she heard car doors slam and voices shouting and the pimp screaming, and she got so sick she vomited all over her bondage bitch costume. And the curtain descended on the last performance of the evening.

Fausto Gamboa was driving when he heard the gut-churning "Officer down" and that an ambulance was racing code 3 to the Sunset Boulevard whore track. He almost gave Benny Brewster whiplash cranking the steering wheel hard left and blowing a stop sign like it wasn't there. Speeding toward Sunset Boulevard.

"Oh, god!" he said. "It's one of the girls. I knew it. I knew it."

Benny Brewster, who had worked with Mag Takara for most of the deployment period, said, "I hope it's not Mag."

Fausto glanced sharply at him and felt a rush

of anger but then thought, I can't blame Benny
for hoping it's Budgie. I'm hoping it's Mag. That
was an awful feeling, but there was no time to
sort it out. When he made the next left he felt
two wheels almost lifting.

The Oracle had been taking code 7 at his favorite taco joint on Hollywood Boulevard when
the call came out. He was standing beside his
car, working on his second *carne asada* taco
and sucking down an enormous cup of *hor-
chata,* Mexican rice water and cinnamon, when
he heard "Officer down."

He was the first one at the scene other than
all the security teams and the paramedics loading Mag into the ambulance. Budgie was sitting
in the backseat of a vice car, weeping, and the
pimp was handcuffed and lying on the sidewalk
near the alley, crying out in pain.

Simmons, the oldest of the vice cops, said to
the Oracle, "We got another ambulance coming."

"How's Mag?"

"Pretty bad, Sarge," Simmons said. "Her left eye
was lying out on her cheek. The bones around
the eye socket were just about crushed, from
what I could see."

"Oh no," the Oracle said.

"He hit her once and she fell back and her

head bounced off the sidewalk. I think she was awake sort of when we first rolled up, but not now."

The Oracle pointed to the pimp and said, "How about him?" And then he saw it in the vice cop's face when Simmons hesitated and said, "He resisted."

"Do you know if FID has been notified?"

"Yeah, we called our boss," Simmons said. "They'll all be here soon."

The vice cop's eyes didn't meet the Oracle's when he finally said, "There's a guy in the liquor store might want to make a complaint about . . . how we handled the arrest. He was yammering about it. I told him to wait until Force Investigation Division arrives. I'm hoping he'll change his mind before then."

"I'll talk to him," the Oracle said. "Maybe I can calm him down."

When the Oracle was walking toward the liquor store, he saw a young vice cop pacing nervously and being spoken to very earnestly by one of the other vice cops. The second ambulance arrived, and the Oracle heard the pimp moan when they put him on the litter.

In the liquor store, the elderly Pakistani proprietor completed a transaction for a customer, then turned to the Oracle and said, "Are you here for my report?"

"What did you see?" the Oracle asked.

"I hear car doors slam. I hear a man scream. Loud. I hear shouts. Curses. A man screams more. I run out. I see a young white man kicking a black man on the ground. Kick kick kick. Curses and kicks. I see other white men grab the young man and pull him away. The black man continues the screams. Plenty of screams. I see handcuffs. I know these are policemen. I know they come to this block to arrest the women of the street. That is my report."

"There will be some investigators coming to talk to you," the Oracle said, leaving the liquor store.

Budgie and one vice car were gone. Four vice cops and two cars were still there. The young cop who had been pacing when the Oracle arrived walked up to him and said, "I know I'm in trouble here, Sarge. I know there's a civilian witness."

"Maybe you want to call the Protective League's hotline and get lawyered up before making any statements," the Oracle said.

"I will," the vice cop said.

"What's your name, son?" the Oracle asked. "I can't remember anybody's name anymore."

"Turner," he said. "Rob Turner. I never worked your watch when I was in patrol."

"Rob," the Oracle said, "I don't want you making any statements to me. Call the League. You have rights, so don't be afraid to exercise them."

It was obvious that Turner trusted the Oracle by reputation, and he said, "I only want you to know . . . everybody to know . . . that when I arrived, that fucking pimp was sitting on her with his hands down inside her pants. That beautiful girl, her face was a horrible sight. I want all the coppers to know what I saw when I arrived. And that I'm not sorry for anything except losing my badge. I'm real sorry about that."

"That's enough talking, son," the Oracle said. "Go sit in your car and get your thoughts together. Get lawyered up. You've got a long night ahead of you."

When the Oracle returned to his car to make his notifications, he saw Fausto and Benny Brewster parked across the street, talking to a vice cop. They looked grim. Fausto crossed the street, coming toward him, and the Oracle hoped this wasn't going to be an I-told-you-so, because he wasn't in the mood, not a bit.

But all Fausto said to him before he and Benny Brewster left the scene was "This is a crummy job, Merv."

The Oracle opened a packet of antacid tablets, and said, "Old dogs like you and me, Fausto? It's all we got. Semper cop."

ELEVEN

EARLY THAT MORNING Mag Takara under-
went surgery at Cedars-Sinai to reconstruct facial bones, with more surgeries to follow, the
immediate concern being to save the vision in
her left eye. After being booked into the prison
ward at USCMC, the pimp, Reginald Clinton
Walker, also went under the knife, to have his
ruptured spleen removed. Walker would be
charged with felony assault because of the great
bodily injury suffered by Officer Takara, but of
course the serious charge of felony assault on a
police officer could not be alleged in this case.

There wasn't a cop on the midwatch who
didn't think that the felony assault and the
pimping allegation wouldn't be the subject of
plea bargain negotiations, but both the area captain and the patrol captain vowed that they'd
do all they could to keep the DA onboard for a

vigorous felony prosecution. However, a caveat was added, because as soon as Walker filed a multimillion-dollar lawsuit against the LAPD and the city for having his spleen destroyed, who could say what the outcome would be?

That afternoon, an hour before midwatch roll call, the floor nurse at Cedars saw a tall man in T-shirt and jeans with a dark suntan and bleached streaky hair enter the ward, carrying an enormous bouquet of red and yellow roses. Sitting outside the room of Officer Mag Takara were her mother, father, and two younger sisters, who were crying.

The nurse said, "Are those for Officer Takara, by chance?"

"Yeah."

"I thought so," she said. "You're the fourth. But she can't see anybody today except immediate family. They're waiting outside her room for her to have her dressing changed. You can talk to them if you like."

"I don't wanna bother them," he said.

"The flowers are beautiful. Do you want me to take them?"

"Sure," he said. "Just put them in her room when you get a chance."

"Is there a card?"

"I forgot," he said. "No, no card."

"Shall I tell her who brought them?"

"Just tell her . . . tell her that when she's feeling better, she should have her family take her to the beach."

"The beach?"

"Yeah. The ocean is a great healer. You can tell her that if you want."

At midwatch roll call the lieutenant was present, along with three sergeants, including the Oracle. He got the job of explaining what had happened and having it make sense, as though that were possible. The cops were demoralized by the events on Sunset Boulevard the night before, and they were angry, and all the supervisors knew it.

When he was asked to be the one to talk about it, the Oracle said to the lieutenant, "In his memoir, T. E. Lawrence of Arabia said old and wise means tired and disappointed. He didn't live long enough to know how right he was."

At 5:30 P.M. the Oracle, sitting next to the lieutenant, popped a couple of antacid tablets and said to the assembly of cops in the roll-call room, "The latest report is that Mag is resting and alert. There doesn't appear to be any brain damage, and the surgeon in charge says that they're optimistic about restoring vision in her eye. At least most of the vision."

The room was as quiet as the Oracle had ever heard it, until Budgie Polk, her voice quavering, said, "Will she look . . . the same, do they think?"

"She has great surgeons taking care of her. I'm sure she'll look fine. Eventually."

Fausto, who was sitting next to Budgie, said, "Is she coming back to work after she's well?"

"It's too soon to say," the Oracle said. "That will depend on her. On how she feels after everything."

"She'll come back," Fausto said. "She picked up a grenade, didn't she?"

Budgie started to say something else but couldn't. Fausto patted her hand for a second.

The Oracle said, "The detectives and our captains have promised that the pimp will go to the joint for this, if they can help it."

B.M. Driscoll said, "Maybe they can't help it. I'm sure he's got half a dozen shysters emptying his bedpan right this minute. He'll make more money from a lawsuit than he could make from every whore on Sunset."

"Yeah, our activist mayor and his handpicked, cop-hating police commissioner will be all over this one," Jetsam said. "And we'll hear from the keepers of the consent decree. No doubt."

Before the Oracle could answer, Flotsam said, "I suppose the race card will be played here. Dealt from the bottom of the deck, as usual."

That's what the lieutenant hadn't wanted, the issue of race entering what he knew would be a heated exchange today. But race affected everything in Los Angeles from top to bottom, including the LAPD, and he knew that too.

Looking very uncomfortable, the lieutenant said, "It's true that the media and the activists and others might have a field day with this. A white cop kicking the guts out of a black arrestee. They'll want Officer Turner not just fired but prosecuted, and maybe he will be. And you'll hear accusations that this proves we're all racists."

"I got somethin' to say about it, Lieutenant."

Conversation stopped then. Benny Brewster, the former partner of Mag Takara, the only black cop on the midwatch and in the room except for a night-watch sergeant sitting on the lieutenant's right, had something to say about what? The race card? White on black? The lieutenant was very uncomfortable. He didn't need this snarky shit.

Every eye was on Benny Brewster, who said, "If it was me that got there first instead of Turner and seen what he seen, I'd be in jail. 'Cause I'da pulled my nine and emptied the magazine into that pimp. So I'd be in jail now. That's all I got to say."

There was a murmur of approval, and a few cops even clapped. The lieutenant wanted to give them a time-out, wanted to restore order, and was trying to figure out how to do it, when the Oracle took over again.

The Oracle looked at all those faces, wondering how it was possible that they could be so young. And he said to them, "The shield you're wearing is the most beautiful and most famous badge in the world. Many police departments have copied it and everyone envies it, but you wear the original. And all these critics and politicians and media assholes come and go, but your badge remains unchanged. You can get as mad and outraged as you want over what's going to go down, but don't get cynical. Being cynical will make you old. Doing good police work is the greatest fun there is. The greatest fun you'll ever have in your lives. So go on out tonight and have some fun. And Fausto, try to get by with only two burritos. Speedo weather's coming up."

* * *

After they had handled two calls and written one traffic ticket, Budgie Polk turned to Fausto Gamboa and said, "I'm okay, Fausto. Honest."

Fausto, who was riding shotgun, said, "Whaddaya mean?"

"I mean you gotta quit asking me if I want you to roll up the window or where do I wanna have code seven or do I need my jacket. Last night is over. I'm okay."

"I don't mean to be a —"

"Nanny. So you can stop now."

Fausto got quiet then, a bit embarrassed, and she added, "The Li'l Rascals didn't want Darla in their clubhouse either. But we're in. So you can all just live with it, especially you, you cranky old sexist."

Budgie glanced sideways at him and he quickly looked out at the boulevard, but she saw a little bit of a smile that he couldn't hide.

Things got back to normal when Budgie went after a silver Saab that pulled out of Paramount Studios heading west a good three seconds late at the first traffic signal. The driver had a cell to his ear.

"Jesus," she said, "what's he doing, talking to his agent?"

When they had the Saab pulled over, the driver tried charming Budgie, whose turn it was to write one. He said with an attempt at a flirtatious grin, "I couldn't have busted the light, Officer. It didn't even turn yellow until I was in the intersection."

"You were very late on the red signal, sir," Budgie said, looking at his license, then at the guy, whose grin came off as smarmy and annoying.

"I would never argue with a police officer as attractive as you," he said, "but couldn't you be a little mistaken on the light? I'm a very careful driver."

Budgie started walking back to her car, putting her citation book on the hood to write while Fausto kept his eyes on the driver, who quickly got out and came back to her. Budgie nodded at Fausto that she could handle this schmuck, and Fausto stayed put.

"Before you start writing," he said, all the charm gone now, "I'd like to ask for a break here. One more ticket and I'll lose my insurance. I'm in the film business, and I need a driver's license."

Without looking up, Budgie said, "Oh, you've

had other citations, have you? I thought you said you were a careful driver."

When she began writing he stormed back to his car, got behind the wheel, and made a call on his cell.

Budgie finished the citation and took it to him, but Fausto stayed glued to the right side of the guy's car, watching his hands like the guy was a gangbanger. She knew that Fausto was still playing guardian angel, but what the hell — it was kind of comforting in a way.

After finishing, she presented the ticket and said, "This is not an admission of guilt, only a promise to appear."

The driver snatched the ticket book from her hand, scrawled his signature, and gave it back to her, saying in a low voice that Fausto couldn't hear, "I'll just bet you get off on fucking over men, don't you? I'll bet you don't even know what a cock looks like that doesn't have batteries included. I'll see you in court."

Budgie removed his copy, handed it to him, and said, "I know what a cassette player looks like with batteries included. This." And she patted the rover on her belt that was the size of a cassette player. "Let's have a jury trial. I'd love for them to hear what you think of women police officers."

Without a word he drove away, and Budgie said to the disappearing car, "Bye-bye, cockroach."

When Fausto got in the car he said, "That is an unhappy citizen."

"But he won't take me to court."

"How do you know?"

She patted the rover. "He said naughty things and I recorded them on my little tape machine."

Fausto said, "Did he fall for that dumb gag?"

"Right on his ass," she said.

"Sometimes you're not quite as boring as other young coppers," Fausto said to her, then added, "How you feeling?"

"Don't start that again."

"No, I mean the mommy stuff."

"I may have to stop at the milking station later."

"I'm gonna keep your gun in the car with me next time," Fausto said.

Farley Ramsdale was in an awful mood that afternoon. The so-called ice he bought from some thieving lowlife greaser asshole at Pablo's Tacos, where tweakers did business 24/7, had turned out to be shitty. The worst part was having to sit there for an hour waiting for the guy and listening to hip-hop blasting from the car of a pair of basehead smokes who were also waiting for the greaseball. What were they doing in Hollywood?

It turned out to be the worst crystal he'd ever scored. Even Olive complained that they'd been screwed. But it got them tweaked, the proof being that they were both awake all night, pulse rates zooming, trying to fix a VCR that had stopped rewinding. They had parts all over the floor, and they both fell asleep for an hour or so just before noon.

When Farley woke up, he was so disgusted he just kicked the VCR parts under the couch among all the dust balls and yelled, "Olive! Wake up and get your skinny ass in motion. We got to go to work, for chrissake."

She was off the couch before he stopped grumbling, and said, "Okay, Farley. Whatcha want for breakfast?"

Farley pulled himself painfully to his feet. He just had to stop passing out on the couch. He wasn't a kid anymore and his back was killing him. Farley looked at Olive, who was staring at him with that eager, gap-toothed grille, and he stepped closer and looked into her mouth.

"Goddamnit, Olive," he said. "Have you lost another tooth lately?"

"I don't think so, Farley," she said.

He couldn't remember right now either. He had a headache that felt like Nelly or some other nigger was rapping inside his skull. "You lose another tooth and that's it. I'm kicking your ass outta here," he said.

"I can get false teeth, Farley!" Olive whined.

"You look enough like George Washington already," he said. "Just get the goddamn oatmeal going."

"Can I first run over to see Mabel for a couple minutes? She's very old, and I'm worried about her."

"Oh, by all means, take care of the local witch," he said. "Maybe next time she makes a stew outta rats and frogs, she'll save a bowl for us."

Olive ran out of the house, across the street and down three houses to the only home on the block that had weeds taller than those in Farley's yard. Mabel's house was a wood-frame cottage built decades after Farley's stucco bungalow, during the 1950s era of cheap construction. The paint was blistered, chipped, and peeling in many places, and the screen door was so rusted a strong touch would make chunks crumble away.

The inside door was open, so Olive peered through the screen and yelled, "Mabel, you there?"

"Yes, Olive, come in!" a surprisingly strong voice called back to her.

Olive entered and found Mabel sitting at the kitchen table drinking a cup of tea with lemon slices. She had a few vanilla cookies on a saucer next to a ball of yarn and knitting needles.

Mabel was eighty-eight years old and had owned that cottage for forty-seven years. She wore a bathrobe over a T-shirt and cotton sweat-pants. Her face was lined but still held its shape. She weighed less than one hundred pounds but had lots more teeth than Olive. She lived alone and was independent.

"Hello, Olive, dear," Mabel said. "Pour yourself a nice cup of tea and have a cookie."

"I can't stay, Mabel. Farley wants his breakfast."

"Breakfast? At this time of day?"

"He slept late," Olive said. "I just wanted to make sure you're okay and see if you need any-thing from the market."

"That's sweet of you, dear," Mabel said. "I don't need anything today."

Olive felt a stab of guilt then because every time she shopped for Mabel, Farley kept at least five dollars from Mabel's change, even though the old woman was surviving on Social Security and her late husband's small pension. Once Farley had kept thirteen dollars, and Olive knew that Mabel knew, but the old woman never said a word.

Mabel had no children or other relatives, and she'd told Olive many times that she dreaded the day when she might have to sell her cottage and move into a county home, where the money from her cottage sale would be used by county bureaucrats to pay for her keep the rest of her life. She hated the thought of it. All Mabel's old friends had died or moved away, and now Olive was the only friend she had in the neighborhood. And Mabel was grateful.

"Take some cookies with you, dear," Mabel said. "You're getting so thin I'm worried about you."

Olive took two of the cookies and said, "Thanks, Mabel. I'll look in on you later tonight. To make sure you're okay."

"I wish you could watch TV with me some evening. I don't sleep much at all anymore, and I know you don't sleep much. I see your lights on at all hours."

"Farley has trouble sleeping," Olive said.

"I wish he treated you better," Mabel said. "I'm sorry to say that, but I really do."

"He ain't so bad," Olive said. "When you get to know him."

"I'll save some food for you in case you stop in tonight," Mabel said. "I can never eat all the stew I cook. That's what happens to old widows like me. We're always cooking the way we did when our husbands were alive."

"I'll sneak over later," Olive said. "I love your stew."

Pointing at her orange tabby cat, Mabel said, "And Olive, if Tillie here comes around your house again, please bring her when you come."

"Oh, I love having her," Olive said. "She chases away all the rats."

Late that afternoon, they were finally on the street, the first day that they'd gotten Farley's car running and Sam's Pinto returned to him.

"Goddamn transmission's slipping on this fucking Jap junker," Farley said. "When we collect from the Armenian, I'm thinking of looking around for another ride."

"We also need a new washing machine, Farley," Olive said.

"No, I like my T-shirts stiff enough to bust a knife blade," he said. "Makes me feel safe around all those greaseballs at Pablo's Tacos." He was thinking, When Cosmo pays me, bye-bye, Olive. Barnacles are less clingy than this goofy bitch.

He lit a smoke while he drove and, as so often happened since his thirtieth birthday three years ago, he started feeling nostalgic about Hollywood. Remembering how it was when he was a kid, back in those glorious days at Hollywood High School.

He blew smoke rings at the windshield and said, "Look out the window, Olive, whadda you see?"

Olive hated it when he asked questions like that. She knew if she said the wrong thing, he'd yell at her. But she was obedient and looked at the commercial properties on the boulevard, here on the east side of Hollywood. "I see . . . well . . . I see . . . stores."

Farley shook his head and blew more smoke from his nose, but he did it like a snort of disgust that made Olive nervous. He said, "Do you see one fucking sign in your mother tongue?"

"In my . . ."

"In English, goddamnit."

"Well, a couple."

"My point is, you might as well live in fucking Bangkok as live near Hollywood Boulevard between Bronson and Normandie. Except here, dope and pussy ain't a bargain like over there. My point is that gooks and spics are everywhere. Not to mention Russkies and Armos, like those fucking thieves Ilya and Cosmo, who wanna take over Hollywood. And I must not forget the fucking Filipinos. The Flips are crawling all over the streets near Santa Monica Boulevard, taking other people's jobs emptying bedpans and jacking up their cars on concrete blocks because no gook in history ever learned to drive like a white man. Do you see what's happening to us Americans?"

"Yes, Farley," she said.

"What, Olive?" he demanded. "What's happening to us Americans?"

Olive felt her palms, and they were moist and not just from the crystal. She was on the spot again, having to respond to a question when she had no idea what the answer was. It was like when she was a foster child, a ward of San Bernardino County, living with a family in Cucamonga, going to a new school and never knowing the answer when the teacher called on her.

And then she remembered what to say! "We'll

be the ones needing green cards, Farley," she said.

"Fucking A," he said, blowing another cloud through his nose. "You got that right."

When they reached the junkyard and he drove through the open gate, which was usually kept chained, he parked near the little office. He was about to get out but suddenly learned why the gate was open. They had other security now.

"Goddamn!" Farley yelled when a Doberman ran at the car, barking and snarling.

The junkyard proprietor, known to Farley as Gregori, came out of his office and shouted "Odar!" to the dog, who retreated and got locked inside.

When Gregori returned, his face stained with axle grease, he wiped his hands and said, "Better than chaining my gate. And Odar don't get impressed by police badges."

He was a lean and wiry man with inky thinning hair, wearing a sweatshirt and grease-caked work pants. Inside the garage a late-model Cadillac Escalade, or most of it, was up on a hydraulic lift. The car lacked two wheels and a front bumper, and two Latino employees were working on the undercarriage.

Olive remained in the car, and when Gregori

and Farley were alone, Farley presented a stack of twenty-three key cards to Gregori, who looked them over and said, "What hotel do these come from?"

"Olive gets them by hanging around certain hotels on the boulevards," Farley said. "People leave them at the front desk and in the lobby by the phones. And in the hotel bars."

Then Farley realized he was making it sound too easy, so he said, "It's risky and time-consuming, and you need a woman to do it. If you or me tried hanging around a hotel, their security would be all over us in no time. Plus, you gotta know which hotel has the right key cards. Olive has that special knowledge but she ain't sharing it."

"Five bucks apiece I give you."

"Come on, Gregori," Farley said. "These key cards are in primo condition. The perfect size and color. With a good-looking mag strip. You can buy those bogus driver's licenses from Cosmo and they'll glue to the front of the card just perfect. They'll pass inspection with any cop on the street."

"I don't talk to Cosmo in a long time," Gregori said. "You see him lately?"

"Naw, I ain't seen him in a year," Farley lied.

Then, "Look, Gregori, for very little money every fucking wetback that works in all your businesses can be a licensed driver tomorrow. Not to mention your friends and relatives from the old country."

"Friends and relatives from Armenia can get real driver's license," Gregori said imperiously.

"Of course they can," Farley said, apologetically. "I just meant like when they first get here. I been in a couple of Armenian homes in east Hollywood. Look like crap on the outside, but once you get inside, there's a fifty-two-inch TV and a sound system that'd blow out the walls if you cranked it. And maybe a white Bentley in the garage. I know you people are real smart businessmen."

"You know that, Farley, then you know I ain't paying more than five dollars for cards," Gregori said, taking out his wallet.

When Farley accepted the deal and was driving back to the boulevard to score some crystal, he said to Olive, "That cheap communist cocksucker. You see what was up on that lift?"

"A new car?" Olive said.

"A new Escalade. That Armo gets one of his greasers to steal one. Then they strip it right down to the frame and dump the hot frame

with its hot numbers. They search every junkyard in the county till they find a wrecked Escalade. They buy the frame, bring it here, and
reassemble all the stolen parts right onto their
cold frame, then register it at DMV. It's a real
Armo trick. They're like fucking Gypsy tribes.
Cosmo's one of them. We shoulda nuked all the
Soviet puppet states when we had the chance."

"I'm scared of Cosmo, Farley," Olive said, but
he ignored her, still pissed off at the price he got
for the key cards.

"Hear what he called his dog? Odar. That's
what Armenians call us non-Armos. Fucking
goat eater. If I wasn't a man of property, I'd get
outta Hollywood and away from all these immigrant assholes."

"Farley," Olive said. "When your mom left you
the house, it was paid for, right?"

"Of course it was paid for. Shit, when my parents bought the house, it only cost about thirty-
nine grand."

"You could sell it for a lot now, Farley," Olive
said. "We could go somewhere else and not do
this thing with Cosmo and Ilya."

"Pull yourself together," he said. "This is the
biggest score of my life. I ain't walking away. So
just deal with it."

"We could stop using crystal," Olive said. "You could go into rehab, and I really think I could kick if you was in rehab."

"Oh, I see," he said. "I've led you into a life of drugs and crime, is that it? You were a virgin cheerleader before you met me?"

"That ain't what I mean, Farley," she said. "I just think I could kick if you did."

"Be sure to tell that to the casting director when he asks you to tell him all about yourself. You were a good girl seduced into the life by a wicked, wicked man. Who, by the way, provides you with a house and car and food and clothes and every fucking thing that makes life worthwhile!"

Farley parked four blocks from Hollywood Boulevard to keep from getting a ticket, and they walked to one of the boulevard's tattoo parlors, one owned by a member of an outlaw bikers gang. A nervous young man was in a chair being worked on by a bearded tattoo artist with a dirty blond ponytail wearing a red tank top, jeans, and sandals. He was drawing what looked like a unicorn on the guy's left shoulder.

The artist nodded to Farley, dabbed some blood from his customer's arm, and said to him,

"Be right back." Then he walked to a back room, followed by Farley.

When Farley and the tattoo artist were in the back, Farley said, "A pair of teens."

The artist left him, entered a second room and returned in a few minutes with the teeners of crystal in plastic bindles.

Farley gave the guy six twenty-dollar bills and returned to the front, where Olive stood admiring the design on the young man's shoulder, but the guy just looked sick and full of regret.

Olive smiled and said to him, "That's going to be a beautiful tattoo. Is it a horse or a zebra?"

"Olive, let's go," Farley said.

Walking to the car, Farley said, "Fucking bikers're lousy artists. People get bubbles under the skin. All scarred up. Hackers is what they are."

They were halfway home and stopped at a traffic signal when Olive blurted, "Know what, Farley? Do you think it might be a little bit big for us? I mean, trying to make Cosmo give us ten thousand dollars? Don't it scare you a little bit?"

"Scare me?" he said. "I'll tell you what I been thinking. I been thinking about pulling the same gag on that cheap fucking Gregori, that's what I been thinking. Fuck him. I ain't doing business with the cheap bastard no more, so I wonder how he'd like it if I phoned him up and said I was gonna call the cops and tell them what I know about his salvage business. I wonder how he'd like reaching in that fat wallet and pulling out some real green to shut me up."

Olive's hands were sweating more now. She didn't like the way things were changing so fast. The way Farley was changing. She was very scared of Cosmo and even scared of Ilya. She said, "I think it will be just awful to meet with Cosmo and collect the money from him. I'm very worried about you, Farley."

Farley looked surprised and said, "I'm not stupid, Olive. The fucker robbed the jewelry store with a gun. You think I'm gonna meet him in some lonely place or something? No way. It's gonna happen in a nice safe place with people around."

"That's good," Olive said.

"And you're gonna do it, of course. Not me."

"Me?"

"It's way safe for you," Farley said. "It's me he hates. You'll be just fine."

At seven that evening, Gregori phoned his business acquaintance Cosmo Betrossian and had a conversation with him in their language. Gregori told Cosmo that he had had a visitor and had bought some hotel key cards from Farley, the dope fiend that Cosmo had introduced to him last year when identification was needed for employees working in Gregori's salvage yard.

"Farley? I have not seen the little freak in a very long time," Cosmo lied.

"Well, my friend," Gregori said, "I just need to know if the thief can still be trusted."

"In what way?"

"People like him, they sometimes become police informants. The police trade little fishes for big whales. They might consider me to be a whale."

Cosmo said, "You can trust him in that way. He is such a worthless addict that the police would not even want to deal with him. But you cannot lend him money. I was stupid enough to do that."

"Thank you," Gregori said. "Perhaps I could buy you and your lovely Ilya a dinner at the Gulag some evening?"

"I would like that, thank you," Cosmo said. "But I have an idea. Perhaps you can do something for me?"

"Of course."

"I would be very grateful next month on a night I shall designate if you would call Farley and tell him you need more key cards because several new employees have arrived from Mexico with family members. Offer him more than you paid today. Then tell him to deliver the cards to your salvage yard. After dark."

"My business is closed before dark. Even on Saturday."

"I know," Cosmo said, "but I would like you to give me a duplicate gate key. I will be at the salvage yard when Farley arrives."

"Wait a moment," Gregori said. "What does this mean?"

"It is only about the money he owes me," Cosmo said reassuringly. "I want to scare the little dope fiend. Maybe make him give me what money he has in his pocket. I have a right."

"Cosmo, I do not do violence, you know that."

"Of course," Cosmo said. "The most I will do is to keep his car until he pays me. I will take his keys and drive his car to my place and make him walk home. That is all."

"That is not a theft? Could he call the police?"

Cosmo laughed and said, "It is a business dispute. And Farley is the last man in Hollywood to ever call the police. He has never worked an honest day in his life."

"I am not sure about this," Gregori said.

"Listen, cousin," Cosmo said. "Drop the key at my apartment after work this evening. I cannot be there because of other business, but Ilya will be there. She will make you her special tea. In a glass, Russian-style. What do you say?"

Gregori was silent for a moment, but then he thought of Ilya. That great blond Russian Ilya with her nice plump, long legs and huge tits.

He was silent too long, so Cosmo said, "Also, I will give you one hundred dollars for your trouble. Gladly."

"All right, Cosmo," Gregori said. "But there must not be violence on my property."

After Cosmo hung up, he said to Ilya in English, "You shall not believe our good fortune. In a few hours Gregori of the junkyard shall come here with a key. I promise to him one hundred for the key. Behave nice. Give to him your glass of tea."

Two hours later when Gregori arrived, he discovered that, true to his word, Cosmo was not there. Ilya invited him in and after he put the salvage yard gate key on the table, he was asked to sit while she put on the tea kettle.

Ilya wore a red cotton dress that hiked up every time she bent over even slightly, and he could see those white plump thighs. And her breasts were spilling from her bra, which Gregori could see was black and lacy.

After putting two glasses and saucers and cookies on the table, Ilya said in English, "Cosmo is gone all evening. Business."

"Do you get the lonesomeness?" Gregori asked.

"I do," she said. "Gregori, Cosmo promises to pay you one hundred?"

"Yes," Gregori said, unable to take his eyes from those white ballooning breasts.

"I have it for you, but . . ."

"Yes, Ilya?"

"But I must buy shoes and Cosmo is not a generous man, and perhaps I may tell him that I paid money, but . . ."

"Yes, Ilya?"

"But perhaps we do like Americans say . . ."

"Yes, Ilya?"

"And fuck the brains from outside of our heads?"

The tea was postponed, and within two minutes Gregori was wearing only socks, but he suddenly began to fret about Cosmo and said, "Ilya, you must promise. Cosmo must never learn we do this."

Unhooking her bra and removing her black thong, Ilya said, "Gregori, you have nothing to fear about. Cosmo says that in America someone fuck someone in every business deal. One way or other."

TWELVE

HOLLYWOOD NATE ALWAYS said that there were two kinds of cops in Hollywood Division: Starbucks and 7-Eleven types. Nate was definitely a Starbucks guy, and lucky for him his protégé Wesley Drubb came from a family that had never set foot in a 7-Eleven store. Nate couldn't work very long without heading for either the Starbucks at Sunset and La Brea or the one at Sunset and Gower. On the other hand, there were Hollywood Division coppers (7-Eleven types) who chose to take code 7 at IHOP. Nate said that eating at IHOP would produce enough bad cholesterol to clog the Red Line subway. He seldom even patronized the ever-popular Hamburger Hamlet, preferring instead one of the eateries in Thai Town around Hollywood Boulevard and Kingsley. Or one of the more health-

314

conscious joints on west Sunset that served great lattés.

The hawkish handsome face of Nate Weiss had now recovered from his battle with the war veteran who insisted on a ride to Santa Monica and La Brea. The last Nate heard about the guy was that he'd plea-bargained down to simple battery and would no doubt soon be returning to drugs and flashbacks and a hankering for another ride to Santa Monica and La Brea.

Nate was back to pumping iron at the gym and jogging three times a week and had an appointment to meet a real agent who might advance his career immeasurably. Being one of the few officers at Hollywood Station who loved to work all the red carpet events at Grauman's or the Kodak Theatre, where sometimes hundreds of officers were needed, he'd met the agent there.

"You know, Wesley," Nate said, "about that little indie film I've been trying to put together? Had a chance to talk to your old man about it yet?"

"Not yet, Nate," Wesley said. "Dad's in Tokyo. But I wouldn't get my hopes up. He's a very conservative man when it comes to business."

"So am I, Wesley, so am I," Nate said. "But this is

as close to a no-brainer as it gets in the film business. Did I tell you I'm getting my SAG card?"

"I'm not sure if you told me or not," Wesley said, thinking, Does he ever stop? The guy's thirty-five years old. He'll be a star about the time USC trades its football program for lacrosse.

"Every time I do a union job as a nonunion extra, I get a voucher. One more job and I'll have enough vouchers and pay stubs. Then I'm eligible to join the Screen Actors Guild."

"Awesome, Nate," Wesley said.

When Hollywood Nate lay in bed after getting off duty, he had latté dreams and mocha fantasies of life in a high canvas chair, wearing a makeup bib, never dating below-the-line persons, using the word "energy" at least once in every three sentences, and living in a house so big you'd need a Sherpa to find the guest rooms. Such was the dream of Hollywood Nate Weiss.

As for young Wesley Drubb, his dream was muddled. Lately he'd been spending a lot of time trying to convince himself that he had not made a horrible mistake dropping out of USC, not graduating and going on for an MBA. He often questioned the wisdom of moving away from the Pacific Palisades family home into a so-so apartment in West Hollywood that he couldn't have easily afforded without a roommate. And not without the personal checks he was secretly receiving from his mother's account, checks that he had nobly refused to cash for several months until he'd finally succumbed. What was he proving? And to whom?

After the hand grenade incident and the fight in which Nate got hurt worse than he pretended, Wesley had confided in his brother, Timothy, hoping his older sibling would give him some advice.

Timothy, who had been working for Lawford and Drubb only three years, knocking down more than $175,000 last year (their father's idea of starting at the bottom), said to him, "What do you get out of it, Wesley? And please don't give me any undergraduate existential bullshit."

Wesley had said, "I just . . . I don't know. I like what I do most of the time."

"You are such an asshole," his brother said, ending the discussion. "Just try to only get crippled and not killed. It would be the end of Mom if she lost her baby boy."

Wesley Drubb didn't think that he was terribly afraid of getting crippled or killed. He was young enough to think that those things happened to other guys, or other girls, like Mag

Takara. No, the thing that he couldn't explain to his brother or his dad or mom, or any of his fraternity brothers who were now going to grad school, was that the Oracle was right. This work was the most fun he would ever have on any job.

Oh, there were boring nights when not much happened, but not too boring. On the downside, there was the unbelievable oversight that LAPD was presently going through, which created loads of paperwork and media criticism and a level of political correctness that a civilian would never understand or tolerate. But at the end of the day, young Wesley Drubb was having fun. And that's why he was still a cop. And that's why he just might remain one for the foreseeable future. But his thought process went off the rails at that point. At his age, he couldn't begin to fathom what the words "foreseeable future" truly meant.

After Hollywood Nate had his Starbucks latté and was in a good mood, they got a call to Hollywood and Cahuenga, where a pair of Hollywood's homeless were having a twilight punchout. Neither geezer was capable of inflicting much damage on the other unless weapons were pulled, but the fight was taking place on Holly-

wood Boulevard, and that would not be toler-
ated by the local merchants. Project Restore
Hollywood was in full bloom, with everyone
dreaming of more and more tourists and of
someday making seedy old Hollywood glam up
like Westwood or Beverly Hills or Santa Barbara
minus the nearby ocean.

The combatants had taken their fight to the
alley behind an adult bookstore and had exhausted themselves by throwing half a dozen
flailing punches at each other. They were now at
the stage of standing ten feet apart and exchang-
ing curses and shaking fists. Wesley parked the
shop on Cahuenga north of Hollywood Boulevard, and they approached the two ragbag old
street fighters.

Nate said, "The skinny one is Trombone Teddy.
Used to be a hot-licks jazzman a truckload of
whiskey ago. The *real* skinny one I've seen
around for years, but I don't think I've ever
talked to him."

The *real* skinny one, a stick of a man of inde-
terminate age but probably younger than Trombone Teddy, wore a filthy black fedora and a
filthier green necktie over an even filthier gray
shirt and colorless pants. He wore what used to
be leather shoes but were now mostly wraps of

duct tape, and he spent most evenings shuffling along the boulevard raving at whoever didn't cross his palm with a buck or two.

It was hardly worth worrying about who would be contact and who would be cover with these two derelicts, and Hollywood Nate just wanted to get it over with, so he waded in and said, "Jesus, Teddy, what the hell're you doing fighting on Hollywood Boulevard?"

"It's him, Officer," Teddy said, still panting from exertion. "He started it."

"Fuck you!" his antagonist said with the addled look these guys get from sucking on those short dogs of cheap port.

"Stay real," Nate said, looking at the guy and at his shopping cart crammed with odds and ends, bits and bobs. There was no way he wanted to bust this guy and deal with booking all that junk.

Wesley said to the skinniest geezer, "What's your name?"

"What's it to ya?"

"Don't make us arrest you," Nate said. "Just answer the officer."

"Filmore U. Bracken."

Trying a positive approach, Wesley smiled and said, "What's the *U* for?"

"I'll spell it for you," Filmore replied. "U-p-y-u-r-s."

"Upyurs?" Wesley said. "That's an unusual name."

"Up yours," Nate explained. Then he said, "That's it, Filmore, you're going to the slam."

When Nate took latex gloves from his pocket, Filmore said, "Upton."

Before putting the gloves on, Nate said, "Okay, last chance. Will you just agree to move along and leave Teddy here in peace and let bygones be bygones?"

"Sure," Filmore U. Bracken said, shuffling up to Teddy and putting out his hand.

Teddy hesitated, then looked at Nate and extended his own hand. And Filmore U. Bracken took it in his right hand and suckered Teddy with a left hook that, pathetic as it was, knocked Trombone Teddy on the seat of his pants.

"Hah!" said Filmore, admiring his own clenched fist.

Then the latex gloves went on both cops, and Filmore's bony wrists were handcuffed, but when he was about to be walked to their car, he said, "How about my goods?"

"That's worthless trash," Hollywood Nate said.

"My anvil's in there!" Filmore cried.

Wesley Drubb walked over to the junk, gingerly poked around, and underneath the aluminum cans and socks and clean undershorts probably stolen from a Laundromat found an anvil.

"Looks pretty heavy," Wesley said.

"That anvil's my life!" their prisoner cried.

Nate said, "You don't need an anvil in Hollywood. How many horses you see around here?"

"That's my property!" their prisoner yelled, and now an asthmatic fat man waddled out the back door of an adult bookstore and said, "Officer, this guy's been raising hell on the boulevard all day. Hassling my customers and spitting on them when they refuse to give him money."

"Fuck you too, you fat degenerate!" the prisoner said.

Nate said to the proprietor, "I gotta ask you a favor. Can he keep his shopping cart inside your storage area here until he gets outta jail?"

"How long will he be in?"

"Depends on whether we just book him for plain drunk or add on the battery we just witnessed."

"I don't wanna make a complaint," Trombone Teddy said.

"Shut up, Teddy," Hollywood Nate said.

"Yes, sir," said Teddy.

"I ain't as drunk as he is!" the prisoner said, pointing at Teddy.

He was right and everyone knew it. Teddy was reeling, and not from the other geezer's punch.

"Okay, tell you what," Nate said, deciding to dispense boulevard justice. "Filmore here is going to detox for a couple hours and then he can come back and pick up his property. How's that?"

Everyone seemed okay with the plan, and the store owner pushed the shopping cart to the storage area at the rear of his business.

While Nate was escorting their prisoner to the car, Trombone Teddy walked over to Wesley Drubb and said, "Thanks, Officer. He's a bad actor, that bum. A real mean drunk."

"Okay, anytime," Wesley said.

But Teddy had a card in his hand and extended it to Wesley, saying, "This is something you might be able to use."

It was a business card to a local Chinese restaurant, the House of Chang. "Thanks, I'll try it sometime," Wesley said.

"Turn it over," Teddy said. "There's a license number."

Wesley flipped the card and saw what looked

like a California license plate number and said, "So?"

Teddy said, "It's a blue Pinto. Two tweakers were in it, a man and a woman. She called him Freddy, I think. Or maybe Morley. I can't quite remember. I seen them fishing in a mailbox over on Gower south of the boulevard. They stole mail. That's a federal offense, ain't it?"

Wesley said, "Just a minute, Teddy."

When he got back to his partner, who had put Filmore U. Bracken in the backseat of the car, Wesley showed him the card and said, "Teddy gave me this license number. Belongs to tweakers stealing from mailboxes. The guy's name is Freddy or Morley."

"All tweakers steal from mailboxes," Hollywood Nate said, "or anything else they can steal."

It seemed to Wesley that he shouldn't just ignore the tip and throw the license number away. But he didn't want to act like he was still a boot, so he went back to Teddy, handed him the card, and said, "Why don't you take it to a post office. They have people who investigate this sort of thing."

"I think I'll hang on to it," Teddy said, clearly disappointed.

Driving to the station, Nate got to thinking

about the secretary who worked for the extras casting office he'd visited last Tuesday. She had given him big eyes as well as her phone number. He thought that he and Wesley could pick up some takeout, and he could sit in the station alone somewhere and chat her up on his cell.

"Partner, you up for burgers tonight?" he asked Wesley.

"Sure," Wesley said. "You're the health nut who won't eat burgers."

And then, thinking of the little secretary and what they might do together on his next night off, and how she might even help him with her boss the casting agent, Nate felt a real glow come over him. What he called "Hollywood happy."

He said, "How about you, Filmore, you up for a burger?"

"Hot damn!" the derelict said. "You bet!"

They stopped at a drive-through, picked up four burgers, two for Wesley, and fries all around, and headed for the station.

When they got there, Nate said to their prisoner, "Here's the deal. I'm giving you not only a burger and fries, but a get-out-of-jail-free pass. You're gonna sit in the little holding tank for thirty minutes and eat your burger, and I'll even buy you a Coke. Then, after my partner writes an FI card on you for future reference, I'm gonna let you out and you're gonna walk back up to the boulevard and get your shopping cart and go home to your nest, wherever that is."

"You mean I ain't going to jail or detox?"

"That's right. I got an important phone call to make, so I can't waste time dicking around with you. Deal?"

"Hot damn!" Filmore said.

When their passenger got out of the car in the station parking lot, Wesley looked at the car seat and said to Filmore, "What's that all over the seat? Beach sand?"

"No, that's psoriasis," said Filmore U. Bracken.

"Oh, gross!" Wesley cried.

B.M. Driscoll and Benny Brewster caught the call to the apartment building on Stanley north of Fountain. They were half a block from the L.A. Sheriff's Department jurisdiction of West Hollywood, and later Benny Brewster thought about that and wished it could've occurred just half a block south.

The apartment manager answered their ring and asked them inside. It was by no means a down-market property. In fact, B.M. Driscoll was thinking he wouldn't mind living there if he could afford the rent. The woman wore a blazer and skirt and looked as though she had just come home from work. Her silver-streaked hair was cut like a man's, and she was what is called handsome in women her age.

She said, "I'm Cora Sheldon, and I called about the new tenant in number fourteen. Her name is Eileen Leffer. She moved in last month from Oxnard and has two young children." She paused and read from the rental agreement, "A six-year-old son, Terry, and a seven-year-old daughter, Sylvia. She said she's a model and seemed very respectable and promised to get us references but hasn't done it yet. I think there might be a problem."

"What kinda problem?" Benny asked.

"I work during the day, but we never see or hear a peep from the kids. The owner of the building used to rent our furnished units to adults only, so this is new to me. I've never been married, but I think normal kids should be heard from sometimes, and these two are not. I don't think they're enrolled in any school. Even on weekends when I'm home, I never hear or see the kids."

"Have you investigated?" B.M. Driscoll asked.

"You know, knocked on the door with maybe an offer of a friendly cup of coffee?"

"Twice. Neither time was there a response. I'm worried. I have a key, but I'm afraid to just open the door and look."

"We got no probable cause to enter," Benny said. "When was the last time you knocked on the door?"

"Last night at eight o'clock."

"Gimme the key," B.M. Driscoll said. "And you come with us. If there's nobody home, we all just tiptoe away and nobody's the wiser. We wouldn't do this except for the presence of little kids."

When they got to number fourteen, Benny knocked. No answer. He tapped sharply with the butt of his flashlight. Still no answer.

Benny called out, "Police officers. Anybody home?" and knocked again.

Cora Sheldon was doing a lot of lip biting then, and B.M. Driscoll put the pass key in the lock and opened the door, turning on the living room light. The room was messy, with magazines strewn around and a couple of vodka bottles lying on the floor. The kitchen smelled of garbage, and when they looked in, they saw the sink stacked with dirty dishes. The gas range was a mess with something white that had boiled over.

B.M. Driscoll switched on a hallway light and looked into the bathroom, which was more of a mess than the kitchen. Benny checked the master bedroom, saw an unmade bed and a bra and panties on the floor, and returned with a shrug.

The other bedroom door was closed. Cora Sheldon said, "The second bedroom has twin beds. That would be the children's room."

B.M. Driscoll walked to the door and opened it, turning on the light. It was worse by far than the master bedroom. There were dishes with peanut butter and crackers on the floor and on the dresser top. In front of the TV were empty soda cans, and boxes of breakfast cereal were lying on the floor.

"Well, she's not much of a housekeeper," he said, "but other than that?"

"Partner," Benny said, pointing at the bed, then walking to it and shining his light at wine-dark stains. "Looks like blood."

"Oh my god!" Cora Sheldon said as B.M. Driscoll looked under the bed and Benny went to the closet, whose door was partially open.

And there they were. Both children were sitting under hanging garments belonging to their mother. The six-year-old boy began sobbing, and his seven-year-old sister put her arm around him. Both children were blue-eyed, and the boy was a blond and his sister a brunette. Neither had had a decent wash for a few days, and both were terrified. The boy wore shorts and a food-stained T-shirt and no shoes. The girl wore a cotton dress trimmed with lace, also food-stained. On her feet she wore white socks and pink sneakers.

"We won't hurt you, come on out," Benny said, and Cora Sheldon repeated, "Oh my god!"

"Where's your mommy?" B.M. Driscoll asked.

"She went with Steve," the girl said.

"Does Steve live here?" Benny asked, and when Cora Sheldon said, "I didn't rent to anyone named —" he shushed her by putting up his hand.

The little girl said, "Sometimes."

B.M. Driscoll said, "Have they been gone for a long time?"

The little girl said, "I think so."

"For two days? Three days? Longer?"

"I don't know," she said.

"Okay, come on out and let's get a look at you," he said.

Benny was inspecting the stain on the bed,

and he said to the girl, "Has somebody hurt you?"

She nodded then and started crying, walking painfully from the closet.

"Who?" Benny asked. "Who hurt you?"

"Steve," she said.

"How?" Benny asked. "How did he hurt you?"

"Here," she said, and when she lifted her cotton dress slightly, they saw dried blood crusted on both legs from her thighs down, and what looked like dark bloodstains on her lace-trimmed white cotton socks.

"Out, please!" Benny said to Cora Sheldon, taking both children by the hands and walking them into the living room, first closing the bedroom door to protect it as a crime scene.

B.M. Driscoll grabbed his rover to inform detectives that they had some work to do and that they needed transportation to the hospital for the children.

"Wait in your apartment, Ms. Sheldon," Benny said.

Looking at the children, she said, "Oh," and then started to weep and walked out the door.

When she had gone, the girl turned to her younger brother and said, "Don't cry, Terry. Mommy's coming home soon."

★ ★ ★

It was nearly midnight when Flotsam and Jetsam were in the station to get a sergeant's signature on a robbery report. A drag queen claimed to have been walking down the boulevard on a legitimate errand when a car carrying two guys stopped and one of them jumped out and stole the drag queen's purse, which contained fifty dollars as well as a "gorgeous" new wig that cost three hundred and fifty. Then he'd punched the drag queen before driving away.

Jetsam was in the process of calling to see what kind of record the dragon had, like maybe multiple prostitution arrests, when the desk officer asked Flotsam to watch the desk while he ran upstairs and had a nice hot b.m.

Flotsam said okay and was there when a very angry and outraged Filmore U. Bracken came shuffling into the lobby.

Flotsam took a look at the old derelict and said, "Dude, you are too hammered to be entering a police station of your own volition."

"I wanna make a complaint," the codger said.

"What kinda complaint?"

"Against a policeman."

"What'd he do?"

"I gotta admit he bought me a hamburger."

"Yeah, well, I can see why you're mad," Flot-sam said. "Shoulda been filet mignon, right?"

"He brought me here for the hamburger and left my property with a big fat degenerate at a dirty bookstore on Hollywood Boulevard."

"Which dirty bookstore?"

"I can point it out to you. Anyways, the degen-erate didn't watch my property like he said he would and now it's gone. Everything in my shopping cart."

"And what, pray tell, was in your cart?"

"My anvil."

"An anvil?"

"Yeah, it's my life."

"Damn," Flotsam said. "You're a blacksmith? The Mounted Platoon might have a job for you."

"I wanna see the boss and make a complaint."

"What's your name?"

"Filmore Upton Bracken."

"Wait here a minute, Mr. Bracken," Flotsam said. "I'm going to talk this over with the ser-geant."

While Jetsam waited for the Oracle to ap-prove and sign the crime report, Flotsam went to the phone books and quickly looked up the law offices of Harold G. Lowenstein, a notorious and hated lawyer in LAPD circles who had made a living suing cops and the city that hired them. Somebody was always saying what they would do to Harold G. Lowenstein if they ever popped him for drunk driving.

Flotsam then dialed the number to the lobby phone. After the eighth ring, as he started to think his idea wasn't going to work, the phone was picked up.

Filmore Upton Bracken said, "Hello?"

"Mr. Bracken?" Flotsam said, doing his best impression of Anthony Hopkins playing a butler. "Am I speaking to Mr. Filmore Upton Bracken?"

"Yeah, who's this?"

"This is the emergency hotline for the law offices of Harold G. Lowenstein, Esquire, Mr. Bracken. A Los Angeles police officer just phoned us from Hollywood Station saying that you may need our services."

"Yeah? You're a lawyer?"

"I'm just a paralegal, Mr. Bracken," Flotsam said. "But Mr. Lowenstein is very interested in any case involving malfeasance on the part of LAPD officers. Could you please come to our offices tomorrow at eleven A.M. and discuss the matter?"

"You bet I can. Lemme get a pencil from the desk here."

He was gone for a moment, and Flotsam could hear him yelling, "Hey, I need a goddamn pencil!"

When Filmore returned, he said, "Shoot, brother."

Flotsam gave him the address of Harold G. Lowenstein's Sunset Strip law office, including the suite number, and then said, "Mr. Bracken, the officer who just phoned on your behalf said that you are probably without means at present, so do not be intimidated if our somewhat sheltered employees try to discourage you. Mr. Lowenstein will want to see you personally, so don't take no for an answer from some snippy receptionist."

"I'll kick ass if anybody tries to stop me," Filmore said.

"That's the spirit, Mr. Bracken," Flotsam said, his accent shifting closer to the burr of Sean Connery and away from Anthony Hopkins.

"I'll be there at eleven."

Filmore was waiting in the lobby when Flotsam returned, saying, "Mr. Bracken? The sergeant will see you now."

Filmore drew himself up on his tiptoes to lock eyeballs with the tall cop and said, "Fuck the sergeant. He can talk to my lawyer. I'm suing all you bastards. When I'm through, I'll own this goddamn place, and maybe if you're lucky I'll buy you a hamburger sometime. Asshole."

And with that, Filmore Upton Bracken shuffled out the door with a grin as wide as Hollywood Boulevard.

When B.M. Driscoll and Benny Brewster went end-of-watch in the early-morning hours, Flotsam and Jetsam were in the locker room, sharing Filmore Upton Bracken adventures with Hollywood Nate and Wesley Drubb.

After the chuckles subsided, Nate said to Flotsam and Jetsam, "By the way, you guys're invited to a birthday party. My newest little friend is throwing it at her place in Westwood. Might be one or two chicks from the entertainment industry for you to meet."

"Any of the tribe coming?" Flotsam asked. "No offense, but I got a two-Jew limit. Three or more Hollywood hebes gather and they start sticking political lapel pins on every animate and inanimate object in sight, which might include my dead ass."

"Why, you filthy anti-Semitic surfer swine," Nate said.

"You inviting Budgie?" Flotsam asked.

"Probably," Nate said.

"Okay, we'll come. My partner admires her from afar."

They stopped the banter when B.M. Driscoll and Benny Brewster came in looking very grim. Both began quickly and quietly undressing.

"What's wrong with you guys?" Jetsam asked. "They taking Wrestlemania off the air?"

"You don't wanna know," B.M. Driscoll said, almost tearing the buttons from his uniform shirt as though he just wanted *out* of it. "Bad shit. Little kids."

"So lighten up," Flotsam said. "Don't you guys listen to the Oracle? This Job can be fun. Get happy."

Suddenly, Jetsam did his Bono impersonation, singing, "Two shots of happy, one shot of saaaaaad."

Benny Brewster peeled off his body armor and furiously crammed the vest into the locker, saying, "No shots of happy tonight, man. Just one shot of sad. *Real* sad."

★ THIRTEEN

EXCUSE ME, PLEASE, Andrea," Viktor Chernenko said late in the morning. There were only
six detectives in the squad room, the rest being
out in the field or in court or, in the case of Hollywood detectives, nonexistent due to the man-
power shortage and budget constraints.

"Yes, Viktor?" Andi said, smiling over her coffee cup, fingers still on the computer keyboard.

"I think you are looking very lovely today, Andrea," Viktor said with his usual diffident smile. "I
believe I recognize your most beautiful yellow
sweater from the Bananas Republic, where my
wife, Maria, shops."

"Yeah, I bought it there."

Then he walked back to his cubicle. This was
the way with Viktor. He wanted something, but
it might take him half a day to get around to asking. On the other hand, nobody ever paid her

the compliments that Viktor did when he needed a woman detective for something or other.

Andi was glad to see that Brant Hinkle was still teamed with Viktor, and because of that she'd probably agree to do whatever Viktor got around to requesting. Ever since Brant had arrived, her belief in his possibilities kept increasing. She'd checked him out by now and found that he'd just turned fifty-three, had only been married and divorced once — a rarity among cops these days — had two adult married daughters, and based on his serial number, had about five more years on the Job than she had. In other words, he was a likely prospect. And she knew he was interested by the way he looked at her, but as yet he hadn't made a move.

Another twenty minutes passed and she was about to go out in the field and call on a couple of witnesses to a so-called attempted murder where a pimp/boyfriend slapped around a whore and fired two shots in her direction when she ran away. Without a doubt, the whore would have changed her mind by now or had it changed for her and all would be forgiven. But Andi needed to go through the motions just in case tomorrow night he murdered her.

"Andrea," Viktor said when he approached her desk the second time.

"Yes, Viktor."

"Will you be so kind to help Brant and me? We have a mission for a woman, and as you see, today you are the only woman here."

"How long will it take?"

"A few hours, and I would be honored to buy your lunch."

Andi glanced over at Brant Hinkle, who was talking on the phone, wearing little half-glasses as he wrote on a legal pad, and she said, "Okay, Viktor. My damaged hooker can wait."

Viktor drove east to Glendale with Andi beside him and Brant in the backseat. Viktor was very solicitous, apologizing because the air conditioner didn't work in their car.

"So okay," Andi said, "all I have to do is tail this Russian guy from his job at the auto parts store to wherever he eats lunch?"

Viktor said, "We have been told that he always walks to a fast-food place, but there are several that are close by."

Brant said, "Viktor's informant says this guy Lidorov is very tail conscious, but he probably won't be looking for a woman to be on him."

"And all we do is get a DNA sample?"

"That is all," Viktor said. "My informant is sometimes reliable, sometimes not."

"Your evidence for a DNA comparison isn't all that reliable either," she said, turning in her seat to look at Brant, who raised his eyebrows as if to say, Viktor is obsessive.

Viktor said, "Andrea, when I did my follow-up investigation and found the cigarette butt in that jewelry store far behind the cabinet, I know in my heart it was left there by the suspect."

"Even though the victim was too terrified to remember for sure if the guy left the butt or took it with him," Brant said doubtfully.

"It is an intestines feeling," Viktor said. "And this Russian in Glendale has two convictions for armed robbery of jewelry stores."

"I've heard you say you're not sure the man from the jewelry store two-eleven is even a Russian," Andi said.

Viktor said, "The accent that the store owner heard from the man was different from the woman's. But everybody is Russian Mafia to people in Hollywood. Actually, Glendale has a very big Armenian population. Many go to the Gulag, where my tip has come from. Criminals from all over former USSR go to the Gulag to drink and dine, including criminals from former

Soviet Armenia. But for now, we have this Russian who was a jewel robber in his past life."

"This isn't much to go on," Andi said.

"We have nothing else," Viktor said. "Except I believe that a theft of mail from a certain mailbox on Gower is where the information about the diamonds was learned about. If only I could get a clue to the mail thief."

"We can't stake out every mailbox in the area, Viktor," Brant said.

"No, Brant, we cannot," Viktor said. "So that is why I would like to try this thing today. I know it is a far shot."

They parked on the next block, and Viktor diligently watched the front door of the auto parts store through binoculars while Andi turned in her seat to chat with Brant about how he liked Hollywood so far and where was he on the lieutenant's list.

Brant was surprised to learn that Andi had a son in the army serving in Afghanistan, and said, "Don't think I say this to all the ladies, but really, you don't look old enough."

"I'm plenty old enough," she said, hoping she hadn't blushed. Next thing, she'd be batting her lashes if she didn't get hold of herself.

"I think Afghanistan's fairly quiet these days," he said.

"Last year he was in Iraq," she said. "I don't like to think about how I felt during those months."

Brant was quiet then, feeling very lucky to have daughters living safe lives. He couldn't imagine how it must feel to have your only child over there in hell. Especially for coppers, whose assertive, in-your-face personality is of absolutely no use in such a situation. To just feel helpless and frightened all the time? He believed it must be extra hard for the parents who are police officers.

Viktor lowered the binoculars, picked up a mug shot from his lap, and said, "It is Lidorov. He is wearing a black shirt and jeans. He has what looks like hair made of patent leather and has a gray mustache and is of medium size. He is walking toward the big mall half a block from the auto parts store."

Andi was dropped on the east side of the mall and walked inside a minute after Lidorov entered. At first she thought she'd lost him, but heading toward the food court she spotted him.

Lidorov paused before the Greek deli, where two Latino men were making gyros, then moved on to an Italian takeout, where another young Latino was expertly tossing a pizza. Then he settled on Chinese fast food and ordered something in a carton along with a soft drink in a takeout cup. From another Latino.

Andi watched from the Italian side and wondered if chopsticks would be better or worse than forks for the collecting of DNA evidence. But Lidorov shook his head when offered chopsticks and took a plastic fork instead. He sat down at one of three small tables in front of the counter and ate from the carton and sipped his drink and ogled any young women who happened to pass by.

When he got up, she was ready to bus his table for him and scoop up the fork and the drinking straw. But she never got the chance. He took the unfinished carton of food with him along with the cup and strolled back toward the entrance, drinking from the straw. She assumed the fork was in the carton, so now what?

Lidorov went out the door into the sunlight, stretched a little, and strolled right past two perfectly good trash receptacles where he could have dropped the carton and the cup.

Litter, you bastard! Andi thought, following as far as she dared. But since there were few pedestrians on the sidewalk, she crossed over to the other side of the street and waited to be picked up.

When Viktor drove alongside, she got in and said, "Sorry, Viktor. He's taking his lunch back to the store."

"Is okay, Andrea," Viktor said.

"Whoops!" Brant said, looking through the binoculars. "He's not a litterbug."

Two minutes later they were parked just east of the little strip mall that housed the auto parts store. Next to the wall in the parking lot was a very tall trash dumpster sitting on a thick concrete slab. All three detectives were standing in front of it with the lid raised.

Viktor and Brant, who were both more than six feet tall, pulled themselves up, their feet off the asphalt, and peered down inside the dumpster.

After getting back down, Viktor said to Andi, "Do you want the news that is good or the news that is not so good?"

"Good," Andi said.

Brant said, "Looks like they dumped the trash this morning. There's hardly anything in there. We can see the Chinese takeout carton and the drinking cup and straw."

"Bad news?"

"We can't reach it without somebody climbing inside," Brant said.

"Well, I guess one of you fashion plates is going to get your suit dirty," Andi said.

"Andrea," said Viktor, "I am so outside of good shape that I truly do not think I can do it. I am thinking that if I spread my coat over the top here so that you do not mess up the beautiful sweater from Bananas, you could lie down over the top here and reach down and get the fork and the straw?"

"And how do I keep from falling in right on my head?"

"We would each hold you by a leg," Brant said.

"Oh, you think it's a good idea too?"

"I swear to you, Andi," Brant said. "I don't think I could do it without a ladder. And if we mess around here much longer, somebody's gonna see us and the element of surprise will be lost. Even if we do get a match, he'll be long gone, maybe clear back to Russia."

"My heroes," Andi said, slipping off her pumps. "Good thing I'm wearing long pants."

With each man holding a bare foot, Andi was boosted up to the edge of the dumpster, lying across Viktor's suit coat, and very reluctantly she allowed herself to be lowered upside down until she got hold of the carton and the cup.

"Get me outta here. It stinks," she said.

When they were back in the car, the fork and drinking straw in a large evidence envelope, Viktor said, "My coat must go to the cleaners. How is your sweater, Andrea?"

"Other than busting a bra strap and bruising my belly and thighs, I'm okay. This lunch better be good, Viktor."

It was. Viktor took them to a whimsically designed Russian restaurant on Melrose, where they had borscht and black bread and blinis and hot tea in a glass. And even got to hear dreamy Russian violins coming from the sound system, with Viktor acting every inch the host.

"Sometimes they make Ukrainian dishes here," he told them, as they drank their tea.

"I don't think I'll do Pilates tonight," Andi said. "You guys stretched every muscle in my body."

"Speaking of muscles, yours are way better developed than mine," Brant said. "Your legs are buff. I mean, they felt strong when I was holding them."

That look again. Andi was sure he'd make a

move after today's little exercise. Maybe after they got back to the station and Viktor was otherwise occupied.

"I try to stay in shape in case I'm called on for dumpster diving," she said. "They should make it an event in the police Olympics."

When Viktor went to the restroom, Brant said, "Andi, I was wondering if maybe sometime you might like to join me for dinner at a new trendier-than-trendy-ever-gets restaurant called Jade that I've been reading about."

Thinking, At last! she said, "I'd like to have dinner with you, but that's pretty pricey. I read a review."

He said, "My daughters're long past child support and my ex remarried ten years ago, so I'm independently comfortable. But on second thought, maybe I'm too old for a place like Jade."

"You look younger than I do," she said.

"Bless you, my child," Brant said. "So is it a date?"

"Yeah, let's try it on Thursday to avoid the weekend rush. Wonder how I should dress."

"Anything you wear would look great," he said, and dropped his eyes in a shy way after he said it.

Andi thought, Those green eyes! This one's

going to take me to heaven or bust me down to the ground. Her heart was pounding when Viktor returned to the table.

"There is one thing for sure," Viktor said to them when he gave his credit card to the waiter, "even if Lidorov is not our robber, it will be good to have his DNA profile. He is a violent thief. And a leopard cannot change its freckles."

It was a different thief, newly seduced by the heady excitement of power and control, who that very afternoon was in the process of committing the second armed robbery of his life. But his chain-smoking companion was not the least bit seduced as they sat in a stolen car in a crowded parking lot, waiting. She wished that his Russian wasn't hopeless, and that she didn't have to convey her fears in English.

"I warn you, Cosmo," Ilya said, looking like a clown to Cosmo in her red wig, wearing big sunglasses. "This is a foolish thing that we do."

"Dmitri told me is okay."

"Fuck Dmitri!" Ilya snapped, and Cosmo impulsively backhanded her across the face, regretting it at once.

He said, "Dmitri say that this is what he plan for long time. He say he is looking for someone like me and you to do it. We are lucky, Ilya. Lucky!"

"We get killed!" she said, wiping her eyes with tissue and touching up her mascara.

"We get rich," he said. "You seen how the man in the jewelry store do when he seen my gun? He piss on his pants. You seen him cry, no? The guards with money do not wish to die. Dmitri say the money is paid back by insurance company. The guards shall see the gun and they shall give the money to me. You going to see."

Cosmo, now wearing a Dodgers cap and sunglasses, had received the call from Dmitri the afternoon prior. Cosmo had thought it was about the diamonds, and when he showed up at the Gulag just before happy hour, he was sent upstairs to the private office.

Cosmo had not been surprised to see Dmitri sitting feet up, much as he'd seen him last time, again watching porn on his computer screen. But this time it was kiddie porn. When Cosmo entered, Dmitri turned down the sound on the speakers but left the screen on, glancing at it from time to time.

"Did you wish to talk about diamonds?" Cosmo said in English, as always.

"No," Dmitri said. "But I been giving much

thinking about the happen-ink guy Cosmo, who is my friend. I think about how you get the diamonds and how we going to do the deal for the diamonds very soon. I think maybe you ready for bigger job."

"Yes?" Cosmo said, and Dmitri knew the look. He had him.

"It feels how? Strong? Sexy? Like fuck-ink when you point the gun in the face of a man. Am I correct, Cosmo?"

"Feels okay," Cosmo said. "Yes, I don't mind."

"So, I have a job where you can get big money. Cash. At least one hundred thousand, maybe lot more."

"Yes?"

"You know the kiosk in the big mall parking lots? The ATM machine kiosk? I know about one. I know exactly when money will come. Exactly."

"Big armor car?" Cosmo said. "I cannot rob the armor car, Dmitri."

"No, Cosmo," Dmitri said. "Only a van. Two guys. They bring money inside a big, how you say, canister? Like soldier in Russia use for ammunition? One man must go behind kiosk, open door with key. Lock self in. Reload machine with nice green bullets from ammunition can."

"Please, Dmitri, how you know about this?"

"Everyone drink at the Gulag sometime," Dmitri said, chuckling in that way of his that scared Cosmo. He could imagine Dmitri chuckling like that if he was slitting your eyes.

"These men have guns, Dmitri."

"Yes, but they be only regular security guard. They are contract out for these deliveries. I know about the two men. They will not die to save money. Insurance will pay anyways. Everybody know that. Nobody lose noth-ink except insurance company. No problem."

"Two guys, two guns, two keys?"

"Yes, two keys for, how you say, internal security. You must take money before first guy get to kiosk. That is why I think of you. You prove at jewelry store you got lot of guts. And you got woman with big tits."

"Ilya?"

"Yes. I give you exact day and time. Ilya is there to do business at ATM machine. Ilya know how to distract man who walks from van with money can. Other guy have a habit. Always the same. He wait until partner get to kiosk. Then he get out and come with his key." Dmitri grinned and said, "One minute all you need, you happen-ink guy. You rock, Cosmo!"

And now here they were, sitting in a busy Hollywood parking lot, waiting in the fifteen-year-old red Mazda that Dmitri's Georgian bartender had stolen for them with instructions to wipe it clean and abandon it somewhere east of Hollywood.

Ilya had gathered herself now, but every time she turned toward him he saw a hateful glare. He had slapped her around before, but this time it was different. He could smell his stale sweat and the fear on her. He thought she might leave him after this. But if Dmitri was right about how much would be in the can, he would just pay her off and let her go.

He had a passing thought about trying to reduce Dmitri's fifty percent by saying that the amount of money in the can was far less than advertised. It gave him a thrill to think about that, but it was tempered when he thought of Dmitri's sinister chuckle. And for all he knew, one of the security guards might be Dmitri's informer. And might know exactly how much money he was delivering.

Cosmo looked at his Rolex knockoff and said, "Ilya, go to kiosk now."

The blue Chevy van looked like anything but an armored car, much to Cosmo's relief. And it sat there a few minutes, just as Dmitri said it would, while the guards looked around but saw nothing out of the ordinary. Just shoppers coming and going to the mall stores. Only one woman, a bosomy redhead, was at the ATM machine, looking very frustrated.

Her black purse was beside her on the tray and she took out her cell phone and appeared to be making a call. Then she threw her cell phone into the purse disgustedly and looked around as though she needed . . . what? She appeared to be trying her ATM card again but failed to make it work and just walked a short distance away, looking toward the electronics store across the parking lot. Maybe for her husband?

One of the guards glanced at the other. This was their last stop of the day and they couldn't sit there all evening because of one goofy woman. The passenger got out, slid open the door of the van, grabbed the only canister remaining, and slid the door closed. Then he walked from the van to the kiosk, and when he got to the front of it he saw that the red-haired woman was crying.

The six o'clock news would give the security guard's age as twenty-five. He was an "actor" who had been in Hollywood from Illinois for three years, looking for work and trying to get a SAG card. He had been with the security service for eighteen months. His name was Ethan Munger.

"Are you okay?" Ethan Munger said to Ilya, only pausing for a moment.

She was wiping her cheeks with the tissue and said, "I cannot make the card work." And when she put the tissue back inside her purse, she pulled out the Raven .25 caliber pistol, one of the cheap street guns that Cosmo had been given by the bartender. Ilya pointed it at the astonished young guard.

The driver of the van keyed his mike, announced the robbery, and jumped out of the van, his pistol drawn. He ran around the back of the van, where Cosmo Betrossian, crouched below a parked car, said, "Drop the gun or die!"

The driver dropped the gun and put his hands in the air, lying facedown when ordered to do so. It was just as Dmitri had promised, no problem.

But Ethan Munger was a problem. The young guard began backing toward the van, unaware that his partner had been disarmed. Ethan Munger had his free hand in the air, the other holding the metal container. And he said, "Lady, you don't want to do this. Please put that little gun away. It will probably blow up in your face. Just put it away."

"Drop the can!" Ilya screamed it. And it was all she could do not to burst into tears, she was so scared.

"Just don't get excited, lady," the young guard said, still backing up with Ilya coming toward him.

It seemed to Ilya like minutes had passed, but it was only seconds, and she expected to hear sirens because several passing shoppers were looking and a woman was yelling, "Help! Somebody call the police!" Another woman was shouting into her cell phone.

Then Cosmo came running up behind the young security guard with a pistol in each hand. Ethan Munger turned, saw Cosmo, and perhaps from having seen too many Hollywood films or played too many action videos tried to draw his pistol. Cosmo shot the young guard with the other guard's pistol. Three times in the chest.

Ilya didn't grab the can. She just put her pistol in her purse and ran screaming back toward the stolen car, the gunfire ringing in her ears. Within a minute, which seemed like ten, Cosmo jerked open the back door of the car and threw the can and two guns inside. And for one terrible moment couldn't get the old Mazda to start. Cosmo turned the key off, then on again three times, and it started and they sped from the parking lot.

Watch 5 was just loading up their war bags and other equipment when the code 3 hotshot call was given to 6-A-65 of Watch 2. And of course all the midwatch officers started throwing gear into their shops, jumping in, and squealing out of the station parking lot. They headed in the general direction of the robbery but really hoped they'd spot the red Mazda containing a dark-haired man wearing a baseball cap and a red-haired woman on the way. It wasn't often that there was a robbery and shooting of a security guard to start off their evening.

Benny Brewster and B.M. Driscoll of 6-X-66 were the last midwatch car out of the parking lot, which didn't surprise Benny. B.M. Driscoll had to run into the station at the last minute to get a bottle of antihistamine tablets from his locker because the early summer Santa Anas were killing him. Benny Brewster just sat and drummed his fingers on the steering wheel and thought about how miserably unlucky he had been in losing a heroic cop like Mag Takara and inheriting a hypochondriac whom nobody wanted.

Benny had visited Mag three times in the hospital and called her every day since she'd been home with her parents. He wasn't sure if her misshapen left cheekbone would ever be rebuilt to look exactly the way it was supposed to look. Mag said that the vision in her left eye was only about sixty percent of what it had been but that it was expected to improve. Mag promised Benny that she was coming back on duty, and he told her sincerely that he longed for the day.

There was still no court date set for the pimp who had assaulted her. Mag had suggested to Benny that with the huge lawsuit filed against the city for internal injuries suffered from the kicks by Officer Turner, maybe some sort of deal was coming down. A deal where the pimp would plea-bargain to county jail time instead of prison hard time, and a settlement would be made with the financially strapped city. Mag said she was very sorry for Turner, who had resigned in lieu of being fired and was awaiting word about whether he would be prosecuted.

"I jist wish I coulda been there, Mag," Benny said when last they'd talked about it.

Mag had looked at her tall black partner and said, "I'm glad you weren't, Benny. You've got a good career ahead of you. I predicted that to the Oracle first time you worked with me."

Benny Brewster was still thinking about all of that when B.M. Driscoll finally got in the car and said, "Let's not roll down the windows unless we have to." Then he sniffed and blew his nose, taking another tissue from the box that he put on the floor beside the shotgun rack.

Benny started the car and drove slowly from the parking lot, saying disgustedly, "Fucking two-eleven suspects that shot the guard're probably outta the county by now."

B.M. Driscoll didn't respond, only taking off his glasses and cleaning them with a tissue so that he could better read the dosage on the anti-histamine bottle.

All that Cosmo Betrossian could think about as he drove away from the scene of the robbery while the young security guard lay dying was the bartender at the Gulag. Cosmo was going to ask Dmitri to torture and kill that Georgian if he and Ilya were not killed themselves in the next few minutes. The stolen Mazda that the bartender assured him was in good working order had stalled at the first traffic light. And as Cosmo sat there grinding and grinding the starter, a police car sped past, light bar flashing and siren screaming, going to the very place from which they had just escaped.

"Let us get out of the car!" Ilya said.

"The money!" Cosmo cried. "We have money!"

"Fuck money," Ilya said.

The engine almost started, but he flooded it. He waited and tried again and it kicked over, and the Mazda began lurching south on Gower.

Cosmo decided that she was right, that they must get out and flee on foot. "Son of bastard!" he screamed. "I kill fucking Georgian that give me this car!"

"We leave it now?" Ilya said. "Stop, Cosmo."

Then the idea came to him. "Ilya," he said, "you know where we be now?"

"Yes, Gower Street," she said. "Stop the car!"

"No, Ilya. We be almost at the house of the miserable addict Farley."

Ilya had never been to Farley's house and could not see the significance of this. "So who gives damn about fucking tweaker? Stop the car! I get out!"

Cosmo realized that he was a block and a half away, that was all. A block and a half. "Ilya, please do not jump out. Farley has little garage! Farley always park his shit car on the street so is easy to push it."

"Cosmo!" she screamed again. "I am going to kill you or me! Stop this car! Let me out!"

"Two minutes," he said. "We be at house of Farley. We put this car in garage of Farley. Our money shall be safe. We shall be safe!"

The Mazda bucked and shuddered its way down Gower to the residential street of Farley Ramsdale. Cosmo Betrossian was afraid that the car wouldn't make the final turn, but it did. And as though the Mazda had a mind and a will, it seemed to throw itself in a last lurching effort up the slightly sloping driveway, where it sputtered and died beside the old bungalow.

Cosmo and Ilya got out quickly, and Cosmo opened the garage door and threw some boxes of junk and an old, rusty bike from the garage into the backyard, making room for the Mazda. Cosmo and Ilya both had to push the car into the garage. Cosmo tucked both pistols inside his belt, grabbed the container of money, and closed the termite-riddled door.

They went to the front door of the bungalow and knocked but got no answer. Cosmo tried the door and found it locked. They went to the back door, where Cosmo slipped the wafer lock with a credit card, and they entered to await the return of their new "partners."

Cosmo thought that now he had more reason than ever to kill the two tweakers, and that he must do it right after they entered the house. But not with the gun. The neighboring homes were too close. But how? And would Ilya help him?

The canister contained $93,260, all of it in twenty-dollar bills. By the time they had finished counting it, Ilya had smoked half a dozen cigarettes and seemed calm enough, except for her shaking hands. Cosmo began giggling and couldn't stop.

"Is not so much as Dmitri promised, but I am happy!" Cosmo said. "I am not greedy pig." That tickled him so much he giggled more. "I must call Dmitri soon."

"You kill the guard," Ilya said soberly. "They catch us, we go to the house of death."

"How can you know he is dead?"

"I saw bullets hit him. Three. Right here." She touched her chest. "He is dead man."

"Fucking guy," Cosmo said, testy now. "He did not give up money. Dmitri say no problem. The guard shall give up money. Not my fault, Ilya."

Ilya shook her head and lit yet another cigarette, and Cosmo lit a smoke of his own while he stuffed stacks of money back into the can, leaving out eight hundred, which he divided with Ilya, saying, "This make you not so much worried about the house of death, no?"

He took the container back out to the car, wanting to lock it in the trunk, but the ignition key did not work the trunk lock. He cursed the Georgian again and put the container in the backseat of the Mazda and locked the door.

When he returned to the house, Ilya was lying on the battered sofa as though she had a terrible headache. He went over to her and knelt, feeling very aroused.

He said to her, "Ilya, remember how much sex we feel when we rob the diamonds? I feel that much sex now. And you? How would you like to fuck the brains outside my head?"

"If you touch me now, Cosmo," she said, "I swear I shall shoot the brains outside your head. I swear this by the Holy Virgin."

★ ★ ★

Less than a mile away, Farley and Olive sat in Sam's Pinto, having borrowed it once again, parked by the cybercafé. They saw several tweakers entering and then leaving after having done their Internet business, but they saw no one who they thought might have some decent crystal for purchase.

"Let's try the taco stand," Farley said. "We gotta get Sam's car back to him before it gets dark and pick up our piece of shit. He musta fixed the carburetor by now. One good thing about tweakers, Sam can sit around his kitchen table with my carburetor in a million pieces and he actually enjoys himself. Like a fucking jigsaw puzzle or something. There's fringe benefits from crystal if you stop and think about it."

"I'm glad the police cars and ambulances stopped their sirens," Olive said. "They were giving me a headache."

She was like a goddamn dog, Farley thought. Supersensitive hearing even when not tweaked. She could sit in a restaurant and hear conversations on the other side of a crowded room. He thought he should figure out a way to use that, the only talent she possessed.

"Something musta happened at one of the

stores in the mall," Farley said. "Maybe some fucking Jew actually charged a fair price. That would cause a bunch of greasers to drop dead of shock and tie up some ambulances."

He was driving out of the parking lot and turning east when a southbound car at the intersection also turned east and drove in front of him, making Farley slam on his brakes.

"Fuck you!" Farley yelled out the window at the elderly woman driver after he flipped her the bird.

He hadn't gone half a block when he heard the horn toot behind him. He looked in the mirror and said, "Cops! My fucking luck!"

Benny Brewster said to B.M. Driscoll, "You're up."

The older cop wiped his runny nose with Kleenex, pushed his drooping glasses back up, sighed, and said, "I'm really not well enough to be working tonight. I shoulda called in sick."

Then he got out, approached the car on the driver's side and saw Farley Ramsdale fumbling in his wallet for his driver's license. Olive looked toward the policeman on her right and saw Benny Brewster looking in at her and at the inside of the car.

"Hi, Officer," Olive said.

"Evening," Benny said.

As B.M. Driscoll was examining his driver's license, Farley said, "What's the problem?"

B.M. Driscoll said, "You pulled out of the lot into the traffic lane, causing a car to brake hard and yield. That's a traffic violation."

Benny said to Farley, "Sir, how about showing the officer your registration too."

Farley said, "Aw shit, this ain't my car. Belongs to a friend, Sam Culhane. My car's at his house getting fixed by him."

When he quickly reached over to the glove compartment, Benny's hand went to his sidearm. There was nothing in the glove box except a flashlight and Sam's garage opener.

"Tell the officer, Olive," he said. "This is Sam's car."

"That's right, Officer," Olive said. "Our car is getting its carburetor redone. Sam has it all over the table like a crossword puzzle."

"That'll do," Farley said to her. Then turning to B.M. Driscoll, he said, "I got a cell here. You can use it and call Sam. I'll dial him for you. This ain't a hot car, Officer. Hell, I just live ten blocks from here by the Hollywood Cemetery."

Benny Brewster looked over the top of the

car to his partner and mouthed the word "tweakers."

Then, while B.M. Driscoll was returning to their car to run a make on Farley Ramsdale and the car's license number and to write up the traffic citation, Benny decided to screw with the tweakers, saying to Farley, "And if we followed you to your house just to verify you're who your license says you are, would you invite us inside?"

"Why not?" Farley said.

"Would there be anything in your house that you wouldn't want us to find?"

"Wait a minute," Farley said. "Are you talking about searching my house?"

"How many times have you been in jail for drug possession?" Benny asked.

"I been in jail three times," Olive said. "Once when this guy I used to know made me shoplift some stuff from Sears."

"Shut the fuck up, Olive," Farley said. Then to Benny he said, "If you don't write me the ticket, you can search me and search this car and you can search Olive here and you can come to my house and I'll prove whatever you want proved, but I ain't letting you do a fishing expedition by looking in my underwear drawer."

"Underwear floor, you mean," Olive said. "Farley always throws his underwear on the floor and I gotta pick them up," she explained.

"Olive, I'm begging you to shut up," Farley said.

Benny looked up and saw B.M. Driscoll returning with the citation book and said, "Too late. Looks like the citation's already written."

B.M. Driscoll looked over the roof at his tall partner and said, "Mr. Ramsdale has a number of arrests for drug possession and petty theft, don't you, Mr. Ramsdale?"

"Kid stuff," Farley mumbled, signing the traffic ticket.

"I didn't write you for not having a registration," B.M. Driscoll said. "But tell your friend, Samuel Culhane . . . where does he live, by the way?"

"On Kingsley," Olive said. "I don't know the number."

B.M. Driscoll nodded at Benny and said, "That checks." Then to Farley he said, "Have a good evening, Mr. Ramsdale."

When they were once again on their way to the taco stand to score some ice that Farley now needed desperately, he said to Olive, "You see what happens when you pin a badge on a nigger? That fucking Watusi wanted to go on a fishing expedition in my house."

"Maybe we shoulda just invited them home to see that you're a property owner and the stuff on your driver's license is correct," Olive said. "And it wouldn'ta mattered if they searched. We got nothing but a glass pipe at home, Farley. That's why we're out here. We got no crystal, no nothing at home."

Farley turned and stared at her until he almost rear-ended a pickup in front of him, then said, "Invite cops home to search? I suppose you'da made coffee for them?"

"If we had any," she said, nodding. "And if they didn't write the traffic ticket. It's always best to be friendly with the police. Being mean will just bring you more trouble."

"Jesus Christ!" Farley cried. "And then what? Maybe you woulda told them you were going to fuck them both to be friendly? Well, I hope not, Olive. Because making terroristic threats is a felony!"

FOURTEEN

BUDGIE AND FAUSTO were the first of the midwatch teams to break away from the hunt for the red Mazda. Virtually every car had driven east toward gang territory and the less affluent neighborhoods where most of Hollywood's street criminals resided, but the suspects' descriptions could have put them anywhere. By now the cars were looking for a male, white or possibly Hispanic, in his midforties, of medium height and weight, with dark hair. He was wearing a Dodgers cap and sunglasses, a blue tee, and jeans. His companion was a female, white, also about forty, tall and full-figured, with red hair that two Latino women said looked like a cheap wig. The woman with the gun wore sunglasses also, a tight, multi-colored cotton dress, and white espadrilles. Both witnesses commented on her large "bosoms."

A supplemental description was given to the

communications operator by Viktor Chernenko during an on-scene interview thirty minutes after the shooting, when the area around the ATM machine was taped off and controlled by uniformed officers. Even though Viktor knew that the Bank Squad from Robbery-Homicide Division would be handling this one, he was confident that these were the suspects from the jewelry store.

When the report call came in on their MDT, Fausto said to Budgie, "Well, by now they're in their hole. Best we could hope for is to spot the abandoned Mazda. They probably dumped it somewhere."

The report they were assigned was for attempted murder, which in Hollywood could mean anything. This was, after all, the land of dreams and fantasy. They were sent to a quite expensive, artsy-craftsy, split-level house in Laurel Canyon, certainly not an area where attempted murders occurred frequently. The fact that there was no code assigned to the call made them think that whoever took the call at Communications didn't think it was worthy of urgent response.

The caller was waiting on his redwood balcony under a vaulted roof. He waved after they parked, and they began climbing the outside wooden staircase. It was still nearly an hour before sunset so they didn't need to light their way, but it was dark from shadows cast by all of the ferns and palms and bird of paradise plants on both sides of the staircase.

Fausto, who was getting winded from the steep climb, figured that the gardeners must make a bundle.

The caller held open the door and said, "Right this way, officers."

He was seventy-nine years old and dressed in an ivory-white bathrobe with satin lapels, and leather monogrammed slippers. He had dyed-auburn transplants and a gray mustache that used to be called a toothbrush. He introduced himself as James R. Houston but added that his friends called him Jim.

The inside of the house said 1965: shag carpets, lime-green-flowered sofa, Danish modern dining room furniture, and even an elaborate painted clown in a gilded frame resembling the ones that the late actor-comedian Red Skelton had painted.

When Fausto said, "By any chance is that a Red Skelton?" and got a negative reply, Budgie said, "Who's Red Skelton?"

"A famous comic actor of yesteryear," the man said. "And a fine painter."

Only after their host insisted did they agree to have a glass of lemonade from a pitcher on the dining room table. Then he said to Fausto, "Even though I don't have the honor of owning a Red Skelton clown painting, I did work with him in a movie. It was in nineteen fifty-five, I think. But don't hold me to that."

Of course, he was implying that he was an actor. Budgie Polk had learned by now that in Hollywood Division, when a suspect or victim says he's an actor, a cop's automatic response is "And what do you do when you're not acting?"

When she said this to him, he said, "I've dabbled in real estate for years. My wife owns some rental property that I manage. Jackie Lee's my second wife." Then he corrected himself and said, "Actually, my third. My first wife died, and my second, well . . ." With that he made a dismissive gesture and then said, "It's about my present wife that I've called you here."

Budgie opened her report binder and said, "Is someone trying to murder her?"

"No," he said, "she's trying to murder me."

Suddenly his hand holding the glass of lemonade began to tremble, and the ice cubes tinkled.

With his long experience in Hollywood crime, Fausto took over. "And where is your wife now?"

"She's gone to San Francisco with her sister-in-law. They'll be back Monday morning, which is why I felt safe to call you here. I thought you might like to look for clues like on . . ."

"*CSI*," Fausto said. These days it was always the *CSI* TV show. Real cops just couldn't measure up.

"Yes," he said. "*CSI*."

"How is she trying to kill you?" Fausto asked.

"She's trying to poison me."

"How do you know that?" Budgie asked.

"I get a stomachache every time she cooks a meal. I've started going out to dinner a lot because I'm so frightened."

"And you wouldn't have any physical evidence, would you?" Budgie asked. "Something that you've saved? Like they do on *CSI*?"

"No," he said. "But it happens every time. It's a gradual attempt to murder me. She's a very sophisticated and clever woman."

"Is there any other evidence of her homicidal intent that you can offer?" Fausto asked.

"Yes," he said. "She's putting a toxic substance in my shoes."

"Go on," Budgie said. "How do you know?"

"My feet are always tired. And the soles sometimes hurt for no reason."

Fausto glanced at his watch and said, "Anything else?"

"Yes, I believe she's putting a toxic substance in my hats."

"Let me guess," Fausto said. "You have headaches?"

"How did you know?"

"Here's the problem as I see it, Mr. Houston," Fausto said. "If we arrest her, a high-priced shyster like the ones Michael Jackson hires would look at all this evidence and say, your wife's a lousy cook, your shoes're too tight, and so's your hat. You see where I'm coming from?"

"Yes, I take your point, Officer," he said.

"So I think what you should do is put this aside for now and call us back when you have more evidence. A lot more evidence."

"Do you think I should risk my life eating her food to collect the evidence?"

"Bland food," Fausto said. "It's not easy to disguise poison in bland dishes. Go ahead and enjoy your mashed potatoes and vegetables and a steak or some chicken, but not fried chicken. Just don't go for the spicy stuff and avoid heavy sauces. That's where it could be risky. And buy some shoes that are a half size bigger. Do you drink alcohol with dinner?"

"Three martinis. My wife makes them."

"Cut back to one martini. It's very hard to put a toxic dose in only one martini. Have it after dinner but not just before bedtime. And only wear hats when you go out in the sun. I think all of this will disrupt a murder plot or flush out the perpetrator."

"And you'll come back when we have more to go on?"

"Absolutely," Fausto said. "It will be a pleasure."

There was no pleasure to be had in the house of Farley Ramsdale. Three hours had passed since Cosmo and Ilya had pushed the car into the little garage, and still Farley and Olive had not come home. At one point Cosmo thought Ilya was asleep, lying there on the couch with her eyes closed.

But when he got up to look out the window at the darkened street, she said, "Stay back from the window. Every police in Hollywood looks for a man in a blue shirt and a woman with the hair that they shall know is a wig. We cannot call a taxi here. A driver shall think of us when he hears about the robbery. Then police may come here and talk to Farley and he is going to know it was us and he shall tell them."

"Shut up, Ilya. I must think!"

"We cannot go to a bus. We may be seen by police. We cannot call any of your friends to come for us unless you wish to share money with them because they shall find out. We are in a trap."

"Shut up!" Cosmo said. "We are not in the trap. We have the money. It is dark now."

"How do we go home, Cosmo? How?"

"Maybe the car will start now."

"I shall not put myself in that car!" Ilya said. "Every cop looks for that car. Every cop in Hollywood! Every cop in all Los Angeles!"

"The car must stay here," he agreed. "We put the money in shopping bags. There are paper bags in the kitchen."

"I understand," Ilya said. "We walk away from this house because we do not dare to call the taxi to come here? And then we call from my cell phone and taxi is going to meet us out on the street someplace where we hide in shadows? And we get taxi to leave us a few streets from our apartment?"

"Yes. That is exactly correct."

"And then Farley and Olive come home to find a car in garage and pretty soon when they turn on TV they see about robbery and the death of the guard and how the killer looks like and you don't think they know who done it? And you think they do not call police and say, Is there reward for the name of killers? The car is here. You do not think this shall happen, Cosmo?"

Cosmo sat down then and put his head in his hands. He had been thinking for three hours, and there was no alternative. He had planned to kill Farley and Olive at the junkyard just before getting the money for the diamonds, but now? He had to kill them when they walked in this house. Yet he could not risk gunfire.

He went over to Ilya and knelt on the floor beside her and said, "Ilya, the two addicts must die when they come home. We got no choice. We got to kill them. Maybe with knife from the kitchen. You must help me, Ilya."

She sat up and said, "I will not kill nobody else with you, Cosmo. Nobody."

"But what must we do?" he pleaded.

"Tell them what we done. Make them partner. Give them half of money. Make them help us to push that goddamn car away from here and leave it or set fire on it. Then they drive us home. And while all this happens, we just got to hope the cops do not see us. That is what we do, Cosmo. We do not kill nobody else."

"Please, Ilya! Think!"

"If you try to kill Farley and Olive, you shall have to kill me. You cannot stab us all, Cosmo. I shall shoot you if I can."

And with that, she drew the pistol from her purse, got up, and walked across the room to the sagging TV viewing chair, where she sat down with the gun in her lap.

"Please do not make fool talk," Cosmo said. "I must call Dmitri. But not now. Not today. I do not talk to Dmitri yet. We must see what is what before I call him."

"We shall get caught," she said. "Or killed."

"Ilya," he said, looking at her. "Let us make love, Ilya. You shall feel much better if we make love."

"Do not come close to me or it shall end here with guns, and you cannot let guns shoot on this quiet street, Cosmo. Or maybe you also wish to stab every neighbor too?"

Budgie and Fausto were back on patrol looking for something to do, when Budgie said, "Let's go by Pablo's Tacos and jam up a tweaker or two. Maybe we'll shake loose some crystal. We could use an observation arrest on our recap."

"Okay," Fausto said, turning east on the boulevard. "But whatever you do, don't order a taco in that joint. You heard about the tweaker at Pablo's that shoved bindles of crystal up his bung and tried to say his partner made him do it? Well, sometimes he cooks there."

Farley was absolutely livid by now, and Olive was getting an upset stomach from the stress. For the tenth time, he cried out, "Ain't there a goddamn teener or two left in this fucking town?"

"Please, Farley," Olive said. "You'll make yourself sick."

"I need some ice!" he said. "Goddamnit, Olive, we been fucking around for hours!"

"Maybe we should try the doughnut shop again."

"We tried it twice!" Farley said. "We tried every goddamn place I can think of. Can you think of a place we ain't tried?"

"No, Farley," she said. "I can't."

Farley raised himself up and looked to his right and saw 6-X-76 parking in the lot. A tall blond female cop got out, along with an old rhino who Farley figured must be a Mexican, or these days a Salvadoran, and that was even worse.

Farley turned his face away and said, "Olive, tell me these two cops ain't gonna jack us up. Not twice in one night, for chrissake!"

"They're looking at us," Olive said. Then Farley heard her say cheerfully, "Good evening, officers."

Farley put both hands on the steering wheel so they wouldn't get goosey and blow his fucking head off, and the female cop said, "Evening. Waiting for someone?"

Farley pointed to Olive and said, "Yeah, she's an actress. Waiting to get discovered."

That did it. Fausto said, "Step outta the car."

Since this had happened to Farley dozens of times in his life, he kept his hands in plain view when Fausto pulled open the driver's door. Farley got out, shaking his head and wondering why oh why did everything happen to him?

Fausto patted him down and said, "Let's see some ID."

When Olive got out, Budgie looked at Olive's scrawny torso covered only by a short T-shirt, revealing a sunken belly and bony hips. Her jeans were child size, and Budgie perfunctorily patted the pockets to see if she felt any bindles of crystal. Then Budgie shined her flashlight beam on Olive's inner forearms, but since Olive had seldom skin-popped, there weren't any tracks.

Farley said, "Gimme a break, *amigo.* Some of your *compadres* already rousted us tonight. They ran a make on us and on the car and then gave me a fucking ticket. Can I reach in my glove box and prove it to you?"

"No, stay here, *amigo,*" Fausto said, painting it with sarcasm. To Budgie he said, "Partner, take a look in the glove compartment. See if there's a citation in there."

She opened the glove compartment and retrieved the traffic ticket, saying, "B.M. Driscoll wrote it right after roll call. Near the cybercafé."

"I'll bet it never occurred to you, *amigo,*" Fausto said, "that maybe the reason you get stopped by so many cops is because you hang out where tweakers score their crystal. Did that ever flash on your computer screen?"

Farley thought he better lose the Spanish words because they didn't work with this fucking greaseball, so he tried a different tack. "Officer, please help yourself. You don't even have to ask. Search my car."

And Budgie said, "Okay," and she did.

While she was searching, Farley said, "Yes, I got a minor record for petty theft and possession of crystal meth. No, I don't have drugs on me. If you want, I'll take off my shoes. If we weren't standing out here, I'd take off my fucking pants. I'm too tired to reason with you guys anymore. Just do what you gotta do and let me go home."

"We even told the other officers they could come home with us," Olive said helpfully. "We don't care if you search our house. You can do a fishing exposition, we don't care."

"Olive," Farley said, "I'm begging you. Shut the fuck up."

"Is that right?" Budgie said. "You're so clean you'd take us home right now and let us search your house, no problem?" To Fausto, "Whadda you think of that, partner?"

"Is that what you'd do?" Fausto asked Farley, as he wrote a quick FI card. "Take us to your crib? You're that clean?"

"Man, at this point I'm just tempted to say yes. If you'd let me go lay in bed, you could turn the fucking place upside down, inside and out. And if you find any dope in that house, it would mean that Olive here must have a secret boyfriend who's supplying her. And if Olive could find a boyfriend, then there really are miracles and maybe I'll win the California lottery. And if I do, I'll move clear outta this fucking town and away from you people, because you're killing me, man, you're killing me!"

Fausto looked at the anguished clammy face of Farley Ramsdale, handed him his driver's license, and said, "Dude, you better get into rehab ASAP. The trolley you're riding is at the last stop. Nothing left ahead but the end of the line."

When Fausto and Budgie were back in their car, she said to Fausto, "I'm tempted to drive by the address on that FI a little later."

"What for?"

"That guy's gotta score some crystal. They'll be smoking ice and getting all spun out tonight or he'll be in a straitjacket. He's that close to losing it completely."

Ilya was on her feet, pacing and smoking. Cosmo was the one on the couch now, exhausted from arguing with her.

"How long we sit at this place?" he asked lethargically.

"Almost six hours," she said. "We can't wait no more. We got to go."

"Without our money, Ilya?"

"Did you wipe all evidence from the car, Cosmo?"

"I tell you yes, okay? Now please shut up."

"Did you empty the cigarette tray in the car? That is evidence."

"Yes."

"Get can of money out from the car."

"You got idea, Ilya? Wonderful. You don't like my ideas. Like we must kill the addicts."

"Shut up, Cosmo. You will put can of money under this house. Find a little door that go under this house. Put can in there."

She began emptying ashtrays into a paper bag from the kitchen, and he said, "Ilya, the car? It cannot travel! What are you thinking about?"

"We are leaving it."

"Here? Ilya, you are crazy person! Farley and Olive —"

In charge now, she interrupted, "Did you take things out from garage?"

"Yes, a bike and few boxes. Goddamn garage, full of junk. Almost no room for a goddamn car."

"As I thought," she said. "Put all junk back in."

"What are you thinking about, Ilya?"

"They are addicts, Cosmo. Look at this house. Trash all around. Junk all around. They do not park car in garage. They do not go in garage almost never. The car must stay for few days. They shall not even know it."

"And us?"

"Take a shirt from Farley. Look inside bedroom. I am going to remove my wig and we shall walk few blocks from here to phone taxi. It is a little bit safe now. Then we go home."

"All right, Ilya," he said. "But you sleep on top of this idea tonight: The addicts must die. We got no other road to travel. You must soon see that."

"I must think," she said. "Now we go. Hurry."

When Cosmo came back into the living room from the bedroom, he was wearing a dirty long-sleeved patterned shirt over his T-shirt. "Hope you happy now, Ilya," he said. "Before we get home I shall be bit a hundred times by tiny creatures that crawl inside Farley's clothes."

After the cops left them in the Pablo's Tacos parking lot, Farley said, "Olive, I think we gotta go home and white-knuckle it. We ain't gonna score tonight."

"There's almost a quart of vodka there," Olive said. "I'll mix it with some packets of punch and you can just drink as much as you can."

"Okay," he said. "That'll get me through the night. It'll have to."

"I just hope it won't make you throw up," Olive said. "You're so thin and tired-looking."

"It won't," he said.

"And I'll make you something delicious to eat."

"That'll make me throw up," he said.

When they arrived at Farley's house, he was almost too tired to climb the porch steps, and when he did and they were inside, Olive said, "Farley, it smells like smoke in here."

He threw himself on the couch and grabbed the TV remote, saying, "Olive, it should. We smoke crystal in here in case you forgot. Every chance we get, which ain't often enough these days."

"Yes, but it smells like old cigarette smoke. Don't you notice it?"

"I'm so fucking tired, Olive," he said, "I wouldn't smell smoke if you set fire to yourself. Which wouldn't be a bad idea."

"You'll feel better after a meal," said Olive. "How does a toasted cheese sandwich sound?"

The PSR putting out the broadcast decided to have a bit of fun with 6-X-32's call to Grauman's Chinese Theater. She put it out as a hotshot.

Flotsam and Jetsam listened incredulously when, after the electronic beep, she said, "All units in the vicinity and Six-X-ray-Thirty-two, see the woman on Hollywood Boulevard west of Highland. A battery in progress. Batman versus Spiderman. Batman last seen running into Kodak Center. Person reporting is Marilyn Monroe. Six-X-Thirty-two, handle code three."

When they got to the scene, Marilyn Monroe was waving at them from the courtyard of Grauman's Chinese Theater and tourists were snapping photos like crazy. B.M. Driscoll and Benny Brewster rolled in right behind them.

Jetsam, who was driving, said, "Which Marilyn is it, do you think? One of them is hot, bro. Know which one I mean?"

"It ain't the hot one," Flotsam said.

Their Marilyn was striking the famous over-the-air-vent pose, but there was no air blowing up her dress. She had the Monroe dress and her pricey wig was excellent. Even her coy but sensuous Monroe smile was right on the money. The problem was, she was six feet three inches tall and wasn't a woman.

Flotsam got out first and saw Spiderman sitting on the curb holding his head and rubbing his jaw. Jetsam went over to him and got the details, which of course involved a turf fight between two tourist hustlers.

While Flotsam was talking to Marilyn Monroe, a tourist begged them to move stage left so he could get Grauman's in the background. Marilyn did it gladly. After a moment's hesitation during which several tourists needled him for being a poor sport, Flotsam moved with her and put up with about a hundred photo flashes from every direction.

Finally Marilyn said, "It was terrible, Officer! Batman struck Spiderman with a flashlight for no reason at all. He's a pig, Batman is. I have always found Spiderman to be a love. I hope you find that cape-wearing rat and toss his fat ass in jail!"

There was quite a bit of applause then, and Marilyn Monroe flashed a smile that could only be called blinding in its whiteness.

As Flotsam was trying to get information from Marilyn Monroe, he was surrounded by all three Elvises. They worked in tandem only on big Friday nights like this one, and seeing the commotion went for the chance at real publicity. And they weren't disappointed. The first TV news van to have heard the police broadcast was dropping a cameraman and reporter at the corner of Hollywood and Highland just as the Elvises gathered.

The Presleys were all talking at once to Flotsam: Skinny Elvis, Fat Elvis, and even Smellvis, he of the yellow sweat stains under the arms of his ice-cream suit, which made tourists hold their breath during his cuddly photo shoots.

"Batman will never eat lunch in this town again!" Skinny Elvis cried.

"Spiderman rules!" Fat Elvis cried.

"I am an eyewitness to the caped crusader's vicious attack!" Smellvis announced to the crowd, and he was so rank that Flotsam had to backpedal a few steps.

Flotsam asked B.M. Driscoll to check out the Kodak Center, and when he asked, "What's the guy look like?" Flotsam said, "Just hook up any guy you see wearing a cape and hanging upside down somewheres. If it turns out to be Count Dracula, just apologize."

The midwatch cops didn't know that there was an undercover team at work in the midst of the crowd, posing as tourists with backpacks and cameras. The UC team had Tickle Me Elmo under arrest for manhandling a female tourist after she'd snapped his picture and refused to pay his three-dollar tariff.

Elmo had grabbed her by the arm and said, "Well you can kiss my ass, bitch!" and next thing he knew, the UC cops had him up against the wall of the Kodak Center and removed his head, inside of which they found more than two hundred dollar bills and a gram of cocaine.

Now the tourists turned on Elmo for photos, but the TV camera crew was still concentrating on Marilyn Monroe, until Benny Brewster said to Flotsam, "Hey man, Elmo had dope in his head!"

Upon hearing this, the news team swung their cameras toward Elmo, who was yelling that his head was dope-free when he'd put the costume on, implying a police frame-up.

Jetsam decided to help search the Kodak Center, where after a few minutes Batman was spotted. It was a brief chase, since Batman's ample gut was hanging over his utility belt, and he was just slogging along in front of the Kodak Theatre when Jetsam jumped him from behind. For a minute or two Jetsam feared that the exhausted Batman was going into cardiac arrest after he was proned out and cuffed.

Jetsam said to B.M. Driscoll, "How do you do CPR through a bat mask and breastplate?"

When Jetsam finally got outside Grauman's forecourt with his handcuffed and forlorn prisoner, crowds gathered, cameras flashed, and the news bunny ran up to him, saying, "Officer, did you have trouble catching up with Batman? Was it an exciting chase?"

The surfer cop struck a semi-heroic pose for the camera and said, "Weak sauce." Then he quickly walked Batman to the black-and-white, where he was put into the backseat.

This particular news bunny was a relentless journalist and proud of it. She hurried after Jetsam and stood next to the police car, making a point of handing her mike to one of the guys in her crew so she could appear to confront the cop empty-handed.

" 'Weak . . . sauce'?" said the news bunny to Jetsam, with arching, perfectly penciled eyebrows, and a lip-licking smile that stopped the surfer cop in his tracks. "Can you translate that term for us? Off the record?"

Jetsam gaped at her cleavage. And goddamn, she licked her lips again! He looked at her camera crew, who were back on the sidewalk and couldn't even see his face, and he leaned down with his mouth close to her ear and whispered,

"It just means, without his Batmobile his shit is puny."

Then with a devil-may-care wink, he whirled and hopped into the car behind the wheel. He was tickled to see the news bunny direct the crew to shoot coverage of 6-X-32 as he was driving off.

What Jetsam didn't see, however, was the news bunny fingering the little mike she had wired inside the collar of her jacket. And the triumphant smile she gave to her sound man was even twice as sexy as the one she'd given Jetsam.

On the late news, the producer bleeped out *shit*, but from the context the audience knew what had been said. Then the news bunny appeared on camera, this time directly in front of Grauman's Chinese Theater.

With her Hollywood insider's saucy grin, she said to her audience, "This is your intrepid reporter coming to you from Hollywood Boulevard, where even superheroes must bow to the forces of LAPD justice — who have anything but . . . weak sauce."

The watch commander told Jetsam that he'd probably get another official reprimand or even a little suspension for the manner of his "interview."

Cosmo did not waken until 1 P.M. the next day. The smell of Ilya's tea brought him around, and at first he felt a stab of panic. What if she'd gone back to get the money? But then he heard her and the sound of dishes being washed, so he entered the bathroom and showered.

When he came into the kitchen, she was at the table smoking and drinking a glass of hot tea. Another glass was poured and awaited him. Neither spoke until he drank some and lit a cigarette of his own, and then he said, "How long you are awake?"

"Three hours," she said. "I am thinking many thoughts."

"And what is the new idea?"

"How much Dmitri is going to give for the diamonds?"

"Twenty thousands," he lied.

"Okay," she said. "Give to him the diamonds. No charge. We keep the money."

"All the money?"

"No, we share with Farley and Olive. We make the best bargain we can. Then we get out of Los

Angeles. Go to San Francisco. Start over. No more guns. No more death."

"Ilya, Dmitri know how much money we got. Do you not turn on TV and hear about it?"

"No," she said. "I have no wish to hear more."

"The news tell how much we got. Dmitri shall want half."

"We may leave Los Angeles with almost fifty thousand, even if Farley take away half. We cannot give Dmitri no money. We give him diamonds."

"Is not enough. He shall kill us, Ilya. I know he is mad now because I did not make a call to him. I know he is very mad."

"We are leaving Los Angeles."

"He shall find us and kill us in San Francisco."

"We take a chance."

"You think Farley and Olive do not tell police about us after we give them money?"

"No. They must have drugs. They must have money for drugs. After they take half of money, they are, how you say it, partners in the crime. They cannot tell police nothing. We shall wait two, maybe three days. I tell you the addicts will not know the Mazda is in garage. And under the house they never go in all their life. We are okay for two, three days. We hide here."

"Ilya, we may keep half money and give other half to Dmitri." Then he almost told the truth about the diamond deal, saying, "I think I may bargain with Dmitri. I think I say to him I must have thirty-five thousands for diamonds. So, we shall have almost eighty-five thousands and we stay in Los Angeles. All of this if you permit me to kill the addicts. I know how. You shall not need to do nothing." He was finished now, but he decided to add a postscript. He said, "Please, Ilya. You love the life here. You very much love the life in Hollywood. Am I correct?"

Ilya's mascara was running when she got up and went to the tea kettle on the stove. She stood there for a long moment before speaking. With her back to him she said, "All right, Cosmo. Kill them. And do not never talk of it. Never!"

★ FIFTEEN

THE SOUTHEASTERN PART of Hollywood Division, near Santa Monica Boulevard and Western Avenue, was the turf of Latino gangs, including Eighteenth Street cruisers and some Salvadorans from the huge MS-13 gang. White Fence, one of the oldest Mexican American gangs, was active around Hollywood Boulevard and Western, and Mexican Mafia, aka MM or El Eme, was only here and there but in some ways was the most powerful gang of all and could even operate lethally from inside state prisons. There were no black gangs in the Hollywood area, like the Crips or Bloods of south central and southeast L.A., because there were very few blacks living in the Hollywood area.

Wesley Drubb was steeped in this what was to him exciting information, having been permitted to gain new experience by working on loan for two nights with 6-G-1, a Hollywood Division gang unit. But now while driving on Rossmore Avenue, which bordered the Wilshire Country Club, his gang chatter seemed ludicrously inappropriate and especially annoying to Hollywood Nate Weiss.

Wesley said, "The California Department of Corrections estimates that El Eme has nearly two hundred members in the prison system."

"You don't say." Nate was gazing up at the luxurious apartment buildings and condos on both sides of his favorite Los Angeles street.

"They're usually identified by a tattoo of a black hand with an *M* on the palm of it. In the Pelican Bay Maximum Security Prison, an MM gang member had sixty thousand dollars in a trust account before it was frozen by authorities. He was doing deals from inside the strictest prison!"

"Do tell." Nate imagined Clark Gable in black tie and Carole Lombard in sable, both smiling at the doorman as they went off for a night on the town. At the Coconut Grove, maybe.

Then he tailored the fantasy to fit Tracy and Hepburn, even though he knew that neither of them had ever lived on the street. But what the hell, it was his fantasy.

Wesley said, "Big homies have been known to order hits from their prison cells. If you're 'in the hat' or 'green-lighted,' it means you're targeted."

"Weird," Nate said. "Green-lighted in the movie business means you got the okay to do the picture. In Hollywood it means you're alive. In prison it means you're dead. Weird."

Wesley said, "They told me that sometimes in Hollywood we might encounter southeast Asian gangsters from the Tiny Oriental Crips and the Oriental Boy Soldiers. Ever run into them?"

"I don't think so," Nate said. "I've only encountered more law-abiding and sensitive Asians who would bury a cleaver in your neck if you ever referred to them as Orientals."

Wesley said, "And the Asian gang whose name I love is the Tiny Magicians Club, aka the TMC."

"Jesus Christ!" Nate said, "TMC is The Movie Channel! Isn't anything fucking sacred anymore?"

Wesley said, "I already knew about the civil injunctions to keep gang members in check, but did you know the homies have to be personally served with humongous legal documents that set forth all terms of the injunction? Two or three gang members congregating can violate the injunction, and even possession and use of cell phones can be a violation. Did you know that?"

Nate said, "Possession of a cell phone by any person of the female gender who is attempting to operate a motor vehicle should be a felony, you ask me."

Wesley said, "I might get to examine the tattoos and talk to some crew members and hear about their gang wars next time."

"Do I detect a 'hood rat in the making?" Nate said, yawning. "Are you gonna be putting in a transfer, Wesley? Maybe to Seventy-seventh Street or Southeast, where people keep rocket launchers at home for personal protection?"

"When I got sent to Hollywood I heard it was a good misdemeanor division. I guess I wanna go to a good felony division. I've heard that in the days before the consent decree, Rampart Division CRASH unit used to have a sign that said 'We intimidate those who intimidate others.' Imagine how it was to work that Gang Squad."

Nate looked at Wesley the way he'd look at a cuppa joe from Dunkin' Donuts or a Hostess Ding Dong and said, "Wesley, the days of LAPD rock 'n' rule are over. It's never coming back."

Wesley said, "I just thought that someplace

like Southeast Division would offer more . . . challenges."

"Go ahead, then," Nate said. "You can amuse yourself on long nights down there by going to drug houses and yelling 'Police!' then listening to toilets flushing all over the block. Cop entertainment in the 'hood. Watching cruisers throw gang signs beats the hell outta red carpet events, where the tits extend from Hollywood Boulevard to infinity, right?"

Wesley Drubb was eager indeed to do police work in gang territory, or anyplace where he might encounter real action. He was growing more and more tense and nervous with Nate boring him to death by directing him far from the semi-mean streets of Hollywood for his endless sorties into Hollywood's past. The gang turf was there and he was here. Touring!

Quiet now, Wesley chewed a fingernail as he drove. Nate finally noticed and said, "Hey pard, you look especially stressed. Got girlfriend troubles maybe? I'm an expert on that subject."

Wesley wasn't far enough from his probationary period to say, "I am fucking bored to death, Nate! You are killing me with these trips through movie history!"

Instead, he said, "Nate, do you think we should be cruising around the country club? This is Wilshire Area. We work in Hollywood Area."

"Stop saying area," Nate said. "Division sounds more coplike. I can't stand these new terms for everything."

"Okay, Hollywood Division, then. We're out of it right now. This is Wilshire Division."

"A few blocks, big deal," Nate said. "Look around you. This is gorgeous."

Hollywood Nate was referring to Rossmore Avenue, where the elegant apartment buildings and pricey converted condos had names like the Rossmore, El Royale, the Marlowe, and Country Club Manor, all of them a short walk from the very private golf course. They were built in the French, Spanish, and Beaux Arts styles of Hollywood's Golden Age.

Seeing that Wesley lacked enthusiasm for the architecture, Nate said, "Maybe you'd like to cruise by the Church of Scientology Celebrity Center? We might spot John Travolta. But we can't hassle any of their so-called parishioners or we'll get beefed by their fascist security force. Do you know they even beefed our airship one time? Said they wanted to make their headquarters an LAPD no-fly zone."

Wesley said, "No, I don't have much interest in Scientology or John Travolta, to tell you the truth."

"This looks like we're in Europe," Nate said, as the setting sun lit the entry of the El Royale. "Can't you see Mae West sashaying out that door with a hunky actor on her arm to a limo waiting on the street?"

"Mae West" was how Wesley Drubb's father referred to the life jackets he kept aboard a seventy-five-foot power yacht that he used to own and kept docked at the marina. Wesley didn't know that they were named after a person, but he said, "Yeah, Mae West."

"Someday I'll be living in one of those buildings," Nate said. "The local country clubs used to restrict Jews. And actors. I've heard it was Randolph Scott who told them, 'I'm not an actor and I've got a hundred movies to prove it.' But then I heard it was Victor Mature. Even John Wayne, and he didn't hardly play golf. It's a good Hollywood story no matter who said it."

Wesley had never heard of the first two actor-golfers and was getting a tightness in his neck and jaw muscles. He was even grinding his teeth and only relaxed when Nate sighed and said, "Okay, let's go find you a bad guy to put in jail."

And at last, with an enormous sense of relief, Wesley Drubb was permitted to drive away from reel Hollywood and head for the real one.

Darkness fell as they were passing the Gay and Lesbian Center, and Nate said, "That's where they can go to let their hair down. Or their hair extensions. There's a place for everyone to dream in Hollywood. I don't know why you can't be satisfied."

A few minutes later, on Santa Monica Boulevard, Wesley said, "Look how that guy's walking. Let's shake him."

Nate looked across the street at a pale and gaunt forty-something guy in a crew neck, long-sleeved sweater and jeans, walking along the boulevard with his hands in his pockets.

"Whadda you see that I don't see?"

"He's a parolee-at-large, I bet. He walks like they do in the prison yard."

"You learned a lot with the gang unit," Nate said. "Maybe even something worthwhile, but I haven't noticed it yet."

Wesley said, "The parole officers are a few months behind in getting warrants into their computer, but we could check him anyway, okay? Even if there's no warrant, maybe he's holding some dope."

"Maybe he's cruising for a date," Nate said. "This is Santa Monica Boulevard, home of boy love and homo-thugs. He might be looking for somebody like the one he left in prison. A guy with a tattoo of a naked babe on his back and an asshole like the Hollywood subway."

"Can we check him?"

"Yeah, go ahead, get it outta your system," Nate said.

Wesley pulled up several yards behind the guy, and both cops got out and lit him with their flashlight beams.

He was used to it. He stopped and took his hands out of his pockets. With a guy like this preliminaries were few, and when Wesley said, "Got some ID?" the guy shot them a grudging look of surrender and without being asked pulled up the sweater sleeves, showing his fore-arms, which were covered with jailhouse tatts over old scar tissue.

"I don't use no more," he said.

Nate moved the beam of his light near the man's face and said, "Your eyes are down right now, bro."

"I drink like a Skid Row alky," the ex-con said, "but I don't shoot up. I got tired of getting busted for eleven five-fifty. I was always under the influence and I just kept getting busted. Like, I was serving life in prison a few weeks at a time."

Wesley wrote an FI card on the guy, whose ID said his name was Brian Allen Wilkie, and ran the information on the MDT, coming back with an extensive drug record but no wants or warrants.

Before they let him go, Nate said, "Where you headed?"

"Pablo's to get a taco."

"That's tweakerville," Nate said. "Don't tell me you're smoking glass now instead of shooting smack?"

"One day at a time, man," Brian Wilkie said. "I wouldn't want my PO to know, but I'm down to booze and a little meth now and then. That's an improvement, ain't it?"

"I don't think that's what AA means by one day at a time, man," Nate said. "Stay real."

A few minutes later, when Wesley drove past Pablo's Tacos, they saw an old car parked in front and a pair of skinny tweakers in a dispute with another guy who also had tweaker written all over him. The argument was so animated that the tweakers didn't see the black-and-white when Wesley parked half a block away and turned out the lights to watch.

"Maybe one of them'll stab the other," Nate

said."And you can pop him for a felony. Or better yet, maybe one of them'll pull a piece and we can get in a gunfight. Would that relieve your boredom?"

Farley Ramsdale was waving his arms like one of those people with that terrible disease whose name she couldn't remember, and Olive was getting scared. Spit was running down Farley's chin and he was screaming his head off because the tiny tweaker that they knew as Little Bart wouldn't sell one of the two teeners he was holding. Farley refused to meet his excessive price and had tried to bargain him down.

Olive thought it was mean and wrong of Little Bart, because Farley had often sold to him at a decent price. But all this screaming was just going to get them in trouble.

"You are an ungrateful chunk of vomit!" Farley yelled. "Do you remember how I saved your sorry ass when you needed ice so bad you were ready to blow a nigger for it?"

Little Bart, who was about Farley's age and whose neck bore a tattoo of a dog collar all the way around, said, "Man, things're bad, real bad these days. This is all I got and all I'm gonna have for a while. I gotta pay the rent."

"You little cocksucker!" Farley yelled, doubling his fist.

"Hey, dude!" Little Bart said, backing up. "Take a chill pill! You're freaking!"

Olive stepped forward then and said, "Farley, please stop. Let's go. Please!"

Suddenly, Farley did something he had never done in all the time they'd been together. He smacked her across the face, and she was so stunned she stared at him for a moment and then burst into tears.

"That's enough," Wesley said, and got out of the car, followed by Hollywood Nate.

Farley never saw them coming but Little Bart did. The tiny tweaker said, "Uh-oh, time to go."

And he started to do just that, until Wesley said, "Hold it right there."

A few minutes later, Little Bart and Farley were being patted down by Wesley and Hollywood Nate while Olive wiped her tears on the tail of her jersey.

"What's this all about?" Farley said. "I ain't done nothing."

"You committed a battery," Wesley said. "I saw it."

"It was an accident," Farley said. "Wasn't it,

Olive? I didn't mean to hit her. I was just making a point with this guy."

"What point is that?" Nate said.

"About whether George W. Bush is really as dumb as he looks. It was a political debate."

Little Bart wasn't really worried, because the ice was under the rear floor mat of his car, which was half a block down the street. So he just had to chill and not piss off the cops, and then he figured he could skate.

When Nate pulled Farley ten yards away from the other two, Farley yelled back, "Olive, tell these guys it was an accident!"

"Shut the fuck up," Nate said. "Where's your car?"

"I ain't got a car," Farley lied, and after he did it, he wondered why he had lied. There was no crystal in his car. He hadn't smoked any glass for two and a half days. That's why his nerves were shot. That's why he was on the verge of strangling Little Bart. He was just so sick of being hassled by cops that he lied. Lying was a form of rebellion against all of them. All of the assholes who were fucking with him.

For the next twenty minutes, the shakes were written, and each name was run through CII, with a rap sheet showing for Farley Ramsdale but none for Olive O. Ramsdale. Farley finally stopped bitching and Olive stopped crying.

Little Bart actually began trying to talk politics to Farley to go along with the George Bush crack, but the cops obviously weren't buying it. They knew that some kind of drug deal was going down, and Little Bart just didn't want to give them a good reason to try his car keys in the doors of the eight cars that were parked within half a block of Pablo's. And he especially didn't want them to look under the floor mat.

Farley thought the cops were going to prolong this for as long as possible, but the younger cop ran up to the other one and said, "Kidnapping in progress, Omar's Lounge on Ivar! Let's go, Nate!"

When Farley and Olive and Little Bart were left standing there outside Pablo's Tacos, Farley said to Little Bart, "Those cops saved your fucking life."

Bart said, "Dude, you need some help. You're way out there. Way, way out there." And he ran to his car and drove off.

Olive said, "Farley, let's go home now and —"

"Olive," he said, "if you say you'll make me a

delicious cheese sandwich, I swear I'll knock your fucking tooth out."

Hollywood detectives had been forced to investigate a number of date rapes, called acquaintance rapes by the police. It was usually "I woke up naked with somebody I didn't know. I was drugged."

The cases were never prosecuted. Evidentiary requirements necessitated an immediate urine test, but the date rape drugs metabolized in four to six hours. It was always too late for the special analysis that had to be done outside the LAPD crime lab, which did only basic drug screening of controlled substances. In fact, as defense lawyers argued, too much booze produced much the same effect as a date rape drug.

The date rape cases were reported to Hollywood Station by persons of both genders, but only once was there a criminal filing by the district attorney's office. The victim had vomited shortly after the encounter, and the drug was able to be recovered and identified.

Six-X-Seventy-six was the unit to receive the code 3 call to Omar's Lounge but Budgie and Fausto were beaten to the call by Wesley Drubb and Hollywood Nate, followed closely by Benny Brewster and B.M. Driscoll, complaining of motion sickness caused by Benny's fast driving.

The first units to arrive gave way to Budgie and Fausto, since they were assigned the call, and Budgie entered the nightclub to interview the victim. Even though Fausto was the report writer on this night and Budgie was driver, she took over with the report because the victim was a woman.

When they were being escorted to a private office inside the nightclub, Fausto whispered to her, "This joint gets sold to somebody new just about every time they change the tablecloths. It's impossible to keep track of who the owner is, but you can bet your ass it's a Russian."

Sara Butler was sitting in the office being tended to by a cocktail waitress who wore a starched white shirt, black bow tie and black pants. The waitress was a natural blonde and pretty, but the kidnap victim, who was about Budgie's age, was both prettier and unnaturally more blond. The straps on her black dress were held together with safety pins, and her pantyhose was in shreds around her ankles. Her knees were scraped and bleeding, as were both her palms. Mascara and eye liner were smeared all over her cheeks, and she was wearing most of her lipstick on her chin. She was angry and she was drunk.

The cocktail waitress was applying ice in a napkin to the victim's right knee when the cops walked in. A faux fur coat was draped across the chair behind the young woman.

Budgie sat down and said, "Tell us what happened."

"I was kidnapped by four Iranians," Sara Butler said.

"When?" Budgie asked.

"About an hour ago," Sara Butler said.

Budgie looked at Fausto, who nodded and went out to broadcast a code 4, meaning sufficient help at the scene, since the suspects were long gone.

"What did you say when you called it in?" Budgie asked. "We were under the impression that it had just occurred."

"I don't know what I said, I was so upset."

"Okay," Budgie said. "From the beginning, please."

After she'd given all of the contact information for the report, and after listing her occupation as actress, Sara Butler said, "I was supposed to meet my girlfriend here but she called me on my cell and said her husband came home from a trip unexpectedly. And I thought I might as well have a drink since I was here."

"You had more than one?"

"I don't know how many I had."

"Go on."

"I got talking to some guy at the bar and he started buying me martinis. I didn't have that many."

Worrying about the liquor license, the cocktail waitress looked at Budgie and said, "We wouldn't serve anyone who's drunk."

"Continue, please," Budgie said to Sara Butler.

"So pretty soon I started feeling weird. Dizzy in a weird way. I think the guy slipped me a date rape drug but I didn't drink enough of it to knock me cold."

"How many martinis did you drink?"

"No more than four. Or possibly five."

"That could knock a hippo cold," Budgie said. "Go on."

"The guy who bought me the martinis offered to drive me home. Said he had a black Mercedes sedan and a driver parked right in front. Said he'd be in the car. I said okay and went to the ladies' room to freshen up."

"Weren't you worried about the date rape

drug?" Budgie asked.

"Not then. I only thought about it after the kidnapping."

"Okay, continue."

"Then I left the club, and there was a long black car at the curb and I went to the back door which was open and got in. And goddamn! There were four drunken Iranians in the car and one of them closed the door and they took off with me, just laughing their asses off. And I realized that it was a limo and I was in the wrong car and I yelled at them to stop and let me out."

"How did you know they were Iranians?"

"I go to acting class with two Iranians and they're always jabbering in Farsi. I know Iranians, believe me. Or Persians, as they prefer to call themselves when they live in a free country, the bastards."

"Okay, and then?"

"They were groping me and kissing me and I scratched one on the face and he told the driver to stop and they pushed me out of the car right onto the street and I ran back here. I want them arrested and prosecuted for kidnapping."

"Kidnapping might be very hard to allege in this case," Budgie said, "but let's get the report finished and see what the detectives think."

"I don't care what the detectives think," Sara Butler said. "I've done half their job for them already."

And with that she produced a tissue that was carefully folded, and said, "These are fingernail scrapings from the Iranian's face. And my coat there can be examined for latent fingerprints."

"We can't get fingerprints from fur," Budgie said.

"Officer, don't tell me what you can't do," Sara Butler said. "My father's a lawyer and I won't have my report swept under the rug by your detectives. The dirt from my dress will identify where I was lying in the gutter in case someone says I wasn't pushed from the car. And those fingernail scrapings will positively identify one of my assailants after a DNA analysis." She paused and said, "And Channel Seven is on the way."

"Here?"

"Yes, I called them. So I suggest you take this case very seriously."

"Tell me, Ms. Butler," Budgie said. "Do you watch *CSI*?"

"All the time," Sara Butler said. "And I know that some cheap lawyer for the Iranians might say I got into the car by design and not by accident, but I have that covered as well."

"I'm sure you do," Budgie said.

"The man who bought me the martinis can testify that he had a car waiting for me, and that will prove I just made a mistake and got into the wrong car."

"And I suppose you have the man's name and how we can contact him?"

"His name is Andrei. He's a Russian gentleman who said he worked as manager at the Gulag in east Hollywood. And he gave me a business card from there. I think you should check on him and see if he's ever been accused of doctoring a girl's drink either at his nightclub or elsewhere. I still think I was affected too suddenly by the martinis."

"Anything else you'd like to add?" Budgie said, intending to get the hell out before a news team arrived.

"Only that I intend to have my father call the Gulag or go to the nightclub in person if necessary to make sure someone from the police department properly investigates my crime report. Now, if you'll excuse me, I've got to get myself together for Channel Seven."

When Budgie got back outside, Fausto, who had stepped into the office during part of the interview, said, "Would you call that a righteous felony or an example of first-stage alcoholism and a slight PMS issue?"

"For once, you sexist old bastard," Budgie said, "I think you got it right."

Dmitri would have been even angrier, if that were possible, had he known that Andrei, his night manager, had been out on his night off trying to pick up a woman who subsequently got herself involved with the police. Dmitri did not want the police at his place of business ever, not for any reason. But this night he had cops all over the place, including Andi McCrea, who'd been called in from home by the night-watch detective Compassionate Charlie Gilford.

When Charlie told Andi that he was having trouble reaching other members of the homicide unit, two of whom were sick with the flu that was going around, she suggested he try one of the detectives from Robbery, and gave him Brant Hinkle's cell number.

Charlie rang up Brant Hinkle and told him there was a murder at the Gulag and asked if he'd be willing to help out Andi. Brant said he thought he could manage and that he'd be there ASAP.

Then Brant closed his cell and looked over at

Andi, naked in bed beside him, and said, "That is a very dirty trick."

She kissed him, jumped out of bed, and said, "You'd rather investigate a homicide with me than lie here alone all night, wouldn't you?"

"I guess I would at that," Brant said. "Is that what you would call a commitment?"

Andi said, "When two cops are committed, the definition is similar to the one meaning residents of an asylum. Let's go to work."

There had been a large private party in the VIP section on the upper level of the Gulag, an area roped off and guarded by a bouncer. Dmitri had assigned two waitresses for the party and wished he'd scheduled three when the party grew much larger than had been expected. Soon the sofas along the walls and every chair was occupied in layers, young women sitting on the laps of any guy who would permit it. Everyone else was standing three deep by a railing, watching the mass of dancers writhing in the pit down below on ground level.

They were foreign students from a technical college attending this gathering put together by a party promoter who dealt with various Hollywood nightclubs. Most at the soirée were Arabs, some were Indians, a few were Pakistanis. And there were two uninvited guests from south L.A. who were members of the Crips gang, out for a night in Hollywood, one of whom claimed to be a cousin of the promoter.

Dmitri had installed a video camera on the patio outside, where customers could go for a smoke, and it was there on the patio that the crime occurred. One of the young Arabs, a twenty-two-year-old student, didn't like something that the taller of the two Crips said to his girlfriend, and a fight started. The taller Crip, who wore a raspberry-colored fedora over a head rag, got knocked down by the Arab with some help from his friends. While several people were separating the combatants, the shorter of the two Crips, the quiet one, walked behind the Arab, reached around, and stabbed him in the belly.

Then both Crips ran from the patio and out through the nightclub's front door as people screamed and an ambulance was called. The young Arab lay thrashing and bled out, displaying no signs of life even before the RA and the first black-and-whites arrived. Still, he was taken straight to Hollywood Presbyterian Hospital while a paramedic worked on him futilely.

It was B.M. Driscoll and Benny Brewster who

sealed off the area and kept as many actual eye-witnesses in place as they could, but the night-club had started emptying fast after word got out about the stabbing. When Andi McCrea and Brant Hinkle arrived (in separate cars so as to stay discreet), Benny Brewster and B.M. Driscoll were writing down information from half a dozen of the Arabs and two of their American girlfriends, who were crying.

Benny Brewster briefed Andi by pointing out the party promoter, Maurice Wooley, a very worried black man who was sitting at the far end of the now-empty bar drinking a tall glass of Jack. He was plump, in his midfifties and wearing a conservative, double-breasted gray suit. He was also bleary-eyed from the booze.

Benny said to him, "Mr. Wooley, this is Detective McCrea. Tell her about the homie that did the stabbing."

"I really don't know much about him," the promoter said to Andi. "He's jist somebody from Jordan Downs, where I grew up, is all. I don't live down there no more."

"I understand he's your cousin," Andi said.

"A much younger cousin to my play cousin," the promoter said quickly. "I don't know his real name."

Benny Brewster abruptly changed tack, glared at him, and said, "So what's your cousin to your play cousin's street name? Whadda you call him?"

The promoter's jowls waddled slightly and he said, "Doobie D. That's all I ever did call him, Doobie D. I swear on my momma's grave."

Benny scowled and said, "Maybe your momma has room for one more in there."

Andi said, "What's his phone number?"

"I dunno," the promoter said, twisting his zircon ring nervously, glancing every few seconds at the tall black cop, who looked about ready to grab him by the throat.

Andi said, "This officer tells me you invited him here as your guest tonight."

"That's 'cause I run into him on the street when I went to visit my momma. He said he wanna go to one of them Hollywood parties I promote. And me, I'm a fool. I say, okay, when I get one, I'm gonna let you know. So I get this job and I let him know and I comp him in here as my guest. With one of his crew. And look at the grief I get."

"If you don't have his number, how did you reach him?"

"I jist have his e-mail address," the promoter

said, handing Andi his cell phone. "His cell company is one of them that you can e-mail or phone."

When they were finished at the Gulag and ready to go, Andi was approached by a man with an obvious hairpiece and a peculiar smile. He extended his hand to both detectives and said, "I am Dmitri Zotkin, proprietor of the Gulag. I am sick to my heart from the terrible think that has een-wolved my club tonight. I shall be of service if you need any-think. Any-think at all."

He gave them his card and bowed slightly.

"We may have some questions for you tomorrow," Andi said.

"On the back of the card is my cell number," he said. "Anytime you wish to call Dmitri. Please, I shall be at your service."

After getting back to the station, Andi Googled Doobie D's Internet provider from the text message. Then she left a phone message with the provider, requesting that the customer's name and phone number be pulled up, with the assurance that a search warrant would be faxed to them in the morning before the provider faxed the account information to her.

Andi said to Brant, "We'll write a three-page search warrant and run it over to the Hollywood court tomorrow. Have you ever done it?"

"I'm real rusty," he said.

"The provider will triangulate from the cell site towers. If we're real lucky and Doobie D uses his phone, the provider will call us every hour or so to tell us where he is. It's like a GPS on the cell phone. If he disposes of the cell, we're outta luck."

"Are we gonna finally get home to get the rest of our night's sleep, do you think?"

Looking at those green eyes of his, she said, "Is that all you're thinking about, sleep?"

"It's *one* of the things I'm thinking about," he said.

★ SIXTEEN

THE ORACLE SHOWED up at roll call that Thursday evening with a detective whom most of them had seen around the station and a few of the older cops knew by name.

The Oracle said, "Okay, listen up. This is Detective Chernenko. He has a few things to say to you, and it's important."

Viktor stood before them in his usual rumpled suit with food stains on the lapels and said, "Good evening to you. I am investigating the jewelry store two-eleven where your Officer Takara was so very brave. And I also have very much interest in the two-eleven of three days ago at the ATM where the guard was killed. I am thinking that the same two people did both of them and now everybody agrees with me.

"What I wish is that you watch out for anybody who might be stealing from a mailbox. It is a crime very typical of addicts, so you might watch for tweakers who are hanging around the blue mailboxes on the corners of the streets. Especially in the area of Gower south of Hollywood Boulevard. If you find a suspect, look for a device like string and tape that they use to fish in a mailbox. If you find nothing, please write a good FI on the suspect and leave it for me at end-of-watch. Any question?"

Wesley Drubb turned and glanced at Hollywood Nate, who looked sheepish, obviously thinking what Wesley was thinking.

Fausto Gamboa, the old man of the midwatch, said, "Why Gower south of the boulevard, Viktor? Can you share it with us?"

"Yes, it is no big secret, Fausto," Viktor said. "It is a very small clue. I believe that information about the jewels was learned from a letter stolen from a mailbox there on Gower."

Wesley Drubb looked at Hollywood Nate again but couldn't wait to see if Nate was going to admit that they might have lost a lead several days ago. Wesley raised his hand.

The Oracle said, "Yeah, Drubb. Got a question?"

Wesley said, "Last week we got a call about two homeless guys fighting on Hollywood Boulevard. One of them said that a couple weeks before, he saw a guy and a woman stealing mail from a blue mailbox a few blocks south of Hollywood Boulevard on Gower."

That didn't elicit too much excitement in itself but Viktor was mildly interested and said, "Did he provide more details than that?"

Looking at Nate again. "Yes, he did. He said the guy was driving an old blue Pinto. And his partner was a woman. And he heard the woman call him Freddy or Morley."

"Thank you, Officer," Viktor said. "I will check recent FIs for the name of Freddy and the name of Morley, but of course that will not be easy."

The Oracle saw Wesley glance at Hollywood Nate again, and he said to Wesley, "I think you're not through, Drubb. Was there something more?"

"Yes, Sarge," Wesley said. "The homeless guy had a card with the mail thief's license number written on it."

Now Viktor's mouth dropped open. "Fantastic!" he said. "Please present me with this card, Officer!"

Wesley looked sheepish, and being loyal to his partner said, "I'm afraid I gave the card back to him."

Hollywood Nate spoke up then, saying, "I told him to give it back. I figured, what the hell, just some tweakers stealing mail, happens all the time. It was my fault, not Drubb's."

"We're not talking fault here," said the Oracle. "What was the name of the homeless guy with the card? Where can Detective Chernenko find him?"

"They call him Trombone Teddy," Nate said. "We wrote an FI on him and the other homeless geezer who knocked him on his ass. But neither one of them has a real address. They don't live anywhere, guys like that."

The Oracle said to Hollywood Nate, "Weiss, you and Drubb are on a special detail tonight. Don't clear for calls. Just stay off the air and go out there and find Trombone Teddy. Get that license number for Detective Chernenko."

"I'm sorry, Sarge," a chastened Hollywood Nate said.

"Do not feel too badly, Officer," Viktor said. "These suspects are no doubt lying down low for a few days but soon must act. Our balls are in their court."

On very busy nights the midwatch units sometimes compared notes for who would get the BHI prize for Bizarre Hollywood Incident of the evening. Six-X-Thirty-two got an honorable mention for a call to east Hollywood, where an Eighteenth Street gang member was loitering by a liquor store with two other homies. A Lebanese store clerk got scared because the guy obviously was hiding something large under his sweatshirt. In the age of terrorism the clerk was afraid that the Eighteenth Street cruisers might be getting ready to bomb his store because he'd once called the cops on one of their crew who had shoplifted a bottle of gin.

Flotsam and Jetsam were the responders, and they had the three cruisers against the wall of the liquor store, assisted by Hollywood Nate and Wesley Drubb, who were tired of looking for Trombone Teddy. Wesley was thrilled that they'd been close enough to provide cover when gang members were involved.

With flashlights and neon from the store lighting him up, the shortest homie, a head-shaved, tattoo-covered, twenty-one-year-old in baggy walking shorts and an enormous cut-off sweatshirt, was looking over his shoulder at them. The cops liked the homie low-slung baggies because they often fell down and tripped them when they ran from cops. But this cruiser had something huge bulging from his chest.

Flotsam drew his nine and holding it down by

his leg, said, "Okay, homes, turn around and raise up your sweatshirt real slow. Let's see what you're hiding."

When he did, they saw the yellow pages of the Los Angeles telephone directory taped to his chest with elastic wrap.

"What in the hell is that?" Flotsam said.

"It's a phone book," the cruiser said.

"I know it's a phone book. But why do you have it taped to your chest?"

The gangster looked around and said, "An old *veterano* from White Fence is after me, man. You think I'm gonna just stand around and take a bullet without some protection?"

"Bro, do you know what you've done here?" Jetsam said to him. "I think you can take this nationwide. You've just designed an affordable bulletproof vest for the inner city!"

On Saturday, two days after Cosmo and Ilya had hidden the stolen car and the money at the house of Farley Ramsdale, Cosmo decided that they had hidden out as long as they dared. He had phoned Gregori at the junkyard that morning and arranged for one of Gregori's Mexicans to drive the tow truck to Farley's address.

Cosmo insisted that timing was important and that the truck should arrive at 7 P.M.

"Why do you buy an old car that will not operate?" Gregori asked him in Armenian.

"For Ilya. We need two cars," Cosmo said. "I will give you the repair job and pay three hundred dollars for the tow because it is on Saturday evening. Also, I shall tip your driver another fifty if he arrives at precisely seven P.M."

"You are generous," Gregori said. "And when do you return to me the spare key for my yard that I left with Ilya?"

"On Monday morning," Cosmo said. "When I come to see how much repairs the Mazda needs."

"All right, Cosmo," Gregori said. "My driver is named Luís. He speaks pretty good English. He will tow the car to our yard."

"Thank you, my brother," Cosmo said. "I shall see you on Monday."

When he finished his call to Gregori, Ilya, who was lying on the bed smoking and staring at an old MGM musical on TV, said, "So today you do what you do?"

"You wish to hear my plan, Ilya?"

"I know I say do not tell me. I have a change of mind about some things. Now I wish you to tell how you get rid of the car and get our money. Do not tell me more than that."

"Okay, Ilya," he said. "I shall be at the house of Farley at seven o'clock to help truck driver to take away the car. I shall give to truck driver fifty dollars to call me when he get the car to junkyard of Gregori. If he do not call me, I shall know that police have him and stolen car he is towing. Then we take our money and our diamonds and fly to San Francisco and never come back."

She said, "But maybe yesterday or today Farley has found the car or found our money and made call to police and they are there to wait for you."

"If I do not phone you at seven-thirty that all is okay, you take taxi to airport and fly to San Francisco with diamonds. And God bless you. Please have good life. I shall never tell the police nothing about you. Never."

"You take big risk, Cosmo."

"Yes, but I think is okay. I think Farley and Olive do not look in garage or under house. All they look for is drugs. Nothing else."

"How you can be sure that Farley and Olive will not be there at the house when you go there at seven o'clock, Cosmo?"

"Now you ask question you say you not wish to know."

"You are correct. Do not tell me."

The unanswered question had a simple answer. Cosmo was going to phone Farley to arrange a business meeting and then arrive at Farley's at six P.M., carrying a canvas bag. In the bag he would have his gun, a roll of duct tape and a kitchen knife that he had sharpened when Ilya had gone to the liquor store for cigarettes. If Farley and Olive were at home, he would knock, be admitted on the pretext of paying the blackmail money, take them prisoner at gunpoint and tape their wrists and their mouths. Then cut their throats. Just another addict murder, the police would think. Probably a drug deal gone bad.

If for some reason Farley and Olive could not be home at the appointed hour, there was an alternate plan that involved the spare key to the junkyard. They would be lured there tomorrow by a call from Gregori about buying more key cards. Cosmo would ambush them there and dispose of their bodies somewhere in east Los Angeles. Just another addict murder.

As for the car, if the tow driver phoned his cell, telling him that the towing had been accomplished, Cosmo would go to Gregori's junkyard on Monday morning and tell Gregori he'd changed his mind about repairing the car and ask him to crush the Mazda for scrap. For one thousand dollars cash Cosmo was sure that Gregori would ask no questions and do it.

He could not see a flaw in his plan. It was foolproof. He wished that Ilya would permit him to tell her about all of it. She would be impressed by how much thought he had put into it. The only thing that worried him was that Dmitri might be so angry Cosmo hadn't called him that he would think he was being betrayed and maybe send Russian thugs looking for him.

His hands were shaking at 5:15 P.M. while driving to Farley's house. He decided to make the two crucial calls that would possibly decide his fate. The first was to the cell number that Dmitri said was the only one he should use after the job was done.

It rang five times, and then, "Yes."

"Dmitri, it is me."

"I know who," Dmitri said. "I am think-ink that you had run away from me. That will be a stupid think to do."

"No, no, Dmitri. We are being quiet for two, three days."

"Do not tell me more. When do I see you for all of our business? You have thinks for me."

"There is more I must complete, Dmitri. Maybe I come to you tonight."

"I like that," Dmitri said.

"Maybe I must wait for Monday morning."

"I do not like that."

"There are two peoples —"

"Enough!" Dmitri said, interrupting him. "I do not want to hear about your business. If you do not call me tonight, I shall be here on Monday. If I do not see you on Monday, you are very stupid person."

"Thank you, Dmitri," Cosmo said. "I shall be correct in my business with you."

After hanging up, Cosmo made the second crucial call, to Farley Ramsdale's cell number, but got only his voice mail. It was the first time this had ever happened. The addict never slept and was always open for business deals. It staggered him. He would try again in thirty minutes. He still had the alternate plan for Farley and Olive, but this did not bode well. He had all of the killing tools with him and he was ready.

Where in the hell was Olive? She knew they were almost down to their last dollar and had to work the mailboxes or maybe try again to pass some of the bogus money they still had. Or just go to a RadioShack or Best Buy and try to boost a DVD player to sell at the cybercafé. Things were that desperate!

But where was the stupid bitch? All Farley knew was she went out searching the goddamn neighborhood for that crazy Mabel's fucking cat! He was about to go out looking for her, when he got a cell call from Little Bart.

When he recognized the voice he said, "Whadda you want?"

"I felt bad the way things were left between us," Little Bart said.

"So you're calling to say you wanna send me flowers?"

"I wanna do a deal with you."

"What kinda deal?"

"I want you to deliver a couple of brand-new computers to a real nice house on the west side of Laurel Canyon."

"Deliver them how?"

"In your car."

"Why don't you deliver them?"

"I lost my driver's license on a DUI."

"That's the only reason?"

"And I hurt my back and can't carry them."

"They ain't very heavy. Tell you what, how about I deliver in your car?"

"They impounded my car when they popped me."

"Uh-huh. So how much do I get for this delivery?"

"Fifty bucks."

"Good-bye, Bart," Farley said.

"No, wait! A hundred bucks. It'll take you a half hour, tops."

"One fifty."

"Farley, I'm not making much on this. They aren't the very best top-of-the-line computers."

"I don't risk my ass delivering hot computers that you're too chickenshit to deliver for less than one twenty-five."

"Okay, deal."

"When?"

"Can you meet me at Hollywood and Fairfax in twenty minutes? I'll be standing on the corner and I'll walk and you follow me to where you pick up and deliver. The merchandise is in a garage there. Then when you got it, I'll ride with you to the drop-off address."

"Why will you walk to the pickup location instead of riding with me?"

"I can't be anywhere near this pickup. I can't explain."

"And you'll have the money?"

"Half. I'll give you the other half when the job's done."

"Can you make it later? I can't find that goddamn bitch of mine."

"You don't need her."

"Who the hell you think does the heavy lifting?" Farley said. "And she goes in first in case there's anything chancy going on."

"We can't wait for her. Twenty minutes, Farley," Bart said.

Farley looked all over the street but still no Olive. He made a quick stop at Mabel's and found the old witch reading tarot cards in which Olive believed with all her heart.

Farley peered through the rusted screen. "Hey, Mabel, you seen Olive?"

"Yes, she's out looking for Tillie. I think Tillie might be pregnant. She's acting peculiar and roaming around as though she's looking for a nest. She was once a feral cat, you know. I took her in and tamed her."

Farley said, "Yeah, I'm sure you got a Humane Society award. If you see Olive, tell her I had to do a quick job and she should wait for me at home."

"All right, Farley," Mabel said. "It might interest you to know that the cards don't look good for you," she added. "Maybe you should stay home too."

She heard him mumble "Crazy old bitch" when he left her porch.

Olive was in the backyard of a neighbor six houses away, looking for Tillie and chatting with the neighbor about the beautiful white camellias that bordered her property. And Olive just loved the pink and white azaleas that climbed the fence. Olive told her that someday she hoped to have a garden. The woman offered to teach Olive the basics and to get her started with the proper seeds and a few young plants.

Olive thought she heard Farley's Corolla, excused herself, and running to the street saw his taillights at the stop sign. She yelled but he didn't hear her and was gone. Olive then went home, hoping he wasn't mad at her.

There he was on the northeast corner of Hollywood and Fairfax, jumping around like he had to take a leak. Or had to score some tweak, more likely, Farley figured. He didn't like any part of this. Little Bart couldn't drive because he had no license? When did that ever stop a tweaker from driving? He couldn't carry a computer because his back hurt? He couldn't ride in Farley's car to the garage where the computers were? What was this shit all about?

Little Bart walked over to his car and said, "Just follow me real slow for half a block. When I get to the house, I'll point with my finger behind my back. Then you drive into the driveway and go to the garage. The door will open manually. Get the computers and pick me up two blocks north."

While he was driving slowly behind Bart, he missed Olive more than he had in the eighteen months they'd been together. This was a very bad deal. Bart was scared to pick up the merchandise, which meant that Bart didn't trust the thief who'd stolen the computers, or the fence who'd hired Bart to deliver them.

If Olive were here, there'd be no problem. He'd drop her off at the pickup address and let her go into the garage and check it out. If the cops were there and grabbed her, he'd just keep on moving down the road. If there was one thing he was sure of, Olive would never rat him out. She'd take the hit and do the time if she had to and come to him when she got out of jail, just as though nothing had happened.

But Olive wasn't here. And that fucking Little Bart was pointing at a house, a modest one for this neighborhood. Then Bart kept walking north. Farley parked across from the house and looked at the garage.

The house wasn't unlike his own. It was in that ubiquitous California style that everyone calls Spanish, which means nothing other than tile roof and stucco walls. The longer he looked at it, the worse he felt about the whole arrangement.

Farley got out of the car and walked across the street to the house. He went to the front door and rang the bell. When he got no answer, he went to the side door, which was only forty feet from the garage, banged on the door, and yelled, "Olive, you there? Hellooooo? Olive?"

It was then that two Hollywood Division detectives came out of the garage, badged him, put him against the wall, patted him down, and then dragged him back into the garage. There was nothing in the garage except a workbench, some tools and tires, and two boxes containing new computers.

"What is this?" he said.

"You tell us," the older detective said.

"My girlfriend, Olive, went to lunch with a pal of hers and gave me the pal's address. This is it."

"Right," the younger detective said. "What've you been in jail for?"

"Petty kid stuff is all," Farley said. "What's this all about?"

"You been busted for burglary?"

"No."

"Receiving?"

"Receiving what?

"Don't fuck with us. Receiving stolen property."

"No, just kid stuff. Drug possession. Petty theft a couple times."

"Are you going to use the S-O-D-D-I defense?"

"What's that?"

"Some other dude did it."

"I'm innocent!" Farley cried.

"Well, partner," the younger detective said to the other. "Let's take kid stuff here to the station. Looks like our surprise party is blown."

"Hey, man," Farley said, "I musta wrote down the wrong address is all. My girlfriend Olive's gonna be looking for me. If you'll let me call her, she'll tell you."

"Turn around, kid stuff," the older detective said. "Put your hands behind your back."

After they handcuffed Farley, they led him out to the street, where a detective car drove up from wherever it had been hidden. Then they searched his Corolla, but of course it was clean. There wasn't even a roach in the ashtray.

When they got to the station, Farley saw some movie posters on a wall. What the fuck kind of police station has movie posters on the wall? Farley thought. And how did he get in this horror flick? All he knew was, if he'd had Olive with him, he wouldn't be here. That dumb bitch just got his ass busted!

It was after five o'clock and Farley hadn't come home and hadn't called. Olive was tired and she was very hungry. She remembered what Mabel had said about saving some food for her. She wondered if Mabel might let her help cook the meal. She'd like that, and getting to eat and chat with Mabel.

When she got to Mabel's the old woman was delighted to see her.

"I'm sorry, Mabel," she said. "I can't find Tillie."

"Don't worry, dear," Mabel said. "She'll turn up.

She always does. She's still a bit of a wild thing. Tillie's got a touch of Gypsy in her soul."

"Would you like me to help you cook?"

"Oh, yes," Mabel said. "If you'll promise to stay and have supper with me."

"Thank you, Mabel," Olive said. "I'll be real happy to join you for supper."

"Then we'll play gin. If you don't know how, never mind, I'll teach you. I know all about cards. Did I ever tell you I used to make good money telling fortunes with cards? That was sixty-five years ago."

"Really?"

"Really. There are certain legal technicalities about foretelling the future that I didn't follow. I was arrested twice and taken to Hollywood Station for ignoring those silly technicalities."

"You, arrested?" Olive couldn't imagine it.

"Oh, yes," Mabel said. "I was a bit of a naughty girl in my time. The old police station was a lovely building constructed in nineteen thirteen, the year my parents got married. When I was born, they named me for the silent-screen star Mabel Normand. I never had any siblings. You know, I used to date a policeman from Hollywood Station. He was the one who arrested me the second time and persuaded me to stop telling fortunes for money. He was killed in the war. One week after D-day."

Loving Mabel's stories and gossip about the old days in Hollywood, Olive hated to interrupt her, but she thought about Farley and said, "Mabel, let me run home and leave a note for Farley so he'll know where I'm at. Be right back!"

"Hurry, dear," Mabel said. "I'll tell you lots of tales about life in the golden age of Hollywood. And we'll play cards. This is going to be such fun!"

★ SEVENTEEN

COSMO BETROSSIAN CURSED the traffic. He cursed Los Angeles for being the most car-dependent, traffic-choked city in the world. He cursed the Georgian bartender who gave him the stolen car that almost got him captured. But most of all he cursed Farley Ramsdale and his stupid woman. He sat in traffic on East Sunset Boulevard looking at all of the signs around him in the languages of the Far East, and he cursed them too.

Then he heard the siren and for a few seconds it terrified him until he saw an ambulance weaving through traffic on the wrong side of Sunset, obviously trying to get to the traffic accident that had him gridlocked. Glancing repeatedly at his Rolex knockoff, he cursed.

First, they left him in an interrogation room for what seemed like an hour, only letting him go to

446

the bathroom once and then watching him piss, just like the goddamn probation officer who used to make him piss in a bottle twice a month. With no sympathy for the fact that it was hard to piss with someone watching to make sure you piss from your own dick and not from a bottle of clean piss stashed in your underwear.

Then one of the two detectives came in and gave him a bad-cop interrogation about a god-damn warehouse burglary of electronic equipment that he knew nothing about. Then the other detective played good cop and came in and gave him a cup of coffee. Then the bad cop took over and played the game all over again until Farley's hands were shaking and his pulse was vibrating.

Farley knew they didn't buy the wrong-address story, but he stuck with it. And he was pretty sure they were starting to think he hadn't been involved in the warehouse burglary but was just some tweaker with exactly $3.65 in his pocket, hired only to pick up and deliver.

He would have given up Little Bart instantly if he thought it would help him, but something in good cop's tone last time around told him he was going to be released. Except that bad cop came in and walked him to a holding tank with a wooden bench, where they locked him in. And every cop walking by could look through the big glass window and gawk at him like he was a fucking spider monkey at the Griffith Park zoo.

When Watch 5 left roll call at 6 P.M., several of them passed by the holding tank and did gawk at him.

"Hey, Benny," B.M. Driscoll said to his partner. "Is that the tweaker we wrote the ticket to?"

"Yeah," Benny Brewster said. Then he tapped on the glass and said to Farley, "What happened, man? They catch you selling ice?"

"Fuck you," Farley mumbled, and when Benny laughed and walked away, Farley growled, "You're the one oughtta be in a zoo with the rest of the silverbacks, you fucking ape."

Budgie and Fausto saw Benny talking to someone in the holding tank, and Budgie looked in and said, "Fausto, that's the guy we FI'd at the taco stand."

Fausto looked at Farley and said, "Oh yeah, the tweaker with the skinny girlfriend. Bet they got him doing a deal at Pablo's. They never learn, they never change."

When Hollywood Nate and Wesley walked past the holding tank, Nate heard Fausto's remark, took a look inside, and said, "Shit, everyone knows that dude. Hey, Wesley, check this out."

Wesley looked in and said, "Oh yeah. That's what's-his-name — Rimsdale? No, Ramsdale."

"Farley," Nate said. "Like the old movie star Farley Granger."

"Who?" Wesley said.

"Never mind," Nate said. "Let's go look for Trombone Teddy. We gotta find him or I'll have stress dreams tonight about chasing an old geezer who keeps holding me off with the slide of his gold trombone."

"Do you really have dreams like that?"

"No," Nate said, "but it would make a good dream sequence in a screenplay, don't you think?"

One of the sergeants on Watch 2 was a forty-year-old black woman, Wilma Collins. She had a good reputation with the troops but had a persistent weight problem that the coppers at Hollywood Station joked about. She wasn't actually obese but they called her a "leather stretcher." Her Sam Browne had a lot to hold in place.

Everyone knew that a few hours before end-of-watch, Sergeant Collins liked to sneak into

IHOP and load up on buttermilk pancakes swimming in butter, with sausages and fried eggs and butter-drenched biscuits. They made lots of cholesterol and clogged-arteries jokes about Sergeant Collins.

When the surfer team were loading their war bags and getting ready to hit the streets, the entire parking lot and the watch commander's office suddenly erupted. Some of those who heard it had to sit for a moment until they could gain control. It became a Hollywood Station moment.

It seems that Sergeant Collins had left her rover behind on the counter at IHOP, because a message was sent on the Hollywood frequency by a Mexican busboy who had keyed the mike and talked into the rover.

The busboy said, "Hello, hello! Chubby black police lady? Hello, hello! You leave radio here! Hello! Chubby black lady? You there, please? Hello, hello!"

Hollywood Nate and Wesley Drubb didn't say much to each other when they left roll call. Nate was driving and Wesley had never seen him so intent on watching the street.

At last Wesley said, "I had to mention Trombone Teddy at roll call."

"I know you did," Nate said. "The real mistake I made was I shoulda told you to take Teddy's license number and at least write the info on the FI card."

"I shoulda done that on my own," Wesley said.

"You're barely off probation," Nate said. "You're still in the yessir boot-mode. It was my fault."

"We'll find Teddy," Wesley said.

"I hope he still has the card," Nate said. Then, "Hey, it was a business card, right? What was the business?"

"A Chinese restaurant. Ching or Chan, something like that."

"House of Chang?"

"Yeah, that was it!"

"Okay, let's pay them a visit."

The tow truck was parked in front of Farley Ramsdale's house and the Mexican driver was knocking on the door when Cosmo Betrossian came squealing down the street in his old Cadillac. The traffic had disrupted everything.

He got out and ran toward the porch, saying to the driver, "I am friend of Gregori. I am the one."

"Nobody home here," the Mexican said.

"Is not important," Cosmo said. "Come. Let us get the car."

He ran to the garage, opened the termite-eaten door, and was relieved to see that the garage was just as he'd left it.

"Let us push it out to the street," Cosmo said. "We must work fast. I have important business."

The Mexican and Cosmo easily pushed the car back down the driveway, Cosmo jumping in to steer after they got it going. The driver knew his job and in a few minutes had the Mazda hooked up and winched. It was all that Cosmo could do to keep from running back up the driveway and snatching the big can full of money from under the house.

Before he got in the truck to drive away, the driver said to Cosmo, "I call you in thirty minute?"

"No, I need more time. Call me in one hour. Traffic very bad tonight. I give you time to get to the yard of Gregori. Then you call, okay?"

"Okay," the Mexican said, waiting for the promised bonus.

Cosmo opened his wallet and gave the driver fifty dollars and said, "Put it back where junk cars go. Okay?"

As soon as the truck was halfway down the

block, Cosmo went to the trunk of the Cadillac and removed the bag of killing tools. He was going to wait at least an hour for them to show up.

He walked quickly back up the driveway to the rear yard of the house and was shocked to see the little access panel hanging open. He dropped the bag and threw himself onto the dirt, crawling under the house. The can of money was gone!

Cosmo screamed an Armenian curse, got up, took the gun from the bag, and ran to the back porch. He didn't even bother slipping the lock with his credit card like last time. He kicked the flimsy door open and ran inside, prepared to kill anybody in the house after he tortured the truth out of them.

There was no one. He saw a note on the kitchen table in a childish scrawl. It said, "Gone to eat with Mabel. Will bring delishus supper for you."

His alternate plan to lure them to Gregori's junkyard, where they could easily be killed, was finished. They had his money. They would never go near him now except to collect the blackmail money from the diamond robbery. They would ask for even more now that they knew about the ATM robbery and the murder of the guard. They must have discovered the Mazda too. Farley had stolen their money, and he would want more money to keep his mouth shut about everything.

Maybe all he could do was give the diamonds to Farley. Give him everything and tell him to do the deal with Dmitri himself. Then beg Dmitri to kill both addicts after they were forced to tell where the money was, and beg Dmitri to be fair with the money split even though so many things had gone wrong. After all, if Dmitri's Georgian bartender hadn't given him a stolen car that could barely run, this would not have happened.

Or maybe he should just go home and get Ilya and the diamonds and head for the airport. It was too much for him to work out. He needed Ilya. She was a very smart Russian and he was far out of his depth. He would do whatever she wanted him to do.

Cosmo took his killing bag and went out to his car. He had never been so demoralized in his life. If the Cadillac failed to start, he would just take the pistol from the bag and shoot himself. But it started and he drove home to Ilya. When he was only two blocks from their apartment his cell rang.

He answered and the driver's voice said, "Mister, I am at Gregori's with the car. No problem. Everything okay."

The stolen car was okay, but of course everything else was far from okay.

At 7:15 P.M. Farley was released from the holding tank and told that he was free to go.

Bad cop said to him, "We know you're connected to those computers, but right now we're gonna let you walk. I suspect you'll see us again."

"Speaking of walk," Farley said. "My car's there where you grabbed me. How about a ride back up there?"

"You got a lotta 'tude, dude," bad cop said. "We're not running a taxi service."

"Man, you hassle me, you keep me here for hours when I ain't done nothing wrong. The least you can do is take me back to my car."

The Oracle heard the bitching and came out of the sergeant's office, saying to Farley, "Where do you need to go?"

Farley looked at the old sergeant and said, "Fairfax, just north of Hollywood Boulevard."

The Oracle said, "I'm going out now. I'll give you a lift."

Fifteen minutes later, when the Oracle dropped him at his car, Farley said, "Thanks a lot, Sergeant. You're okay."

The Oracle offered the Hollywood mantra: "Stay real, Farley. Stay real." But he knew that this tweaker would not. Who in Hollywood ever did?

"Teddy?" Mrs. Chang said when Hollywood Nate had a Latino busboy call her from the kitchen. "He eat here?"

"He's a bum," Nate said.

"Bum?" she said, grappling with the English meaning.

"Homeless," Wesley said. "Street person."

"Oh, street person," she said. "Him I know. Teddy. Yes."

"Does he come here?"

"Sometime he come to back door," Mrs. Chang said. "Come at maybe seven o'clock, sometime later. And we give him food we got to throw away. Teddy. Yes. He sit in kitchen and eat. Nice man. Quiet. We feel sorry."

"When did you last see him?" Wesley asked.

"Tuesday night maybe. Hard to remember."

Nate began writing in his notebook and said,

"When he comes again, I want you to call this number. Ask that Six-X-Seventy-two come right away. I've written it down for you. We don't want to arrest him. We just have to talk to him. Understand?"

"Yes, I call."

The house was dark when Farley got home, and the garage door was open. Why would Olive go in the garage? There was nothing in there but junk.

He unlocked the front door and entered, yelling, "Olive! You here?"

She was not, and he went into the kitchen to see if there was any orange juice left and found the back door kicked open!

"Son of a bitch!" he said.

This was the first time that burglars had struck his house, although several houses on the block had been hit by daytime thieves in the past two years. But the TV was still there. He went into the bedroom and saw that the radio-CD player was still there. Nobody had ransacked the bedroom drawers. This wasn't like house breakers. It wasn't the way he worked when he himself was a daytime burglar fifteen years ago.

Then he saw the note on the kitchen table.

Mabel. He should have known. The fucking old ghost probably was reading tarot cards for Olive and time had gotten away from the skinny moron. He went into the bedroom to strip down and take a shower and then he saw that something was different. The closet was half empty. All of Olive's clothes were missing, including the jacket he'd shoplifted for her Christmas present. He opened the drawer and saw that her underwear and socks were gone too. She'd bailed on him!

The note. He ran out the front door and across the street to Mabel's. It was such a warm evening that her door was open, and he could see that the TV was on. He put his hands up to the screen door to peer inside and said, "Mabel!"

The old woman shuffled in from the back bedroom of the cottage, wearing pajamas, a bathrobe, and fuzzy slippers, and said, "Farley? What're you doing here?"

"Do you know where Olive is?"

"Why, no."

"She left a note saying she was having supper with you."

"Yes, she did. And Olive found Tillie under your house where she'd made a nice little den for herself. Tillie's in my bedroom now, the

little brat. I never have completely domesticated
her."

"Did Olive say where she was going when she
left?"

"Yes, home."

Farley had to sit down and ponder that when
he got back to the house. Everything was going
wrong lately. His entire world was upside down.
Without a dollar to her name, that toothless
fucking scarecrow had abandoned his ass! This
was impossible! That imbecile Olive Oyl had actually dumped Farley Ramsdale, who'd given her
everything!

This time it was Cosmo who was lying on the
bed trying to quell a throbbing headache. He
had quickly briefed Ilya on what had happened
and then fell on his knees beside her chair and
kissed her hands.

He is beaten, Ilya thought. Cosmo is crying for
Mommy. He would never strike her again.

Ilya prepared her third glass of hot tea and lit
a cigarette with the butt of the last and finally
said, "Cosmo, all is a fuckup."

"Yes, Ilya," he murmured painfully.

"I think we must pack the suitcase and make
ready to fly away."

"Yes, Ilya," Cosmo said. "What you say, I do."

"On other hand," she said, looking from one palm to the other for emphasis, "we do not know for absolute truth that Farley has our money."

"Ilya, please!" Cosmo said. "The money is gone. Farley is gone. I cannot get to Farley with cell. Farley always have cell with him. He is addict. Addict must have cell."

"One way we find out," she said. "Sit up, Cosmo!"

He obeyed instantly.

"Call Farley. Go with plan. Tell him Gregori need key cards. Many more. Will pay top money. Let us hear what he shall say."

Cosmo's head was aching too much for this but it was impossible not to obey her. He felt as though he was back in Soviet Armenia and the Comrade Chairman himself had spoken. He was afraid of her now. He dialed.

"Hello!" Farley yelled into his cell.

Cosmo was stunned. He couldn't speak for a moment and Farley said, "Olive? Is that you?"

Looking at Ilya, Cosmo said, "Is me, Farley."

"Cosmo?" Farley said. "I thought it was Olive. That fucking tweaker has up and disappeared!"

"Olive?" Cosmo said. "Gone?"

He saw the wry smile turn up the corners of

Ilya's mouth, and he said, "You know where she go to?"

"No," Farley said. "The cunt. I ain't got a clue."

Ilya was mouthing the words "Ask him," and Cosmo said, "I very sorry, Farley. You know Gregori? He need more cards right away."

"Key cards? Cosmo, you forgot that you and me got a little business deal coming up? You think I'm gonna keep waiting? You think I'm gonna fuck around with key cards?"

"Please, Farley," Cosmo said. "Do this for me. I owe big favor to Gregori. Just drop off cards at his junkyard tonight. He work to midnight. He will give you fast hundred fifty. You buy crystal."

The word "crystal" struck a chord with Farley. He wanted to smoke ice more than he'd ever wanted anything in his life. This was the kind of deal where he desperately needed Olive. If she were here, he'd drive her over there to the junkyard and send her in. If Cosmo had a plan to waste them, he'd have to settle for Olive. Goddamn her!

"I only got about ten of the primo cards left," Farley said.

"Is enough," Cosmo said. "Gregori got a bunch new worker who must have driving license.

Gregori so cheap his old worker not stay long. Always new worker."

"Is that dog in the yard?"

"I tell Gregori to tie up dog. No problem."

"You tell Gregori to call me. If he says come, I come. He ain't a violent type. He's a business-man. You I ain't so sure about."

"Okay, I call Gregori now," Cosmo said. "And if he say come?"

"Then I'll be there at nine o'clock. Tell Gregori to put the money in a bag and stick the bag between the links of the gate. If the money's there, I'll drive in and give him the cards."

"Okay, Farley," Cosmo said. Then he added, "Call me if Olive come home."

"Why?"

"I think I got good job for her."

"You better have my big bucks this weekend, Cosmo," Farley said. "Let me worry about Olive if she comes home."

When Cosmo closed the cell, Ilya took a great puff from her cigarette, sucked it into her lungs, and with her words enveloped in smoke clouds said, "If he go to junkyard tonight, he don't know nothing about ATM robbery."

"But I shall kill him anyways. The diamond blackmail shall end."

"Blackmail still there, Cosmo. Olive has our money and Olive know all about both our jobs. Olive is full of danger for us. Not Farley so much."

"But I shall kill him anyways?"

"Yes, he must die. Olive may give up the blackmail. She got lot of money now. She buy lot of drugs and die happy in two, three years."

"Our money," he said.

"Yes, Cosmo. She got our money, I think so. Call Gregori now. Say again and make him to believe you only scare Farley to pay a debt he owe you. Tell Gregori you will pay money for the Mazda on Monday."

Before phoning Gregori, Cosmo said, "Ilya, you tell me. When Gregori come to bring key to junkyard, you fuck him. No?"

"Of course, Cosmo," she said. "Why?"

"If he getting scared about Farley, scared about Mazda that I want to crush to scrap, is okay if I tell him you wish to make him glass of tea one more time? To make him calm?"

"Of course, Cosmo," she said. "My tea is best in all of Hollywood. Ask Gregori. Ask anybody who taste my tea."

Six-X-Seventy-two got the call twenty minutes after they'd left the House of Chang. Hollywood

Nate spun a U-ee and floored it. He craved redemption.

When they got back to the restaurant, Mrs. Chang tossed her head in the direction of the kitchen. And there they found Trombone Teddy sitting at the chopping block by the back door, happily scarfing down a huge bowl of pan-fried noodles.

"Teddy," Nate said. "Remember us?"

"I ain't causing no trouble," he said. "They invited me in here."

"Nobody says you're causing trouble," Nate said. "A couple questions and you can sit and enjoy your noodles."

Wesley said, "Remember the fight you had on the boulevard? We're the officers that got the call. You gave me a card with a license number on it. Remember?"

"Oh yeah!" Teddy said, a noodle plastered to his beard. "That son of a bitch sucker-punched me."

"That's the night," Nate said. "Do you still have the card? With the license number?"

"Sure," Teddy said. "But nobody wants it."

"We want it now," Wesley said.

Trombone Teddy put down his fork and searched inside his third layer of shirts, dug into a pocket with grimy fingers, and pulled out the House of Chang business card.

Wesley took it, looked at the license number, and nodded to Nate, who said, "Teddy, what kind of car was it that the mail thief was driving?"

"An old blue Pinto," Teddy said. "Like I wrote down on the card."

"And what did the guy look like?"

"I can't remember no more," Teddy said. "A white guy. Maybe thirty. Maybe forty. Nasty mouth. Insulted me. That's why I wrote down the license number."

"And his companion?" Wesley said.

"A woman. That's all I can remember."

"Would you recognize either of them if you saw them again?" Nate said.

"No, they was just dark shadows. He was just a dark shadow with a nasty mouth."

"Tell us again what she called him," Wesley said.

"I don't remember," Teddy said.

"You told me Freddy," Wesley said.

"Did I?"

"Or Morley?"

"If you say so. But it don't ring a bell now."

"Have you seen them either before or after that?"

"Yeah, I saw them try to hustle a clerk in a store."

"When?"

"A few days after he insulted me."

"What store?"

"Coulda been like a Target store. Or maybe it was RadioShack. Or like a Best Buy store. I can't remember. I get around."

"At least," Nate said, "you got another good look at them, right?"

"Yeah, but I still can't remember what they look like. They're white people. Maybe thirty years old. Or forty. But they could be fifty. I can't tell ages no more. You can check with the guy at the store. He gave me a ten-buck reward for telling him they were crooks. They had a bogus credit card. Or bogus money. Something like that."

"Jesus," Nate said, looking at Wesley in frustration.

Wesley said, "If we can find the store and find the guy who saw them, at least you can say that they're the same two people who stole from the mailbox, isn't that right?"

"He stole from the mailbox," Teddy said. "She didn't. I got a feeling she's okay. He's a total asshole."

Wesley said, "If the detectives need to talk to you, where can they find you?"

"There's an old empty office building on that street on the east side of Hollywood Cemetery. I'm living there for now. But I come here a few nights a week for supper."

"Can you remember anything else?" Hollywood Nate said, taking a ten-dollar bill from his wallet and putting it on the chopping block.

"Hell, half the time I can't remember what day it is," Teddy said. Then he looked at them and said, "What day is it, anyways?"

Viktor Chernenko was known for working late, especially with his obsession to solve the jewelry store robbery and the ATM robbery-murder, and most of the veteran cops from Hollywood Station were aware of it. Nate knew it and was busting stop signs and speeding to the station faster than he'd driven to the House of Chang.

They ran into the detective squad room and were overjoyed to see Viktor still there, typing on his computer keyboard.

"Viktor," Nate said. "Here it is!"

Viktor looked at the business card, at the license number and the words "blue Pinto" written on it, and he said, "My mail thief?"

★   ★   ★

Since he had been on the initial callout, Brant worked all day in southeast L.A. with Andi on the Gulag homicide. Doobie D, whom they had identified through data received from his cell provider, was Latelle Granville, a twenty-four-year-old member of the Crips with an extensive record for drug sales and weapons violations. He had begun using his cell in the afternoon.

With a team of detectives from Southeast Division assisting, the cell towers eventually triangulated him to the vicinity of a residence on 103rd Street known to be the family home of a Crips cruiser named Delbert Minton. He had a far more extensive record than Latelle Granville and turned out to be the Crip who had been fighting with the slain student. Both were arrested at Minton's without incident and taken back to Hollywood Station for interview and booking. Both Crips refused to speak and demanded to call their lawyers.

It had been a very long day, and the detectives were hungry and tired from working well into an overtime evening. Then Andi returned a phone call from a cocktail waitress, one of the people she'd interviewed at the Gulag on the night of the murder. At that time, the waitress, Angela Hawthorn, had told Andi she was at the service bar fetching drinks when the fight broke out and had seen nothing. So why was she calling now? Andi wondered.

"This is Detective McCrea," Andi said when the woman answered her cell.

"Hello," Angela Hawthorn said. "I'm at home. I don't work at the Gulag anymore. Dmitri fired me because I wouldn't put out for one of his rich Russian customers. I have some information that might help you."

"I'm listening," Andi said.

"Up in the corner of the building by the window to Dmitri's office there's a video camera that sees everything on the smoking patio. During the party I'm pretty sure it was there like it always is. But when you showed up it wasn't there. Dmitri probably took it down so you wouldn't see it."

"Why would he do that?"

"He's paranoid about bad publicity and cops and courtrooms. And he doesn't want trouble with black hoodlums. In fact, he doesn't want black customers. He just wouldn't want to be involved in your murder case. Anyways, if you get that camera from him I'll bet you'll see that black guy sticking the knife in that kid. Just keep my name out of it, okay?"

When Andi hung up, she said to Brant, "Do you need money?"

"Why?"

"You're going to be getting even more overtime. There might be video at the Gulag with our murder shown right there on it!"

Brant looked around, but all the other detectives had gone home. Only the night-watch detective Compassionate Charlie was there, with his feet up on the desk, sucking his teeth as usual, reading the *L.A. Times* sports page.

"I'm all you got?" he said.

"Don't be a wuss. This is more fun than being an IA weasel, isn't it?"

"I don't know," he said. "I'm starting to miss the Burn Squad. At least I got fed every once in a while."

"When we're all through tonight, I'm making you a very late supper with a bottle of good Pinot I've been saving. How's that sound?"

"Suddenly I'm renewed," he said.

"One thing, though," Andi said. "I think I should call Viktor. We might find a Russian translator very useful if this nightclub owner starts lyin' and denyin' like he probably will. Viktor is a master at handling those people, a kick-ass skill he learned in the bad old days with the Red Army."

"He's just getting home by now," Brant said. "He won't be pleased."

"He owes me," Andi said. "Didn't I do a dumpster dive for him? Didn't it cost me a busted bra strap?"

Eavesdropping as usual, Compassionate Charlie said, "Hey, you guys looking for Viktor? He left in a hell of a hurry with Hollywood Nate and that big kid Nate works with. I love to watch Viktor run. Like a bear on roller skates."

EIGHTEEN

THE BLUE PINTO was registered to a Samuel R. Culhane who lived on Winona Boulevard. Viktor Chernenko was sitting in the backseat of the black-and-white, concerned about whiplash with Hollywood Nate still driving in his high-speed redemption mode.

Wesley said to Viktor, "You know, Detective, the only problem here is that the first time we talked to Trombone Teddy he said the guy's name sounded like Freddy or Morley."

"Maybe Samuel sold the car to a Freddy," Nate said. "Stay positive."

"Or lent the car to Morley," Viktor added.

The house was almost a duplicate of Farley Ramsdale's old Hollywood bungalow except it was in good repair and had a small lawn in front with geraniums along the side of the house and a bed of petunias by the front porch.

Wesley ran to the rear of the house to prevent escape. It was dusk, and he didn't need a flashlight yet. He took cover behind the garage and waited.

Viktor took the lead and knocked, with Nate standing to his left.

Samuel R. Culhane wasn't as thin as Farley but he was in a late stage of methamphetamine addiction. He had pustules on his face and a permanent twitch at the corner of his right eye. He was several years older than Farley and balding, with a bad comb-over. And though he couldn't see Hollywood Nate standing beside the guy at the door, he knew instantly that Viktor was a cop.

"Yeah?" he said cautiously.

Viktor showed his badge and said, "We need to talk to you."

"Come back with a warrant," Samuel Culhane said and started to close the door, but Viktor stopped it with his foot and Nate pushed past and into the room, touching the badge pinned to his shirt, saying, "This is a brass pass, dude."

When the back door opened and Nate whistled to him, Wesley entered and saw the tweaker sitting on the couch in the living room looking glum. Viktor was formally reading the guy his rights from a card that every cop, including Viktor, had memorized.

Nate handed Samuel Culhane's driver's license to his partner and said, "Run him, Wesley."

After Viktor had finished with the rights advisement, he said to the unhappy homeowner, "You are not pleased to see us?"

"Look," Samuel Culhane said, "you ain't searching my house without a warrant, but I'll talk to you long enough to find out what the hell this is all about."

"We must find out where you were on a certain night."

"What night?"

"Three weeks ago. You were driving your Pinto with a lady friend, no?"

"Hah!" Samuel Culhane said. "Driving with a lady friend? No! I'm gay, dude. Gayer than springtime. You got the wrong guy."

Persisting, Viktor said, "You were driving on Gower south of Hollywood Boulevard that evening."

"And who says so?"

"You were seen."

"Bullshit. I got no reason to drive down Gower in the evening. In fact, I don't even go out till around midnight. I'm a night person, man."

"There was a woman in your car," Viktor said.

"I told you I'm gay! Do I gotta blow you to prove it? Wait a minute, what crime was I supposed to've done?"

"You were seen at a mailbox."

"A mailbox?" he said. "Oh, man, now I get it. You're gonna try to fuck me with a mail theft."

Wesley came in then and handed an FI card to Viktor on which he'd scribbled some of Samuel R. Culhane's rap sheet entries.

Reading, Viktor said, "You have been arrested for fraud . . . one, two times. Once for counterfeiting. This is, as they say, consistent with the theft of U.S. mail from a public mailbox."

"Okay, fuck this," Samuel Culhane said. "I ain't spending a night in jail till you guys get your shit together and figure out you got the wrong guy. I'll come right out and tell you what's what if you'll go away and leave me be."

"Proceed," Viktor said.

"I rented my Pinto for a week to a guy I know. I got another car. He lives down there off Gower with an idiot tweaker who calls herself his wife but they ain't married. I warned them both, don't fuck around and do any deals in my Pinto. They didn't listen to me, did they? I'll show you where he lives. His name's Farley Ramsdale."

Hollywood Nate and Wesley Drubb looked at each other and said it simultaneously and with such gusto that it startled not only Samuel Culhane but Viktor Chernenko as well.

"Farley!"

That goddamn Olive, she never puts anything in its proper place. Farley was still thinking of Olive in the present tense although he knew in his heart that she was in the past. He had to admit there were things he was going to miss. She was like those Bedouin women who walk through minefields while the old man stays fifty yards behind on the donkey and follows in her footsteps. Never less than obedient. Until now.

Finally he found the key cards in the bottom drawer of the kitchen together with the egg timer she'd never used and a badly burned skillet that she did use. They were the best key cards they'd ever stolen, and they had always fetched a good price. Just the right size and color, with just the right mag code to look exactly like a righteous California driver's license once they slapped the bogus facsimile on the front. He was going to have to find another woman partner to hang around that particular hotel and get more of them. Maybe a halfway classy woman who would never arouse suspicion. He tried to think of a halfway classy woman he might know but gave up trying immediately.

Of course he knew that the junkyard rendezvous was very dangerous and might be a trick of Cosmo's to kill them, but after he'd told Cosmo that Olive had boogied and Cosmo still wanted him to make delivery, he figured it was probably okay. That fucking Armo wouldn't dare try to kill him with Olive out there able to dime him to the cops if Farley went missing. Would he?

He might. Farley had never dealt with anyone as violent as Cosmo, so that's why he'd devised a little plan of his own. Sure, he was going to drive to that lonely junkyard on that lonely fucking road in east L.A., where no white man in his right mind would roam around at night. But he wasn't stepping one toe out of his car, no way. He was going to drive up, wrong side of the road to that fence, reach out, and grab the paper bag. And if the money was in there, he'd pull into the yard, spin a sweeping U-turn, blow his horn until Gregori came out, toss him the paper bag with the key cards in it, and zip on out of that yard and back to white man's country — if Hollywood could be called white man's country these days.

And if there wasn't a trap at all and Gregori got insulted by his method of delivery and threatened not to do business with him anymore, too fucking bad. Gregori shouldn't hang with gun-packing Armos like Cosmo. He should stick with thieving, chiseling, blood-sucking Armos like himself. Yeah, Farley thought with waxing confidence as he fantasized about the glass he'd be smoking tonight, where's the glitch in *that* plan?

Suddenly he was hungry from all that thinking, but he couldn't bear the thought of a cheese sandwich. He had a yearning for Ruby's doughnuts, especially for a couple of those big fat cream-filled, chocolate-covered specials. He found the emergency twenty-dollar bill he had stashed in his underwear drawer, where Olive would never look, then propped up the broken back door as best he could and left for Ruby's. Like Pablo's Tacos and the cybercafé, Ruby's Donuts was one of the last stops on the Tweakerville Line.

He saw a couple of tweakers he knew in the parking lot, looking hungry but not for doughnuts. Come to think of it, this was the first time he'd ever gone to Ruby's looking for something to put in his stomach. The Hollywood nights were growing more and more strange and weird and scary for Farley Ramsdale, and he couldn't seem to stop it from happening.

They didn't really need Samuel R. Culhane to lead them to Farley's house. A call took care of that. The FI file was full of shakes involving Farley Ramsdale and Olive O. Ramsdale, and it also had their correct address as shown on his driver's license. Like other tweakers, they were always getting stopped and FI'd. But Viktor pretended that Culhane's presence was needed just to be sure that if left alone, he wouldn't make a warning call to Farley.

Driving his Pinto, Samuel R. Culhane did as he was told and led 6-X-72 and Viktor Chernenko to Farley's house, where he slowed and indicated the house with his left-turn signal. Then he took off for home while the cops parked and piled out of the black-and-white, approaching the house with their flashlights off.

As before, Wesley went to cover the back door. He found it partially ajar, one hinge hanging loose, and propped in place by a kitchen chair. Nate and Viktor got no response and there were no lights on in the house. Wesley checked the empty garage.

"He's a typical tweaker," Nate said to Viktor. "Out hunting for crystal. When he finds it he'll come home."

"I must arrange for a stakeout," Viktor said. "I feel very strong that this Farley Ramsdale stole the letter from the mailbox that led to the jewel robbery. Yet it is only a feeling. But I am positive that the jewel robbers are the ATM killers. This shall be the biggest case of my career if I can prove that I am correct."

"This could be one for the TV news and the *L.A. Times,*" Hollywood Nate said.

"It is more than possible," Viktor said.

Hollywood Nate paused for a moment and only one word came to him: "publicity." He thought about walking into a casting office with a *Times* under his arm. Maybe with his picture in it.

"Viktor," he said, "since we've been in on this with you so far, how about calling us if the guy shows up? We'd be glad to transport for you or help you search for evidence — whatever. We were there during the grenade trick and we sorta feel like this is our case too."

"Detective," Wesley added. "This could be the biggest thing I've ever accomplished in my whole life. Please call us."

"You may be sure," Viktor said, "that I shall personally call you. I am not going home tonight until I have a talk with Mr. Farley Ramsdale and his friend who calls herself Olive O. Ramsdale. And if you wish, you can go now and look for them at tweaker hangouts. Perhaps we do not have enough to tie them into crimes but we do not have to just sit back and cool our toes."

Now Ilya was lecturing Cosmo as she would a child, and he sat there with a cigarette in his nicotine-stained fingers, taking it gladly, a man bereft of ideas.

"Understand me, Cosmo, and trust," she said. "Olive is gone and Farley will not get out of his car in the junkyard of Gregori. He will not, because of you. Do not think all people are as stupid as . . ." She stopped there and said, "You must kill him in his car. Outside the yard."

"Ilya, I cannot find no place to hide myself outside. It is open road and no cars parked on the road at night. Where can I hide myself?"

"Think on it," Ilya said. "Use the brain. After you kill him you take him away in his car. You park one mile away. You leave. You go back to the yard and get our car."

Interrupting, "How must I get back to the yard? Call taxi?"

"No!" she said. "You do not! You want police to find out that taxi takes somebody from a scene of dead body to the junkyard of Gregori? Goddamn, Cosmo!"

"Okay, Ilya. Sorry. I walk back."

"Then you and me, we drive to Dmitri. You have some diamonds in your pocket. Not too many. You give diamonds to Dmitri. His man inspect diamonds. You say, please bring money downstairs to the nightclub. Give to Ilya. I shall be sitting at the bar. He give me money, I go to ladies' room and get the remaining diamonds from where I hide them in a safe place. Lots of people around in the nightclub. We shall be safe."

"But Ilya," Dmitri said. "You forget about ATM money."

"No, I do not forget. You must tell Dmitri mostly truth."

"Ilya! He shall kill me!"

"No, he wants ATM money. You tell him we know where to find Olive. You tell him we shall find her tomorrow. We shall get money and kill her. We shall bring half of money to Dmitri like our deal say we do."

"He shall be very angry," a despairing Cosmo said. "He shall kill me."

"Dmitri wish to kill someone? Tell him to kill

his goddamn Georgian who give us a goddamn car that don't run!"

"Then, what we do tomorrow? We cannot find Olive. We cannot get money to Dmitri."

"The Americans have saying, Cosmo. I am not for sure what each word mean but I understand the idea. Tomorrow we get the fuck out of Dodge."

The Oracle was having a bad night. The lieutenant was off and he was watch commander, so he had to deal with the angry phone call from the lawyer, Anthony Butler.

"Mr. Butler," he said, "the detectives have gone home, so if you'll just call back tomorrow."

"I have been waiting all day for your detectives!" the lawyer said. "Or rather my daughter has. Do you know she was given a date rape drug at a place called Omar's Lounge?"

"Yes, I've pulled the report and looked it over as you requested, but I'm not a detective."

"I talked to your nighttime detective twenty minutes ago. The man's an idiot."

The Oracle didn't argue with that one but said, "I will personally make sure that the detective commander knows about your call, and he will send someone to your office tomorrow."

"The man Andrei who tried to drug my daughter knows she got in the wrong car. He probably knows the police were called. And how do we know that he's not a friend of the Iranians? Maybe he can identify them. What if this was a filthy little plot involving Andrei and the Iranian pigs? I'm shocked that nobody has been to the Gulag to at least identify this Andrei."

The Oracle said, "If he's really the manager of the Gulag, he's got a good job and he's not going anywhere. He'll be there tomorrow. And being an attorney, you must understand how impossible it would be to prove that she'd been given a drug last night."

The lawyer said, "I want to know if the man has a history of this sort of thing. Sara is my only child, Sergeant. A security officer from our corporation is going to accompany me and my daughter to the Gulag this evening, and she's going to point him out if he's there, and we're going to get his name and address. I intend to make the bastard's life a misery with or without the help of detectives from Hollywood Station."

"No, no, Mr. Butler," the Oracle said. "Don't go to the Gulag and stir things up. That'll just end up a real mess for everyone. Tell you what, I'll go there myself tonight and talk to the guy and get all the necessary information that the detectives can act on. How's that?"

"You give me your personal guarantee, Sergeant?"

"You have it," the Oracle said.

After he hung up, the Oracle called 6-X-76 to the station while he read through the report in its entirety. This was the kind of petty crap that wore him down more than anything, that made him feel old.

Whenever anybody asked him how old he was, the Oracle always answered, "I'm the same age as Robert Redford, Jack Nicholson, Jane Fonda, Warren Beatty, and Dustin Hoffman."

He'd always figured that ageless images of Hollywood stars would somehow mitigate what the mirror was showing him: jagged furrows running down his cheeks and encircling his neck, a sagging jawline, deepening creases between his hazel eyes.

But the trick didn't work anymore. Many of the young coppers would say, "Who's Warren Beatty?" Or ask what movie Jane Fonda ever played in. Or say, "Jack Nicholson's the dumpy old guy that goes to the Laker games, right?" He opened the desk drawer and swallowed a dose of antacid liquid from the bottle.

When 6-X-76 entered the watch commander's office, the Oracle said, "This so-called kidnapping at Omar's Lounge is a piece of shit, right?"

"A smelly one, Sarge," Budgie said. "The woman insisted on a kidnapping report. She threatened lawsuits. She called a TV news crew, but I didn't hear anything more, so I guess they also figured it was a piece of shit. Her old man's some kind of politically connected lawyer, according to her."

"He just called."

"She's an actress," Fausto said, and at Hollywood Station that explained a lot.

The Oracle nodded and said, "Just to keep the peace I'll run up to the Gulag later tonight and get Andrei's name and address so that when her daddy calls, the detectives can pacify him. We don't need any more personnel complaints around here."

"What time you going?" Fausto asked.

"In a couple hours."

"We'll meet you there and take you to Marina's."

"What's that?"

"New Mexican restaurant on Melrose."

"I'm not rich enough for Melrose."

"No, this is a little family joint. I'll buy."

"Is there a rehab for Tex-Mex addiction? I've got permanent heartburn."

"Whatever you say."

The Oracle hesitated and said, "Home-made tortillas? And *salsa fresca?*"

"I been hearing good things," Fausto said.

"Okay, I'll call and let you know when I'm at the Gulag," the Oracle said.

"Catch you in five, Fausto," Budgie said, obviously going to the bathroom.

When she was gone, the Oracle said, "I'm doing car assignments for the next deployment period. How do you feel about Budgie?"

"Whaddaya mean?"

"You didn't want to work with a woman, but you did me a favor. I don't wanna ask for a favor two months in a row if you still feel the same way."

Fausto didn't speak for a moment. He looked up at the ceiling and sighed as though it were a tough decision and then said, "Well, Merv, if you're on the spot again and need me to help out . . ."

"We're so shorthanded that figuring out deployment is awful hard these days," the Oracle said. "It would make things easier for me."

"She's a good enough young copper," Fausto said, "but I think she could benefit from having an old dog like me as a shepherd for a while longer."

"I'm glad you feel that way, Fausto," the Oracle said. "Thanks for helping me out."

"Well, I better go collect her," Fausto said. "These split tails take a long time to get unrigged just to take a pee. We oughtta come up with some kind of loincloth uniform for them."

The Oracle saw Fausto go out the back door to the parking lot to wait, and he caught Budgie coming out of the bathroom.

"Budgie," he said, "you got any objections to working another deployment period with the old walrus?"

"No, Sarge," she said, smiling. "We have an understanding, Fausto and me. We're actually a pretty good team."

"Thanks," he said. "Working with you has done wonders for him. He looks and acts ten years younger. Sometimes I think I'm a genius."

"We all know that, Sarge," Budgie said.

★   ★   ★

Farley arrived at the junkyard at the appointed
time and parked fifty yards away with his lights
out. If any shadow figure that even slightly re-
sembled Cosmo Betrossian walked up to that
fence, he was going to drive away, money or no
money. But in ten minutes nothing moved. He
had to get close to see if the gate was open and a
paper bag was stuffed through the chain link, so
he drove slowly toward the yard, lights still out.
He heard dogs barking at another yard closer to
his car. It reminded him of Odar, the oversize
Doberman guard dog that was named for non-
Armenians.

He was on the wrong side of the road now,
but there was so little nighttime traffic on the
junkyard road that it didn't matter. Behind the
fences were stripped and wrecked cars on both
sides of the road as well as huge cranes. He saw
small office buildings, or RVs serving as office
buildings, and larger buildings where cars could
be dismantled or reassembled. And all was dark
except for security lights on some of the buildings and along some of the roadside fences.

When he was drifting close to Gregori's car
gate, lights out, he could see by moonlight that it

was open. And he could see something white in the chain-link mesh. Apparently the bag containing the money was there.

He lowered his window, snatched the bag from the wire, and drove back up the road a safe distance, where he parked. He opened the bag and turned on the overhead light, and there it was — $150 in tens and twenties. He counted it twice. Then excitement began to replace his fear. He thought about the ice he'd be smoking tonight. That was all he could think about for a moment, but then he realized he had to deliver.

Farley drove back boldly now and wheeled into the junkyard with his lights on and his windows rolled up and the doors locked. Odar, tied to a long wire line that allowed him to run from the gate to the office, was barking and snarling, but there was nobody around the gate at all, nothing except an oil drum up against the fence. Farley felt so safe that he made a leisurely U-turn in the yard, blew his horn three times, lowered the window, and tossed the bag of key cards onto the asphalt and headed back to the gate.

His headlight beams caught just enough of Cosmo Betrossian climbing out of the empty drum! Farley had time to step on the accelerator hard, but by the time he got to the gate, Cosmo had swung it closed!

The Corolla slammed into the gate and stopped, its left headlight broken and its front fender driven into the tire. The engine died, and in utter panic Farley turned the key off and on as Cosmo ran up to the car, a pistol in his hand.

"Stop, Farley!" Cosmo yelled. "I shall not hurt you!"

Farley was sobbing when the engine finally kicked over, and he slammed the shift into reverse and backed all the way across the yard, bashing into the door of the office, breaking both taillights and jerking his head back.

Odar was going mad! The dog was snapping and snarling and barking hoarsely, his muzzle white with froth. He was lunging at the car that was crashing and smashing things. Lunging at the running man who had showed up two hours after his master leashed him to the wire and left him. Odar wanted to attack! Anybody! Anything!

Farley dropped the shift into low and gunned it, aiming at Cosmo, who leaped aside and fired a shot through the passenger window behind Farley's head. Farley drove for the gate and rammed it a second time. The car shuddered and recoiled again but the gate still stood. He looked in his side-view mirror and saw Cosmo running toward the car, gun in one hand, flashlight in the other.

Farley reversed it again and floored the accelerator. The tires spun and burned and smoked and the car jetted in reverse and Cosmo leaped out of the way again and fired a second shot and a third, the recoil taking both rounds over the top of the Corolla's roof.

The car was hurtling backward with its driver not knowing which way to turn, but turn he did, this time avoiding a rear-end crash into the office building. Then Farley slammed on the brakes and spun to a stop, his head still reeling.

He could see the blur in his headlights and knew it was Cosmo Betrossian coming to kill him, so he dropped it in low and gunned it and jerked the wheel left, uncertain if Cosmo was still there, even though he could hear the gunfire and see muzzle flashes coming at him. Farley's damaged left front fender just clipped Cosmo on the hip and he flew twenty feet across the asphalt, landing on that same hip, losing his pistol in a jumble of scrap metal and grease rags.

Farley knew he'd hit Cosmo and he floored it again, driving right at the gate, but at the last second he mashed on the brakes, got out, and ran to the gate, expecting to be struck in the back of the head by a bullet. Farley threw back the steel bolt and swung the gate almost open but when he turned he saw Cosmo staggering toward him, without a pistol now but carrying a metal bar that he'd picked up from the scrap heap. Cosmo was limping and cursing in his language. And coming at him.

Farley got the gate all the way open and headed for the driver's seat but he was too late. Cosmo was on him and the bar smashed the driver's side window after Farley ducked. Then Farley was running with Cosmo after him, running into the darkness, running toward the rows of stacked cars waiting to be crushed, then toward another row waiting to be stripped and sold for parts.

Odar had had all he could handle. These two intruders running through his yard were too much for him. His canine adrenaline was overflowing and he took a run, a long run at both men, and the leash drew as tight as piano wire and the overhead line that held the leash snapped. And Odar, eyes aflame, fangs bared, his entire face covered in foam, narrowed those demon eyes and came at them.

Farley saw Odar first and scrambled on top of a wrecked Plymouth, pulling himself onto the roof. Cosmo saw Odar too but had no time to swing at him with the bar, and taking a cue from Farley, he leaped onto the deck lid of a wrecked Audi, scuttling up onto the roof with Odar behind him, his black coat glistening in the moonlight.

The dog vaulted up, slipped, fell from the car onto the ground, then tried again and in a few seconds was standing on the Audi roof dragging his leash. But Cosmo had jumped from the roof of the Audi to the hood of a Pontiac and from the Pontiac across to the roof of a nearly stripped Suburban. Suddenly, Odar abandoned the chase of Cosmo and switched his attention to Farley, who was also leapfrogging cars and partially stripped car bodies, until he turned around, horrified to see the goddamn dog doing the same and coming after *him!*

Cosmo's injured hip began to freeze up on him now, and Farley caught his breath on the roof of an old Cadillac while the confused dog crouched on the hood of a Mustang between them, looking from one man to the other, uncertain which he should attack.

Cosmo began speaking to the dog in Armenian then, trying to win him over with the language the animal was used to hearing. He began issuing gentle commands in his mother tongue.

Farley, who was not as badly injured as Cosmo but every bit as exhausted, also tried persuading the dog, but when Farley tried to speak, he was blubbering and hysterical and tears ran down into his mouth as he cried, "Don't listen to him, Odar! You're like me! I'm an odar, too! Kill him! Kill the fucking Armo!"

Odar started for Farley then and Farley screamed like a woman. The scream of terror triggered something in the attack animal. The dog whirled, hurtled from deck lid to hood to roof, flying at Cosmo like a missile, driving Cosmo off the car onto the ground. The dog's momentum took him with Cosmo and he landed on the ground at a twisting angle, yelped in pain, and came up limping badly. Within seconds he was unable to walk at all on his left rear leg, and hardly at all on his right.

By then Farley was running for his car, and he made it and jumped in but was unable to start it. Weeping, he flooded the engine, then turned off the ignition and locked the door as Cosmo limped to the scrap heap where he'd lost the pistol. But Cosmo's flashlight was gone too, and he could only dig his hands into the twisted metal until he found the gun, cutting a finger to the bone in the process.

Farley tried the ignition again and the car started! He dropped it into low and stomped the accelerator at the same instant that Cosmo appeared at the passenger window and fired five rounds through the glass, missing with the first four. The fifth and last round entered through Farley's right armpit as his hand was cranking the wheel left and the car was digging out and burning rubber.

Out of the fight, the dog sat on his right hip, snarling and howling at Cosmo, who limped to his Cadillac which had been concealed behind the office building, started it up, and tried to drive after Farley. But Cosmo hadn't driven a quarter of a mile before he had to pull off the road, rip off his T-shirt, and use it to stem the blood that was flowing from a nasty head gash and running into his eyes and blinding him.

Farley is a quarter of a mile down that junkyard road before he knows he's been shot. He reaches down with his left hand, feels the warm wetness, and begins bawling. Still, he keeps driving, one headlight lighting the road in front, smashed fenders scraping both front tires.

Farley loses track of time but just follows his instincts onto east Sunset Boulevard, where it begins near downtown Los Angeles. Sometimes Farley stops for traffic lights, sometimes not, and he never sees the police car that spots him cruising through a red light at Alvarado as several motorists slam on brakes and blow horns and yell at him.

He is driving leisurely now through all those ethnic neighborhoods where people speak the languages of Latin America, Southeast Asia, and the Far East as well as Russian and Armenian and Arabic and a dozen other languages he hates. Heading west, heading toward Hollywood, heading home.

Farley Ramsdale does not hear the police siren either and of course has no knowledge that a Rampart Division unit has broadcast a pursuit of a white Corolla along with his license number and his location and direction, causing Hollywood Division cars to start heading for Sunset Boulevard, everyone convinced that this incredibly reckless drunk will blow at least a .25 on the Breathalyser because he's weaving along

Sunset at only thirty miles an hour, causing on-
coming traffic to veer right and stop, and is apparently oblivious to the sirens and the queue of
black-and-whites that have joined in behind the
pursuit car.

At Normandie Avenue Farley crosses into Hollywood Division, still heading west. But he's not
in a car any longer. Farley Ramsdale is fifteen
years younger and is in the gymnasium at Hollywood High School shooting hoops in an intra-
mural game, and they are all three-pointers that
find only net. *Swoosh!* And that cheerleader
who always disses him is now giving him the
big eye. He'll be boning her tonight, that's for
sure.

At the corner of Gower Street his foot slips
from the accelerator and the car drifts slowly
into the rear of a parked Land Rover and the engine dies. Farley never sees the officers of Hollywood Division midwatch who know him —
Hollywood Nate and Wesley Drubb and B.M.
Driscoll and Benny Brewster and Budgie Polk
and Fausto Gamboa — and those who don't.

All out of their cars, guns drawn, the cops run
very warily toward the Corolla now that Nate's
broadcast has alerted all units that the pursued
car is wanted in connection with a robbery in-

vestigation. They are yelling things, but Farley doesn't hear that either.

Hollywood Nate was the first to reach the car, and he smashed the rear driver's side window open and unlocked the driver's door. When Nate jerked open the door and saw all the blood, he holstered his nine and yelled for someone to call an RA.

Farley Ramsdale's eyes were rolled back showing white, his eyelids fluttering like wings as he went into shock and died long before the rescue ambulance reached Sunset Boulevard.

NINETEEN

COSMO COULD NOT stop cursing as he drove west toward Hollywood. He kept looking at his watch without knowing why. He kept thinking of Ilya, of what she would say, of what they would do. He kept wondering how long it would take that miserable addict Farley to phone the police and tell them about the jewelry store robbery. At least Farley couldn't tell them about the ATM robbery and the killing of the guard. Ilya was correct. Farley did not know about that or he would not have come to Gregori's tonight. But that was very little consolation now.

His finger was throbbing and so was his head. He had a laceration just inside the hairline and it was still oozing blood. His finger would need suturing and maybe his head would as well. Almost every bone and muscle ached. He wondered if his hip was broken. Should he go home? Would the police be waiting for him there?

Tonight he had used the Beretta 9-millimeter pistol that he'd taken from the guard. He thought it would be much more accurate than the cheap street gun he had used in the robberies. And what good did it do him? But at least he still had rounds left in the magazine. He had no intention of living his life in prison like an animal. Not Cosmo Betrossian.

He opened his cell and phoned Ilya. If she did not answer, it meant that the police were already there.

"Yes?" Ilya said.

"Ilya! You are okay?"

"Yes, I am okay. Are you okay, Cosmo?"

"Not okay, Ilya. Nothing is correct."

"Shit."

"I am bleeding on my hand and head. I need bandage on my wounds and I need a new shirt and I need a cap to hide blood. Not the cap from that day."

"I threw the baseball cap away, Cosmo. I am not so stupid."

"I shall be home soon. I must be putting gas in my car. I think there is more safety if we drive to San Francisco."

"Shit."

"Yes, Farley may be calling police now. Make all things ready to travel. I shall see you soon."

Before she began packing their clothes Ilya went to the closet shelf and removed the bag of rings and earrings and loose diamonds. She left a sufficient sampling of each for Cosmo to show to Dmitri. Then she put the rest in a very safe place.

The intersection of Sunset Boulevard and Gower Street was a very busy place, completely blocked off by police. Viktor Chernenko was there, having left the stakeout at Farley Ramsdale's house. The house would now be the object of a hastily written search warrant as soon as Viktor got back to the office. After Hollywood Nate told him that the homicide victim was definitely his person of interest, Farley Ramsdale, Viktor began to think of Farley as having been much more ambitious than a petty mail thief. Whatever his connection to the Russian robbers it had gotten him killed.

And when word got to the detective squad room that the pursuit suspect had ended up dead, shot at some location east of Hollywood Division but wanted by Viktor Chernenko, it stirred a lot of interest from the usually disinterested night-watch detective Compassionate Charlie Gilford.

Andi McCrea and Brant Hinkle were just getting ready to leave for the Gulag to follow up on their own homicide case and try to get their hands on Dmitri's videotape, when Compassionate Charlie looked their way.

Andi said, "Don't even think about it, Charlie. The guy was shot somewhere outside Hollywood, and I've got all I can handle anyway."

Compassionate Charlie shrugged and started making calls. When he was through, he put on his checked sport coat and headed for Sunset and Gower so as not to miss a chance to offer commentary on another Hollywood dream gone terribly wrong.

Wesley Drubb was so excited that Hollywood Nate told him to hang on to his seat belt for fear of levitation. Viktor Chernenko had spoken to Robbery-Homicide Division detectives from the Bank Squad who were on the ATM case and had phoned his lieutenant at home. Things were happening so fast it was hard to decide what to do next other than to write a search warrant for the Ramsdale house and hope that they could

locate the woman who called herself Olive Ramsdale. Another Hollywood robbery team had the
house under surveillance, waiting for her.

There wasn't anything else for 6-X-72 to do at
the moment, so Nate and Wesley reluctantly had
to go back to the streets and return to ordinary
police work.

Viktor said to them, "I shall write you a com-
mendation for your good performance whether
or not we solve this case. And do not forget
Olive. You know her. You might see her at the
taco stand or the doughnut shop or the cybercafé."

"We'll be looking," Nate said.

"Keep the eyes skinned," Viktor said. "And
thank you."

Andi and Brant had decided to have a quick bite
before going to the Gulag. One thing about Russian nightclubs, they stayed open until the last
minute the law allowed, so Andi figured they
had plenty of time left.

They were in Thai Town, Andi working on a
green papaya salad and Brant devouring a red
curry with chicken, his eyes watering from the
chilis. They each drank two Thai iced coffees,
both to soothe their burning mouths and be-

cause they needed the caffeine jolt, having had so little sleep in the past two days.

Brant said, "Since I'm the new kid on the block and bouncing from robbery team to helping you, I think I'll talk to the lieutenant about working homicide full-time. You're shorthanded."

"Everybody's shorthanded," Andi said, sipping the iced coffee through a straw.

"It's not that anybody would fight over me," Brant said. "The boss knows I'll only be around here until the promotion list gets down to me and I'm appointed."

"Lieutenant Hinkle," Andi said. "It has a nice sound. You'll be a good watch commander."

"Not as good as you," Brant said. "I expect you to knock 'em dead and be near the top of the next list. The troops will love working for you."

"Why is that?"

"You have a good heart."

"How do you know what's inside? You've only seen the outside of me."

"Cop instinct."

"Careful, buddy. I'm at the age where I get all giddy when a man flatters me like that. I might do something stupid. Like taking you seriously."

"I'm several years older than you. I'm ready to be taken seriously."

"Let's postpone this conversation until end-of-watch," Andi said, "when I can focus on it."

"Whatever you say, partner."

"I say, let's go get a videotape and clear a homicide."

"Is Viktor still gonna meet us there for a little Russian fast talk?"

"He's a very busy guy tonight but he said he would."

"To the Gulag, comrade," Brant said with a smile that crinkled his heavily lashed green eyes and made Andi's toes curl under.

Cosmo was a shocking sight to Ilya when he limped up the stairs. She helped him clean up the head wound and stanch the ooze of blood. As to his finger, she did her best to hold the laceration together with butterfly Band-Aids, then wrapped and taped the finger until they could get to a doctor tomorrow and have it sutured. Where they would have that done, where they would be tomorrow, was anybody's guess. Ilya just wanted to concentrate on getting the money from Dmitri tonight.

"We may run away now, Ilya," Cosmo said. "We have diamonds. We find somebody in San Francisco."

"We are very much hot," Ilya said. "Too much happening. We got no time no more. The police shall be coming when Farley informs to them about us. No time to fish for diamond people in San Francisco. We need money now. You know, Cosmo, I may run clear back to Russia. I do not know."

He didn't know either. All he knew was that he was very much afraid to face Dmitri tonight without the ATM money. And to try to sell him a lie. Dmitri was very smart. More smart than Ilya, he thought.

He made the phone call to the cell number Dmitri had given to him.

"Yes," Dmitri answered.

"Is me, brother," Cosmo said.

"Do not say your name."

"I shall like to come in thirty minute."

"Okay."

"You ready to finish business?"

"Yes, and you?"

Cosmo swallowed and said, "Ready, brother."

"See you in thirty," Dmitri said, and somehow Cosmo could see that smile of his.

Cosmo put on the black beret to hide his head wound. It was something that Ilya wore with her black sweater and boots when she wanted to look very sexy. He wore a pale white sport coat and blue slacks and his best cordovan shoes. He tucked the Beretta inside his waistband in the small of his back. He cinched the leather belt tight to hold the pistol there.

Ilya was wearing the tightest red skirt she owned, and a shell with a deep V neckline, the one that made her breasts swell out, and a short black jacket over that, one trimmed with sequins. And since they were going to a Russian club she wore her black knee boots with three-inch heels. She was not short on bling, she thought. Ilya liked that American word: "bling."

Cosmo forced a brave smile and said, "We go to get our thirty-five thousands, Ilya. We go to the Gulag."

The Oracle looked at the clock. He was getting hungry and this had been a very busy night what with the pursuit driven by a dead man, and Viktor Chernenko tying up one of his midwatch cars, along with more ordinary Hollywood madness breaking out here and there as though there was a full moon. He felt a stab of heartburn and popped a couple of antacid tablets.

He said to the Watch 3 sergeant, "I gotta go do

a PR job to keep some dirtbag of a lawyer from making a personnel complaint on everybody in Hollywood Division who met or failed to meet his goofy daughter who's made a bogus crime report. I just gotta get the name and address of the manager of a nightclub, if the guy really is the manager. Maybe he just has business cards made up to impress the chicks he meets in bars."

"Which nightclub you going to?" the sergeant asked.

"A Russian joint called the Gulag. You know it?"

"No, but I imagine it's a Russian Mafia hangout. They change owners and names more often than they change underwear."

The Oracle said, "After that, I'll be taking code seven with Fausto and his partner. They found a hot new mama-and-papa Mexican eatery. Call if you need me."

When the Oracle drove out of the Hollywood Station parking lot, he sent a message to 6-X-76 telling them he was on his way to the Gulag and shouldn't be there for more than fifteen minutes.

The Gulag parking lot was jammed when Cosmo wheeled his Cadillac in. He had to park in the far corner by the trash containers.

"Dmitri should hire valet boys," Ilya observed nervously.

"Too cheap," Cosmo said.

They could hear the place rocking the moment they stepped out of their cars. Cosmo snuffed out his cigarette, touched the pistol under his coat, and limped to the entrance with Ilya.

Ilya went to the bar, joined the rows of drinkers trying to get service, and called to the sweaty bartender, "Excuse me, please."

A boozy young guy sitting at the bar turned and looked at her face, then at her tits, got up from the bar stool, and said, "I'll give you my seat if you'll let me buy you a drink."

Ilya gave him her best professional smile, took his bar stool, and said, "That is lovely, darling."

Smiling at her accent, he said, "Are you Russian?"

"Yes, darling," she said.

"How about I order you a Black Russian?"

"I prefer a white American," she said, and the young guy laughed out loud, drunk enough that anything was funny.

Ilya wished that the world had not stopped smoking. She would have given a diamond for a cigarette at this moment.

★ ★ ★

As busy as he was, Viktor Chernenko had made a promise to Andi McCrea, and a promise was a promise. He looked at his watch and told Compassionate Charlie that he had to quickly run to a Russian nightclub called the Gulag to do a verbal muscle job for Andi in the proprietor's own language. As for the outside detectives who were on their way to the station to help piece together the puzzle of the Ramsdale murder and Hollywood robberies, Viktor planned to stay tonight as long as there was hope of finding Farley Ramsdale's woman. He had a copy of her minor rap sheet for petty theft and drug possession and saw that the name "Olive Ramsdale" must be a recent alias. She'd given the name "Mary Sullivan" when she'd been arrested, but who could say if that was her true name?

Then he put in a quick phone call home and got his wife, Maria, on the phone.

"Hello, my darling," he said. "This is your most loving husband."

Compassionate Charlie said, "What the hell?" and looked at Viktor like he'd just burped pepper spray. Charlie couldn't bear telephone canoodling.

"I am working on the most important matter

of my entire career, my little sweetheart," Viktor said. "It is possible that I shall be sleeping here in the cot room tonight. I do not know for sure."

Then Viktor listened with a dopey smile on his broad Slavic face, said, "Me too!" and actually did kisses into the receiver before he rang off.

"Is this your first marriage, Viktor?" Charlie asked him.

"My first, my last," Viktor said.

Charlie shook his head and said, "Must be a Russian thing."

"I am not Russian," Viktor said patiently. "I am Ukrainian."

Compassionate Charlie said, "Bring me back some kielbasa if the Gulag looks like a clean joint."

"That is Polish, not Russian," Viktor said, heading for the door.

"Polish, Russian, Ukrainian. Gimme a fucking break, Viktor," Compassionate Charlie whined.

Cosmo knocked at the door to Dmitri's office and heard "Come."

When he limped into the office, he saw Dmitri in his high-back chair behind the desk, but not with his feet up this time and not watching exotic porn on the computer screen. An older man in a dark suit and a striped necktie, bald except for a scraggly fringe of gray, was sitting on the leather sofa against the wall.

Standing by the window that looked down on the smoking patio where the murder had occurred was the Georgian bartender, wearing a starched white shirt, a black bow tie, and black pants. His wavy black hair was even thicker than Cosmo's and he had a square, dark jaw that no razor could ever shave clean. He nodded to Cosmo.

Dmitri smiled that unreadable smile and said, "The happen-ink guy is here! Please to meet Mr. Grushin, Cosmo. And show to him your goods for sale."

"I have some sample," Cosmo said, and Dmitri's smile faded and his face seemed to grow pale around the corners of his mouth. So Cosmo quickly added, "All other diamonds downstairs with Ilya. Not to worry, brother."

"I do not worry," Dmitri said, smiling again. "Why are you so injured?"

"I shall explain after," Cosmo said. Then he removed a plastic sandwich bag from his jacket pocket and poured out two rings, three sets of earrings, and five loose diamonds onto Dmitri's desk.

Mr. Grushin got up and walked to the desk. The Georgian pulled the client chair close so he could sit. Mr. Grushin took a jeweler's loupe from his pocket and examined each item under the light of the desk lamp and when he was through nodded to Dmitri, got up, and left the office.

"I may see money now, brother?" Cosmo said.

Dmitri opened the top desk drawer and withdrew three large stacks of currency, placing them on the desk in front of him. He did not ask Cosmo to sit.

"Okay, my friend," Dmitri said. "Tell me of ATM. And when I shall receive my half of money you got from there."

Cosmo felt the dampness under his arms, and his palms were wet when he pointed his uninjured hand at the Georgian and said, "He gave us a no-good car. The car die when we leave ATM!"

The Georgian said something quickly in Russian to Dmitri that Cosmo couldn't understand, then turned a scowl toward Cosmo and said, "You lie! The car is good car. I drove car. You lie."

Now Cosmo felt his stomach gurgle and his bowels rumble and he said, "No, Dmitri. This Georgian, he lie! We have to drive the car away from ATM and park at the house of guy I know. We almost get caught by police!"

"You lie!" the Georgian said, taking a menacing step toward Cosmo until Dmitri held up his hand and stopped him.

"Enough," Dmitri said to both men.

"I tell you truth, brother," Cosmo said. "I swear."

"Now, Cosmo, where is money from ATM?" Dmitri asked.

"The man where we must take no-good car, his woman steal our money and run away from her man. But not to worry. We shall find her. We get money."

"This man," Dmitri said calmly, "he does not know noth-ink of me? Noth-ink of the Gulag?"

"No, brother!" Cosmo said. "Never!"

"And what of this man? What is his name?"

"Farley Ramsdale," Cosmo said. "He is addict."

Dmitri looked in disbelief at Cosmo, then at the Georgian and back to Cosmo, and said, "You leave my money with addict?"

"No choice, brother!" Cosmo said. "This Georgian give us car that don't run. And Farley not at home so we got to hide car in his garage and hide money under his house. But goddamn addict woman, she find it and run away!"

Cosmo's mouth was dry as sand now and it made a popping sound each time his lips opened. The Georgian was glaring at him dangerously but Cosmo could hardly take his eyes from the thirty-five thousand dollars. It was a bigger pile of money than he'd imagined.

"Go get Ilya," Dmitri said. "Brink her up and I buy you drinks and we complete diamond deal and you tell me how you catch addict woman and tell me when you goink to get me my money from ATM."

This was the moment he dreaded. This is what Ilya said he must do regardless of the outcome. Cosmo swallowed twice and said, "No, brother. I take money now and your Georgian come with me down to the bar and Ilya go to bathroom and get diamonds from safe place and give to this Georgian. Lot of peoples down there. Safe for everybody."

Dmitri laughed out loud at that and said, "Cosmo, is information on TV and in newspaper correct? How much you find in the box?"

"Ninety-three thousands," Cosmo said.

"TV lady say hundred thousand," Dmitri said, "but never mind, I believe you. So this mean you owe to me forty-six thousand and five hundred dollars and I owe to you thirty-five thousand dollars. So we do mathematics and we discover eleven thousand, five hundred dollars you owe to me. And the diamonds, too. Is very simple, no?"

Cosmo was dripping sweat now. His shirt was soaked and he kept wiping his palms on his trousers, standing there like a child, looking down at this Russian pervert and up at the Georgian thug standing beside him. And he wanted badly just to touch the Beretta, cold against the sweat on his back.

Cosmo said, "Please to give me three minute to explain how the car this Georgian steal for us is reason for every problem!"

The Oracle was very surprised to see the detective car parked in the red zone on the east side of the nightclub, where he too was forced to park, the packed parking lot being an impossibility. He wondered which detective was in there and why. As he was walking toward the door, a black-and-white slowed and stopped and Fausto gave a short toot to get his attention. The Oracle walked over to the curb, bent down, and said, "I won't be long, Fausto."

"Want some company?" Budgie said. "I've never been inside one of these Russian glam palaces."

"Okay, but we'll scare the crap outta them," the Oracle said. "There's already a detective team in there."

"For what?" Fausto said.

"Maybe the murder the other night," the Oracle said. "Five cops? They'll think they're back in the USSR."

When the Oracle entered, followed by Fausto and Budgie, he spotted Andi and Brant standing back by the restrooms talking to a guy in a tuxedo who the Oracle figured might be the manager Andrei.

The decibel level was astounding and multi-colored lights and strobes were playing all over the dance-floor pit, where couples, mostly young, were "get-tink down," as Dmitri called it. From her seat at the end of the bar, Ilya couldn't see the three uniformed cops who entered and headed toward a narrow corridor by the kitchen. The Oracle, Fausto, and Budgie attracted some attention but not much, and they surprised the detectives.

Andi had to shout over the music. "What're you doing here? Don't tell me there's another murder on the patio I haven't heard about?"

The Oracle said to the unhappy-looking guy in the tuxedo, "Are you Andrei?"

"Yes," the manager said.

"We'll give you cuts in line with this one," Andi said to the Oracle. "We're waiting to see Dmitri, the proprietor."

The Oracle said to Andrei, "I need to have a chat with you and get your name and address. I'll explain when we get to a quiet place, if such a thing exists around here." Then, with a wink at Andi, he indicated Fausto and Budgie and said to Andrei, "These two're my bodyguards. I take them with me wherever I go."

Andrei had a what-else-can-go-wrong look on his face then. Just as something else was about to go very wrong.

Dmitri's eyes were half closed as Cosmo glossed over the aftermath of the ATM robbery, leaving out his confrontation tonight with Farley Ramsdale.

And when Cosmo was through, Dmitri said, "You had to shoot the guard?"

"Yes, Dmitri," Cosmo said. "He did not give up money like you say."

Dmitri shrugged and said, "Sometimes information on enemy is not correct. Ask President Bush."

Cosmo was getting his hopes built until Dmitri turned to the Georgian and said, "Okay, maybe is a little piece of truth about the car. Maybe the car is not so good as you think."

"Dmitri!" the Georgian said, but he saw the look in Dmitri's eye and stopped his protest.

"So, Cosmo," Dmitri said, "you are going to get ATM money tomorrow when you catch addict woman, no?"

"That is exactly correct," Cosmo said.

"Okay, here is what I do for you, Cosmo," said Dmitri. "You owe me eleven thousand, five hundred plus diamonds. I am go-ink to cancel the money what you owe me! You get Ilya up here and give me all diamonds and we are even. Tomorrow when you catch addict woman, you keep all ninety-three thousand dollars. Your share, my share. I could not be more generous with my own brother, Cosmo."

Then Dmitri looked up at the Georgian for validation and got a nod of agreement that said Dmitri was a very reasonable and very generous man.

It was hopeless. Cosmo was the image of despair. As Cosmo was staring at the money on Dmitri's desk, the Russian opened the top drawer and put the first stack back inside. When he reached for the second stack, Cosmo felt that he was outside his body and watching himself pull his coat back and reach behind him for the Beretta.

"Dmitri!" the Georgian yelled, coming up with a small pistol, from where, Cosmo didn't see.

And Dmitri shouted in Russian and opened a second drawer and reached inside for a gun of his own.

Andi said to the other cops and to Andrei the manager, "We've waited long enough. I'm going to knock on Dmitri's door."

She was interrupted by one shot followed by two more followed by five! And the two detectives and three uniformed cops ran upstairs. Andi was getting her pistol out of her purse when Fausto and Budgie passed her and both crouched down on one knee, guns extended in two hands aimed at the door of Dmitri's office. The Oracle ran to the other side of the door, and with his old six-inch revolver extended, he backed up, so that all guns, high and low, were deployed diagonally, pointed at the door.

Inside the office, Cosmo Betrossian had pain in his left arm that far exceeded anything he'd suffered this night either from Farley Ramsdale or the killer dog. Cosmo had a through-and-through wound in the biceps that had chipped the bone before exiting, and it burned like liquid fire.

The Georgian was sprawled across Dmitri's desk, spurting blood from an arterial penetration in the neck. But his chest wounds were even more devastating.

Dmitri was sitting back in his chair with a hole in his forehead that was actually a coup de grâce delivered by Cosmo as Dmitri lay dying, having fired the round that wounded Cosmo.

The thundering sounds from the pit below Dmitri's office had actually muffled the sound from the patrons' area, and everyone rocked on. From time to time Ilya gazed across the dance floor, wondering why Cosmo had not returned.

Cosmo hoped he didn't faint before he got down to Ilya with the stacks of money inside his shirt against his skin. The money felt good. He was about to put his gun back into his waistband, but thinking that an employee from the kitchen might have heard the shots, he held the gun in front of him with his one good hand and opened the door.

In such confined space it sounded to Fausto like automatic weapon fire that he'd heard in Nam. Budgie later said that it sounded to her like one huge explosion. She couldn't differentiate the separate weapons firing.

Cosmo Betrossian got off exactly one shot, which hit the wall above their heads. He in turn was shot eighteen times with nine rounds missing him, probably as he was twisting and falling. All five cops shot him at least twice, with Fausto and Budgie scoring the most hits.

This being her first shooting, Andi McCrea later said during the FID investigation that it truly was like a slow-motion sequence. She could see, or thought she could see, hot shell casings ejecting into the air from various pistols and slapping against her face.

The Oracle said that in forty-six years, this was the first time he'd ever fired his weapon outside of the police pistol range.

Budgie had the most interesting commentary. She said that in such close confines, all the muzzle blasts and gun smoke had created a condition that, with her mouth wide open and sucking air, got her chewing gum full of grit.

The pandemonium that followed was worse than what occurred on the night of the patio stabbing. The customers did hear the roar of the multiple gunshots from the upstairs hallway. Budgie and Fausto ran down the stairs to grab the manager and anybody else who looked like he might know what the hell had happened upstairs to cause the original gunfire. The Oracle made urgent calls on his rover.

By the time Viktor Chernenko pulled up in front, people were pouring from the front door and running for their cars. The parking lot was in such chaos that the cars in the back of the lot could not move. Headlights were flashing and horns were honking. Viktor bulled his way through emerging hysterical customers and took the stairs two at a time.

When he got to the scene of carnage, he said to the Oracle, "One of these Russians may be the one I am looking for! Maybe the one who shot Farley Ramsdale!"

The Oracle, who was pale and had the worst heartburn of his life, said, "A busboy told us the one in the chair is the owner. The one lying across the desk is a bartender. The one we shot . . ." — and he pointed to the ragged, bloody heap lying in the corner just beyond the door — "I don't know who he is. He killed the other two."

Viktor said, "You have latex gloves?" and when the Oracle shook his head, Viktor said, "Hell with it!" and pulled Cosmo's wallet from his back pocket and ran back down the stairs, his hands stained by Cosmo's blood.

When he got to the sidewalk in front he could hear sirens wailing as patrol units were arriving from all directions.

"Come with me!" Viktor yelled to Wesley Drubb, who had just leaped from their car as Nate was double-parking it.

Wesley followed Viktor to the parking lot, where Viktor looked inside each and every car with his flashlight as the cars took turns trying to funnel out of the narrow driveway. Most cars had couples in them or single men. Less than ten percent of the cars were driven by single women, but for every one that was, Viktor's flashlight beamed squarely into the driver's face.

He was starting to think that he'd been wrong when he got to the last row of cars, but then he saw a big blond woman with huge breasts behind the wheel of an older Cadillac. Viktor turned to Wesley, his flashlight on Cosmo's driver's license, showing Wesley the name. Then he shined his light on the Cadillac and said, "Please get a DMV on this license plate! Very fast!"

Viktor hung his badge on his coat pocket, walked up to the driver's door, and tapped on the window with his flashlight, his pistol in hand concealed just below the window ledge. And he smiled.

The woman rolled down the window, smiled back at him, and said, "Yes, Officer?"

"Your name, please," Viktor said.

"Ilya Roskova," she said. "There is a problem?" Then she looked to see if the queue of cars was moving, but it was not.

"Maybe," Viktor said. "And is this your car?"

"No, I borrow this car from a friend. She is a neighbor. I am so stupid I do not even know her family name."

"May I see the registration?"

Ilya said, "Shall I look in glove box?"

"By every means," Viktor said, shining his light on her right hand as well as the glove compartment. His gun coming up a bit higher.

"No," she said. "No papers in there."

"This car belongs to a woman, then?"

"Yes," Ilya said. "But not to this woman who sits before you in traffic." Her smile broke wider, a bit coquettish.

Hollywood Nate and Wesley came running

back, and Wesley whispered, "Cosmo Betrossian. Same as on that driver's license."

"So you know the owner of the car, then?" Viktor said to Ilya.

"Yes," Ilya said cautiously. "Her name is Nadia."

"Do you know Cosmo Betrossian?"

"No, I do not think so," Ilya said.

Viktor raised his pistol to her face and said in Russian, "You will please step from the car with your hands where we can see them at all times, Madame Roskova."

As Wesley handcuffed Ilya's hands behind her back, she said, "I shall be calling my lawyer immediately. I am completely full of outrage!"

When they were transporting her to Hollywood Station, Nate said to his partner, "Well, Wesley, what do you think of your misdemeanor division now?"

TWENTY

AT 3 A.M. Ilya Roskova was sitting in the detective squad room, which was more crowded with people than it ever was during daylight hours. There were Force Investigation Division people, there was the area captain, there was the Detective Division commander — everyone had left their beds for this one. And the Gulag had more LAPD cars and personnel swarming around than they ever had customers during happy hour.

What was known so far was that the diamonds found on the desk at the Gulag under the body of the Georgian bartender matched descriptions given by Sammy Tanampai of his jewelry store inventory. The serial number on the Beretta 9-millimeter pistol used by Cosmo Betrossian to kill Dmitri and the Georgian proved to belong to the weapon taken from the surviving security guard during the ATM robbery.

Viktor Chernenko, the man who had been instinctively correct from the beginning, was told that, along with the captain, he should be prepared to speak to the media in the late morning after he got some much-needed sleep. Viktor predicted that ballistics would show that the bullet that killed Farley Ramsdale came from the same Beretta, and that Farley Ramsdale must have been an accomplice to the robbery and had a falling-out with Cosmo Betrossian.

There was a person in the squad room, being guarded by Budgie Polk, who knew if Viktor was correct in both theories, but she wasn't talking. Ilya's wrist was handcuffed to a chair and she'd said *nyet* to every question asked, including whether she understood her constitutional rights. Everyone was waiting for Viktor to find time to try an interview in her language.

Andi McCrea along with the others who had participated in the officer-involved shooting were being separately interviewed by FID and were scattered among several of the station's offices. Andi was the third one finished, and when she came back into the busy squad room, she played the videotape that had been seized along with the other evidence from the desk of Dmitri.

When she watched the video with Brant Hinkle looking over her shoulder, they nodded, satisfied. The stabbing of the student was caught vividly. The identity of the assailant was unmistakable.

"He'll cop a plea when his lawyer sees this," Andi said.

After packaging the videotape for booking, she looked at Ilya Roskova, sitting in the chair glaring at her stoic guard, Budgie Polk, who had been interviewed for one hour by FID.

Andi pulled Viktor aside and said, "Have you gotten any information out of her?"

"Nothing, Andrea," Viktor said. "She will not speak at all except to ask for cigarettes. And she keeps wanting to go to the bathroom. I was just going to ask Officer Polk to take her."

Andi kept eyeing Ilya, looking particularly at her lower body squeezed into that low-rise red skirt, as tight as Lycra. She said, "Let me take her. Where's her purse?"

He pointed and said, "Over there on the desk."

"Does she have cigarettes in there?"

"Yes."

Andi went to the desk and picked up the purse, then walked over to Ilya Roskova and said, "Would you like us to take you to the bathroom?"

"Yes," Ilya said.

"And after that maybe a cigarette?" Andi said.

"Yes."

"Take the cuff off her, Budgie," Andi said.

Budgie unlocked the handcuff and the prisoner stood, massaging her wrist for a second, prepared to accompany the cops.

As they started to walk, Andi opened the purse and said to Ilya, "Yes, I see you have cigarettes in —" Then the purse dropped from Andi's hand onto the floor.

Ilya looked at Andi, who just smiled and said "I'm sorry" but made no effort to pick up the purse.

Ilya angrily bent over to pick it up, and Andi stepped forward, put her hand on Ilya's shoulder, and forced her down into a full squat with one hand, reaching down toward the purse with her other, saying, "Here, let me help you, Ms. Roskova."

And when Ilya was held in the squatting position for a few seconds, making a fish mouth, a diamond hit the floor. Then another. Then a ring with a four-carat stone plinked against the floor and rolled across the squad room, stopping when it hit Viktor's shoe. Diamonds were shooting from that "safe place" where she'd promised Cosmo to hide them.

Andi reached under Ilya's arm and raised her up, saying, "We'll let you pee in a urinal and we'll be watching. And Viktor, I think you better put on gloves before you pick up the evidence."

"Bitch!" Ilya said, as the two women, one on each arm, led her to the door.

"And you can use our bidet," Budgie said. "Like the one I have at home. It's called a sink. You jump up on it, but we'll keep the stopper in."

Brant Hinkle said to Viktor, "I think she might talk to you now."

"How did Andi know?" Viktor marveled.

"She noticed right away and told me. No panty line, no thong line, nothing. She guessed that Roskova might want to get rid of them in a hurry first chance she'd get at privacy."

"But the trick? To put her down in that position? How did she know that trick?"

"Viktor, there're some things you and I didn't learn at detective school that women just know," Brant Hinkle said.

When Andi and Budgie returned with the cache of diamonds, Budgie said, "I'm sure glad I didn't have to remove the evidence. I can't even clean out my rain gutters for fear of spiders and other crawly things."

Late the next day, after getting five hours' sleep in the cot room along with a wardrobe change driven to the station by his wife, Maria, Viktor Chernenko completed his investigation by supervising a thorough search of the car and apartment of Cosmo Betrossian, as well as the house of Farley Ramsdale.

They found Cosmo's Lorcin .380 pistol and the Raven that Ilya had carried during the ATM robbery. At Farley's house they found some stolen mail, a glass pipe for smoking meth, and the usual litter and detritus that are found in the homes of tweakers. There were a few articles of women's clothing, but it appeared that Farley Ramsdale's companion had disappeared.

Viktor and two other detectives inquired at every house on both sides of the street but learned nothing of value. The next-door neighbor, an elderly Chinese man, said in barely understandable English that he had never spoken to Farley and never noticed a woman. The neighbor on the other side was an eighty-two-year-old Romanian who said that she only saw the man and woman coming in late at night and that her night vision was so bad she'd never recognize them in the daylight.

Interviews of other, mostly elderly, residents on the block were equally fruitless. Even when Olive's old mug shot was shown to them, nobody could say that she looked very familiar. She was the kind of person, it seemed, who would live and die on the streets of Hollywood utterly invisible.

Upon reading the news accounts about Farley Ramsdale and the massacre at the Gulag, a very frightened Gregori Apramian called Hollywood Station early in the afternoon to offer information. And after that call, his junkyard was deemed a crime scene and was sealed and scoured by criminalists and detectives from downtown.

Gregori stood in front of his office next to a leashed Doberman who, despite the cast on his rear leg, was snarling and still ready to fight. And scaring the crap out of every cop who got within ten yards.

What Gregori said for the record and what was transcribed onto a police report was: "I just promise Cosmo to tow the Mazda that night. I don't know about no robberies. Maybe Cosmo bring this guy Farley to my yard to destroy the

Mazda? That is what I think. They are going to burn up the Mazda to do the covering up of robberies. But something happen. They get in fight and hurt my Odar. And Cosmo shoot the man Farley. I do not know Farley. I do not know the Russian woman you arrest. I only know Cosmo because we go to same Armenian church sometimes. I am trying to be a friend to a fellow immigrant and be a, how you say, credit to America."

At the end of his long day, Viktor Chernenko played a tape of Ilya Roskova's interview for the detective lieutenant and both area and station captains. Ilya had stopped saying *nyet* after the diamonds were excreted onto the squad room floor. She had then voluntarily removed the rest in the Hollywood Station bathroom where they were packaged and booked.

Ilya had been advised of her rights in both English and Russian, and she declared her understanding. The interview about her role in both robberies was long and tedious and self-serving. She kept claiming to have been totally in thrall to Cosmo Betrossian, calling herself a mental captive who lived in fear of him.

When one of the captains looked at his watch, Viktor advanced the tape to the portion dealing with the last pieces of the puzzle that remained missing: Olive and the ATM money.

Ilya's voice said, "Olive was there when Farley did blackmail on Cosmo. When he gave big threat to tell police about the stolen letter. But Olive is, how you say, imbecile. Her brain is in a destroyed condition from drugs. I am very astounded that she have enough of the brain left to find the money Cosmo steal from ATM. Very astounded that she can take the money and vanish into thin smoke."

Then Viktor's voice said, "Do you think it is possible that Cosmo was holding back from you? Is it possible that Cosmo hid the money somewhere because he did not wish to share with you?"

After a long pause on the tape, Ilya's voice said angrily, "Is not possible!" Then she obviously realized that she was blurring her portrait of enslavement and said, "But of course I was so much in fear that I may be incorrect about what Cosmo can do. He was very much clever. And had two faces."

Viktor turned off the machine then and said to his superiors, "So far as I am concerned, we have hit a stone fence. I believe that Cosmo Betrossian took the ATM money from under the house of Farley Ramsdale on the night that the car was towed to the junkyard. I believe that Cosmo Betrossian has disposed of the ATM money with a friend, probably another woman. The Russian pride of Ilya Roskova does not wish to admit such a possibility — that he could have another secret woman and would be leaving her. I believe that Cosmo then tried to tell to Dmitri Zotkin a false story of Olive stealing the money, but Dmitri was too smart to buy it. And that's when the shooting started."

"You've been right on so far," the area captain said. "So what do you think happened to this woman Olive?"

"I think she finally got scared enough of Cosmo Betrossian to run away from Farley Ramsdale. She is probably living now with some other tweaker. Or maybe just living out on the street. We shall find her dead sometime from an overdose. Truly, she is of no further use to this investigation."

"Do you think we'll ever find the ATM money?" the station captain asked.

Viktor said, "We have learned that Cosmo Betrossian loved Russian women. There is probably one of them shopping on Rodeo Drive with the ATM money. Right now as we talk."

"Okay, it's a wrap," the area captain said. "When you do press interviews on this, just try to avoid mention of the missing money. The other pieces fit perfectly."

"Yes, sir," Viktor Chernenko said. "That is the only fly in the jelly."

TWENTY-ONE

By THE TIME the June deployment period was in full swing at Hollywood Station, things were back to normal. The surfer cops were hitting the beach at Malibu every chance they got. B.M. Driscoll was sure that he had a sinus infection from what to him was a severe allergy season. Benny Brewster had persuaded the Oracle to stick B.M. Driscoll with one of the recent arrivals who didn't know him, and the Oracle complied. Fausto Gamboa and Budgie Polk were an effective team, particularly after Budgie convinced Fausto that he absolutely had to treat her more like one of the guys. Wesley Drubb got his wish and was assigned to a gang unit with a chance to do more hardcore police work. And in a pinch, caused by summer vacations, Hollywood Nate agreed to be a temporary training officer to a brand-new probationer named Marty Shaw, who made Nate nervous by constantly calling him sir.

But best of all for the midwatch, Mag Takara came back to duty. The Oracle thought she should be assigned to the desk until her vision improved a bit more, and she agreed. Mag wore glasses now and would soon be taking sick days for future plastic surgery, but she wanted very much to put on the uniform again, and it was permitted. She learned that she was going to be awarded the Medal of Valor for her actions in the jewelry store on the night of the grenade incident. She said her parents would be very proud.

Mag even thanked Flotsam for the beautiful roses he had brought to the hospital, telling him he was a "choiceamundo friend." Flotsam actually blushed.

When Budgie Polk saw Mag, they hugged, and Budgie looked at the cheekbone that showed a slight darkened crater where tissue had not yet fully recovered and said, "You're still the most gorgeous slut that ever hustled tricks on Sunset Boulevard."

The deployment period was ending on a night when the homicide team of Andi McCrea and

Brant Hinkle was working late after having arrested an aging actor who walked into his agent's office, cold-cocked the guy with an Oscar replica that the actor used as a paperweight, and then threatened to return with a gun.

When Hollywood Nate heard about it he said no jury made up of SAG members would ever convict the actor, and they might even make the agent buy him another fake Oscar.

They were just finishing up that evening when the Oracle entered the detective squad room looking very grim. He said, "Andi, can you come to the captain's office, please?"

"What's up?" she said, following the Oracle to the captain's office, where she saw a U.S. Army sergeant major holding his hat in both hands.

"Noooo!" Andi cried out, and Brant Hinkle heard and ran to the sound of her voice.

"He's not dead!" the Oracle said quickly. "He's alive!"

He put his arm around her and led her into the office and closed the door.

The sergeant major said, "Detective McCrea, we've been informed that your son, Max, has been wounded. I'm really sorry."

"Wounded," she said, as though the word were foreign to her.

"It wasn't a roadside bomb, it was an ambush. Automatic weapons and mortars."

"Oh, my god," she said and started weeping.

"It's his leg. I'm afraid he's lost his right leg." Then he quickly added, "But it's below the knee. That's much better."

"Much better," Andi murmured, hardly hearing, hardly comprehending.

"He's been flown to Landstuhl Regional Medical Center in Germany, and from there he'll go to Walter Reed Army Medical Center in Washington."

The sergeant major expressed his and the army's gratitude, offered to assist her in any way he could, and said a lot of other things. And she didn't understand a word of it.

When he was finished, Andi thanked him and walked out into the corridor, where Brant Hinkle took her in his arms and said to the Oracle, "I'll drive her home."

There wasn't a more excited homeowner in that part of Hollywood than Mabel was these days. She had so much to do. There just weren't enough hours in the day.

First of all, she got a new screen door. It was a

nice aluminum door that the man said would last a lifetime. Then he looked at Mabel and she knew he was thinking, It will surely last your lifetime.

Then came the painting of the exterior, which was still going on. Mabel had to keep the windows open all the time in this hot weather, even though there was the awful smell of paint from outside. But it all just added to the excitement. They were going to start painting the interior of the house very soon and putting wallpaper in the kitchen and bathroom. Mabel thought she'd buy a couple of air conditioners before the interior painting started. It was a thrilling time to be alive.

When they were having breakfast, Mabel said to Olive, "Do you think you're up to going to an NA meeting this afternoon, dear?"

"Oh, sure," Olive said, still looking pale from having to white-knuckle it.

"I started going to AA when I was sixty-two years old," Mabel said. "After my husband died, the booze got the best of me. I've been in recovery ever since. You'll meet some grand people there who will always be just a phone call away. I'm sure that the NA meetings are like

AA meetings, just a different drug is all. But I have no doubt you'll prevail. You're a strong girl, Olive. You've never had a chance to prove it."

"I'll be okay, Mabel," Olive said, trying to eat some scrambled egg.

Mabel's physician had told Olive that a diet of nutritious food was essential for her, and Mabel hadn't stopped cooking since Olive arrived. Mabel had seen that Olive's attempt at unassisted withdrawal from methamphetamine addiction was very hard on her, so Mabel had taken Olive by bus to a doctor who'd treated Mabel for thirty years.

The doctor had examined Olive and given her medication to ease withdrawal symptoms but said that healthy eating was the best medicine, along with abstaining from all drugs forever.

Mabel was pleased watching Olive eat a forkful of scrambled egg and a bite of toast, washing it all down with orange juice. A week earlier she couldn't have done that.

"Dear," Mabel said, "do you feel well enough today to talk about the future?"

"Sure, Mabel," Olive said, realizing that this was the first time in her life that anyone had ever mentioned her future. Olive never thought that she had a future. Or much of a past. She'd always lived in the present.

"As soon as you're well into recovery I'm going to do a quitclaim deed. Do you know what that is?"

"No."

"I'm going to deed this house to you with the provision that I can live here for the rest of my life."

Olive looked at Mabel with a blank expression, then said, "I don't think I understand what you mean."

"That's the least I can do for you after what you've given me," Mabel said. "I was going to leave the house to the Salvation Army so the state doesn't get it. That's what will happen to Farley's house, you know. He had no heirs and no will, so the state of California will take it. I think Governor Schwarzenegger is rich enough. He doesn't need my house."

Olive clearly couldn't grasp it. "Me?" she said. "You're giving me your house?"

"All that I ask is that you take care of me as best you can for as long as you can. We can hire one of those nice Filipino girls to help with the unpleasant nursing when I get to that point. I would like to die at home. I think my doctor will help me achieve that wish. He's a good and decent man."

Suddenly tears ran down Olive's cheeks, and she said, "I don't want you to die, Mabel!"

"There there, dear," Mabel said, patting Olive's hand. "My parents both lived until they were nearly one hundred. I expect I've got some years left."

Olive got up and took a tissue from the box beside Mabel's chair, then came and sat down at the table again, wiping her eyes.

Mabel said, "I never use that silly sewing room anymore, so that will be your bedroom. We'll decorate it up real pretty for you. And it has a good closet. We'll take you shopping and fill up that closet."

Olive just kept looking at Mabel with eyes as quiet and devoted as a dog's and said, "My own bedroom?"

"Certainly, dear," Mabel said. "But of course we'll always have to share the bathroom. You wouldn't mind not having your own bathroom, would you?"

Olive started to say that in her whole life she'd never had her own bathroom. Or her own bedroom. But she was so overwhelmed she couldn't speak. She just shook her head.

Mabel said, "I think we'll buy a reliable car right away. You can drive, can't you?"

"Oh, yes," Olive said. "I'm a good driver."

"I think when we get our car, the first thing we'll do is take a drive to Universal Studios and do the tour. Have you ever been to Universal Studios?"

"No," Olive said.

"Neither have I," Mabel said. "But we'll need to buy one of those fold-up wheelchairs. I don't believe I could manage the long walk. You wouldn't mind pushing me in a wheelchair, would you?"

"I'll do anything for you, Mabel," Olive said.

"Do you have a driver's license?"

"No," Olive said. "When I got arrested for DUI, they took mine away. But I know a real nice guy named Phil who makes them. They're very expensive. Two hundred dollars."

"All right, dear," Mabel said. "We have plenty of money, so we'll buy you one of those for now. But someday you should try to get a proper one."

Thinking of the driver's license, Mabel said, "Dear, I know your real name is not Olive Oyl."

"No, that's the name Farley gave me."

"Yes, he would," Mabel said. "What's your real name?"

"Adeline Scully. But nobody knows it. When I got arrested I used a alias."

"Adeline!" Mabel said. "Sweet Adeline. I used to sing that song when I was a girl. That's the name that will go on the driver's license. That's who you are from this day forward. Adeline. What a lovely name."

Just then Tillie, the striped tabby who was lying on the coffee table — a cat who had never heard a negative word spoken to her since Mabel rescued her — finished a can of tuna and slapped the empty can from the table in disgust.

"Oh, goodness," Mabel said, "Tillie's getting cross. We'll have to open another can of tuna. After all, if it wasn't for Tillie, we would never be able to have this new and wonderful life, would we?"

"No," Adeline said, smiling at Tillie.

"And mum's the word, Tillie," Mabel said to the cat.

"I'm real happy, Mabel," Adeline said.

Looking at her smile like that, Mabel said, "Adeline, you have such nice thick hair I'll bet a stylist could give you a beautiful cut. Let's both go get our hair done and a manicure. And I was wondering, would you like to have some teeth?"

"Oh, yes!" Adeline said. "I'd love to have some teeth."

"That's going to be something we tend to first thing," Mabel said. "We're going to buy you some nice new teeth!"

By the start of the new deployment period things were getting better insofar as car assignments were concerned. The Oracle liked the way Mag Takara was recovering and her vision was improving. He was thinking about putting her back on patrol.

Andi McCrea had been to Washington for a week, where she'd visited her son in Walter Reed every day. When she came back to Hollywood, she said she'd seen courage beyond words and that she'd never underestimate her son's generation, not ever again.

There are no worse gossips in the world than cops, and few can keep a secret, so the word got around Hollywood Station that Andi McCrea and Brant Hinkle were getting married. Compassionate Charlie Gilford quickly offered his usual brand of commentary.

"Another double-handcuff ceremony," he said

to Viktor Chernenko. "Right now they're calling each other darling babycakes and little buttercup. In another six months they'll blow each other's brains out. That's the way it is in Hollywood."

Viktor was especially happy, having learned that he'd been named Hollywood Station's Detective of the Quarter, and paid no attention to Compassionate Charlie's unromantic notions. He loved the sound of those terms of endearment.

That evening before going home, he phoned his wife and said, "I am so joyful, my darling babycakes. Would it be pleasing if I picked up some Big Macs and strawberry ice cream for my little buttertub?"

TWENTY-TWO

WITH THE JULY Fourth holiday approaching, the Oracle thought he had midwatch well sorted. When Fausto and Budgie brought in a report for signature, he said, "Fausto, it's time we took code seven at that other new Mexican restaurant — what's it called?"

"Hidalgo's," Fausto said.

"I'm buying."

"You hit the lottery?"

"Time to celebrate. It's summer in Hollywood," the Oracle said. "I feel expansive in the summer."

Fausto looked at the Oracle's ample belly and said, "I see what you mean."

"You should talk," Budgie said to Fausto. Then turning to the Oracle she added, "I have him on a six-burrito diet. He's already had five this week so he only gets one tonight."

"Give us a few minutes," Fausto said. "I gotta get a DR for a report."

The Oracle was alone again when he started to feel pain in his upper stomach. That damn heartburn again. He was sweating for no reason and felt he needed some air. He walked out into the lobby, passing below the hanging photos of those slain officers whose names were outside on the Hollywood Station Walk of Fame.

The Oracle looked up at the full moon, a "Hollywood moon," he always called it, and sucked in air through his nose, blowing it out his mouth. But he didn't feel better. There was suddenly a dull ache in his shoulder and his back.

A woman was coming to the station to make a report on the theft of her son's bicycle when a loud motorcycle roared by and she saw the Oracle grab his chest and fall to the pavement.

She ran into the station, screaming, "An officer's been shot!"

Fausto almost knocked her down as he threw open the glass door and ran out, followed by Budgie and Mag Takara, who'd been working at the front desk.

Fausto turned the Oracle over onto his back and said, "He hasn't been shot."

Then he knelt beside him and started chest compressions. Budgie lifted the Oracle's chin, pinched off his nostrils and started breathing into his mouth as Mag called the rescue ambulance. Several officers ran out of the station and watched.

"Come on, Merv!" Fausto said, counting compressions silently. "Come back to us!"

The RA arrived quickly, but it didn't matter. Budgie and Mag were both crying when the paramedics loaded the Oracle into the ambulance. Fausto turned and pushed two night-watch cops out of his way and wandered alone into the darkness of the parking lot.

One week later at roll call, the lieutenant said to the midwatch, "There will not be the usual police funeral for the Oracle. His will was very specific and stated that he'd made other arrangements."

"He should get a star on the Walk," Flotsam said.

The lieutenant said, "Well, that's for our Hollywood Division officers killed on duty."

"He was killed on duty," Hollywood Nate said. "Forty-six years around here? That's what killed him."

"How about a special star for the Oracle?" Mag Takara said.

The lieutenant said, "I'll have to talk to the captain about this."

"If anybody deserves a star," Benny Brewster said, "that man does."

Jetsam said, "No funeral? We gotta do something, Lieutenant."

B.M. Driscoll said, "The Oracle always said he was staying on the job till his ex-wife died so she couldn't get any of his pension. What about her? Did they have kids who might want a funeral?"

Getting rattled, the lieutenant said, "It's out of my control. He'd made special arrangements, I've been told. He left everything he owned to the L.A. Police Memorial Foundation for scholarships. That's all I know."

Fausto Gamboa stood up then, the first time he'd ever done such a thing at roll call in his thirty-four-year career. He said, "The Oracle didn't want any fuss made over him after he was gone. I know that for a fact. We talked about it one night many years ago when we were having a brew up at the Tree."

B.M. Driscoll said, "But what's his ex-wife say about it?"

"There is no ex-wife," Fausto said. "That was

his excuse for being crazy enough to stay on the Job all this time. And if he'd lived, someday they woulda had to tear the badge off his chest to get rid of him. He wouldn'ta liked that at all. He was nearly sixty-nine years old and enjoyed his life and did some good and now he's gone end-of-watch."

"Didn't he have . . . anybody?" Mag asked.

"Sure he did," Fausto said. "He had you. He was married to the Job and you were his kids. You and others before you."

The room was still then until Hollywood Nate said, "Isn't there . . . one little thing we can do for him? For his memory?"

After a pause, Fausto said with a quivering voice, "Yeah, there is. Remember how he said the Job is fun? The Oracle always said that doing good police work is more fun than anything you'll ever do in your entire lives. Well, you just go out there tonight and have yourselves some fun."

As soon as darkness fell on Hollywood, 6-X-76 went on a very special mission. A secret mission known to nobody else at Hollywood Station. They didn't speak as Budgie drove up into the Hollywood Hills to Mount Lee. When they got to their destination, she pulled up to a locked gate and stopped.

Fausto unlocked the gate, saying, "I had to practically sign in blood to get this key from the park ranger."

Budgie drove as far as they could on the fire road and then parked. There was no sound but cicadas whirring and a barely audible hum of traffic far below.

Then Budgie and Fausto got out and she opened the trunk. Fausto reached into his war bag and lifted out the urn.

Budgie led the way with her flashlight, but it was hardly needed under the light from a full moon. They walked along the path until they were at the base of the sign. It was four stories high and brilliantly lit.

Budgie looked up at the giant *H* looming and said, "Be careful, Fausto. Why don't you let me do it?"

"This is my job," Fausto said. "We were friends for more than thirty years."

The ground by the *H* had fallen away, so they walked to the center, to the *Y*, where the ground was intact.

The ladder was in place beside scaffolding,

and when he had climbed halfway up, Budgie yelled, "That's high enough, Fausto!"

But he kept going, puffing and panting, pausing twice until he was all the way to the top. And when he was there, he carefully opened the lid from the urn and turned it upside down, saying, "Semper cop, Merv. See you soon."

And the Oracle's ashes blew away into the warm summer night, against the backdrop of HOLLYWOOD, four stories high, under magical white light supplied by an obliging Hollywood moon.

When they were finished with their mission and Budgie had driven them back down to the streets of Hollywood, she broke the silence by saying, "I've been thinking about cooking a turkey dinner. How about coming over and meeting Katie? I want a photo op of you burping her. I'll buy a small bird for just you and me and my mom."

"I'll check my schedule," Fausto said. "Maybe I can make time."

Budgie said, "My dad's been dead for three years but Mom hasn't started dating yet, so it probably won't do you much good to hit on her."

"Oh, sure," Fausto said. "Like I'd hit on an old lady."

Budgie looked at him and said, "The old lady is nearly ten years younger than you are, pal."

"Yeah?" said Fausto, cocking that right eyebrow. "So what's she look like?"

"Well, Marty," Hollywood Nate said to his rookie partner. "We're going to do some good police work and have some fun tonight. You ready for that?"

"Yes, sir," the young cop said.

"Goddamnit, Marty," Nate said, "save that 'sir' crap for your real training officer, who'll probably turn out to be one of those GI junkies who grew up watching TV war movies. Me, I watched Fred Astaire and Gene Kelly musicals. My name's Nate. Remember?"

"Okay, Nate. Sorry."

"By the way, you like movies?"

"Yes, . . . Nate," Marty said.

"Your old man wouldn't be rich by any chance, would he?"

"Lord, no," Marty said.

"Oh, well," said Nate. "My last rich partner didn't help my career anyway."

There was a good crowd on the boulevard,

and the young cop turned to Nate and said, "Sir — I mean, Nate, there's a fifty-one-fifty raising heck over there in front of Grauman's Chinese Theater."

Without looking, Nate said, "What's he doing?"

"Waving his arms around and yelling at people."

"In Hollywood, that's just called communication," Nate said. "Nowadays it's hard to tell ordinary boulevard lunatics from people with headsets talking on cells." But then he glanced toward the famous theater, saw who it was, and said, "Uh-oh. That guy's a known troublemaker. Maybe we should talk to him."

Nate pulled the car into a red zone and said to his partner, "Marty, on this one, you be contact and I'll be cover. I'm gonna stay by the car here and see how you handle him. Think you can deal with it?"

"For sure, Nate," Marty said with enthusiasm, getting out of the car, collecting his baton, and putting on latex gloves.

The wild man waving his arms saw the young cop coming his way and stopped yelling. He planted his feet and waited.

Young Marty Shaw remembered from academy training that it's usually better to address mental cases in personal terms, so he turned around for a moment and said to Nate, "Do you remember his name, by chance?"

"Not his full name," said Hollywood Nate. "But they call him Al. Untouchable Al."

ABOUT THE AUTHOR

Joseph Wambaugh, a former LAPD detective sergeant, is the *New York Times* bestselling author of sixteen prior works of fiction and nonfiction, many of which have been adapted for the big and small screen, including *The Onion Field* and *The Choirboys.* He is a Grand Master of the Mystery Writers of America and lives in Southern California.